# THE CASSANDRA SYNDROME

# The Cassandra Syndrome

Also by

Eleonor Mendoza:
The Bells of Balangiga

iUniverse, Inc.
Bloomington

# The Cassandra Syndrome

This is a work of fiction. All of the characters, names, incidents, organizations, and dialogue in this novel are either the products of the author's imagination or are used fictitiously.

iUniverse books may be ordered through booksellers or by contacting:

iUniverse
1663 Liberty Drive
Bloomington, IN 47403
www.iuniverse.com
1-800-Authors (1-800-288-4677)

Because of the dynamic nature of the Internet, any web addresses or links contained in this book may have changed since publication and may no longer be valid. The views expressed in this work are solely those of the author and do not necessarily reflect the views of the publisher, and the publisher hereby disclaims any responsibility for them.

Any people depicted in stock imagery provided by Thinkstock are models, and such images are being used for illustrative purposes only.
Certain stock imagery © Thinkstock.

ISBN: 978-1-4759-7215-3 (sc)
ISBN: 978-1-4759-7217-7 (hc)
ISBN: 978-1-4759-7216-0 (ebk)

Library of Congress Control Number: 2013901115

Printed in the United States of America

iUniverse rev. date: 02/25/2013

For God, country, and family,
my sources of strength and inspiration

# CONTENTS

# Part I

# THE CRUISE

# 1. To Copenhagen

June 6, 2012

Anne and her son Mark were going on a cruise of Scandinavia and Russia. Anne was supposed to have been ready much earlier, but as usual, Anne was behind schedule as she took care of other things that cluttered her life.

"Why did you not just answer the phone?" Mark said reprovingly.

"Sometimes I just want to get so much done before we leave. Anyway, I've endorsed the printing of invitations to another committee member. Just hold on; I'll finish packing even if I don't sleep," Anne said patiently.

"I'm packed—I'm going to bed," said Mark, who went to bed with a shrug.

"Two hours before departure means we have to be at the airport at four a.m.," said Anne's husband, Edward, grumbling as he headed for the sofa.

"I'll be done soon," Anne said, and she looked at the clock, which was striking midnight.

They made it on time to the Kansas City airport and then to their international flight going through O'Hare, in spite of the tight connection.

Anne led the way out of the plane and into the terminal. "Take this photocopy of my passport and put it in your wallet. I have yours in mine. Here's the list of the toll-free numbers to call if our credit cards are stolen," Anne said as she looked around at the restaurants.

"Got it." Mark put the folded paper in his wallet and followed. He was used to his mom acting like this, even if he squirmed at times. He suddenly smiled at the thought of his cousin calling his mom a control freak.

"Let's eat here. Chinese food will do. We have less than an hour to eat," Anne said, and she started for the line.

"Cheap and fast it is." Mark followed her.

The flight to Copenhagen was full. Anne sorted and arranged their itinerary sheets, passports, money, and other papers before she settled down. Mark was already asleep when she opened a paperback book and began to read.

Copenhagen

"Two days in Copenhagen is barely enough, but we will make the most of it." Anne suddenly stretched to free Mark's backpack from a moving luggage cart. "Is it that necessary to bring your computer?"

"Mom!"

"Okay! Okay!" Anne rolled her eyes and followed the bell captain pushing the luggage cart toward the hotel elevator.

"Are we going to see the Lorelei before dinner then?" Mark asked as they entered the room.

"Yes, and we can walk around that area and get dinner before we come back to the hotel. We'll sleep early so we can make the most of tomorrow."

Anne and Mark were at Tivoli Gardens by nine o'clock in the morning. They appreciated the scenery and chose among the rides that were available.

"How beautiful! I'm so glad I'm not missing the gardens this time!" Anne said.

"It's worth our time and trouble all right!" Mark agreed.

Next they went for the world-famous, tallest carousel, the Star Flyer.

They sat down next to each other as the carousel began to fill with people getting on the ride.

"I can do this, but I'm not going to ride that wooden roller coaster or the Vertigo, okay, Son? You go, but I'll wait nearby. I've had enough of those thrill rides. Oh! That jarring motion makes me nervous."

Anne looked around when she heard raised voices just outside the carousel perimeter. "Son!" she called.

"Huh?" Mark pointed out the scene to his mom.

Just then the carousel started, but with a slow motion at first. As Anne and Mark looked at the commotion, they suddenly heard a shot.

"Oh no! A man just got shot! I hope the mechanic lets us get off this ride," Anne said.

The carousel sent them on a spin, faster and faster, and then suddenly stopped with a loud, jarring noise. Anne and Mark were wide-eyed as they disembarked right near the scene of the commotion. Sirens were blaring, and a crowd of curious people formed around the disturbance.

Anne and Mark left the carousel and stood aside from the scene, not wanting to be involved. An ambulance came, and several people were taken away in police cars.

"Let's eat. Maybe then we can think better," Anne said.

"Okay, but I'm trying not to let that spoil our day," Mark said. "Shall we stay here for the day as originally planned?"

"I agree, and we should do some shopping and walking around town tomorrow, just before we go to the cruise ship," Anne said.

They arrived at the cruise ship in good time, ate a casual dinner, and went to the lower deck to book their shore excursions.

"We don't need to see Berlin again if you remember it from last time," Anne said, looking up from the brochure.

"I need to see it because I don't remember that long ago," Mark countered.

"Okay, I hope I can still have some time to walk around Warnemunde after we return—maybe just the market square." Anne sighed.

## 2. Warnemunde, Berlin

On the excursion bus to Berlin, Mark was in the window seat and admiring the scenery when Anne nudged his elbow.

Mark looked up and saw a tall Caucasian man going toward the restroom. Mark tried to act casual, while his mom prayed her rosary.

The tourist bus brought them to Brandenburg Gate, Checkpoint Charlie, bombed sites from World War II, and the old Reichstag building. They were then given time to walk and shop along Unter den Linden.

Anne and Mark were quiet but observant; realizing that the man they'd seen at the Tivoli Gardens shooting was with them on the tour. The man had a pretty female companion, which somehow allayed their suspicion.

Anne was anxious to talk as soon as they returned to the cruise ship.

"Did you get a funny feeling when you saw that guy?"

"Yes, he was at the scene of the shooting at Tivoli Gardens," Mark said.

"I can't put a finger to it, but even if I did not see him clearly there, I just have that sense. I hope it doesn't mean anything. We'd better shake it off, or we won't enjoy this trip," Anne said.

"Rather odd, but I agree. Let's go to the computer room and check our messages." Mark led the way out.

"Dad's okay—he says the stock market is up, so he's happy. Jim's okay—he'll go out with friends tomorrow after their volunteering is done."

"I'll come with you to the gym tomorrow," Anne said. "I'm uncomfortable staying in the room alone. We will be at sea tomorrow, and we are on first seating for our formal dinner."

It was still daylight outside, but along the corridors leading to the main dining room, men and women were dressed for the occasion, nodding in approval at the beautifully groomed crowd, and exchanging friendly banter with those waiting in line to be seated.

Mark smiled to himself as he noticed the admiring gazes shot in the direction of his mother. She was petite at five feet one, was always well dressed, looked expensive, and had the right jewelry to boot; but it was her quick friendliness and wit that made people warm up to her.

The waiter led them to a table for eight, and the man they'd been talking about earlier was there.

"Hi! I hope we did not keep you waiting." Anne was quick to hide her apprehension. "I'm Anne Cortez, from Kansas City, Kansas."

"Hi! I'm the son, Mark."

"We just got seated a few seconds ago. How do you do? I'm Barry Eastbrook, and this is my wife, Mabel."

The blonde wife waved her bejeweled hand to all and said, "Hi! We're from Maine."

"Hello! I'm Fawzi Senawi, and this is my wife, Janan. We're from Iran."

Janan waved to everyone with a shy smile and said, "Hi!"

"That's interesting!" The portly man with crew-cut hair chuckled in a friendly way. "I'm Noel Pietz, and my wife is Cheryl. We're from Illinois." He turned to Senawi. "I'm just kidding; I suppose you get that all the time."

"You can say that again. Worse, I'm a physicist," Senawi said with a smile.

"Oh! Oh!" Pietz bantered.

Senawi raised one eyebrow with a sardonic smile. "Can I have a vacation in peace?" he said.

Anne blinked for just a second. "Absolutely! Nice to meet you!" she said with a nod from across the table.

"Nice to meet you," the others added.

"I'm buying the wine," Eastbrook said. "This trip is for our thirtieth wedding anniversary."

"Congratulations!" the others chorused.

"We don't drink wine, but we'll settle for soda," Senawi said.

"Soda it is," Eastbrook said, and he motioned to the waiter.

"This is the first time we are having a leisurely dinner," Mark observed.

"Same here," Pietz answered. "This cruise is not leisurely at all, and to think that we were at Tivoli Gardens when there was a shooting! They closed down the gates! We were near the carousel."

"We were on the carousel, quite near the scene of the commotion. The view was wonderful, but that shooting got me worried," Anne said.

"I was actually near the scene," Senawi said deliberately, making the others look at him. "People were looking around, and the whole area was cordoned off, with us in the circle. We were all questioned closely at the police precinct."

"Oh! I'm so sorry to hear that," Mabel Eastbrook said, looking puzzled.

"I hope we can still enjoy the rest of the trip," Senawi said.

"Don't worry! We'll make sure you do," Pietz said.

"Right!" Cheryl chimed in.

The others at the table put up their glasses in a toast. "Right!" they said.

Eastbrook turned to Anne and said, "I'm a retired real-estate broker, how about you?"

"I'm a retired doctor," Anne answered. "My husband is an investor and doesn't leave the USA that often, because he trades stocks. I love to travel, so my two sons take turns accompanying me. Mark is in college."

"Well, I'm a retired lawyer," Pietz countered.

The waiter came back to serve their salads.

Anne and Mark made the sign of the cross and prayed silently before they began eating, as they always did. They returned to the conversation without much fanfare.

Fawzi Senawi looked at them before he started eating his salad.

"Just call me Noel," Pietz said to Anne. "Shall we call each other by first names? You too, Mark," Pietz said as he saw the younger man hesitate. Everybody nodded, and they each repeated their first names.

## 3. Talinn, Estonia

Feeling more comfortable with their company, Anne and Mark were more relaxed as they boarded the bus for the trip to downtown.

"What a quaint scene," Anne said as she took a picture of people outside a church, gathered around a baby in baptismal dress.

As soon as they came down from the bus, the tourists got busy taking pictures; then they took pictures for each other. They formed into groups, posing with the scenic backdrop.

Anne and Mark posed with the Eastbrooks, and when they came near the Senawis, they also had a picture together.

"Let's exchange pictures by e-mail. Do you have a pen? I'll write down my e-mail address, and you give me yours," Eastbrook said to Mark.

"Here's a pen. Okay, write down my e-mail address too," Mark said.

"Here's mine," Senawi said as he wrote on a piece of paper and gave it to Mark.

"Here's mine," Pietz said. "What's yours?"

"Oh! My pen . . ." Mark looked around and then said, "Thanks!" as Senawi handed him a pen.

Anne watched the exchange of e-mail addresses. The Senawis were behaving like most people, and she felt relieved. *They're normal,* she thought.

The camaraderie was catching, with Eastbrook singing funny songs on the drive back. He then suggested they play cards on the cruise ship.

"Make that gin rummy and I'll play you," Senawi answered.

"No betting," Pietz said. "I'll play too."

"I'm going for a swim," Mark said.

Anne and Mark ate dinner at the poolside buffet.

"Wait, Mom," Mark said. "Let's pass by the group playing cards. I seem to have Senawi's pen."

They went to the game room, but Senawi had just left.

"Maybe you can return it tomorrow," Eastbrook said. "Needless to say, he won. He's so competitive, I doubt if he ever losses."

"Oh! Thanks," Mark said.

"Good night! Tomorrow should be exciting." Anne waved as they left.

## 4. St. Petersburg, Russia

As though primed for adventure, most tourists lined up early to disembark for the shore excursion.

Anne's yellow outfit got some nods from the men, and she added a scarf to ward off the morning cold. "Good morning," she said pleasantly.

"Top of the morning, my dear! You are brighter than the sun today," Eastbrook joked.

"At least I can help the tour guide if you wander off and miss us," Anne bantered.

"Look who's just coming! Yo! Senawi, over here!" Pietz signaled the Senawis, who were arriving in a hurry.

"Haah!" Janan said, catching her breath as they came closer. "We did not get our morning call, and the clock in our room was late!"

"Write a complaint and put it on your door outbox, or be sure to let the steward know when we return. Our schedule is hectic, and you could easily miss the excursion if you don't get up early," Mabel advised.

"Right! I'm not taking chances. I'll also set the alarms on our cell phones," Senawi said in between breaths.

The tour director was really knowledgeable, so Mark listened intently.

Anne saw an unusual building and looked back. "Wasn't that a church?"

Mark was chuckling at the tour director's joke, but Anne looked forward to hide her apprehension. She had looked back for a better view of the church, but it was Senawi's face she saw, beads of perspiration on his brow as he whispered to Janan.

The tourists came off the bus in a hurry. The Winter Palace was so huge and breathtaking; they all wanted to take a lot of pictures and found themselves pressed for time.

"Hurry up, Mom," Mark said, wondering why his mother was behind.

"Would you take our picture, Mark?" Mabel Eastbrook asked. "Then I'll take yours with your mom against that fountain there."

Mark nodded, and Anne followed. Their group took turns photographing each other, and Anne tried her best not to worry.

*Maybe I'm imagining things,* she thought as she saw Janan and Senawi taking pictures of the fountain.

It was a full day's excursion going to the Winter Palace and seeing the Amber Room. Lunch, dinner, and a show were included. The Kirov Ballet was performing, so Mark sat attentively for the first ballet he would see. Their group was impressed, and Anne heard a whispered comment from Pietz behind her.

She turned in agreement, smiling, but then she quickly looked down at the program to hide her concern. Anne thought she had shaken off her worry about the Senawis, but she had just seen Fawzi sweating and looking behind him apprehensively.

"What a wonderful day, but I'm tired." Mark stretched out on his bed even before he could change into pajamas.

"It's been hectic but well worth it. I didn't tell you that something was bothering me—I didn't want to spoil your day—but Fawzi Senawi has been acting scared." Anne explained what she had seen.

"I'm getting spooked. I too have been trying to shake off the feeling. I hope it's nothing," Mark said.

Anne sighed. "We'd better sleep early. It's another long day tomorrow."

"I'm looking forward to the Hermitage Museum," Mark said with a yawn.

"All right! I've tried to show you about a fourth of the most important paintings in this museum," the tour guide said. "Even if we spent an entire week here, we couldn't cover everything. It's not possible. Look up what interests you most. We will meet in the bus parking lot in two hours. The Rembrandts and the Reubens are in this pavilion." The guide pointed to his left and, with a nod, left them.

Anne and Mark looked at their wristwatches and quickly moved left. They made an effort to concentrate on each famous painting and yet move quickly to the next. When they approached the third room, Anne glanced back at their outdistanced group, and then she noticed that there was a man already in the room, looking at a painting. She felt a movement nearby and saw that Senawi had entered the room too.

The man came toward Senawi and spoke in low tones, but from behind Senawi, another man raised his voice and pointed a gun. The man talking to Senawi also pulled a gun.

"Look out!" Mark shouted, at the same time pushing Anne out of the way.

From behind them, they heard a shot, and they took cover behind a post. There was a scuffle, and then one of the men ran away, followed by the other one. The tourists screamed and scattered in different directions, tripping over each other.

The security police arrived and started firing at the two men, but each of the men ran in an opposite direction. More police arrived, and the chase continued outside the museum.

The tourists stayed hidden and petrified until the police returned to tell them it was safe. Most went for the door, half-running out of the museum, and they sat panting at the foot of the steps. Mark and Anne sat on the steps too, catching their breath.

"The gunman is dead," the tour guide reported, and he went back inside to check with the police.

"Thank God!" Mabel said.

Fawzi was pale, and Janan Senawi was crying. The group looked at them, and Eastbrook went over to them.

"Take it easy," he said.

Fawzi nodded, wiping his sweat with a white handkerchief.

"Thanks for the warning," Mabel said to Mark.

The others repeated, "Thank you!"

Mark just nodded, still looking shaken.

Their guide returned. "We are free to go. The police does not have any more information."

The tourists went back to the bus, but after what had happened at the museum, most of them just went back to the ship. Somehow their group ended up going to the swimming pool.

They chatted during the poolside dinner.

"There is something going on here—I'm telling you. I feel we're in a cloak-and-daggers game," Mabel said.

"I'm not the spy; don't look at me," Eastbrook jokingly countered.

"Has anybody heard on the news about the Nationalists complaining about leaks regarding intelligence?" Noel Pietz looked around him. "Who knows about the Stuxnet cyberworm?"

Anne did not answer yes, but Senawi looked at her closely.

"It's supposed to attack the Iranian nuclear program's computers, where I work," Senawi said deliberately, making the group look at him. "That's all in the past."

"Really? You've countered it?" Pietz challenged.

"Whatever," Senawi said with a shrug. "There's always stuff going on."

"Is that why there was that man in the museum?" asked Cheryl.

Eastbrook looked around, Senawi hesitated, and Pietz looked like he was waiting.

"Search me," Senawi said with a shrug.

"Let's just eat! I'm already hungry," Anne said.

"Me too! We can't solve the world's problems," Mabel said.

"I'm part Finnish, so I'm looking forward to seeing Helsinki," Barry Eastbrook said, changing the topic. He then proceeded to tell them about his family's migration.

They all felt better when they dispersed.

"Let's check our e-mail," Mark said, and he led the way to the computer room. "It feels good to be in touch, even if we are far away. This iPhone with the international use option is handy. Dad said my iPad is ready when we get home. Nice pictures! Mom?"

Anne came over to look at the pictures. "Nice! Barry really likes to clown around. Did you send ours already?"

"Sent, but there's something funny going on. Either there's a virus from one of those e-mails I've received, or my computer was hacked. The pictures we've sent to Dad and Jim seem to have been sent to practically everybody in our address book. Look!"

Anne took a look. "Oh no! They've gone to my committees and classmates—even my tennis group! Hurry up! E-mail all the groups to warn them! Unbelievable!"

## 5.  Helsinki, Finland

"Waking up early again for this shore excursion is not that fun," Mark complained.

"Sorry, you stayed up a little later containing that virus, Son. It's not our fault if somebody has the malice to spread a virus. Come on; let's eat at that fancy restaurant where Kissinger went. We can at least feel like those guys once in a while," Anne consoled.

"That's where I had my picture taken long ago." Anne pointed. "Let me see if I can get up there, and you can take my picture with the Sibelius façade."

13

"Let me help you." Senawi picked up Mark's camera bag from the ground as the younger man moved back to get the Sibelius façade in the picture frame. "That looks like a neat picture; can you take our picture next?" Without waiting for Mark's answer, he turned to Janan and said, "Up there! Let's have that picture like Anne's."

Others followed, and Mark also got his picture taken with the same scene.

A similar commotion occurred when their tour bus landed at the Rock Church.

"Let's get our group picture here," Eastbrook suggested. "Would you take our group picture, please?" he asked the tour director.

She graciously complied, and one after another, the cameras were handed to her.

"Thanks to you," Anne said with an amused smile, "nobody was left out from the picture."

The tour director smiled amiably. "Okay. For those planning to have lunch at the Havis Amanda, we can drop you off there."

The rest of their group decided to have lunch there too, and they all enjoyed the food and the ambience. They walked in the market area near the wharf as Anne suppressed her anxious feeling. There was no bad incident that day.

## 6.  Stockholm, Sweden

"So if we do this city on our own, you'll get the ambience of *The Girl with the Dragon Tattoo*? Okay. Let's also visit one of their Internet cafés; maybe we will meet a hacker or something," Anne said, and she let Mark take the lead. "We're quite early, though."

They were in the town square, where quaint shops were festooned with banners, just like the merchant guilds of medieval times. The stores were beginning to open, and they looked around, unsure of where to start.

"A lace shop!" Anne said.

"Not exactly what I had in mind," Mark said crossly.

"Okay, just a few minutes," Anne said, and she led the way.

They came out of the shop with some purchases, squinting as they met the full glare of the morning sun.

"Mom," Mark said in a hushed voice.

Anne turned and was suddenly face-to-face with Fawzi Senawi. "Oh, hi!" She tried to hide her surprise.

"Hello," Senawi said in a calm voice. "I need your help. I have nowhere else to turn."

"Oh!" was all the stunned Anne could say, her eyes wide; while Mark just stood there.

"My son was kidnapped because those bad guys want something from me. Even if I give them what they want, there is no assurance they will return my son. Help me!"

"Let's call the police!" Mark said.

"They won't understand," Janan said, standing beside Fawzi.

Anne started thinking. "Okay. What can we do?"

"Those guys will soon show up. I hope I can have a satisfactory meeting with them; if not, help Janan get my son back." He showed his son's picture. "This is Andre."

"Son! Dial 911. We need help, and we can't be choosy!"

As Mark pressed the numbers on his iPhone, a car screeched in front of them. He instinctively pushed Anne toward the store, and Anne pulled Janan along with her.

Senawi stood frozen in the street for a while, and then he went forward alone, holding an object in his hand. A well-dressed man stepped out of the car and took the object; then he gave orders. Three men came out of the car and grabbed Senawi, pushing him inside the car. There was a scuffle inside. Anne and Mark stood terrified, and then they heard a shot. Janan screamed.

Anne cried, "Help! Help!"

Mark pressed the emergency numbers on his iPhone and also recorded the car's license plate. The car sped off, and before it turned the corner, the body of Senawi was thrown out of the car and onto the pavement.

Anne and Janan were not thinking. They both ran toward the body, and, panting, they turned it face-up. Senawi was bleeding from a head shot. Janan tried to cradle his head on her lap.

"My son . . ." Senawi died before he could say more.

The police sirens jolted them, but Janan's reaction again startled Anne.

"We have to go; I don't trust the police," Janan said.

"What? But your husband!" Anne was wide-eyed as Janan left Senawi's body on the street and ran to hide behind a parked car.

Anne followed her just as the police cars stopped in the middle of the square. Mark had ducked back into the store where they had bought the lace.

It seemed like an interminable wait as Anne and Janan watched the police go over the body and consult by phone, until the ambulance arrived. An area was cordoned off, and arriving onlookers were allowed to go in a roundabout way.

Anne watched Janan cry silently and refrained from hugging her. Janan looked determined, with her jaw set and her fists clenched.

"Let's go to the lace shop and meet Mark; then we can talk somewhere," Anne said as she gently touched Janan's shoulder. They got up from their crouched position.

The police did not mind them walking by, and they entered the shop. The shop owner merely nodded, understanding that the tourists were just taking cover.

"Thank you very much," Anne said to the shop owner with a smile, and she reached out to touch Mark's shoulder as they left, aware that her son looked quite anxious.

Anne guided her companions to a smaller café farther from the square and ordered pancakes, sausage, coffee, and juice. She suddenly felt so hungry, and she presumed that everybody else was hungry too. "Eat. You will need to think," Anne said as she shoved the plate in front of Janan.

Janan was dry-eyed by now, but her sad demeanor was mixed with some determination.

Anne forced herself to eat hurriedly, feeling that her appetite was fast disappearing as she realized the danger they were in. She looked at Janan.

"I cannot return to the cruise ship. My life might be in danger. You have to be careful too," Janan said.

"Tell us more. We don't even know what we are facing," Anne said softly.

"Fawzi works with the Iranian nuclear program and would have been on his way to a conference after this cruise. The North Koreans kidnapped Andre and called us when we were already on the cruise. Those thugs want Fawzi to give them important information about his work.

"It seems that they wanted to take him too. I cannot return to Iran after what happened. Either I will be under suspicion, or they will be blaming me too," Janan said sadly.

"But that's not right! All the more reason they should protect you!" Mark interrupted indignantly.

"You don't know them," Janan answered.

"What else is there? This does not look that simple to me," Anne said with a frown.

"The less you know, the safer you will be," Janan answered.

Anne was half-indignant. She felt trouble brewing, and Janan was not helping. She gulped her coffee, paused, and finally said, "Okay. What are you going to do now?"

"I'll hide here in Stockholm until I can find help in some communities."

Anne sized up Janan—probably ten years younger than she was and not making any sense. "Do you want us to help with sending your stuff home?"

"Yes," Janan said softly, handing Anne the room key.

Anne felt frustration welling up inside her. She almost wanted to shake Janan's shoulders; then Janan started crying again. Anne and Mark looked at each other.

"All right," Anne said softly. "Do you need money?"

Janan looked at Anne blankly; then she opened her purse. "Fawzi had most of the money. I don't have much."

Anne sighed. "I'll give you some cash, and I'll just get more from the ATM. Come to think of it, if we could be in trouble, we will need some money too. Worse, our credit cards might become useless." Anne opened her bag and counted out her money. "I have a thousand in euros here." She gave the money to Janan, who cried some more.

A noise outside the café made them turn. Four men in business suits were gesticulating, as though fanning the area for a search.

Anne quickly left the money for their breakfast on the table, and they left through the upper staircase, which connected to a small street that led back into the square.

"We're better off here," Anne said. "That's the bus stop for the route that goes around the city." Anne pointed to Janan. "This mall has an ATM that Mark and I can use, and over there I saw an Internet shop. We have to move fast."

17

Anne looked at Janan and decided to tie her scarf around Janan's lustrous brown hair, partly hiding the hair and also altering Janan's appearance. Anne then hugged Janan good-bye, but Janan was shaking so badly that Anne held her until the shaking stopped. "God be with you," Anne said.

"Take care," Mark said, shaking hands.

Janan could not say anything through her tears; then she slowly walked away.

They waited for Janan to get on the bus before they headed for the ATM.

"Call your dad on the iPhone first. He's going to be shocked we need more money. Wait, I'll talk to him," Anne said.

Mark called on his iPhone, and after three rings, his dad answered. Mark just gave the phone to Anne.

## 7. Emergency Password

"Edward, please listen carefully. We are in some kind of trouble. I'll withdraw three thousand now from this ATM here. We gave our money to somebody. Just listen, please. We could be in danger. Don't talk! Please, just listen carefully. Get a pen and write this down. Now!" After a pause, Anne continued. "E-mail everybody in my address book that we will be out of town and out of communication indefinitely."

"What! What have you done?" Edward interrupted.

"Please! Just listen—we don't have time. We will use the e-mail address copinski6054@yahoo.com when we communicate with you. Check your spam mail. Our emergency code word is *Kidapawan*. Please put all my papers from the dining room cabinets, all my jewelry from the safe, and other valuables in storage. Do not talk to strangers, police look-alikes or whatever. Take all the computers and get out of there so you cannot be taken hostage. Go somewhere on vacation, and communicate to us on e-mail. We will call Jim so he can ask for a temporary leave!"

"No!' Edward was upset.

"We got involved in a spy intrigue here. We don't know what will happen. We are trying to protect our family," Anne continued.

"No!" Edward said again.

Anne got mad and turned the phone off. "Call your brother!"

Mark dialed his brother, but there was no answer.

"Text him! Tell him this: 'We got caught in a spy intrigue here; ask for temporary leave, and go into hiding. Do not communicate with friends or relatives, or you will compromise them. Talk to your dad.'" Anne was trying to say this softly, but she might have been above a whisper. She looked around and was glad nobody was nearby.

Mark looked tired from the strain, and they proceeded to the ATM, glad they were able to get enough money.

Next stop was the Internet café.

They entered slowly, adjusting their eyes to the relatively low lighting. A short, thin brown man was in the inner part of the store. Having just finished, he got up and almost collided with Anne, who hesitated before she sat down.

"Sorry," he said, and he smiled.

"Sorry," Anne said as she moved her chair sideways.

"Filipino?" the man asked.

"Yes," Anne answered. Then, looking at him closely, she asked, "Are you Guzman?"

"Yes." He nodded and motioned for her to be quiet.

"What are you doing here?" Anne asked softly.

Rolando Guzman sat on the chair next to hers and talked softly. "I could not get a job in a legitimate computer world because nobody would trust me. I've been doing work on and off here—some legal, some questionable."

"What are the terms of your visa?" Anne asked.

"I had a temporary work permit for a computer company who fired me. Actually, they wanted me to spy by hacking into other companies' computers. I was going to quit because it was illegal, but the SOBs fired me instead."

"I might need you for government work," Anne said on a wild guess. "Would you be interested?"

"Yes, ma'am!" Guzman said.

"Give me info on how we can reach each other." Anne opened her purse and got a piece of paper. He wrote his e-mail address on one end, and she wrote the copinski6054@yahoo address. They split the paper, and Anne also gave Guzman one hundred euros.

"See you, ma'am!" Guzman smiled happily before he left.

19

Anne watched Mark get to work on a new computer address. "E-mail your dad and Jim on our old e-mail address and ask if they followed instructions. Let's go. We will check the replies later; the ship leaves earlier today."

"Mom, do you remember that tomorrow we will be at sea, before we reach Copenhagen?" Mark asked.

"What? Oh my God! Let's go to the ship now." Anne led the way out and called a taxi.

They arrived almost breathless at the cruise ship and went straight for the Senawis' room. They did not have to use the key Janan had given Anne. The door was ajar, and the room had been ransacked. They backed off, and Anne decided to wipe the room key clean with her skirt hem and tissue paper. She then dropped it on the floor.

"It is not safe here. We must leave," Anne said unnecessarily, and they hurried to their cabin.

They packed very quickly and left a note on the table, signing their names.

*We have to fly home. Emergency! Husband in hospital.*

They dragged their suitcases and carry-on bags over the gangplank, to the surprise of the cruise ship personnel.

"So sorry! Emergency at home! My husband is in the hospital. We will fly home now. Thank you very much!" she said effusively, and Mark waved with a smile.

They took a taxi to the airport and made it as chance passengers on the flight leg to Copenhagen. Anne had changed their route; instead of O'Hare to Kansas City, she'd booked them for Washington, DC.

## 8. Copenhagen to O'Hare Airport

At the Copenhagen airport, Mark opened his computer to check their e-mail. He also opened his camera bag to take out the film disc, but there was something else inside. He took it out and, puzzled, looked at it.

"Senawi must have put something in my camera bag—a disc with Arabic writings was in one of the pockets."

Anne looked at it surreptitiously. "Remember when we were talking about the Stuxnet cyberworm? Fawzi made me feel uncomfortable; that's why I did not say I'd read about it. He must think we know a little more than we let on. In the *Smithsonian* magazine, I read an interview with a man who could help us—Richard Higgins, the former head of counterintelligence. The people who could help us save Andre should be the ones in Washington, and now we have to deliver this disc too. Let's find the address of Richard Higgins now."

Mark looked puzzled for a while, tapping on his computer. "Okay. The official address is in Arlington, Virginia, but there's a mention of a Washington, DC, office. I just got the latter by doing a different search based on the other article."

"We're going to the Washington, DC, office," Anne said.

As usual, there was a delay in their connection at O'Hare airport. Anne advised Mark that they should both be discreet and alter their appearance; however, there were not many options while they were in the airport.

"Give me a pair of your shorts," Anne said. "Get them out of your carry case when you go to the restroom."

Mark rolled his eyes. At five feet five, he was the shortest of the three men in the family. Since his mother did not have rugged clothes, every now and then she would borrow his shorts when she had to work in the garden. "You can have my last clean pair of shorts; but I'm not changing into some drastic disguise," he answered.

After Anne changed out of her skirt and into Mark's shorts, they ate at Chili's and bought a Chicago Cubs baseball cap for Mark. They took opposite chairs in the boarding area so that each one could look out for the other's back.

Anne stood up when a man changed something on the departure notice.

"We're changing gates." She moved out, and Mark followed.

"It's quite far!" Anne remarked as the other passengers also hurried in the same direction.

Mark saw Noel Pietz first. Pietz was coming to their boarding gate in a hurry, keeping right, while they were on his left, keeping right while going in the opposite direction.

"That was Noel Pietz, Mom!"

"I saw him too. I hope he is not after us. If he does see us, I hope he won't recognize us," Anne whispered, and she walked faster.

"Mark!" Noel Pietz was suddenly running after them, still some distance away but letting his voice carry.

Ahead of them, Anne saw a group of soldiers wearing camouflage uniforms, young men bantering in a low voice, with knapsacks and parcels of recent purchases in their hands.

"Mark! Anne!" Pietz called, still behind them, but louder.

"Help!" Anne ran toward the soldiers. "That's a bad guy trying to get us! Stop him!"

The reaction was swift. The soldiers formed a wall of their bodies, and Pietz collided head-on with the burliest of them all.

Anne and Mark barely made it to the boarding gate, showing their passes and hauling their carry-ons to the bin.

The plane was quickly on the move, as though making up for lost time. Anne sighed in relief when they were airborne and Pietz was nowhere to be found.

Part II

# STUXNET AND THE HOSTAGE

# 9. Washington, DC

When they arrived in Washington, DC, they looked around, just in case Pietz shows up. They quickly claimed their luggage and took a cab. They directed the driver to the office address of Richard Higgins.

They felt out of place hauling their luggage through the elevator and into Higgins's office.

"We would like to see Mr. Higgins. It is urgent," Anne said.

"No. He is very busy today," the middle-aged secretary said, hiding her surprise at their appearance.

Anne thought that obviously she was not worth listening to. "Look! I know we look horrific, but this is urgent. Tell Mr. Higgins it is about the Stuxnet cyberworm."

The secretary gave them a second look before ringing Mr. Higgins's room. She put the phone down and relayed the message. "Please come back tomorrow."

"We are not leaving," Anne countered irritably. "An Iranian nuclear physicist has been killed, and his son has been kidnapped. Our lives may be in danger here. We have to talk to him."

The secretary rang Mr. Higgins again, this time using what sounded like a code word. "You may go in."

Richard Higgins stood waiting for them. He was a tall, white-haired, serious man.

Anne and Mark told him what had happened, filling in each other's gaps in the story, and pleading for help to save Andre Senawi. They were almost out of breath from excitement by the time they finished. They waited for him to speak without offering the disc. Higgins buzzed his secretary and told her to get hold of somebody.

"You look fatigued," Higgins said.

"Sorry, but for fear of somebody following us, I needed a disguise, and this is the best we could come up with," Anne said ruefully, and she looked at the shorts she was wearing.

"No way I was gonna wear her skirt." Mark smiled.

Higgins buzzed his secretary again. "While waiting for Levi, call Luke Mattheson and tell him to come ASAP too. Also, get us some food."

The phone rang, and Higgins immediately picked it up.

"Could you come over ASAP, Levi? There's something very important you need to decipher here . . . Okay." Higgins sat down and explained his plan. "Levi is an Israeli whose parents grew up in Iran. The parents moved back to Israel, but they talked to Levi in Farsi and trained him on the ways of the Iranians, knowing that it would be necessary as a Mossad agent. He is very good but sometimes brusque—just bear with him. He will decipher your disc. He said that he has heard of the Mossad agent killed at Tivoli Gardens."

"Whoa! Mossad?" Mark could not help exclaiming.

"And at the Hermitage?" Anne asked.

"He will tell us a lot more when he comes. The fight was to get to Dr. Senawi and find out his sympathies. They suspect he passed on some information before he was killed; so, yes, spies are looking for you two, but they do not know about this disc." Higgins looked at Anne and Mark, who both turned pale. "You apparently outsmarted some of the spies. Levi has just come from a meeting where the Mossad was trying to figure out the Senawi fiasco."

The food arrived quite quickly, to Anne's relief. "Thanks." She smiled at the secretary.

The secretary smiled back and said, "I was wondering where I've seen you before; otherwise, I would have called security to throw you both out. You sure looked funny when you arrived, but you spoke so persuasively. Now I know you are the author of *The Bells of Balangiga*, which my Filipino friend gave me as a gift."

"Oh, wow!" Anne exclaimed. "How did you like it?"

"Very much! I learned a lot of history. I'll get you to talk about it sometime."

"I'll be glad to!" Anne said; but became subdued when she glanced at Higgins.

The secretary hurriedly left.

"So you are an author too?" Higgins asked. "Is your bio out there on Facebook and all that?"

"No, because I don't do Facebook, and I specifically instructed my publisher that I want to stay private." Anne paused to think. "We told you that I told my husband to remove all files and papers and leave the house. Only we can contact him. My other son is in school, but he was instructed to be on the lookout and temporarily stay somewhere else other than his own apartment. Come to think of it, we haven't had time to check if they have done as instructed." Anne looked worried.

Mark opened his computer but looked at Higgins first.

"Get a new e-mail address and contact them," Higgins instructed.

While Mark was typing, a tall, well-built man arrived.

"How urgent is this? I was going out on a date." He turned to shake hands with the newcomers and said, "Luke Mattheson."

"I'm Mark."

They shook hands.

"Anne Cortez," Anne said automatically, looking up at a clean-shaven, handsome man.

"Urgent, as in somebody's life," Higgins said, pointing to a chair and the food. "Let's eat. It's going to be a long night."

Anne handed Mark a pizza and a Coke and then sat down near her son with her own food. Higgins updated Mattheson in between bites of food, and both men finished eating quickly. Anne found herself hurrying to finish and nudged Mark.

"No answer yet." Mark looked worried and started eating.

The door opened, and a tall, ruggedly good-looking, well-built man walked in. He directly looked at Anne and Mark. Only then did the others realize that the man's shoulder was smudged with dirt and there was a tear in his suit jacket.

"Either your office has been watched, or I was followed randomly. I had to knock out some idiot who was pretending to beg but wanted me to get into a car. I had to go roundabout to be sure there were no more stragglers following me. Let me see that." He opened his palm to Mark, who obediently gave him the disc.

"Sorry, I'm Levi Cohen." He quickly shook Mark's and Anne's hands. "Tell me your story again from beginning to end, including the people, especially Senawi." Levi went to the computer on Higgins's desk and inserted the disc.

Anne and Mark repeated their story with no interruptions while Mattheson took notes, and Higgins put on the video recorder. It took them a little longer to tell it, adding the little, unusual things they'd noticed, describing the people they'd met on the cruise and the episode with Pietz.

"By the way, who's Pietz?" Anne asked.

"He's CIA," Levi said. "He was supposed to guard Senawi but not directly approach him. It seems that you knew more of what was happening than he did. He was waiting for the Senawis on the Stockholm excursion tour bus, but the Senawis did not show up. Pietz arrived at the Stockholm square when Senawi was already dead."

"Sorry. We eluded Pietz because we didn't know if we could trust him," Anne said.

"So you know more current events than most people, and this guided you to elude all the spies?" Mattheson asked.

"I do read a lot of history and novels of international intrigue, like John le Carré, Robert Ludlum, and Tom Clancy," Anne answered.

"She's an author too, of a historical romance novel," Higgins said. "I remember my secretary spending her break time reading that book, and out of curiosity, I looked at the cover.

"Well, there are some puzzles in the information that you have told us. When the Iranians were trying to build a nuclear program, the North Koreans were actually helping them get the materials they needed, and shared their know-how from the scientific point of view.

"At that time, there was no Dr. Senawi in their physicist profiles. It is possible that with his coming, the Iranians made greater strides and advanced faster than the North Koreans, who now want their share but are not being given it. Thus, the scenario of them kidnapping Senawi's son, to get what they could not obtain by subtler means.

"I have to warn you that the North Koreans and Iranians are both persistent and terribly violent in their means."

"Could we be safe to go now that you have the disc?" Anne said. "Can you take care of finding Andre Senawi?" She was looking at Higgins and then at Luke and Levi, when she caught a glimpse of her reflection in a mirror. She looked horrified and suddenly felt embarrassed.

Levi looked up. "Not so fast. I'm reading a position paper which I think is what the Iranians are proposing in the coming talks. They want to be allowed to enrich more uranium, and they claim that it is their right. This is confidential information, but the Mossad and the CIA guessed this already. What I'm trying to find out is whether Senawi has something hidden here that I need to decrypt. Also, the Mossad agent who was killed was supposed to pass on to Senawi some secret formula to disable the upcoming missile test, but the Mossad did not know that Senawi had just sent feelers to the CIA."

After working on different possibilities through the computer, Levi threw up his hands. "Nothing more. Are you sure this is all he gave you?" Levi made a copy of the disc.

"He did not give it. I found it in my camera bag after Senawi was killed," Mark answered with a frown. "As you know, his cabin was ransacked by the time we got there."

"There's still something somewhere. Those were Iranian agents trying to get me. Did he tell you something?" Levi persisted, handing Mark the original disc.

Anne and Mark looked at each other. "Janan, the wife, is somewhere in Stockholm. Could it be with her?"

"Janan is his sister," Levi explained. "Senawi's wife and daughter were not allowed to leave Iran, so the government could be sure that Senawi returned. Dr. Senawi was their top nuclear physicist, but his position was deputy because he was Christian. He was probably the one who could make sure that the coming missile test was a success.

"The cruise was like a diversion. Senawi liked to travel, and for a long time he could not. Since he was their prized physicist, he was rewarded with this cruise, just before he would attend the negotiations and presentation to the commission.

"Before he left, however, he surreptitiously dropped a note to a CIA agent at one of the Swiss embassy functions. Neither the CIA nor the Mossad could ascertain whether he was playing a game or indeed wanted to defect. If he were to defect, he was supposed to tell the CIA the locations of their nuclear program and other information, so we could stop it.

"Our gut feeling was that Senawi was for nonproliferation, and he was also a Christian, actually a Chaldean Catholic. He was close to his grandfather, who was a Christian and a history professor.

"Did he talk to you in a strange way or say something out of turn? He could have been giving you a password."

"He did have a curious way about him and would say something out of turn now and then," Anne answered, trying to think. "When we were talking about the Stuxnet cyberworm, he said to me, 'You could be Cassandra.' That scared me, so I never looked him in the eye again until just before he died."

"How does the Stuxnet cyberworm connect with Cassandra?" Mark asked with a knitted brow.

"You know that in Greek mythology Cassandra was the daughter of King Priam of Troy," Anne explained. "She was red haired, blue eyed, and considered second in beauty to Helen. She was given the gift of prophecy by Apollo, but she spurned him. Apollo could not revoke a gift a god had already given, so Apollo made it so that people would not believe Cassandra. She predicted the fall of Troy, but nobody believed her.

"The *Smithsonian* article I read was actually entitled 'The Cassandra Syndrome.' That's because upon being interviewed, Higgins said that the USA released the Stuxnet cyberworm without a defense. If our enemies use it like a boomerang against us, it will destroy our defense, electrical, and financial systems, leading to disaster."

Mark nodded. "I actually liked Senawi, but I did try to keep a distance from him because of the shootings. Instead, he seemed to like to talk to Mom and me. One time when I went to the computer room, he came near me as I turned on my computer. He said, 'Use a Mexican mythology for your password.'"

"That might be it! Let me check it out." Levi tapped on the computer. "Spell those Mexican gods for me."

"Huh?" Mark said.

"Spell *Quetzalcoatl*, Son," Anne said.

"Q-u-et-z-a-l-c-o-a-t-l," Mark said.

"Not that—try another," Levi said.

"Can't think. Pachamama, Cities of Gold, Machu Picchu, Montezuma—I quit," Anne said.

"Right! We talked about Cities of Gold, Lake Titicaca, anacondas, the Amazon, the Caribbean," Mark added.

"Titicaca! There's one," Levi said. "Keep going."

"Okay. Galapagos, Kukapetl, Ecuador, Guatemala," Mark said.

"Kukapetl. That's another." Levi looked up from the computer.

"What's the Indians' or natives' name, the tall ones?" Anne added. "Uh . . ."

"Don't know. I'm tired," Mark said.

"Can we just go now? We'll try to stay hidden until you guys have solved this," Anne said.

"Wrong," Mattheson said drily.

"We will have to take you into a safe house, and it will be a while before this is over, sorry," Higgins said. "If Levi had to shake off those trailing him, then there are still a lot of questions unanswered. You are not safe. You have the original disc for safekeeping because we don't know what we are up against."

"Oh no!" Anne exclaimed, and she covered her face.

"But I still have work to do," Mark protested.

"All that will have to wait," said Higgins, who then tried to reassure them. "We will help you, but there are probably more questions still for you to answer."

"How about our family?" Anne asked.

"We will take them to a safe house," Higgins said. "Don't get in touch with them now. It will be too dangerous."

"But we just got here! The enemy hasn't had time to get to them yet! Can we just join our family in hiding?" Anne persisted.

The phone rang, and Higgins quickly picked it up.

"Oh God! No! Release her, you SOB! We don't have what you are talking about." Higgins slammed the phone down.

Everyone looked at Higgins with apprehension.

"That was a North Korean agent. They grabbed Donna, the secretary, and are using her as a hostage until we give up the blueprint."

"Blueprint?" Anne and Mark looked at each other, puzzled.

"This guy was saying that we have the blueprint from Dr. Senawi. Apparently they kidnapped Senawi's son and threatened to kill the boy if Senawi didn't give them the information to use for their own nuclear bomb. They abducted the son in international waters while he was on his way to a US prep school. Senawi promised he would hand over the blueprint during his cruise."

"That must be the one at the Hermitage," Mark said.

"Son!" Anne said. "Why did you not tell me?"

"I myself could not figure out what was going on. Mom and I made a point of concentrating on the paintings and being quick about it, so we were ahead of the others. That Asian guy was already there ahead of us at the Reuben gallery.

"Senawi was suddenly behind me, and the Asian guy turned from looking at a painting. He talked to Senawi, but only briefly because there was another guy behind Senawi who pulled a gun. The Asian guy also pulled a gun; that's when I yelled, and everybody ducked. The gunmen fought, with the Asian guy kicking the other one's gun away. A lot of security police arrived, and both gunmen fled.

"The museum security apprehended the Middle Eastern guy with a gun. I've noticed him before. He shows up now and then at the cruise ship," Mark said.

"You did not mention that the first time, you know," Levi said.

"We're confused as it is, as to what is important and what is not," Anne said. "One of the gunmen in the museum was killed, wasn't he? Was it the North Korean guy? What happened to the other one who was apprehended?"

"The North Korean agent was shot by museum security when he turned to shoot at them," Levi said. "The other gunman was Iranian; he claimed diplomatic immunity."

"So Senawi had a lot of dealings on this trip! And therefore we need to know which side he was really on," Anne said.

"Right! Now think again if there is more that you can add," Higgins said.

"I'm thinking about whether there were hints he dropped when we were talking about the Stuxnet virus," Mark said thoughtfully. "Mom nudged me to stay quiet when we were talking, but I know she was observing the other people at dinner."

The phone rang. Higgins picked it up.

"I'm sorry, but I was really mad when you first called. We don't have whatever blueprint you are talking about. Please release my secretary . . . What? Okay. Come on in." Higgins put the phone down and motioned to a paper, where he started writing. "They said they are coming for a peaceful negotiation. They want to come in with Donna. What arrogance! They said that they have disabled our security."

Anne got her cell phone and pressed the numbers 911.Mark made calls while looking at the pizza boxes in front of him. Mattheson looked at them and also called the DC police on his cell phone. Mark and Anne ran to the receptionist's desk and hid their suitcases under it. They grabbed their carry-on bags and headed out the door.

"Where are you going?" Higgins asked.

"To hide somewhere!" Anne said. "They don't know about us."

"Wait!" Higgins handed them an envelope before they ran off.

"I'll stay here with Higgins." Levi smiled wryly.

Mattheson got his revolver out and hid behind the bathroom door.

Anne and Mark hid in the bathroom at the reception area. To their right was the elevator. Anne nudged Mark and pointed to her face. She was breathing hard but did not make noise, as she breathed through her mouth. Mark nodded. Next Anne pointed to the elevator. "We'll bolt as soon as they all enter Higgins's office."

They sweated as minutes passed. It had already been fifteen minutes when the elevator opened up.

"Hello! Hello! Pizza delivery here!"

"Over here!" Levi answered distinctly from inside the office.

The delivery boy's noise almost made Anne laugh hysterically, and she covered her mouth. Suddenly the elevator opened again.

"Pizza! Pizza!" Another delivery had arrived.

"Over here!" Levi said again.

Anne peeped through the door. "Did you pay for the pizza?"

"No, I did not want to use my card. I copied the info on the receipt of the pizza that we ate," Mark whispered.

"You're learning fast, Son," Anne whispered with relief. "None of the pizza guys have left yet. Higgins and Levi will probably use them to foil the enemy."

"It did occur to me that Higgins, Levi, and Mattheson could switch clothes with the pizza guys, but our guys are all too well built," Mark answered.

"Something is happening there." Anne started to worry, when they heard the elevator open again.

Both quickly closed the restroom door. They could hear the heavy footsteps of several men and the whimpering voice of the secretary. They heard the footsteps pass through into Higgins's office. Afterward, they peered through the door and, seeing it clear, bolted for the elevator. The elevator door suddenly opened with another pizza delivery boy.

"Pizza! Pizza!" he said.

Anne saw that the boy was in ordinary clothes, not in uniform, so she let the boy pass, pointing to Higgins's office. She then pressed the button for the ground floor and, after some hesitation, also pressed the button for the second floor.

"Let's try to walk out of here casually and quickly grab the first cab. We'll go straight to the airport."

"Is that good, or should we travel by bus?" Mark asked.

"That might be better. Bus it is," Anne said.

The ground floor was swarming with police, with more arriving. Sirens were blaring. Mark stared blankly, but Anne led the way.

"Officer, which way is Pennsylvania Avenue? We're lost. This is where the cab dropped us," Anne said.

"Get lost! There's trouble here. That way, to your left," the officer said, shooing them out of the way.

"Thanks!" Mark said.

Anne was already out the door and heading left. There was no traffic there, as the police had blocked all intersections. It was already getting dark outside, and Anne quickly checked her wristwatch. "Almost eight p.m.," she said to Mark.

They were able to find a cab on the third block west.

"The bus depot, please, just for Maryland," Anne said unnecessarily.

Mark glanced at his mom and nodded.

The cabdriver was quiet and dropped them at the Greyhound terminal without even thanking them for the tip.

They looked around as they bought their tickets and, not seeing anybody following them, decided to go to New York instead.


## 10. New York

"The only hotel we could get without showing an ID would be neither fancy nor safe," Anne said worriedly.

"Can we stay with somebody you know?" Mark wondered.

"I have my address book, but we cannot compromise anybody," Anne said with a sigh. "Let's sleep when we can on the bus; we might find someplace to stay by daylight. We need a place to meet up with your dad and Jim and go into hiding."

Mark fell asleep on the bus, but Anne dozed on and off, worrying and often checking their surroundings. It was early morning when they reached New York. They followed the crowd of people disembarking from the bus and looked around for a place to eat. They headed for the brighter lights and soon saw Times Square from a distance.

"I'm so tired. Maybe we can eat at a McDonald's if it is open already. You can then check on your computer what is going on," Anne said.

Mark pointed instead to a Starbucks with a Free Wi-Fi sign.

Anne arranged their carry-on bags on a chair and motioned to Mark. "I'll go; what do you want?"

"Any meat sandwich and coffee," Mark answered without looking, and he sat down at a table.

It was five o'clock in the morning and they were the first customers, so Anne came back with their orders quickly. Mark had already opened the e-mail and was looking puzzled.

"I don't understand what Dad is saying," he said with a frown.

"Let me get some calories down first. Eat! I'm famished," Anne said, and she chewed several bites, followed by sips of coffee. She then glanced at the computer and looked shocked. "The time on this e-mail is eight p.m. central yesterday, when we were in DC. 'Come home, not feeling well. No problem here.' The e-mail before that was nine a.m. central time, saying, 'Suspicious character knocked for a long time at our door. I called police.' But your dad sent this on our emergency e-mail address already."

"The second one was sent on the same emergency e-mail address too," Mark said.

"Something's wrong! Why can't he just follow instructions?" Anne said angrily; then tears streamed from her eyes. "Darn!" she said. "Let's check where we can sort this out and get some sleep. We need a shower and a change of clothes. It's daytime, less danger."

Pulling their carry-on luggage, they walked along the sidewalk until they noticed a crowd outside a Best Buy store. People were looking at the TV screens inside. They joined the crowd but could not hear amid the noise, so they went inside the store to listen.

"Mr. Richard Higgins was wounded and is in critical condition at the hospital. His secretary received a concussion and several bruises. She was released from the hospital this morning. Two Asian men are dead. Two pizza delivery boys were wounded; one was released this morning, and the other is still in the hospital. Three Asian guys, probably North Koreans, are in police custody. The interpreter said that the Koreans insisted there were other men in the office, but the police could not find them. Our reporter is checking on the rumor that the Koreans will be released on diplomatic grounds."

Anne and Mark looked grim as the disaster scene of Higgins's office was briefly shown. Anne nodded a signal, and they headed for the door.

"What's that?" the announcer said excitedly, making Anne and Mark stop in their tracks. "Two suitcases were found behind the secretary's desk. They seem to belong to persons from a tour or cruise! There are identification tags! One reads 'Mark M. Cortez,' and the other is 'Anne M. Cortez'! The mystery is deepening, folks! The police are looking for those people now!"

Anne and Mark became pale after hearing the news; then their smiling pictures were flashed on the screen.

"Let's go," Anne whispered, and they left with heads down, quickly putting on their sunglasses. "Let's buy new cell phones; there's a shop over there," Anne said.

The sidewalk stall sold cell phones and took cash. They bought two.

"These might have been stolen," Mark protested.

"Precisely. It would be hard to trace our call. As much as possible, we will even use the public phones, just before we leave a place," Anne said.

One block off Broadway, they saw the Belvedere Hotel, and they checked in, paying cash. They showed their IDs and hoped that the clerk was not yet any wiser.

They just waved to the bellboy, signifying they did not need help, and quickly stepped inside the open elevator.

"The people working at this hotel are not yet aware of the search for us. We just have a little time," Anne said once they were inside their room. "Check our e-mails while I check what's in this envelope Higgins gave me. Here it is: e-mail addresses and phone numbers of Higgins, Luke Mattheson, and Levi; a VISA card with Higgins's name; and some kind of ticket. Hmmm. E-mail Levi and Mattheson! I presume that these are safe addresses."

"What should I say?" Mark said. "By the way, I'll use a new e-mail address, talinneston6054@yahoo.com."

"Okay. Just say that we are in hiding, awaiting instructions. Say we need help tracking your dad, and ask how Jim is."

"Here goes!" Mark typed hurriedly and was surprised at the quick answer.

"We are in hiding too. We will check on your dad and Jim. Lie low, but stay in touch." The message was signed by Luke.

"Where are you?" Levi asked. "I need to figure out more passwords. I have the disc."

"Try the words *Mendoza* and *Esteban,*" Anne said to Mark, and they saw that Luke's e-mail address was added.

"Yes! *Mendoza* worked . . . Yes! *Esteban* is the other," Levi typed. "Give me more."

"Golden Condor, Burning Mountain, Olmec," Mark typed.

"*Olmec* is the fifth!" Levi typed. "I'll let the CIA and the Mossad know. This is the disable code. We'll now go to the second level."

"What level?" Anne said, and Mark typed.

"My theory is that Senawi made five different grades, one for each level, and they go stepwise deeper into the system of the nuclear site. I'm not even done with the second level yet, and there are three more to go. Each level has at least five different passwords. Hurry up and think; I need your help. You seem to think along the same lines as Senawi did."

"Oh no!" Anne exclaimed.

"Darn!" Mark said. Then he typed, "Can we come out of hiding? Why are you in hiding?"

"We don't know whom to trust," Luke answered. "Until the Iranian nuclear setup is completely disabled, we are the only ones working on this level. We let the CIA know some information, not all, because we don't completely trust them.

"Higgins is still critical at the hospital, under guard, no visitors allowed. As soon as Higgins can be taken out of the hospital, we will care for him ourselves until this crisis is over."

"Come on, let's finish level two," Levi typed.

"Looks like Senawi used *The Mysterious Cities of Gold,*" Anne said, and Mark typed it.

"What?" Levi typed.

"What's that?" Luke typed.

"It's a children's adventure series about South America, with myth and geography thrown in," Anne said to Mark, and he typed.

"Magellan, St. Elmo's fire," Anne added.

"Marinche, Amazon," Mark typed.

"Magellan, stelmosfire, marinche! More!" Levi typed excitedly.

"Yucatán, Campeche," Mark typed, thinking about geography.

"Mazatlán, Tegucigalpa," Anne added.

"Yucatán, Campeche, Tegucigalpa!" Levi repeated. "Next! Level three!"

Anne and Mark looked at each other. "That might be another set of characters," Anne said to Mark. "How about Greek mythology?"

"Jupiter, Cronus, Aegis, Aphrodite, Hera, Athena, Ares, Neptune," Mark typed quickly.

"No hit," Levi typed.

"Try Gilgamesh, phoenix, Babylon, ziggurat, Megiddo," Anne said, and Mark typed.

"*Gilgamesh* and *ziggurat* are hits! Keep going!" Levi typed.

"Nebuchadnezzar, Melchizedek, Abraham, Isaac, Ishmael," Anne said, and Mark typed the names.

"*Nebuchadnezzar, Melchizedek,* and *Ishmael* are hits!" Luke typed.

"Huh?" Mark typed.

"We copied the disc so that we each have a copy, and a third one is for Higgins. I'm in another hotel, but we know where each other is. Tell us where you are," Levi typed.

"Better not," Anne said, and Mark typed. "We're so spooked."

"Okay. Your way," Levi typed.

"You're more paranoid than most spies," Luke typed.

"We're amateurs and not feeling comfortable," Anne said, and Mark typed.

"Okay. Some more. What happens is this: after some words seem to click, there are irregular gaps where I scramble numbers to fit in," Levi typed.

"Jerusalem, Mazada, Tiberias." Mark typed as Anne spoke.

"*Mazada* and *Tiberias* are hits! I can finish level three today," Levi typed.

"Isn't that longer and longer?" Anne asked.

"Yes, you noticed! The first was five, then six, now seven. Let's resume tomorrow. I still have to fit scrambled numbers here."

"What a relief!" Mark typed without prodding as Anne sighed.


## 11. The Storage Box

Their hotel room window faced east, and Anne pulled the curtains to avoid the glare on the TV screen as they watched the news that indeed the North Koreans had diplomatic passports and would be escorted to the airport to leave the country. "We still need to check this out, where the order is coming from," the female newscaster said with a frown.

Anne frowned too but continued with her task. "This envelope has so many things on it that look like treasures. It'll be a big help if we can figure this out. This ticket says 'Grand Central Station locker.'" Anne gave the ticket to Mark.

Mark looked at it. "It says 'Grand Central Station' but gives an address. Let me check . . . No, it is not in Grand Central Station. There is no more locker service there, but Schwartz Travel Services has locker storage. The address is 34 West Forty-Sixth Street, between Fifth and Sixth Avenue, on the fourth floor. They can store your luggage with them at ten dollars per bag per day."

"We will need money if we stay in hiding for a long time," Anne said. "Our family accounts are already under watch. If your dad is already compromised, we would still need to help him. All we know is that he and Jim are alive. Let's presume that it's the CIA guarding them. Once we get in touch with them, the enemies will swoop in. Let's check out that locker as soon as possible."

"Can we get some sleep or rest first?" Mark yawned.

"Okay. Come to think of it, I'm tired," Anne said, and she glanced at Mark, who was already on his bed after removing his shoes.

Anne brushed her teeth and used a warm-water-soaked towel to wipe her face. She needed to get some sleep.

They woke up after two in the afternoon, and Anne showered quickly. She had to do more to alter her appearance, so she checked herself at the mirror, figuring out what she needed to buy when they go out.

"Let's go." Mark dressed quickly after coming out of the shower.

"Son, let's try one thing, if you don't mind." Anne took her comb and parted Mark's hair in the middle and made him wear her reading glasses. "You look different now. If you're okay with this, we only need to buy you some eyeglass. For me, I'll need scissors to cut my hair, hair dye, and some ordinary but deceiving outfit."

"Okay by me; after all, it's a matter of survival," Mark answered with a shrug.

They took the elevator and tried to look nonchalant, but Anne was getting edgy. They started at a brisk pace at once.

"Let's walk," Anne said. "Taking a taxi could be trouble if the taxi driver saw us on TV. Besides, we can start buying our eyeglasses and other contraptions from the sidewalk vendors."

On the way to Grand Central Station, Anne bought three pairs of light sunglasses and a visor; Mark already had his baseball cap on.

"You're going to be hot with that; just use the eyeglasses, and use that as backup," Anne said, pointing to the cap.

"Mom!" Mark protested, and he adjusted his cap. "On second thought, the scholarly look is more ingenious." Mark put on the eyeglasses and stuffed the cap in his backpack.

"A drugstore! Let's get what we need now; we can also get a bag for whatever is in the locker," Anne said, and she hurried in.

They bought toiletries and disguise paraphernalia. They paid in cash.

"I remember in *The Day of the Jackal* that the assassin put on makeup that made him look ill," Anne explained to Mark as they continued to walk at a brisk pace.

They arrived at the address for Schwartz Travel Services and gave the ticket to an attendant. Anne opened her bag to pay.

"It's prepaid already with a credit card." The young man handed them a duffel bag with a smile.

"Thank you," Mark said pleasantly, and he took the bag.

"I'm really hungry now," Anne said with a side glance as soon as they were back on the street. "Is it heavy?"

"Not very, but yes. I can't wait to open it. Can we eat a big meal? Nobody seems to be following us."

"About time—a square meal, nothing fancy, or we are out of place," Anne agreed, and she pointed to a diner.

They bought some food from a grocery before heading back to the hotel.

Anne and Mark were both laden with parcels when they arrived at the hotel, glad that they looked like the rest of the passengers hurrying to the elevator.

"That's why it was heavy," Mark said as he placed two guns wrapped in several layers of paper on top of the table.

Anne sat across from him on another chair and tried to open another paper-bound bundle. "I need the scissors now," she said as she got it out of the grocery bag and cut the tape. "Money? How much is this?" She split it with Mark, and they started counting.

"A hundred thousand dollars! Let's count it again." Anne started from one stack of bills while Mark started on another. "That's what it is," she said exhaustedly. "What have we gotten ourselves into? If this mystery is going to take a while to solve, then we need that money; but that's not even worth our lives."

Mark lay on his bed and looked tired. "I don't even know how to use a gun."

"I took one lesson, so I can fire it, but that's all. I wouldn't even know if it was loaded, and I'd be afraid to check. Can't think," Anne said, and she lay on her bed, closing her eyes.

## 12. The Hostage

Both must have dozed off since it was dark when they woke up. Anne turned on the TV and rummaged through the food bags. Suddenly she looked up as the screen showed the North Korean party that would soon be deported.

"Son, wake up!" She pointed at the TV screen at the same time.

Mark sat up. "That's Andre! Senawi's son!" Mark opened his computer and e-mailed Levi and Luke to check out the news.

"Stop them! They're taking Senawi's son to North Korea and will use him as a pawn!" Anne dictated beside Mark by the computer, feeling very agitated.

"The attorney general's office has given the final approval to let the North Koreans leave, citing diplomatic protocol," the news anchor said.

"No answer from Levi or Luke?" Anne's eyes widened as Mark shook his head. "We have to do something! That poor kid! Is that Dulles Airport or JFK? Let's call somebody!" Anne took out the envelope and called Higgins's cell phone number.

"Mattheson here," said a voice Anne recognized.

"Luke! The Koreans are taking Senawi's son with them! Stop them!"

"What!" Levi could be heard from a distance.

"Is that Dulles Airport? Stop them!" Anne said louder.

"Good Lord! I'll call the CIA," Levi said.

"I'm calling airport security; I know Jack Wilson," Luke said.

Anne and Mark held their breath as the phone line went dead. Finally Anne's cell phone rang.

"I've temporarily stopped the plane from departing, but the CIA may need to physically snatch Senawi's son. The North Koreans are claiming it's their diplomat's son," Levi said.

"With those eyes!" Anne said sarcastically.

"Higgins is not much help. He took a downturn; that's why Luke and I rushed to the hospital," Levi explained.

"If he is breathing and his surgery wound is all right, I'll remove Higgins and take him to an undisclosed location," Anne said angrily.

"Where would that be?" Levi countered, getting angry.

"How about Mt. Sinai Hospital?" Anne thought aloud.

"I'm going to Dulles Airport; you take care of Higgins," Levi said to Luke.

"Use the Mossad then, not the CIA!" Anne couldn't help saying.

Levi looked at Luke and called on his cell phone. "Hello, Ben? You saw the TV report too? I'll meet you at the airport."

Anne angrily dialed the number again. She got angrier when it kept ringing and nobody was answering.

"Hold your horses! Geez!" Luke said irritably when he picked up. "I'm alone here making arrangements to move Higgins, and Levi is having problems!"

"I'm sorry. What problems?" Anne said anxiously.

"The North Koreans are adamant that they should leave now."

"They're not even supposed to have an embassy in Washington, right? Why are they there?" Anne said in a raised voice.

"Don't take it out on me! I didn't do it!" Luke answered back, getting irritated. "You are right! That's a lot of clout they are enjoying with this administration, and looks like Levi can't stop them!" Luke said.

"What plane are they taking? How could it leave?" Anne asked, but the line went dead. She looked at the TV screen and pointed to Mark. "Not a commercial plane, and they are about to board."

They looked at each other helplessly; then Anne had an idea.

"Go back to our old e-mail address and look for the e-mail address of my classmate who is in the U.S. Air Force! His e-mail starts with *mister*." She sidled over to Mark as he changed his e-mail address. "This one! Quick! Write the following: 'Urgent! Please call me right now! Need air force help! Write your new cell phone number!'" Anne paused and prayed.

"An answer, Mom!" Mark could not believe it; then his cell phone rang.

"Larry!" Anne said breathlessly. "Thank God! Have you been watching TV? I need your help! Those North Koreans are taking as hostage the son of a nuclear physicist we met on our cruise. The Koreans killed Dr. Senawi already. Don't let them leave the USA with Andre!" she said.

"Anne? Hold on, I can't understand you!" Larry answered.

Anne took a deep breath before repeating herself. "Andre is the son. Sorry, I'm so distressed here. My son and I were there when Dr. Senawi was killed. The North Koreans kidnapped the son so that Senawi would tell them how to perfect their nuclear bomb, but apparently Senawi was also about to defect to the USA. We're trying to decipher something he gave us, but please help save the son!" Anne looked at the phone when it went silent. "Hello? Hello?"

"Anne! Take it easy. I'm thinking . . . Okay. I'm calling my buddies. I'll call you back on this line," Larry said.

Suddenly Anne's cell phone rang.

"Levi is not answering, and his phone is dead, which means he is in trouble," Luke said slowly. "Levi and I both have a GPS device on our leg, so I know he is still at Dulles. I'm going!" Luke said.

"No! It's a trap!" Anne said, somehow having a premonition. "My classmate will try to stop the plane from leaving, or at least not let it reach its destination. Let's secure Higgins's safety first and then . . . Oh! I can't think. Is it better for us to be in Washington? Where could we be safe?"

"Where will Higgins be safe?" Luke asked. "We'd better take him somewhere closer."

"Luke," Anne said in between breaths, "would you take the ambulance carrying Higgins to the Israeli embassy instead? Take your computers and the discs with you. At least the enemy—or whoever—is not yet expecting this move. If you are at the embassy, you can get more of their guys to go to Dulles and check out what happened to Levi and Ben.

"It might be better for us to be closer to Washington, but we're not sure if it is wise for all of us to be in the same place. Wait"—Anne picked up the other cell phone and listened—"my classmate said that the private plane belongs to an Asian businessman. If it continues to prepare for departure, they will fly over it so that it goes back to the airport. This will cause an international incident and his friends might be court-martialed, but they will take the risk . . . Oh!" Anne started to cry helplessly.

Luke was silent for a while. "Okay. I think taking Higgins to the embassy is a good idea. I'll call you when I get there."

Mark held his mother's shoulders and let her cry.

"The plane is delayed. There's a stalemate." The TV announcer's excited voice made Anne and Mark look at the screen. "Wait! It's leaving! Folks, this is the plane carrying the North Koreans with diplomatic passports through the UN. For those who are just joining us now, these people were involved in a fiasco at Richard Higgins's office, where Richard Higgins was shot. Higgins is in critical condition, two North Koreans are dead, and several pizza boys are wounded."

Anne and Mark waited for either phone to ring, but the phones were silent.

"Shall we pack?" Anne said.

"Where to?" Mark asked.

"I don't really know. We've been safe for a while, but I don't know how long it'll last. I'm thinking of going to Virginia or Maryland, closer to Washington, but for what? How else can we help?"

Both jumped when the phone rang.

"Take the Amtrak to DC, and then take a cab to this embassy. Call me when you are getting close; we'll be waiting for you," Luke said.

"Where is Levi? Is he on the plane? Where is it going?" Anne asked.

"Levi is on the plane, but he's nonfunctional. I don't know if he is alive. Your classmate's buddies almost succeeded, but the order came from the secretary of defense to let them go."

"All right, we're coming back. By the way, what happened to our suitcases?" Anne asked.

"What? Oh! Of all things! They've been sent to your address." Luke sounded exasperated.

"I'm done packing," Mark said.

"I'll be done in a minute. Let's split the money and the gun. We have to keep the gun under wraps; maybe it was packed this way to escape detection. At least if it is in our overnight carry-on luggage, they might not inspect it. After all, it's Amtrak, not an airport. We have to bring the food; we don't have time for any real meal," Anne said as she packed. They were soon out of the hotel and hailing a cab.

"How safe is a taxi?" Mark asked.

"We can chance it once. After all, we've altered our appearance, even if we are carrying some luggage," Anne said as a taxi stopped.

They quickly got into the taxi. Anne had put a scarf around her hair in a fashion that could be mistaken for a cancer patient after chemotherapy, or a religious person covering her hair. With eyeglasses on, she felt she looked different enough already to pass first glance.

The Amtrak trip was uneventful; the two dozed on and off and ate whatever food they had leftover. Just before reaching DC, Anne wiped her face with a napkin wet with water from their water bottle. She handed one to Mark too.

"This will help me clear my mind a bit. We need to be on the alert once the cab nears the embassy. I need to make sure the taxi driver speeds up if necessary," Anne said, beginning to tense up. "There have been no calls in the meantime. I don't like it."

It took some time for a taxi to come, and Anne hoped the taxi driver did not notice how she hesitated for just a second. She came in and put her luggage with her in the passenger seat. Mark did the same. The cabdriver had a turban.

"Please take us to the Israeli embassy. Do you know where it is?" Anne said in a soft voice.

"Yes, ma'am," the taxi driver said with just a backward glance, "but it might be closed."

"I'll call when we're nearby. Our plane was badly delayed, and we had to take the Amtrak. The person sponsoring my treatment told us to just go there."

The taxi driver merely nodded.

## 13. The Israeli Embassy

Mark called on Luke's phone as soon as they turned unto the street where the embassy was located. The embassy gate opened, and the guard had his gun ready when the taxi dropped them off.

Embassy personnel helped them carry their bags to a room where Luke was waiting. It was like a clinic room, and Higgins was on a stretcher bed with IV fluids infused from bags hanging from poles. There was a doctor in attendance.

"It was a good decision to bring him here. We have doctors who can take turns to be sure that he recuperates fully. There was indeed some degree of questionable medication, and we don't know if it was due to tampering. I'm Doctor Eli Zeev." He shook hands with Anne and Mark.

"Thank God for that!" Anne said with relief; then she turned to Luke. "If Higgins can be safe here, we can pursue the kidnappers of Andre Senawi and Levi. That's more urgent. It may still be tied to our deciphering the disablement disc."

A big guy in camouflage gear came into the room. "I'm Captain Aaron Talmor. The plane carrying Andre Senawi and Levi was going to North Korea, but your air force friends forced it out of direction. It might land in northern France instead, before the plane's fuel runs out. Our men were instructed to apprehend them, but we are not sure how the French government will cooperate."

"Can we go there?" Anne said. "I feel responsible for Andre. Also, where can we safely return him? What's happening to his family? Where is Janan?"

Captain Talmor called on his cell phone instead.

Luke Mattheson sighed and, looking around, sat on a nearby chair. "Can we get some coffee?"

The embassy personnel left to get it just as a medium-sized, muscular man came in.

"Moshe Goldfarb, Mossad," he said, and he shook hands with each of them. He went to the TV in the room and put it on a special channel. He also had a pointer and used it to indicate a map on the screen. "We are getting ready to apprehend the kidnappers. They are not the only problem. The Iranians are somewhere here, looking for whatever Dr. Senawi might have given away regarding their nuclear program. Dr.

Senawi held the key to complete it and might have already formulated everything. When you said that it was a disable code that Levi was decrypting, we figured that Senawi had completed his formulations. Now we hope you succeed in decrypting this disc."

"Can we come?" Anne repeated.

"Yes. We realized that Levi decrypted the disc faster with your help, and it is possible that there might still be things that will unravel when we see Senawi's son. We leave as soon as possible for the airport."

"Oh!" Anne and Mark said.

"We'll give you soldiers' fatigues. You can carry only what will fit in a backpack." Goldfarb looked at Anne's perplexed face. "We'll give you a backpack."

The coffee arrived, and they hurriedly prepared their own cups.

Anne breathed a sigh of relief when their fatigues arrived along with a backpack for her. She placed her essentials in the backpack and approached Mark. He nodded. She then left to change in the ladies' room.

Luke and Mark changed in the men's room.

"We'll put your other things in safekeeping in the meantime," the embassy personnel said as she picked up the bags.

"Just a sec," Anne said. She opened one bag and took out a bag of candies. "This helps; I easily get hungry." She folded the sleeves and pant cuffs of her fatigues, which were too long. "One more second, if you don't mind." She got the other bag, dug out the scissors, and cut off her sleeves.

The female personnel helped her finish the cutting.

"Ready," Anne said finally.

They were a little crammed in the SUV going to the airport since Goldfarb and Talmor had other people on their team. They were all quiet as they boarded the private plane.


## 14. From France to Switzerland

Anne and Mark fell asleep on the plane and were roused only when they heard the plane making a hissing noise prior to landing.

"Where are we?" Anne asked Talmor.

"We are at Charles de Gaulle Airport. We are changing to helicopters. The kidnappers have landed in Lyon, France, and commandeered a van to take them to Switzerland. We think that they are heading for the Chinese consulate. The attack helicopter will get there ahead of us."

The soldiers and Mossad agents left the airplane first. They boarded two helicopters that were awaiting them with engines already running. Goldfarb led the way to the last helicopter, with Luke helping Anne get aboard the chopper. With a heave and a grunt, Mark got aboard last. Goldfarb curiously looked at the two carrying their backpacks with them but said nothing.

"We are ahead of the van the North Koreans have taken," Goldfarb updated them. "The other helicopter will block its way, but we have to be careful since they have Andre and Levi as hostage."

Their helicopter landed in a clearing just before the Swiss border. The Israeli soldiers and agents had already taken positions along the ditches, the rocks, and the trees.

After a while, Goldfarb impatiently looked at his watch. The buzz from his Bluetooth lit up his eyes, but it quickly changed into a frown.

"We will commandeer some cars too and give chase. Keep us posted on where they are going." He signaled his men for a briefing. "They took an unexpected turn and then hid in a tunnel. We need cars to get there, because it's hard for a helicopter to land in that mountainous area."

The soldiers started commandeering the cars on the highway. Goldfarb arranged a car for them, and the driver agreed to come with them. Goldfarb took the front seat next to the driver, and Anne sat between Luke and Mark in the back.

Their car quickly sped up the mountain, following the other cars. At the mouth of a tunnel under a mountain, one Israeli helicopter guarded the rear while the soldiers and agents moved toward the entrance. There had been no movement from inside for a while.

Most motorists had driven their cars onto the road shoulder, trying to get out of the confrontation.

Minutes went by, and Anne could see the sweat on Goldfarb's brow as he stood waiting with his gun pointing at the entrance. Anne and Mark tensed up at the rustling sound of leaves being stepped on.

An Asian man came out, pushing a young man ahead of him, with a gun pointing at the hostage's head. Five more men followed after him. They walked closely together while pointing three AK-47s toward the Israeli group.

"You will let us go, or we will kill this hostage. If you move against us, we will kill this young man and detonate the bomb tied to your friend over there in the back of the van." The leader spoke with assurance and calmly motioned for two cars to be vacated.

"How do we know our friend is safe?" Goldfarb asked.

"You can go and see him yourself," the leader said.

"Keep your hands up while we check and you will be free to go," Goldfarb negotiated.

One of the soldiers went inside the tunnel. Suddenly, a deafening blast startled those who were outside; then they could see fire coming out of the tunnel.

The impact, the noise, and the fire caused enough diversion that the Asians were able to hijack two cars and take off with the hostage.

"No!" Goldfarb cried, and he ran inside the tunnel with several of the soldiers.

"After him!" Anne said, running back to the car they had used, with the driver still inside. Mark followed, and as the car screeched in reverse, Luke climbed in too.

Anne had learned from Mark to have her backpack on most of the time, and she quickly took out her cell phone. She suddenly hesitated and asked Luke, "Who do I call?"

Luke looked blank for a while and then took the phone. "Let's call the embassy . . . Is this international? Hello? Reporting an incident . . . Awaiting instructions . . . We are in pursuit of the kidnappers. We need backup. They are heavily armed, in two cars . . ." He listened and then took a pen from his pocket. Anne straightened out a small piece of paper in front of him, and he wrote down instructions.

Anne reached out to the average-sized, brown-haired driver of the car. "Thank you." The driver merely nodded and concentrated on his pursuit. Only then did Anne notice the driver's demeanor. "Are you American?"

"Yes. I was here on a backpacking tour when you guys commissioned me. I'm glad to help. Name's Alain."

"Oh! God bless you, Alain! Those guys over there kidnapped the son of a scientist who wanted to help us. We have to save the hostage. We don't know what has happened back there, but we need to pursue those guys."

"Okay. Watch out, a lot of dangerous curves ahead," Alain said, and then he was silent and tense as the winding roads became narrow and just one lane each way.

Anne got thrown toward Mark and resolved to hold on tighter, when the phone rang.

"Yes?" Luke listened and then said, "Okay." He closed the phone. "The Swiss are cooperating, and helicopters are going to shadow the cars. The man inside the van was badly burned and needs to be taken to the hospital. Goldfarb is okay. The first soldier who went in is dead."

"Why are we always several steps behind? I don't understand it!" Anne said in frustration.

Luke looked at her and then said, "You are paranoid."

"Mom is right!" Mark said. "We should have solved this problem already! We had the upper hand in Washington, DC. That's our territory!"

Suddenly they heard shots. The cars they were pursuing were shooting at them.

"Oh yeah? I know this road!" Alain said angrily. "Watch me!" He slowed down to put a little distance between the cars; then suddenly sped up to ram their car against the shooting car, just as the winding road was heading downslope.

"Oh God!" Anne screamed and closed her eyes just as their car slammed into the car ahead of them, which in turn slammed against the first car. The first car was pinned against a tree.

"The gun!" Anne opened her eyes and looked at Mark, shaken but wide-eyed. She opened her backpack quickly and unwrapped the revolver.

Mark did the same.

Luke looked at them, unhooked his seat belt, and took Anne's revolver.

"Let me have that!" Alain held out his hand, and Mark gave his.

Luke and Alain ran forward and took cover from a tree nearby. Anne and Mark followed cautiously behind them.

There was motion in the car ahead, and the door opened. One man staggered out, bleeding. Another man came out of the lead car, holding his AK-47. Alain shot him.

Anne's eyes widened; she took a gulp and moved forward behind Alain. She had no weapon, so she bent over and filled her hand with road dirt.

Mark saw her and did the same.

Alain approached the first car from the left and shoved the bleeding man aside. He picked up one AK-47 and turned to give the revolver to Anne. He took a cursory look at the car and, with a signal to Luke, moved quickly to the forward car.

Luke advanced from the right and inspected the car. He disarmed the dazed men still strapped by their seat belts. He also took an AK-47 and gave his revolver to Mark after cocking it.

Anne had shaken when Alain had given her the revolver, but she moved forward with resolve and inspected the man who was face down on the ground. The man seemed alive, and surmising that the man was not capable of hurting them, she turned the man face up.

"Levi! It's Levi!" she said.

Levi was bleeding from his side.

"Here's the hostage!" Alain said from the front.

Suddenly a shot rang out. Anne and Mark hit the ground. Luke was only momentarily stunned; he moved forward and unloaded the AK-47 clip on the North Korean who'd shot Alain. Blood splattered on Andre too, but the young man took it stoically.

Anne ran forward to help Alain. Alain was bleeding from the stomach.

Mark ran around the back to help Andre come out of the car. "Are you all right?"

The man on Andre's left moved, and Luke shot him too. Like a madman unleashed, Luke moved forward and shot the other Asians sitting in the front seats.

Anne stared at Luke, who was suddenly transformed. "No!" she said, and she was about to move forward but thought better of it. "Luke, it's all right now. We'll call for help. Let's hope our guys will be all right," she said softly.

Luke blinked and then put down his AK-47.

"Let's call on the cell phone," Anne said softly. "We need an ambulance for three men. I'm not sure if Andre is all right."

It took a second before Luke called on the cell phone.

"Son, take care of Alain. I'm putting a pressure on Levi's side." Anne looked up.

Mark was already on Alain's side, opening the shirt and putting a pressure on the stomach wound.

"Ambulance helicopter is on the way. The Swiss were confused at first about whether it was the same site," Luke said, and he sat on the ground, looking sad.

"Oh Luke!" Anne said, coming over. She uncharacteristically touched his hand. "You did the right thing. You had no choice, or we would be dead too. Those guys were merciless. They must have beaten up and drugged Levi. I don't know who was left in the van and got burned. It might be Ben." Anne ended up crying.

Luke stared at her and then put his hand on her shoulder. "I'll be all right," he said.

Anne and Mark checked Levi and Alain again, trying their best to lay them comfortably on the ground by the shade of the car. Anne then signaled to Luke and Mark, and they talked together with Andre.

"Something terrible has happened to your family," Anne started.

"Is my father dead?" Andre asked.

Anne looked at Mark and Luke, not wanting to say the awful truth, but she saw Andre softly crying. She just nodded.

"I want to see my father," Andre said.

"Stockholm," Anne said. "It will not be easy, even from diplomatic channels. Both North Koreans and Iranians will be watching."

"I know," Andre said simply.

They checked their watches several times before the helicopter came.

Anne and Mark helped put the intravenous lines into the patients and assisted in whatever ways they could.

"Hurry! These two are seriously wounded." Anne tried not to sound impatient. She turned to Andre and said softly, "We will follow you to the hospital. You need to be checked. Don't talk to anyone about this."

Andre nodded.

"You have to drive to the hospital where we will take the patients. We don't have room for you. Here are the directions," the nurse said, writing them down.

Luke looked at the paper and frowned. "It's in French. Wait!"

Mark came forward and looked at the directions. "I can translate this."

"You'll have to help me navigate," Luke said as they prepared to follow. "I hope this car can still move; we have no other choice."

Anne sat tensely in the back as Luke drove the car. It moved in fits and starts, and they kept checking their direction. What normally would have taken two hours became three, but they arrived at the hospital. Luke parked on the street.

The hospital staff was friendly and seemed to be expecting them. Levi and Alain had been rushed to the operating room, and the nurse in the waiting room area assured them that the operation was going on smoothly.

"Let's check on Andre. I'm worried," Anne said.

"I want to see my father! I'm all right!" Andre's voice could be heard through the slightly ajar door of the room where the emergency-room doctor was examining him.

Anne unceremoniously said, "Excuse me," and she entered the room. Luke and Mark followed.

The ER doctor had just finished examining Andre and looked at the intruders with a frown.

"Doctor, this patient has been the cause of an international incident. We will take him now if you are done. Are the findings normal? Does he need a psychiatrist?" Anne said.

"His physical exam is fine. Take him. I couldn't care less with all these diplomatic incidents," the doctor said irritably.

"Let's go, Mr. Senawi." Anne tried to appear noncommittal and hurried Andre out of the room.

They went back to the operating room waiting area and bought some food from the vending machines. They talked while they ate.

"Andre, do you want to go back to Iran?" Anne asked.

"If my father is dead, I will not live there, but I have to bury my father in our ancestral land," Andre answered.

"Can you tell us why? Your aunt may still be in Stockholm—I'm not sure—but she was also going to hide," Anne said gently.

"My father said that if something happened to him, I should not live in Iran until it is peaceful, because my family will be persecuted. We are Chaldean Catholics, and our family is the last of our clan," Andre said calmly. "Aunt Janan could take care of me, but I am the man of the family now. I have to get my mother and sister out too."

"Where would you like to go?" Anne asked.

"Help me go to Stockholm. I need to see my father's body and say good-bye. Then help me find Aunt Janan. She will know better what is going on back home."

"I can't promise you that," Anne said tentatively, "but maybe we can ask other government people to help us. The North Koreans kidnapped you to get secrets about the nuclear bomb. That's because your father had moved the Iranian program much faster than theirs."

"My father had many secrets that he would reveal only to me," Andre answered.

"We will have to ask our government to protect us if you want to see your father. The Iranians and North Koreans have a stake in what your father knew. We cannot approach without those people knowing."

"Help me find a way, please!" For the first time, Andre was tearful.

Anne looked at the lanky young man with his curly auburn hair. He looked like a juvenile Greek god. Anne sat there unable to think, so she raised her hand as if she were calling a time-out and hurriedly finished eating. She was clearing up when there was a noise from the far end of the surgery pavilion.

"You can't go in there. The surgery is just finishing. I'll call security!"

The nurse's voice was followed by a scream and then the sound of several heavy footsteps approaching.

Luke pushed Andre toward a closet. Anne and Mark hid behind a laundry cart, and Luke stood with a revolver behind the door. The footsteps passed the waiting room, and the operating room buzzer sounded several times. They heard a door opening, a friendly voice turning into a protest, and then the door closing.

Anne signaled to go silently, with her finger across her lips. Luke pulled Andre from his hiding place. Mark was already ahead of them and pressing for the elevator. The others got there as the elevator opened. Mark pressed the button for the lobby.

"Let's use the side door; there might be somebody watching. Mark and I will go first, followed by Luke and Andre. We'd better not use the car. Let's get a cab," Anne said in between breaths.

There were no cabs by the side door, so Luke got one waiting by the main door. As the cab turned around, the others got in. They were just a few paces ahead. Anne looked back to see several men coming out of the main door and gesticulating.

They directed their taxi to the Eurail, and Anne got tickets.

Part III

# The Trail to the Solution

## 15. Return to Stockholm

"Where are we going?" Mark asked.

"I got tickets that should take us to Stockholm. We can make several stops or go straight through. What do you think? We can throw this away if you don't like it." She looked at Luke and Andre.

"I like it!" Andre said.

"Search me . . . okay," Luke said with a sigh.

"Maybe when we've lost our tail, you can call to check on Levi and Alain," Anne said to Luke.

"Let's do that in the next country. We also have to change clothes," Luke answered.

Mark and Andre smiled as Anne suddenly looked at their fatigues and sighed.

"Maybe we should change now, but it's quite late already. Even if it's not safe to travel in these fatigues, let's hope we can shop in the next town by morning. Let's hop on this train now; I'll buy the clothes tomorrow. Let me write down your sizes." Seeing Luke frown, Anne added, "What? I'm just like a mother shopping for people here. It'll be too obvious if we all go shopping in fatigues. Come to think of it, I still have the euros we exchanged in Stockholm last time."

Luke glared at her and then led them to the back of the train. "All right, mother hen, over here. If some bad guys come, we can easily hop out."

They sat down without comment and were soon asleep, Luke securing the aisle.

The rising sun streamed its golden light on Anne's face as soon as the train emerged from the tunnel. She woke up with a start and woke Mark up too. She checked her watch and was glad she had slept. Across from her sat Andre, still asleep with his mouth open.

Luke had sat along the aisle on Andre's right, and he was awake already, looking ahead and deep in thought. "We're now in Germany. We'll all come down, eat, and shop together. It would not be good to get separated. We should change our clothes before we board the train again."

"I think so too. Okay," Anne agreed.

Once the train stopped at a big town, they disembarked and ate at a small café. They took a window seat and observed the market square, which was surrounded by quaint shops and a department store.

They moved quickly and bought their clothes with an eye on comfort and the nondescript. They bought a backpack for Andre and filled it with changes of clothing. Anne paid for it in cash, and then each one changed clothes in the restroom. They hurried up to catch the next train on the schedule.

"If anybody searches for us, I hope it takes them a long time to identify us on the store camera," Mark said as they boarded the train.

They sat in the usual arrangement, with Luke and Mark in the aisle seats.

"How do we get Andre to see his father's body?" Anne asked Luke.

"We're not using diplomatic channels; we have to see the body in the morgue secretly, if that's enough for Andre," Luke answered.

"That would suffice. I just need a knife," Andre said.

"What for, Andre?" Anne tried to sound calm.

"We have a family code hidden in my father's leg," Andre said.

"Oh! Is that purely related to your family, or are there state secrets?" Anne asked before she could check herself.

"I don't know, but my father told me this again and again," Andre replied.

"Wait, I . . ." Anne was at a loss for words. "What does that mean?"

"You will see it. I can't tell you," Andre replied.

"Is that fair? I mean, it's so dangerous, and we can't leave you, but we don't know what's at stake," Anne protested, and she looked at Mark and Luke.

"I need your help! Please stay with me!" Andre pleaded.

Luke had been silently observing, and he addressed Anne and Mark instead of Andre. "We will go with you, and we must do it quickly. It is possible you are not completely aware of what your father had in mind."

Andre smiled thankfully while Anne looked flabbergasted, and Mark just nodded.

They went on an express train schedule, so they arrived in Stockholm the next day. The trip had been uneventful, and Anne breathed a sigh of relief, hoping that they had indeed eluded whoever might be pursuing them.

They came out of the central station with their backpacks, squinting at the bright sunlight.

"Let's go to a hotel room so we can plan things and get organized. I don't even know where to start," Anne said.

"Radisson, Royal Blue, Viking Hotel . . ." Mark read out the hotel signs.

"Still too central—we need a more discreet one," Anne said.

They booked at the Scandic Sergel Plaza on Brunkebergstorg Street. It had free Internet, and it was nearby the posh shops.

Anne saw a newspaper stand and went to buy newspapers, including older issues. She joined the group in a hurry and paid cash for two adjoining rooms with the last of her euros.

"I'm running low on euros," Anne said. "I'll exchange the dollars I have left." She exchanged them at the hotel desk while the guys waited nearby.

"We'll keep the door open between the rooms," Anne said. "Shall we meet in thirty minutes for conference?"

Luke and Andre nodded.

"I'll take a shower first," Anne said to Mark. "I can then inventory what we have."

Anne was out of the shower in fifteen minutes. She hurriedly trimmed her hair shorter and used a hair gel from Mark's backpack to keep the hair off her face. *Wrong sequence,* she thought. *I should have cut my hair before the shower.* She sighed, knowing that she'd needed to get in there first so that she wouldn't keep the group waiting. With the short hair, she looked androgynous, and she wore a knee-length skirt so she would look less noticeable.

She turned on the TV, opened up some packed food, and then scanned the newspaper headlines. There was no news referring to them. Just then she heard a knock.

"Come in," Anne said without looking.

Luke and Andre came in just as Mark was bringing out his computer. Mark searched for information about hospital morgues in the white pages.

"We might need to talk to somebody in the pathology department to help us," he said with a frown. "There's no information here on exactly where the morgue is or what the procedure is."

"Are we sure which hospital he's in?" Anne asked.

"No," Mark answered. "There's no listing for it."

Luke looked up and hurriedly turned up the TV volume.

"The Iranian government is adamant that the body of Dr. Senawi be returned to Iran. They also denounce whoever has killed Dr. Senawi, and their ambassador is certain that their complaint will be filed in the international court at The Hague. Let's hear from Marcus Schmidt."

The TV anchor let the local reporter talk. "This is Marcus Schmidt, in front of the Karolinska University Hospital. The body of Dr. Senawi is in the hospital pending a resolution of a claim by the Chaldean organization in the USA. The Chaldean organization wants to bury Dr. Senawi following their tradition, which is different from that of the Iranian government." The TV screen showed the anchorman speaking again. "Now back to the Olympics . . ."

"What a break!" Mark said.

"We must do it tomorrow," Luke said. "We'll have to play it by ear."

"It won't be easy going about town when all we know are the landmarks. Let's get help. Maybe that Guzman guy can help us. Also, what has happened to Levi and Higgins? Could you get in touch through the Israeli embassy? Our phones have no international SIM card."

"Slow down," Luke said patiently. He seemed to have finally acclimatized himself to Anne's rapid questioning. "We'll have to use the computer. Mark, put in this address." Luke sidled over to Mark and gave an e-mail address. "Just write this: 'Status report on Richard Higgins and Levi. Sign in Luke.'"

They waited.

Anne looked through her backpack, where she had transferred some of her important things from her carry-on luggage. "I was afraid I'd lost it. Here, enter this information now. E-mail Guzman to meet us. He could be a big help. Also, he could be a big help if Levi is out. Are you familiar with Guzman?" She turned to Luke.

"That Love Virus guy?" Luke asked.

"Yes, we met him here in Stockholm shortly after Senawi was killed." Anne looked at Andre. "We still have a lot to talk about when we get the chance."

"An answer!" Mark said, and he read it aloud. "Those were Iranians who arrived in the hospital after the helicopter fiasco. The Swiss security system locked down the operating area when the Iranians tried to shoot through the bulletproof glass. More security came afterward, but the Iranians had already escaped. So Levi and Alain are still alive, but Levi is still in critical condition. He was beaten up, and drugs were all mixed up in his system when the North Koreans wanted him to talk."

"I can't understand how those thugs have been close at our heels. Are they tracking our computer, cell phone, or what? We haven't used our old cell phones! They have spies all over!" Anne said.

Luke was thoughtful. "You still kept your cell phones originally from the USA, right? Okay. We'll toss them out today. You can keep the ones that you bought cheap; those are basically untraceable, but we need to put in an international SIM card. I also have a GPS device on me."

"What? Oh! We know that from Higgins's office. Who's supposed to know it? I thought only your group knows that. Who's your group, by the way?" Anne asked.

Luke sat down. "I suppose this is as good a time as any to tell you guys something. Higgins was the counterterrorism czar under three presidents, and after retirement, he had an office as a consulting firm.

"He was vocal about a need to disable the Iranian nuclear program, and in 2009, we unleashed our Stuxnet cyberworm to do just that. The Stuxnet cyberworm had been formulated while Higgins was still with the government, but by the time it was released, Higgins was already retired. It was a complex undertaking, and I was part of the team of lawyers who sifted through the legal ramifications of how and when it would be unleashed.

"Higgins knew even before we did that there was a flaw in the virus. The virus does four levels of confirmation, all specific to the Iranian nuclear site at Natanz. Were it to spread to computers other than the nuclear site, it would stay inactive. The flaw is that the virus could mutate, or be mutated, and be used as a boomerang to hurt the USA instead, spreading through computers that regulate our electrical system, our defense system, and our financial system.

"By his own initiative, Higgins had formed his own network of men he could trust his life with, and I and Levi are on it, along with other Israeli agents and several ex-CIA officers. We are sworn to prevent a major catastrophe, should a reverse malware infect the U.S. system.

"I'm beginning to think that there is a rat somewhere. Pietz is a CIA officer who was assigned to babysit Senawi until Senawi could be brought to the US embassy for asylum in Copenhagen after your cruise.

"Apparently, the North Koreans kidnapped Andre Senawi on his way to Philips Exeter, the school he goes to. It is possible that Senawi had already made arrangements for his wife and daughter to visit relatives in the Chaldean area of Syria. He had done this quietly, even before he surreptitiously gave a note to our CIA in the Swiss embassy at Teheran. The only problem was that the North Koreans had been lying in wait to get him, because he was the main physicist of the nuclear program—hampered from being the chief, because he was a Catholic Chaldean.

"The North Koreans certainly complicated what was already a difficult task. Senawi was always guarded by two trigger-happy Iranian agents. One of them killed the Mossad agent who was trying to establish contact with Senawi at Tivoli Gardens. The other agent was the one who had an altercation with the North Korean at the Hermitage Museum. I think that the Iranians did not know until days later that Senawi was under pressure because of his kidnapped son.

"I believe that Senawi was for nonproliferation not just because of his religious faith, but also because he was a decent, peace-loving man. He came from a family rich in oil money and also steeped in tradition, trained to be leaders. He was working on strengthening the Chaldean group by having a revival or a renaissance, because their ethnic number has remained small.

"Higgins became aware of the Senawi fiasco through his connection with the CIA. We could not confirm where the wife and daughter are, because of the rebellion in Syria.

"When you showed up, Higgins could not believe his eyes. From your story, it is possible that Senawi chose you because he trusted your strong faith in religion, also probably identifying with your strong family relationships.

"The disc you brought was what Senawi was going to give to the CIA. It is for disabling the nuclear program; albeit it is not easy to decrypt. Now we are stuck because Levi is our genius in computer cryptography. Maybe this Guzman guy could help us—I hope so.

"I don't know what he could have given the North Koreans, because he was about to embark on the cruise when they threatened him. I suppose that the North Koreans really wanted to speed up their program, so they decided to kidnap Senawi instead. He must have fought and ended up getting himself killed."

"Oh!" Anne said, and she saw Andre crying silently. She held his shoulders, and they were quiet for some time.

"That's a lot of information—just when I suspect there's a rat somewhere. Let's finish eating first. I hope Guzman answers soon. We have to do this first thing in the morning."

"Check for any response on the e-mail, Son," Anne said. "E-mail your dad and brother that we are okay, and ask how they are. Make it vague so we cannot be traced. Could we still get phones with international SIM cards tonight, or do we wait till tomorrow?" she wondered aloud.

"An answer!" Mark said. "It's Guzman; he can come over tonight."

"Could you let him sleep in your room?" Anne turned to Luke. "If he is here early, we can go to the hospital with his direction. He can also help us get other cell phones for you, plus international SIM cards."

"No problem with me," Luke answered.

Andre just nodded.

Guzman knocked at their door an hour later, carrying his own backpack.

"Where have you been staying?" Anne asked. "What did you do with your other things? Are you ready to travel?"

"I've been living in a hostel. I've put the rest of my few things in two lockers at the Central Station. I have two untraceable cell phones here with international SIM cards. I know the way to the hospital. We'll take a taxi and pay to keep it waiting," he answered.

Luke smiled. He was getting used to the way these people thought and talked.

"Eat something. We have a few things here," Anne said.

"I had gone out to eat when your e-mail came," Guzman said. "When I saw your problem, I bought some cold meat you can use for sandwiches. I have six extra bottles of water, too. Here."

Luke laughed softly. "Do you always think of food in case of emergency?"

"I take care of that first always," Anne said with a smile. "I can't think or run if I'm hungry."

"Same here." Mark grinned.

"Our game plan is to get to Dr. Senawi's body so that Andre can say good-bye," Anne explained to Guzman. "Then we also have to get the GPS out of Luke's leg. I can do it myself . . ."

"No!" Luke said.

"Of course I could!" Anne glared at him.

"We can get the emergency-room doctor to do it," Mark intervened. "If it is a teaching hospital, there will be residents at the ER, and we can get it done without causing a fuss."

"What's your problem?" Anne asked Luke irritably.

"I'm shy toward female doctors," Luke answered, reddening.

"Hmmph! Okay. Andre, let's try to contact Janan. I don't know if your aunt is still here or has left for somewhere," Anne said, giving the e-mail address to Mark.

"Andre, how do you read this?" Mark asked as he typed the e-mail address.

Andre read it for him, and Mark tried to pronounce it too.

"After that, maybe we can try working on the disc tonight. We have some time still," Anne said.

"Maybe not," Guzman said. "They might be able to trace you by your computer. If we finish at the hospital early enough, we can buy a computer and work on that disc. None of those spies would be able to quickly trace a new computer working from someplace they did not expect."

"Okay. We sleep early," Luke said, and the three men left the room.

They all went down for breakfast, which was included in the hotel room charge. Anne paid extra for Guzman as their guest.

*Maybe I should pay more,* she thought after seeing Guzman unload the contents of the salt and pepper shakers into two napkins.

They were soon squeezed together in a cab that almost refused five people.

"The two are minors," Luke said in German, and he sat in the front.

Anne wondered whom he meant.

Luke decided to dismiss the taxi, and Anne paid.

The hospital was part of a large campus, but Anne and Mark knew what to expect. They led the way with Andre, while Luke and Guzman followed. They went first to the emergency room and registered Luke, complaining of a pain in his leg. They then pretended to need a restroom and, one by one, drifted off to the basement. Following the signs, they ended up at the morgue, but the room was closed.

Anne looked around and decided to grab a doctor's coat hanging by the corridor. She gave it to Luke. "You'll look authoritative in this. Just speak in German and order the first person you see to open the morgue for you. Pretend you are a visiting doctor who left something there when you visited yesterday."

"All right, you guys, stay hidden until I get the door opened," Luke said.

He walked down the corridor and saw a janitor with a pail. He spoke in German, gesticulating at the door, and the janitor opened the door for him.

As soon as the janitor turned the corner, they all went inside.

"Wait, I'll be the lookout," Mark offered, and he stood just behind the door, which he kept ajar.

"Where is it?" Anne said, quickly going through the vertical file of corpses in their respective shelves. "S . . . Let's check this." She pulled one drawer after another until she saw the face of Senawi. "Oh . . ."

Andre was behind her at once. They moved the corpse to the demonstration table. Andre went over to the covered instrument set that lay on top of a moving table. He put on gloves, picked up a scalpel, went toward the corpse, and raised the corpse's left leg. There was a lump on the medial side of the left leg. Andre used the scalpel to cut through the skin and took out a tiny metal piece. He rinsed it in the sink, wrapped it in gauze, and then placed it in his shirt pocket. Next Andre went toward the instrument set and got a bigger knife, to the surprise of the others. He then stabbed hard just to the left of the sternal bone, went downward, and cut toward the side.

Anne stood frozen while Luke and Guzman stood speechless.

Andre then moved the knife upward and back toward his starting point. He then dug with his right hand and took out the heart.

Anne was so galvanized that she could not scream.

Next Andre wrapped the object with cloth, placed it in a tin pail that was in the room, and removed his gloves. He washed his hands and then moved to the foot of the corpse. He then made the sign of the cross and sang a short hymn in a language Anne did not know.

Luke moved first. "Are you done? Let's go."

Andre nodded, picked up his pail, and walked to the door.

"Hurry, I hear voices," Mark said.

"Let's return the corpse—quickly!" Anne finally said something.

"No time!" Luke answered.

"Now!" Anne said stubbornly. "We must, or they will know we have been here.

Guzman helped her move the corpse back to its shelf, and they ran toward the door.

Luke had grabbed a doctor's clipboard and stood outside the door, pretending to read a memo. He talked to Mark in German, as though directing a lost person. He waved at two janitors going the other way. "All clear," he said, and they all scampered quickly to the staircase leading up.

Once on the first floor, Luke removed the doctor's coat and dumped it in the laundry bin by the emergency room. He then checked whether it was his turn for surgery yet for his leg. The emergency room surgeon checked out his record and proceeded to remove the lump he was complaining about.

"What's this?" the ER doctor asked after the object was removed from Luke's leg.

"That's what I got for serving in Iraq. I don't need it anymore; it's bothering me," Luke said nonchalantly as he took the disc, getting a tissue to wrap it with before putting it in his pocket. "Thank you," he added as the doctor stitched up the incision.

His four friends got up from the waiting room as soon as he showed up. Without speaking, they headed for the door, one by one.

Luke hailed a taxi, speaking in German, and once more prevailed for all of them to be taken in.

"Let's stop at a grocery for a small cooler and fill it with ice first. Mark and I can dash in while you guys wait," Anne said to Luke.

"Done," Luke answered, and he told the taxi driver what to do.

Next they stopped at a computer store and bought two computers and an iPad.

"One computer is for backup. The iPad will be easier to use if we are on the run. We also need some software. I can do this quickly," Guzman said.

Anne paid for the items, and they went back to their hotel.

Andre transferred his father's heart from the pail to the cooler and then put ice around it.

"We've never stayed more than one day in a hotel. Is this safe?" Anne couldn't help asking.

"We need to change computers because it is possible to get tracked through them," Guzman said. "First we need to transfer all your information; then we get rid of all gadgets that could possibly be tracked. That includes your old cell phones and the GPS device on Mattheson. We will throw them all out in the sea or river—whatever—so that they'll get damaged and won't be useful if anybody tries to recover them to track us or use them against us." Guzman was in his element with this technology, so everybody just nodded.

"So after you are done, we leave?" Anne asked.

"Your call. That's probably safest. I'll try to do it as fast as I can," Guzman said.

Luke took care of updating the iPad, muttering to himself about addresses. He then put the iPad in his backpack.

Guzman worked on transferring the information from Mark's computer to the two new computers.

"You take care of one." Luke handed the first computer to Mark.

"Where's that disc? On second thought, we'll work on it after we get out of here. I'm getting nervous already," Guzman said, and he put the second computer in his backpack.

Anne had been cleaning up both rooms to remove any of their traces. She took all the toiletries in her room and stuffed them in her backpack. Mark helped by doing the same in the other room.

"Fingerprints!" Andre whispered, and he did the job of wiping down whatever he could. Anne also grabbed a hand towel, giving another to Mark.

They did the best they could, stuffing the towels into their bulging backpacks.

"On second thought," Anne said, and she took two more hand towels for Luke and Guzman.

Guzman and Luke double checked everything; before they got ready to go.

"Is that enough?" Anne asked Luke.

"The best you could do. Let's go," Luke said, and he let Anne get out with Mark first.

Luke, Andre, and Guzman followed at a close distance; then Guzman hurried up toward Anne and Mark.

"Let's take a turn from Vasagatan to Vasabron. I'll walk toward the water and just pitch this laundry bag containing all the gadgets we have to dispose of," he said.

Anne nodded and let him take the lead. She had almost blinked, forgetting about that part. She was exhausted and beginning to feel it.

Guzman carried the hotel laundry bag as he led the way past the Central Station, toward Vasabron, and looked around. A policeman was walking by, and he waited. Anne pretended to be taking a picture, distracting the policeman.

"Right there—move left so there's a view of the Royal Palace," she said.

Luke and Andre obliged while Mark watched.

Guzman tossed the bag right into the water, making a splash.

"All right," Anne said, hoping the policeman hadn't heard the splash, "we've got to visit city hall. Let's go to the shops first." She smiled at the policeman, letting Luke and Andre walk ahead, while she and Mark waited for Guzman.

Once at the Central Station, Anne hesitated.

Andre moved toward Anne. "I have to bury my father's heart in our homeland," Andre said deliberately.

Luke looked at him, while the others were surprised. They stood aside from the line, and Luke went toward the different maps. They followed. Luke traced a route with his fingers and quietly whispered,

"Let's go by Germany, to Hungary. It will be closer. We'll talk on the train."

## 16. To Hungary

Anne bought the tickets for two adjoining cabins, paying for a roomier one with an extra berth for Guzman. They boarded the first trains available and convened at Anne and Mark's cabin to discuss what to do.

"I'm so tired that you surprised me," Anne said to Andre.

"In a way, I expected that," Luke said. "Senawi was brilliant. He was not going to make it easy for anybody to decrypt the codes without him. There must be more mystery to this that we can only decipher by following his instructions. It is possible that Andre is only following his father's instructions, but somewhere along the way, there will be clues to unravel this mystery."

Guzman looked thoughtful. "Better clue me in on what's going on, or I won't be able to help as much," he said.

"You better tell him, Luke," Anne said.

"Wait!" Guzman took out the iPad and typed as Luke began.

Everybody else was silent, and Guzman looked tense as Luke finished.

"I see some clues!" Guzman said. "Mark, you did not realize that Senawi put that disc in your camera bag, right?"

"Right," Mark said thoughtfully, and then his eyes widened. "Wait! I have Senawi's pen!" Mark got his backpack and took out the pen.

Luke looked at it, Andre touched it reverently, and Guzman proceeded to examine it.

"Let's see if it writes." Guzman took a napkin and tested it. "It works." He then dismantled the pen, to Andre's surprise. "There's a paper inside it."

He handed the paper to Luke.

Luke looked it over, holding it close to the light. "Looks like a Swiss bank account number with codes. Are you familiar with this, Andre?"

"Yes, my father said that when he was gone, I was to look after my family, including Aunt Janan. We are the last of our clan. My father said that we have funds outside of Iran if we are to flee because of religious or political persecution. He wants our tribe to increase, because we are being killed off one by one by other groups. My grandfather was assassinated."

Anne sighed and waited.

"Okay," Luke said. "I still don't understand why you have to bury your father's heart in Iran."

"It is our Chaldean land. He must go back to our homeland; his heart will always be in it. My heart will always be in it, even if I am far away," Andre answered passionately.

Luke turned to Guzman. "You think that there will be clues along the way? I'm going, but I'm not sure the others should risk their lives too."

"I want Anne and Mark to come; my father chose them!" Andre persisted.

Luke nodded for Anne and Mark and turned to Guzman. "You have to come; you are our only chance to decipher this while Levi is out."

Guzman nodded. "I'm free and ready for adventure." He then proceeded to assemble the pen.

Luke gave the pen back to Mark. "Maybe you ought to take care of this, since you've done an excellent job so far," he explained to Andre, who just nodded.

"Let's get some rest; don't open your cabin unless you hear our voice," Luke said, and they went to their cabin.

"Ohh!" Anne said.

"Let's rest; maybe we can think better," Mark said.

Anne nodded, picked up two blankets, and gave one to Mark. "You're right. Too many things are happening; I need to think it out." She then curled up on her bed and fell asleep.

It was late afternoon before anybody was awake. Anne got up to answer the knock on their door.

"It's Luke. Let's eat now, so we can use the computer when we get to Germany."

"Okay. Meet you in the dining area in five minutes," Anne said.

"No. Knock on our door when you are ready; we will go together," Luke answered.

"Right. Make that ten minutes," Anne said. She suddenly realized that people on the train might be quite nicely dressed compared to their scruffy appearance. They would be more conspicuous if badly dressed than if they dressed up a bit. She used the sink first to freshen up before she woke up Mark.

She quickly exchanged her cotton shirt for a silk blouse, put on her pearl earrings and necklace, and applied some quick, light makeup. She took out a clean collared shirt for Mark and found another one for Guzman. She gingerly went out to knock on the other cabin.

"If we eat in the dining area, use the extra shirts with collars that we bought last time. This is for Guzman." She handed over the shirt.

"Oh!" Luke sounded put off but then said, "Okay."

Two minutes later, Andre knocked on their door, and everybody was ready.

"We'd better eat well. We seldom get the chance," Anne said with anticipation, looking at the menu.

"I've been looking forward to a nice meal," Andre said, more relaxed than his usual stoic demeanor.

Luke was on Mark's left, pointing to the steak, and Guzman nodded.

"I'll take the lamb," Andre said.

"I'll take the steak. Mark or any one of you can finish it off for me," Anne said.

Luke waited for the waiter to go before he gave his instructions in a whisper. "We will come off the train during a busy daytime hour in one of the German towns. That way, we will be less obvious when we go to a free Wi-Fi area and take care of deciphering things through the computer.

"After that, we stay on the train until we get to Hungary, where we go straight to the Israeli embassy for help. Hungary is close enough for us to be flown by private plane to either Tel Aviv or Armenia, whichever the embassy thinks is best.

"From a closer starting point, we can drive to the area in Iran where Andre wants to bury his father's heart. We've been lucky recently, but that's because we've made moves that were unpredictable to the enemy."

Anne's brows were knitted for a while; then she nodded. "You are right. I've looked at the papers we bought, and Iran is getting involved in the rebellion in Syria. It is complicating the easy path."

"Thank you," Andre said happily to everyone.

For once, they all ate heartily without worrying.

When they returned to their cabin, Anne aired Mark's shirt and changed her blouse. "I'll wash some stuff when I get the chance. With you guys, we can just pitch those cheap shirts and keep the dressy ones. We still have to maintain our disguise somehow."

Mark let her go around doing her stuff while he checked his computer. "No Wi-Fi," he said, closing his laptop.

They slept without incident and felt better the next day.

Luke knocked gently early in the morning. "We'll eat whatever food we have for breakfast in our cabins. I'll only get coffee here with Guzman. Andre can wait here with you. I can't believe how lucky we have been, so far."

They ate their breakfast in Anne and Mark's cabin.

Anne saw that Luke was worried, and she too was wondering. She took out the newspapers she had not finished reading and laid them out.

They took turns reading from different pages and dates, and they talked about the rebellion going on in Syria.

"I wonder what we may be missing. We seem to be on a news blackout. Let's buy more papers when we disembark," Luke said.

The three then went back to their cabin afterward and waited.

At noontime, they got off the train. Guzman pointed at the first Internet café he saw, right off the town square.

Luke motioned for him to move on, and Guzman moved on to another street.

They ate lunch silently in the next commercial area, feeling tense and trying not to show it. There were several Internet cafés and electronics stores, and with a nod from Luke, Guzman went into an Internet café.

Luke talked in German to the person at the desk, and Anne paid.

"We can use our own computer. We paid for the Wi-Fi," Luke said.

Guzman eagerly opened the computers, but Mark got through his settings faster because he just typed the passwords automatically.

Guzman opened up his palm, and Mark gave him the disc. "No time to decipher this here, but I'll make a copy for myself; you keep this. Don't put it in the computer."

Mark nodded and returned the disc to his camera bag. "No answer from Dad or Jim, Mom. Hmm . . . There's an answer from Janan!" Mark whispered excitedly.

Andre and Luke immediately stepped behind him and read the message over his shoulder:

*I am in northern Syria with Andre's mother and sister. We are waiting for Andre. I'm so happy he is with you. Hurry, we are not sure how long it will be safe here. You know how to contact me.*

Andre shed tears of joy. Anne wiped her tears silently. Luke sat down to think.

"Do they know how to get from Syria to your gravesite in Iran?" Luke asked.

"Yes, we know our land. The only problem will be if there are hostile neighbors."

Andre said it easily, but Luke was still deep in thought. "We will need a lot of help. That's very hostile territory for me. We'll see what we can do at the Israeli embassy tomorrow."

"Here, Andre, answer Janan any way you want—something like 'I hope to see you soon.'" Luke tapped at Mark's shoulder so that Andre could type it himself.

Luke and Mark could not understand what Andre typed.

"It's in Aramaic; she'll know it is me," Andre explained.

Anne was thoughtful. "You wrote to her in Aramaic, but she answered us in English?"

"But you wrote to her in English, didn't you?" Andre asked.

"Yes, but . . ." Anne frowned.

Instead of feeling better, Anne was worried. "Could it be a trap? Was she captured?" she asked Luke.

"I'm worried too, but the only way to solve this is to take the risk of going there," Luke said. "Okay. Let me e-mail the embassy now. Where's the place we are going to, Andre?"

"It is in the foothills of the Abidar Mountains, in the western part of Sanandaz." Andre went over to Luke to spell it for him. Then he felt overwhelmed and sat down.

Mark touched Andre's shoulder in sympathy, and the younger man suddenly burst into tears. Mark was taken aback, and then he held Andre by the shoulder.

Anne came nearer and held both of them by the shoulder, at the same time using her body to shield the emotional scene from other people who might come into the store.

"No other news," Guzman said.

"I'm done. We'll wait for the answer in Hungary," Luke said.

They moved on to a grocery store, and Anne bought newspapers, food, and other essentials they needed. Just before paying, she asked Andre to grab a bag of ice.

"You'll need to keep what's inside, at a cool temperature. The ice in there may be water by now," she said to Andre, and she motioned with her eyes for the men to go to the restroom and replace the ice in Andre's cooler.

She waited for them restlessly, and then they made their way back to the train.

On the way to the train, they passed an electronics store with a TV screen facing the square. Luke was up front, encouraging them to hurry, when he saw the news flash. He signaled for Anne to wait. On the screen was a TV reporter standing in front of Karolinska University Hospital. The reporter spoke in German, so Luke went inside the store with Mark, pretending to look at TV sets.

Anne, Andre, and Guzman waited outside, pretending to converse. After a short while, Luke and Mark came out, with Luke saying some pleasantries to the staff.

Once outside, they increased their pace and got into the next train. They had two cabins, but they all huddled in Anne and Mark's room.

"The reporter said that the body of Dr. Senawi was vandalized, and organs were taken. She either does not have accurate information or is being intentionally misled. The reporter also said that the Chaldeans in northern Iran are being persecuted. There were pictures of hangings and beheadings. The Chaldean organization in the USA protested, but nobody is willing to face the camera. The Kurds are calling the Chaldeans traitors."

Andre started crying again. Anne held him by the shoulder, but she herself was getting emotionally exhausted. Mark and Guzman sat down on the opposite seat, while Luke sat beside Anne and held her shoulder.

"We'll stay in our cabin throughout the trip," Luke said. "Take out one gun, Mark. I'll hold on to the other revolver. Let's read those newspapers."

They divided the work and read aloud any information they felt might be relevant to their mission.

"The Egyptians accuse the Islamist radicals of killing the soldiers guarding the Sinai checkpoint," Guzman read.

"Standard Charter PLC is being investigated for its dealings with the Iranians," Mark read.

"Tehran vows to stand by Assad regime in Syria," Anne read.

"Syrian rebels are holding forty-eight Iranians who traveled to Syria through a travel agency, ostensibly to support the Assad regime," Luke read. He then continued, "Here's a small entry on the back page. A Stockholm policeman came forward saying that he heard a splash somewhere near Vasabron yesterday. The policeman only came forward after a tourist claimed that a suspicious-looking man tossed something into the water. However, the police could not find that tourist. The reporter will follow up after a team is sent to find out if indeed there was something sinister about the event."

That was more than enough to dampen everybody's spirits. They sat slouched in varying positions, until finally Anne brought out the food.

"Let's eat," she said as she opened the parcels.

They ate slowly, each trying to think aloud; but without appetite, they took a while.

"There's been no direct threat to us so far," Luke said. "Whoever is looking for us has not found us yet. I'm beginning to think you are right, Anne. The enemy has gotten Janan and is waiting for us."

"Do you know what will happen, Andre?" Guzman asked, making everybody turn.

Andre did not seem bothered. "If we can get there, my people will protect me. My father must be buried in the tomb of the Chaldean kings."

Anne looked up. "Is there a rite? Are you saying there is a lineage of kings?"

"Yes! That's what I meant!" Andre smiled.

Guzman opened his computer. "Forgot! Okay. We need to work as soon as we are in the embassy."

With Andre smiling, Anne tried to smile too. The three went to their cabin shortly afterward. Luke nodded to Mark as he went out, and Mark nodded in the direction of his revolver.

"Let's try to sleep while we can." Anne held her son's shoulder. "How do you feel, Son?"

"We'll see it through. I feel like it is a responsibility. Like you said, we are at bat. We can't give the job to somebody else. It will be our play."

Anne hugged her son and blessed him with a sign of the cross.

Somehow Mark snored through the night, and hearing him, Anne tried hard to sleep. The only other thing she could do was pray, so she got out her rosary.

The next morning, they did their routine of eating breakfast in their cabin. At lunchtime, Anne prepared sandwiches with the cold meat that Guzman had brought. It was a light meal, but they had pears and grapes, along with some chocolates, so it was filling enough. Then they got ready for the train arrival at Budapest.

Luke, Andre, and Guzman knocked at Anne and Mark's cabin by four in the afternoon. Mark quickly let them in.

"We've wiped off our fingerprints," Guzman volunteered.

"We just finished," Mark answered.

They were ready as soon as the train stopped. Luke came out first, holding Anne's hand. A few seconds later, Mark led the way for Guzman and Andre. According to their previous plan, Luke got a taxi, and without fuss, the other four got in. The taxi driver was about to complain, but Luke waved one hundred euros in his face.

"The Israeli embassy, please," Luke said, opening his cell phone at the same time. "Step on it."

They arrived at the embassy without speaking and quickly got out of the taxi. Israeli soldiers, with their guns ready, were waiting for them.

A large black sedan sped toward the taxi as it exited the embassy gate. The taxi was sideswiped, and it hit a post. As the dazed taxi driver got out of the cab, two men got out of the black sedan with guns drawn. Five Israeli guards came out of the gate and fired into the air. The men from the sedan jumped back into their car and sped away. The embassy guards picked up the taxi driver and took him into the compound.

"Do you have a family or a girlfriend?" Anne could overhear the guard beginning his interrogation.

"They'll help him," Luke told his group, and they followed the official who met them.

They were ushered into a conference room where the ambassador was waiting.

"Welcome! I'm Ambassador Ehud Nussbaum," he started.

They all said their names and shook hands. They next sat around an oval table while they were served hot croissant sandwiches, appetizers, and salads. A secretary came in with coffee and offered soda or water for those who wanted something else.

"Pardon me, would you happen to have some ice for our cooler?" Anne asked the secretary while looking at the ambassador, who nodded in their direction.

The secretary seemed to have anticipated this already. She gestured for Anne to wait and was right back with a cooler full of ice.

Anne looked at Andre, who quickly took the cooler.

Andre then also picked up his cooler and went to the restroom.

The ambassador helped himself to some sandwiches and ate with them, thus making them feel at home.

"We're ready," Luke said after they ate. He took out his iPad, and Guzman and Mark took out their computers.

Andre watched, fascinated, as the discs were inserted and Luke explained to the ambassador what had transpired so far.

The ambassador then explained other developments. "We were able to piece together some of the puzzles. Pietz was a CIA agent assigned to babysit Senawi until he returned to Copenhagen and got asylum at the US embassy. Pietz did not know at that time that Senawi's son had been kidnapped. Even without returning his son, the North Koreans wanted Senawi to give them information about the nuclear program, but Senawi did not have the papers. He offered a blueprint instead. If the North Koreans wanted the real information, Senawi said that they had to wait until he was back in Iran. He couldn't come home until after the conference, or he would be under suspicion.

"The North Koreans got impatient and wanted Senawi to give up this blueprint at the Hermitage Museum, aware that Senawi had only one guard left. As a North Korean agent was talking to Senawi, Senawi's guard showed up and had an altercation with the North Korean. Senawi's second guard was detained in Russia.

"Senawi had no guard left when the North Koreans threatened to kill his son. He signed up for the Stockholm shore excursion, and Pietz waited there on the bus. Senawi hoped to resolve the issue by meeting the North Koreans at the square in Stockholm. Maybe Senawi did not expect that the Iranians would help him get his son back.

"Pietz realized that Anne and Mark might know something when those two left at Stockholm. He traced them to O'Hare airport, but they eluded him, blocking him with a group of marines. Pietz butted heads with a burly guy, and was knocked to the floor. When he got up, the North Koreans were pointing something at him. Pietz was taken, and he was given medicines to make him talk. He must have really sung like a canary, because he knew that Anne was aware of the Stuxnet cyberworm, pointing to Higgins's office. That's why the North Koreans arrived at Higgins's office. However, Pietz's descriptions of Anne and Mark, and also their pictures, were so different from their assumed disguises that those two were able to elude the agents.

"Senawi was important for the Iranians to complete their bomb, so they were very mad at the North Koreans when Senawi died. The Iranians were also mad at the USA and Israel because they sensed that the Mossad who approached Senawi was sending feelers for defection. We don't know if the Iranians are aware that Senawi planned to defect. We don't know where Senawi's wife and daughter are, but we think that the sister, Janan, was taken by the North Koreans.

"At the airport, the US allowed the North Koreans to leave with Andre because the North Koreans had Pietz as a hostage, bound up in a warehouse.

"We don't know where Janan is or how to help her, because she will surely be used as bait. We cannot establish communication lines through Syria now. There's chaos; it's too risky."

They were all quiet after the explanation, and the typing stopped. Anne did not know where to begin. Luke helped himself to more coffee.

"I answered Janan's e-mail in Aramaic, to be sure it is her," Andre said, breaking the silence. "We will learn more information when she answers. We have codes for different emergencies," he said.

"I'm not fluent in Aramaic; I'll call someone," the ambassador said, pressing a button.

"We still have to go, don't we?" Luke said. "It would be of very high value to finally deactivate the Iranian nuclear threat. However, can we possibly succeed in such hostile territory? We don't even actually know what we are looking for."

"We are ready with all the support," Ambassador Nussbaum said. "Your idea of going through Armenia is most plausible. It is close enough for us to have Land Rovers speed through that area in Iran, with tank support along the way. Attack helicopters will try to stay within the Armenian border as much as possible. We flew two platoons to Armenia yesterday. This is a very high-value effort—I agree. We must succeed," he said gravely.

The Aramaic interpreter arrived and spoke to Andre. They seemed to hit it off well, and Andre smiled.

"I'm Aaron Stein," he said, and he shook hands with everyone.

"Could you type in this computer that prayer you said at your father's side, Andre?" Guzman said.

Anne was surprised at how Guzman's mind worked in unusual circuits.

Aaron was quick to pick the drift. "Why don't you recite it, Andre, and I'll type it in?" Aaron took over Guzman's computer.

Andre made the sign of the cross first, so Anne and Mark did the same and bowed their heads. Andre then recited his Aramaic prayer in a cadence that was regular, half-chanted and half-sung.

When Andre finished, they were all quiet, but Anne was just waiting.

She then asked, "Is there a different ritual at the burial site?"

"Yes, but it is not very long," Andre said.

"Do we need candles or something?" Anne asked gently.

"Yes, thank you for reminding me," Andre said comfortably, and he enumerated a list.

Aaron wrote the list on a piece of paper and showed it to the ambassador, who rang his secretary and gave it to her.

"Okay. We start out early tomorrow. The sooner, the better, so the enemy cannot yet prepare," the ambassador said. Noticing a raised brow from Anne, the ambassador added, "I'm a colonel."

Guzman looked around. "I have a lot of work to do with this disc. Could Anne and Mark stay? I think I should solve some of this before we go."

Anne looked at Mark, who nodded. "We'll stay with you."

"I'll hang around too," Luke said, edging Mark sideways. "I'll type, and you think."

"I'm staying too," Andre said.

"We might as well send for stuff we need through the night," the ambassador said, and he rang for his secretary. "More coffee and food. Bring blankets and pillows. We're camping."

Guzman was like a man possessed. He asked Aaron to repeat the prayer again and again, and his eyes lit up. He would write something down, look up, and write circles and arrows pointing in different directions.

"There is a pattern in the cadence of words," Guzman said. "I don't know where it fits yet, but it is a different set. Now I'll work back on the mythology pattern with Anne and Mark."

"Where were we?" Anne asked.

"We start at level four. The other levels look incomplete, but I guess they can only be completed when the other passwords are in," Guzman said.

"Will you please repeat the passwords that were in?" Anne asked.

Guzman obliged.

"We've done *Cities of Gold* and a mixture of Middle Eastern characters and places—no Greek gods. Shall we try Greek characters? The other thing would be Chaldean kings." She looked at Mark.

"Okay," Mark said. "Looks like we'll try random Greek characters, say Odysseus, Agamemnon, Menelaus, Electra."

"Theseus, Perseus, Andromeda, Penelope, Telemachus, Priam, Hecuba, Cassandra, Antigone, Tantalus, Clytemnestra, Astyanax," Anne said.

Guzman typed furiously and then said, "Wow! We have eight: Odysseus, Penelope, Telemachus, Agamemnon, Clytemnestra, Antigone, Tantalus, and Astyanax. They're all level-four passwords, but I still have to work on the random numbers. Can we try level five now? Some of these things will come into place when we finish the passwords."

Anne felt exhausted, but Mark made an attempt.

"From your suggestion, let's check the web for the names of the Chaldean kings." Mark turned to his mother.

Luke searched for "Chaldean history" and called out the names of kings and proper names to Mark, who wrote them down.

"Okay," Mark said, reading off the names slowly. "We already have Nebuchadnezzar. Try *Belshazzar* and *Nabopolassar*. Also, Nineveh, Carchemish, Nimrud, Ur, Hormizd, Aramaic, Diyarbakir, Assyria, Karchemish, Etemenanki, Zedekiah, Psammetichus, Mesopotamia, Phoenicia, Amel-Marduk, Neriglissar, Labashi-Marduk—"

"Slowly," Guzman said. "I need help with some spellings. Spell Belshazzar and Nabopolassar."

Mark spelled them slowly.

"Those two are hits," Guzman said, and then he looked up. "Say the words and then spell them for me, please."

Mark slowly repeated them, with spellings.

"We have nine hits: Belshazzar, Nabopolassar, Carchemish, Etemenanki, Zedekiah, Psammetichus, Amelmarduk, Neriglissar, and Labashimarduk!" Guzman rejoiced. "I'll work on the numbers while you guys try to sleep. Maybe I can sleep on the plane. I'm almost sure there's something other than just the levels, like a coordinating net. Hang on . . ." He then proceeded to work on transferring information back and forth from the computer to the iPad and the disc.

Andre got a pillow and a blanket and lay down on the floor. "I'm here if you need me."

Mark did the same, and one by one, they each camped in varying positions in the room. Ambassador Nussbaum stretched out on a chair.

Guzman was humming as he worked through the night. He fell asleep with his head on the table.

When morning came, the secretary walked in and saw the sleeping bodies scattered throughout the room. She left. Half an hour later, she reentered with a rolling table filled with food, coffee, and other things, including disposable shaving kits and toiletries.

Anne blinked, got up, and washed her face in the restroom.

One by one, the other bodies moved, and they all started eating.

"In one hour, the cars taking you to the airport will be ready," the secretary said, addressing the ambassador, who just nodded. "The guest rooms are on the next corridor if any of you need to use them."

Anne looked at her wristwatch and grabbed her backpack. Mark followed. Andre took one room with Guzman, while Luke took another. The ambassador had his own room. They were all in the foyer in less than one hour. Anne made a visual check of their backpacks and saw that Andre had his small cooler with him.

## 17. Armenia to Iran

There were two armored cars. One preceded them, and the other followed right behind the two embassy cars. Ambassador Nussbaum, Aaron, and their group of five were in the two embassy cars driven by soldiers.

The embassy front was on a wide avenue, with cars parked along the street across from it. There was also a back door, heavily guarded, which opened unto a smaller street.

The secretary came running after them just before the car doors closed. She spoke urgently to the ambassador, and Nussbaum stepped out of the car and raised his hand.

"Plan B!" Nussbaum announced to the team, and he went back to his seat.

"Stay down!" Luke ordered from the front seat.

"Oh!" Anne's eyes widened as she sat in the back with Mark and Andre. They held hands and ducked, closing their eyes.

Another car suddenly came from behind them, sirens blaring. It shot forward to the main avenue ahead of them. Suddenly there was a deafening blast, followed by fumes and smoke that went up into the sky. The four cars barreled right through the smoke and flying debris, speeding through the streets until they arrived at the airport. The plane was ready for take—off, and they all hurried aboard.

They were all panting yet somehow sighing in relief. Anne looked at Nussbaum as she passed him.

"It was a dummy car. They were lying in wait for us," Nussbaum explained to them.

Guzman got busy as soon as they were seated. "I'll let Aaron hold the iPad, I'll hold one computer, and Luke can take the other. One disc is on my computer, but Luke's does not have it. This disc goes to Mark's backpack. Andre, when you do perform the rite, say it slowly so that Aaron can catch it."

Andre nodded.

The ambassador looked very serious. "Our straight flight to Yerevan, Armenia, will be about three hours. When we arrive there, we will immediately transfer to helicopters that will bring us close to the Iranian border. Once at the border, we will go by Land Rovers to the area at the Abidar foothills that Andre described. There are tanks that will cross the border to help us if there is trouble, and the helicopters will assist. We have to be alert and hope for our lucky stars so that we can get back without incident."

"I'll catch some sleep," Guzman said as he took a seat beside Aaron.

Anne sat tensely on her seat and started to pray. Mark closed his eyes to get more sleep.

Some turbulence woke everybody up just as they were already close to Yerevan. It was an opportune time for bathroom breaks, for as soon as the plane landed, they were all pointed to the waiting helicopters.

There were tribal costumes for them to change into. Anne looked around uncomfortably since she was the only female. She put on the white lace blouse over the shirt she was wearing and put the dirndl-like skirt over her own skirt. The men put on the twisted cloth headbands, and Anne picked a bandana cloth and used it as a banded hairpiece.

The helicopters landed with a thud. Luke was quick to help Anne come down. It was difficult with her short stature to just jump over the metal frame of the door or to jump like a panther onto the ground.

"Thank you," Anne said with a sigh. "I'm obviously short and not nimble."

Aaron gave a hand to the ambassador. Guzman jumped off without assistance and was caught from a bad fall by Mark. Mark then helped Andre.

"The soldiers will help us later," Ambassador Nussbaum noted. He realized the implication of having civilians who were not fit for battle.

Four Land Rovers arrived precisely a minute later. Heavily armed soldiers rode in one, while the other two vehicles were obviously for their group. Kevlar vests were on their seats. Anne removed the lace blouse, put the Kevlar vest over her own blouse, and buttoned up the lace blouse over it.

The driver of their car had goggles and a mask on. He handed them their masks and goggles and then drove quickly, right behind the third Land Rover.

Anne was glad to have the mask and goggles; dust was all over them from the parched road, and it was difficult to see or breathe. She felt her whole body being shaken to the bone.

Sanandaz, Iran

*I must have dozed off in spite of the rough ride,* Anne thought, checking her wristwatch and realizing that three hours had passed.

It was quite a long drive over unpaved country road, going up and down some hills, seeing the Zagros Mountains in the distance.

"Senna!" Andre pointed to the city they were approaching.

Anne looked at Andre and realized that it was the name he used for Sanandaz. She smiled and touched his hand.

Luke signaled with his right hand out of his window, and their driver slowed down. "We will take the lead and slow down a bit so as not to attract any attention. Please direct me, Andre."

"Over there, toward the foothills of Abidar Mountain. Go toward Amiryeh Park, but do not go farther. There in the foothills, with those two cypress trees!" Andre said excitedly.

Their car took the lead until they came to an open space just before the park. Two cypress trees stood like sentinels on each side of what looked like a simple stone marker.

Andre led the way as they all came down from the Land Rover. He turned to Aaron, who was holding a box. From among its contents, Andre took a headpiece with an emblem on the front, and he put it on.

Next Andre picked up the candles and lit them. He gave one each to Anne and Mark to hold.

Guzman held the box while Aaron got his iPad out.

Andre then got one of the four plows and dug at the foot of the stone marker. Luke and two soldiers helped him. After twenty minutes, they hit a wooden casket. Andre went over to the box and took out a flare and then lit it.

Anne stood, surprised, looking at the bright streak in the afternoon sky. Then, anticipating a musty smell at the sight of the casket, she held her breath; but Andre had lit the incense, and swung the censer gently back and forth as he started to chant a Chaldean prayer. Aaron was at once typing on the iPad. The ambassador stood beside him, while their soldiers formed a circle around them.

Andre took his father's heart out of the small cooler. It was still wrapped in hospital cloth, and he simply placed it near the head of the wooden casket. At the foot of the casket was a metal box with a handle. Andre picked it up and placed it on the box that Guzman was holding. Once more, he chanted another prayer.

The sound of voices startled them, except Andre. People from the city arrived by foot and in cars; some were cheering noisily. They rushed to Andre and bowed to him. There was joy for a moment; then a voice cried out.

"Andre!" It was Janan, but beside her was her captor, holding her arm and pointing a gun at her.

"Hand me the box and the blueprint," the captor, who was disguised in tribal costume, said.

There were ten men—four around Janan—disguised in tribal costume, and they moved slowly forward as the villagers let them pass.

But the captors had taken the Chaldean villagers for granted. The villagers closed in on the captors, and one villager clubbed with his fist the head of the captor holding Janan. Another villager grabbed Janan, and they hit the ground. Other villagers rushed the other kidnappers so unexpectedly and quickly that their weapons were useless. The North Koreans were bound hand and foot by the very costumes they had dared to use.

Andre joyfully hugged Janan. Then he spoke in Aramaic to his people, reassuring them, and they exchanged pleasantries—but all too briefly.

A plume of dust heralded the coming of army jeeps. Andre waved his hand, and with a nod from the villagers, the visitors and Janan quickly went back to the Land Rovers.

A hailstorm of bullets preceded their pursuers, but the ambassador and his men were more than ready. They had carried petrol with them, and the Land Rovers had been filled up while the ceremony was going on. The pursuers were stalled by smoke bombs that were thrown by the departing group. Smoke mixed with road dust, so the soldiers who were in pursuit could not see clearly. After an hour, the pursued group could no longer see the army jeeps; however, they could hear attack helicopters coming from a distance.

Ambassador Nussbaum called on his cell phone, and their helicopters got ready for confrontation. The tanks had been at the border all the while, covered with camouflage, and their soldiers removed their camouflage to be on the ready.

There were two pursuing helicopters, but there were four helicopters coming from the Armenian border. After a brief exchange, the Iranian helicopters went back.

"There is definitely safety in numbers," the ambassador said to the ladies as Luke and Aaron helped them up into a helicopter.

Anne smiled gratefully, when she noticed that Janan looked ill. Anne gave Janan some water and wiped her face and hands with a wet washcloth. Only then did Anne see some of the bruises and hematomas on Janan. Anne asked for the medicine kit and started first aid on the wounds she could see. "Please radio for an ambulance; I can't tell how much injury there is."

Andre turned pale just as Janan fainted.

## 18. Working in Budapest

Andre rode in the ambulance that took Janan to the hospital. Anne, Mark, and Luke followed in another car. Guzman, Aaron, and Nussbaum went straight to the Israeli embassy, carrying their backpacks, their computers, and the iPad.

"This will open the box," Andre told Guzman before getting on the ambulance. Andre opened the cooler, which now contained only the GPS from his father's leg. "Without this, you cannot open it."

Janan had been beaten, and she had bruises and hematomas underneath her clothes. She had long incision wounds along her trunk, as though it had been slowly lengthened, day by day, in the interrogation process. She had also been drugged. X-rays and scans were taken, as well as blood tests, before the surgeons started work in the OR.

Andre cried in the waiting room, losing the struggle to maintain his composure. Luke paced the floor, saying nothing. Anne and Mark sat beside Andre, trying to console him.

"I will avenge her!" Andre said.

"Hush," Anne said gently. "The villagers caught them, and when they are turned over to the Iranian soldiers, there will be no mercy."

The surgeon approached them and turned to Andre. "Hi, I'm Dr. Nazarian. We have to operate. I'm just letting you know, but we will have to get consent from the administrator since you are still a minor. We will do an exploratory laparotomy, meaning we'll open up her abdomen. She is bleeding from somewhere; it is hard to tell where, because so many organs have hematomas."

He nodded toward Anne; then left in a hurry.

"I'll be eighteen in two years!" Andre protested, but the surgeon had hurried out before Andre could grasp what was said.

Anne soothed Andre before explaining in less morbid terms what was going to happen.

"I don't even know where my mother and sister are; the villagers were not certain," Andre added miserably.

Anne wished they had their backpacks with them. They were once more in the waiting room, and she was getting hungry. The door opened, and an embassy staff member brought in hot food and coffee. A hospital aide followed, bearing blankets, washcloths, and some toiletries. When they left, there were two guards at the door.

"Let's eat; then we can sleep while waiting," Luke said.

They helped themselves to a pasta meal with fruits and bread, talking desultorily. Anne was thankful for the washcloth; she was the first one in the restroom, wiping off all the dust. Each of them then took different positions to sleep. Luke and Mark got the sofas. Andre dragged two loveseats to face each other, and put a bench in the middle; while Anne contented herself on a wing chair made longer—like a chaise lounge—by adding two chairs.

Anne stirred when she heard a tray table being pushed in. She checked her watch and realized that she had been out for six hours. Luke and Mark began to stir too, but Andre was still asleep.

Dr. Nazarian came in with another surgeon. "She was bleeding from her spleen, which had to be removed. We also had to remove the hematoma from her intestine because it was causing an obstruction. She might need a blood transfusion. I recommend that you get typed and cross-matched if you can donate. Overall, however, she has passed the most critical phase. If you want to go home, this is a good time."

Luke and Mark nodded. Andre looked grim.

"Thank you," Anne said to the doctors.

A laboratory technician came in next and drew blood from Luke and Mark. They waited for the results, and Luke was a match. Luke donated blood; then they got into the waiting car to go to the embassy.

Guzman and Aaron had been busy while the others were at the hospital. "We are getting there!" Guzman announced as they came into the conference room.

"How long?" Anne asked. "I'd really like to freshen up. Give us thirty minutes."

"Oh! I don't really know. Depends on how much we can piece the puzzle together with Andre's help. Go ahead. We'll take a break," Guzman said.

Thirty minutes later, they were all seated around the table and had breakfast with coffee, Danish, eggs, and bacon.

"Okay," Guzman started. "The metal box contained the list of all Chaldean kings dating from Nebuchadnezzar. We entered all the names, and each name has one consonant that formed a sequence, like an outer ring. The Aramaic prayers had a cadence in which the vowels formed an inner ring. Together with the five levels, we are very close to finishing the entire face. I need to ask Andre some questions. There are gaps that may be due to my not understanding the nuances of Chaldean Aramaic as his family practiced it. Okay, Andre, if you can come over . . ."

Andre sidled up to Guzman and Aaron, and the three worked together at one end of the conference table, filling out the missing gaps.

The others were silent, as though sensing the importance of solving the code. An hour passed and then two. Mark went to sit in an armchair and closed his eyes. Anne leaned back on her chair and closed her eyes. Luke and the ambassador leaned back on their chairs too.

It was already past noontime when a rolling table came in. It was their lunch. The others ate quietly, but Guzman and Aaron were still at it.

"Here, this part—could you pronounce this, Andre?" Guzman asked.

"Maybe it fits with one consonant instead of two, like the *z* or *c* when used by the Germans or the Turks," Aaron said. "Okay, if we replace this letter with . . ."

It was past three o'clock in the afternoon when the others were startled.

"We're done!" Guzman and Aaron remarked loudly, waking up the others.

Guzman, Aaron, and Andre were sweating, but their faces showed elation.

The ambassador sat up with a start. Luke got up and went over to where the three were huddled. Anne brought the lukewarm food over to their end, and the three ate hungrily.

The ambassador made several calls before going over to the computers. Luke and Mark made way for him. The others sighed in relief as they let the three eat their belated lunch; then the ambassador spoke.

"This is a huge breakthrough, and we need to be very careful. All the codes and inscriptions will be double-checked in Israel. Guzman, Aaron, and Andre will have to be flown in also, both for confirmation and to answer if there are any questions.

"Janan will also be flown there with us, and she will have to finish recuperating there. It is safer all around.

"Luke, Anne, and Mark should come also. This is something you worked hard for, but when the final decision to trigger the disable comes, how committed are you? One reason we have to do this in Israel is to ascertain that the disable does not trigger a nuclear reaction, and that's something we are not so sure of."

Somehow the thought must have already been in their minds; the group just nodded. Guzman gave back the box with the small metal key to Andre.

"This has to be placed back in the tomb when I die," Andre said. "The GPS key will be placed in my leg when I am eighteen."

They all looked askance at the young man, except the ambassador.

"We leave by plane tomorrow morning," the ambassador said.


## 19. Tel Aviv

The sky was a bright blue when the plane carrying the group arrived in Tel Aviv. There was no other chance to savor a beautiful day; they were all ushered to waiting cars and then into a facility with closed rooms and long conference tables.

A team of computer experts and physicists looked over the information from the disc, the metal box, and the entered passwords. They sifted through the information and studied what was done; then they asked for time to double-check it again.

Aaron and Guzman worked with the scientists. Luke, Andre, Anne, and Mark were allowed to entertain themselves by playing ball, but only within the compound. They played tennis and table games desultorily, trying to relax but continuing to worry.

Then one night, Andre received a request to go to the computer room after dinnertime.

The next morning, Ambassador Nussbaum was very solemn as they ate an early breakfast. Aaron and Guzman looked exhausted.

"We will go to the computer room before nine a.m.," he said.

They arrived at the computer room early, but all the other scientists were already there. There was palpable excitement as the minister of defense arrived.

"Good morning, I am Dr. Litwak. With the work of these people here, and confirmation by our team of scientists and physicists, we have indeed discovered the disable code to deactivate the nuclear facility in Natanz, Iran. We were able to verify by isolated computer testing that Dr. Senawi built a complex program so that the deactivation would proceed without a nuclear trigger—meaning that there will be no explosion. Instead, the deactivation will occur through a sequential shutdown of electrical power to the nuclear plant, so the disable will be orderly. A malware virus then takes over so that all the previous calculations will have to be revised, and the isotopes will reconfigure to something less radioactive. Dr. Senawi did a very brilliant job, which I can only understand as coming from a man with a love for humanity, in order to keep us from destroying ourselves.

"Let us have a moment to pray to God and remember Senawi before our minister presses the start button."

They were all silent. Andre stood erect even as his tears flowed freely.

The minister then stepped forward and pressed a button. They all looked up at the TV screen, where the Iranian nuclear plant in Natanz was indicated by a green-emitting circle, signifying high levels of nuclear activity. Minutes turned into half an hour, then an hour, before the assembled crowd could discern that the green emissions had become lighter.

"It will take days before the green will turn gray; then become a black circle, signifying that the plant is inactive," Dr. Litwak said. "That's because those isotopes need to be slowly reconfigured to an inactive form. Suffice it to say that we consider ourselves successful. It cannot be reversed at this point."

The room exploded with loud cheers and applause. Anne cried and held Andre's hand. Mark and Luke sighed in relief. Guzman and Aaron congratulated each other, and several scientists and experts congratulated them too.

They were next herded to another room, a more graciously decorated one, obviously for receptions. The tables were set for an elaborate lunch with champagne and caviar.

Their group was together at a big, round table, while the ambassador joined the defense minister at another table.

Finally they had a wonderful, unhurried lunch, and this time they were able to laugh about their adventure.

"What do you plan to do, Andre?" Anne gently asked. "Janan will have to stay here for a week at least, and we don't know about your mother and sister yet. After that, what are your plans?"

"I will stay here with Janan. She made it clear that the North Koreans kidnapped her just outside of Stockholm. She has not been able to reach my mother and sister. Her e-mail answer was ordered by her captors. I'll stay here, where I can get help from the Israeli network about my mother and sister. Afterward, I will continue my studies, but I'm not sure where I'll be safe," Andre said.

"We can get you a change of identity so that the enemies cannot trace you," Luke said. "Of course you have responsibilities to your clan, but for the moment, you need to lie low. I'll give you the information on how to contact me when you are ready. You will be safe in the USA." Luke then turned to Anne. "What are your plans?"

"As soon as it is safe, we are going home, but only to make arrangements to move. I might want to change our address and a lot of things, because I don't feel safe after encountering those spies."

"I have put all your names into a witness protection program," Luke said. "Higgins is already back to his usual self and will definitely be your advocate to that effect. He thanks you, by the way. Levi and Alain are back in the USA, doing better by the day.

"By the way, Levi is fighting for your air force friends, who are being reviewed for court-martial by the Department of Defense.

"There is a fund in our Defense Department allocated for the disablement of the Iranian nuclear program. There is also a fund in Israel for that. Together, this whole group is due to be given compensation from that program. Unless you live unusually lavishly, you can all retire. Guzman is welcome to stay in the USA, not only with his reward money but probably with an added job in the Department of Defense as well."

"I thought that was possible," Anne said. "But somehow it does not foretell a peaceful existence. There will always be fear, making us look behind our backs all the time," she said sadly.

"How about if we all take a couple of days off? We'll see the sights in Israel. I'll contact a tour group," Luke said.

"We have prepared a five—or seven-day excursion for you, with our compliments," the ambassador said, and they all turned. "We know Janan has to recuperate before Andre can make final plans. They can stay here or go to the USA.

"Luke told you of the reward money, but the government here also has awards for you. The excursion will help you unwind. I've worked with you for just a few hectic days, but you have been on the run for quite a long time. The excursion will give you a chance to get back to normal. How about it?"

"Great Idea!" Guzman said.

Mark and Luke nodded. Andre smiled.

"Let me check my family there first," Anne said.

"They're all right according to Higgins," Luke said.

"Okay. We'll call them and then enjoy the vacation," Anne said.

"Can I leave my box in a safety-deposit at a bank?" Andre asked.

"Right," Luke said. "We'll do that this afternoon."

"You might want to deposit this there now," Mark said, handing Andre his father's pen.

Luke accompanied Andre to the bank; then they spent the remaining afternoon on a city tour, with Aaron acting as driver and guide in a comfortable van.

Anne's eyes lit up when they were in the commercial district. "Let's do some shopping; we can exchange the leftover money from Higgins's storage box," she said. "We do need to look like tourists if we are starting to travel the country tomorrow."

Luke smiled. "I was wondering when I would hear a female wanting to shop."

"We are tired of our scruffy outfits!" Anne said, and she led the way to a department store.

They came out laden with assorted sizes of bags, looking happy. After a light supper, they slept early with no alarms to worry about.

Early the next morning, they were ready. Each wore a new outfit, pleased to look like tourists for once. In place of the backpacks, they had rolling carry-on luggage and computer bags. Their tour took them to Jerusalem and Bethlehem. After that, the majority prevailed, and they went north, visiting little towns on the way to Nazareth and the

Sea of Galilee. They drove along the coast on the way back, and Anne was glad to see Caesarea. They laughed and argued and bantered along the way, slowly easing into a life without tension, and they were glad to return to Tel Aviv.

They exchanged information on how to get in touch with one another and got ready to head back to the USA. Anne and Mark decided to go by California instead of going directly back to Kansas. Somehow Anne wanted to be sure that Edward and Jim were really alright. She and Mark were going to return through an unexpected route.

"You are really paranoid," Luke said with a smile.

Luke was going back to Washington, DC, with Guzman.

Janan had recovered well, although she was still pale, and she and Andre were staying in Tel Aviv. They were anxious to hear more from the intelligence agents who were following some leads regarding Andre's mother and sister.

Part IV

# THE ADVERSE
# ADMINISTRATION

## 20. A Circuitous Route

"We have one day in San Francisco," Anne said, once again checking things out, planning ahead, and hurrying. "We then take the flight to Denver. From there, we go by land.

"In San Francisco, we can go to Fisherman's Wharf, the Embarcadero Center, and Lombard Street before we spend the afternoon at the Golden Gate Park area. What do you think?"

"Fine." Mark knew his mother was hyperactive, and he was not the kind to argue for the sake of arguing. His mother was usually right.

They arrived in the morning, took the shuttle to their hotel, and then went sightseeing. They walked to the Embarcadero Center and looked at the shops around the area. Mark sighed in relief when his mother did not enter the department stores. Anne hailed a taxi to take them to the crooked street; then they had lunch at Fisherman's Wharf. As they were waiting for a taxi, a crowd carrying placards passed by.

Farther on, toward the Embarcadero Center, a bigger crowd was beginning to chant. "Down with Wall Street! Occupy Wall Street!"

"The Occupy Wall Street movement was quite long ago," Anne commented, and they were about to get into a stopped taxi, when one of the demonstrators yanked Mark away from the taxi.

"Get in here, buddy—join the crowd!"

"Yeah! Yeah!" another hippie said.

Anne was surprised, but she was still able to think. "Please wait for us," she said to the taxi driver. She walked away from the taxi and followed the mob, pretending to get along. "Where are we going?" she said as though enthusiastic, catching up with the mob and holding on to the man on Mark's left.

"We're making a speech over there—lots of stuff!"

"Right on!" she said, and she took hold of Mark's arm. "Forward!"

Mark had been wide-eyed, stunned by the hippie's move, but he realized that his mother had been able to think.

"Okay! Forward!" he said, moving farther away from the hippie group.

"Yeah!" the hippies said.

There was a platform in the center of the Square, where a thin man wearing eyeglasses was screaming his complaints through a bullhorn. The gathering was a rally against all kinds of things, ranging from lack of jobs, to the need for marijuana, to the problems of polluted beaches and smog, along with an assortment of incoherent complaints by drunkards unable to formulate their thoughts. Among the crowd were some college kids and middle-aged people who were also airing their complaints. There was a party-like atmosphere; people seemed to be there just for fun, with no serious thought for possible trouble. A number were just chatting or talking on their cell phones, and some were taking iPhone photos to send to friends.

Anne and Mark had been able to free themselves from the mob that had grabbed Mark, so they skirted away from the crowd, toward the back.

Just then another speaker took the bullhorn. "Listen up, people! Look at our accomplishment! We've put a stop to that nuclear plant in Iran. Reelect Olama for president!"

The crowd roared approval, and the encouraged speaker became bolder.

"Yes, I was among the team that made it possible to stop the Iranian nuclear plant. We are rocking, man! I'm telling you the great strides this administration has done!"

The speaker was in his thirties, dressed in rolled-up shirt sleeves; Anne could tell from a mile away that he was a rabble-rouser. She was aware of his kind, present in crowds to incite them into disorder and to bait the naïve into actions that lead to chaos, all the while working toward a sinister goal that was not apparent until it was too late.

Anne and Mark listened, disbelieving, as the speaker wove an elaborate scenario of how the current administration had saved the world. Anne's temper finally exploded. Mark braced for trouble at the foot of the platform when he realized his mother was going up to speak.

"Do you recognize this face? Not that it is much to talk about, but do you remember that the police was searching for me after there was a shoot-out at Richard Higgins's office in Washington, DC?" She paused while some in the crowd scratched their heads, trying to remember.

"Yeah! Yeah! Did you shoot the North Korean?" the bespectacled previous speaker said sarcastically off to the side.

"Listen!" Anne shouted into the bullhorn. She raised her hand. "I was in that office because I had knowledge of the Stuxnet cyberworm. There was a shoot-out because the North Koreans kidnapped a scientist's son just to get information about nuclear bombs. As you know, Richard Higgins was seriously wounded. Check the news. I had to go into hiding. Now the nuclear plant in Natanz, Iran, has been disabled—not through the effort of this liar but through other channels. This guy is full of crap!" Anne pointed to the liar. "Seize him, and find out who planted him here to cause you trouble!"

"You liar!" One hippie went up the platform and shoved the bespectacled previous speaker.

There was a commotion as the previously apathetic crowd chanted, "Get the liar out of here!"

Anne went down from the platform calmly and faded off into the crowd with Mark; then they walked faster toward the taxi. She directed the taxi to Golden Gate Park, where they stayed in the car as it went around, just for a panoramic view. They came off and took another taxi to their hotel and had it wait. They claimed their carry-ons from the courtesy room and told the taxi to head for the airport. They checked in for Denver.

"Can't be helped," Anne finally said as they took seats in the boarding area of their flight.

"That was scary!" Mark said. Then both of them burst out laughing.

"What a wacky day!" Anne said. Then she became serious. "I thought we were on our way to a quiet life."

"Attention, please," the desk clerk said, using the microphone. "There is a gate change."

Anne and Mark picked up their rolling carry-on luggage and walked through the central terminal for the gate change. There was a food-court area on their right as they hurried through, with TV screens above to update the commuters on recent events.

Mark suddenly stopped. "That's us!" he said, pulling Anne aside.

The news channel carrying it was CNN; then Fox and CNBC followed with cell phone photos of the event in San Francisco.

"Now we have a glimpse of what could have happened several weeks ago when Richard Higgins was seriously wounded and some North Koreans were killed in his office. The administration was mum about it then. Now we have the real participant of that event speaking up, but we are still looking for her. She seems to have disappeared in the crowd." A cell phone photo of Anne and Mark appeared onscreen, showing them as they calmly walked away from the crowd. Anne's scarf was being blown gently by the wind.

Anne quickly removed her blue silk scarf and put on sunglasses.

Mark parted his hairline in the middle with his fingers and put on sunglasses too.

They arrived at the boarding gate and warily seated themselves in the corner.

Anne called Edward. "Did you see the TV news? Simmer down. You better leave the house and stay in a hotel on the Missouri side. Call us on this cell phone. From Denver, we will go by land to Kansas City on the Missouri side. We might have to take the Greyhound bus. Please just do it. You said you don't have the CIA babysitting you anymore."

"I can imagine this event going viral. People like half mysteries rather than outright news. They had a lot of photos—talk about a new age." Mark sighed.

Anne took a deep breath. "Just can't take it sitting down, I suppose. I can't stand liars taking credit that's not theirs, while others die to do what is right. Besides, that's my idea of campaigning for my candidate in the coming election."

They burst out laughing and then looked around just as the boarding gate opened.

Mark took out his computer from his backpack as soon as they were seated. "Let's see what transportation is available from the Denver airport to Kansas, Missouri, if we go by land . . . Yes! There's an Amtrak service from Denver to Kansas City going through Galesburg, Illinois."

"We'll pay cash," Anne said.

They slept on the plane and ate at the Denver airport before they took the bus downtown. From there they took the Amtrak.

When they arrived in the Kansas City terminal, they called Edward.

He arrived shortly. The family embraced each other and cried with a sense of relief; then they rode the car in silence. They went up to their hotel room, and as soon as they closed the door, Edward turned on the TV.

"You are all over the news!" he said angrily. "Now you want us to go into hiding?"

"It's a precaution," Anne sighed. "You cannot risk those North Korean and Iranian agents getting revenge for what happened to them. We will be in a witness protection program, and there's reward money. That might take time, but just the same, it is not that we are going to lose our possessions; we just have to relocate."

"We are moving? Who said so?" Edward said.

"Don't you think it is better to be safe than sorry? Even our neighbors won't like us around if they feel threatened by attacks from those spies!" Anne could not believe that she had to spell things out this way.

"I'm not moving, period. This is your fault; you straighten it out," Edward shot back.

"Look!" Mark pointed to the TV.

"The administration is seeking those people involved in the disablement of the nuclear plant in Iran for actions that were not sanctioned by our Department of Defense. They must come in for questioning; we cannot afford rogue individuals making decisions that we, as a government, should be making. We cannot afford frayed relationships with other countries just because some citizens choose to take sides in international problems." The press secretary announced the message slowly and clearly.

Anne sat on the bed and cried. Mark held her by the shoulder and sighed.

What was supposed to be a joyful reunion became an acrimonious confrontation. After a period of silence, Anne made up her mind.

"We're leaving for a country that has no extradition treaty with the USA. I was afraid of this. I've realized that we made decisions that did not involve the US government, but that was because the Israelis were available and more committed. We also doubted how much to trust the CIA. As a matter of fact, we were not sure the administration would do it the way we did—no hassle or bureaucracy, just getting it done. The interest of the Israeli country was once allied with the USA, but with this administration, we were not even sure. I admit I made my decisions on an individual basis, and Mark agreed. Are you still with me, Son?"

With a nod from Mark, Anne continued. "I'll use the card that we have from Higgins's storage and withdraw one hundred thousand dollars. We will live on that until it is safe to come home. If you are coming with us, let's pick up your passport, Edward; if not, we will get the money, fly from LA to the Philippines, and hide there."

Edward shook his head. "You're just into one trouble after another."

"Let's see if we can contact Higgins or Luke," Anne turned to Mark. "Guzman might need to come with us."

"We just have Higgins's phone number; there was no answer. I only have Luke's old cell phone number; I'll leave a cryptic message. What do we say?" Mark asked.

"Just say, 'Please advise. Guzman can come with us. Will use LAX,'" Anne said. "Now use the e-mail address of Luke and Levi; that might work. Same message."

After a few tense minutes, they received Luke's answer via e-mail. He provided them with his new cell phone number and e-mail address, along with the following message: "Where are you? Agree with plan. Guzman will call you when he is at LAX. Get new cell phones, and e-mail me the numbers. Higgins and Levi are better. I have to lie low also. Must stay here to monitor events; otherwise, I'd come with you."

"Huh?" Mark said, and Anne wondered what that was about.

"Okay. We'll get money and go to the airport for Los Angeles. From there we can fly straight to the Philippines." Anne turned to her husband. "I'm sorry, but this was a fight for world peace; that's what we think it is. Other people choose to see it in some other way and aim to persecute us. We need to hide until this misunderstanding is over. If you don't agree, then Mark and I will just go. We'll stay in touch."

Edward shook his head.

Anne and Mark left the hotel with their luggage and withdrew money from an ATM using Higgins's card. The maximum withdrawal allowance was $20,000 in one-hundred-dollar bills, which scared Anne, but she took it. They then took a taxi to the airport. At the Kansas City airport, they used the ATM again and withdrew another $20,000.

Anne looked around. "Take this other half. We have to camouflage this money to get through security. I'm so tired; I can't think. Any ideas?"

Mark looked around and then signaled toward a trash can. A man in a fedora was throwing a newspaper away and missed. Mark picked it up. "I could read it while waiting." He waved away the man trying to put it in.

"Oh, here's another one," the man said, and he left.

"Thanks," Anne said, taking the paper. She looked toward the restrooms and nodded. "We'll wait for each other out here. Putting the money in between the newspaper pages might do the trick."

They each went to the restroom. After a while, they came out and went to the ticket counter. They paid cash.

It was not until they were seated on the plane on the way to Los Angeles that Anne cried. She was used to functioning on her own without her husband's counsel, mostly because it was a hindrance to bother. They generally agreed on the big things but not on the small things. This was a big thing, and it was a disappointment that her husband was of a different opinion.

Anne had always been headstrong, independent, and capable of going it alone. At least Mark thought the same way she did, but now the two of them were in trouble.

Mark put his arms around Anne's shoulders; she tried not to make noise as she cried. After a while she stopped, just as the drinks were being served.

They looked around when they arrived at the Los Angeles airport.

"I could get our tickets at this computer kiosk here. It has a printer," Mark said.

"I want to be sure Guzman is on the same plane as we are. I don't know if Luke gave him some funds. So far, we have the money," Anne said.

They went toward the Philippine Airlines ticket counter and waited nearby. It was about an hour before they saw Guzman hurrying with a worried look. Mark waved, and Guzman broke into a smile when he saw them.

"Luke got me on the flight here but instructed me to let you get the tickets. He gave me five thousand dollars. Am I supposed to give this to you?" he said excitedly.

"Keep it. It's good to divide our assets just in case we get separated. We don't know what we are facing. I might cash in more money when we arrive in the Philippines, before somebody shuts down this account or uses it to trace us," Anne whispered. "I'll get our tickets now. I'll pay cash—it's less traceable. Let's go together."

They moved together to the ticket counter and went through the security check without their money being discovered. Even Guzman's passport was okay. Anne made a mental note to check that out later.

"That was too easy. I hope it's not a trap," Anne commented.

Later, while they were in the food court, a TV screen caught their attention. A reporter was standing outside the Cortez residence.

"Here is Mr. Cortez's residence, but he has not answered the doorbell or any phone calls. A few minutes ago, Mr. Cortez rode off in his Lexus, and without any comment, he left. We don't know where he went. Here is his neighbor, Mr. Schnuck. Sir, could you tell us anything about Mr. Cortez and his family?"

Anne and Mark looked resigned, and Guzman just went ahead in the McDonald's line, motioning for them to follow him.

Anne had no appetite, but Mark pushed the food in front of her and pointed to his wristwatch. Anne felt as if she were chewing poison as she tried to eat automatically.

There was a delay while the plane was on the tarmac, and the three looked at each other. After thirty minutes, the plane left.

A stewardess sidled up to them when she served their drinks. "An FBI agent was trying to stop the flight. He was not sure if you were here, and he did not have the required paper, so we left."

Anne looked up from her aisle seat. Mark was in the middle, and Guzman was in the window seat.

"This is a straight flight; can they still stop us?" Anne asked.

"They can, but not if we are over international waters, which will be soon. The pilot is aware that you might be on this flight," the stewardess whispered.

"Thank you," Anne said.

Mark and Guzman sighed in relief, but Anne became restless. Just the same, there was not much to do on the plane. They slept through the flight and woke up just as the plane arrived. It was morning, Philippine Time. The straight flight was available only through PAL, and it had the advantage of letting the travelers avoid jet lag.

## 21. In the Philippines

They arrived without any incident at the Ninoy Aquino Airport. It was the usual warm, humid day, and since they had no check-in luggage, they all proceeded to the taxi area.

"To Makati. Do you know the Prince Plaza Condotel on Dela Rosa Street"? She asked the driver.

The driver nodded, and they were off.

"We'll just be in the Condotel for two days," Anne said. "We will then move to a place where we don't have to register with our passports. By the way, we'll get a suite."

The suite was actually a bigger room with a bunker-type sofa for a third bed, along with two twin beds.

"I can take the bunker bed—I'm smaller—but I'm first in the bathroom, okay?" Anne was quick to negotiate.

"No problem," Mark said.

Guzman nodded.

"Will you check our cell phones? What can we still use, and do we need SIM cards?" Anne turned to Guzman.

"Let me check," Guzman said. He then started tinkering with the phones. "Let's buy two cheap ones, one each for Mark and me, plus get international SIM cards. We can use those two for this country and still have a lot of access with the phones from Stockholm."

"Let's eat first," Mark said.

The Glorietta shopping complex was just across the block from their hotel. They gorged on native dishes at a specialty restaurant. They checked different shops and bought casual shirts and shorts. Anne also bought some skirts.

They took a taxi to another side of town to get the cell phones.

When they came back to their room, Anne turned on the TV while Mark and Guzman sorted out their purchases.

"The authorities are looking for Edward Cortez," the TV anchor said. "He will have to be questioned regarding his wife and son. As you know, folks, Anne and Mark Cortez were involved in the disablement of the Iranian nuclear plant in Natanz, Iran. The whole affair has caused an international incident, which the UN is trying to mediate. Here is the UN secretary general being interviewed by Stan Brooks . . ."

"What? Those clowns are really something!" Mark said angrily.

"SOBs!" Guzman said.

"You miserable, Godforsaken piece of crap!" Anne said to the TV screen.

They then sat on the beds, feeling depressed, as the news continued.

"We also have a follow-up on a previous report from Stockholm, where a bag was fished out of the water, just off Vasabron. The bag seems to contain computers and cell phones, but they have all been corroded because of an unknown substance. The authorities are figuring out if this was related to the disablement of the nuclear plant," the announcer said.

Guzman nodded. "That's where the pepper, salt, and lemon went."

"At least one problem is out of the way, thanks to you." Anne sighed. "Whatever the truth is, it can only come out with us. Those heels in the administration are on the Iranian side. Imagine what they are saying. Those stupid cowards! That's not all. They are making demons out of us. Problem is, they are in power," Anne said angrily. Then she burst out crying in frustration.

Mark and Guzman sat forlorn for some time.

"It's almost six o'clock; let's eat and give ourselves time to think," Anne said.

They went to eat in the open plaza of the mall. It was a merry scene with people singing karaoke, but their appetite was gone. They discussed possibilities, but they had neither the idea of the actual situation nor the knowledge of possible options. They argued in whispers, which amounted to no decision.

"Let's listen to the news," Anne said, "and then call Luke when we get back to our room. Let's fight back. We'll check the news and opinions from the time we were out of circulation."

They headed back to the Condotel, picking up some food along the way, and Anne passed by the reception desk to request Wi-Fi access for their rooms.

"First thing, Mark, please e-mail your dad and brother. Just say we are in the Philippines and doing okay. We're twelve hours ahead of USA Eastern Time; let's review the news and all other events before we call Luke. Whatever he says, we can then form our own decision,"

Anne said. She turned on the TV to CNN, placed it on a low volume, and listened.

Mark and Guzman turned on their computers and started checking.

"I'm looking at *USA Today*, starting from two weeks ago, after we disabled the nuclear site," Guzman said. "The Iranians at first denied that something happened at Natanz, although USA scientists said they detected a lack of radioactivity where there used to be immense activity going on. Next Iranians blamed the USA for a cyberattack on their nuclear plant . . . North Koreans had no comment . . . Pizza delivery boys are being represented by O'Hearn Law Firm, which is seeking compensation for pizza boys injured in the fiasco at Higgins's office and also seeking international justice at The Hague for the trespass of US sovereignty to foment mayhem . . . President Olama instructed Ambassador White to address the UN in a conciliatory speech directed toward Iranians . . . North Koreans protested . . . The US ambassadors to England and to France resigned in protest . . . President Olama's poll advantage was up after the administration claimed credit for disablement of the nuclear plant. Then his lead was lowered by ten points on the poll reading, after the truth came out . . . Challenger Kit Rooney is ready to choose among six potential vice presidential running mates . . . Talk-show host Hal Breitbart is angry over the 'spineless administration' and doesn't know where it is going . . . An evening report anchor decried 'dirty campaign tactics' . . . The search is on for Mr. Edward Cortez to shed light on the Iran fiasco."

"Okay," Mark said, "I'm looking at the *Wall Street Journal* and reading through the international news and politics. I'll just call out headlines that seem pertinent, information not mentioned yet: 'Chartered PLC accused of financial dealings with Iran,' 'China claims more islands in South China Sea,' 'Philippines and Vietnam protest,' 'Japan protests South Korean claims to disputed islands,' 'Egyptian court sentences 14 members of militant Islamic group to death for attacks six days ago in Sinai Peninsula,' '46 people killed by 14 suicide bombers in Afghanistan,' 'Earthquakes hit northwest Iran, demolishing villages—More than 200 dead,' 'Syrian PM defects,' 'Syrian rebels clash with government troops.'"

"Okay. Let's call Luke," Anne said.

The TV flashed a news release, and Mark turned on the volume. It was a conference by the press secretary. "Mr. Edward Cortez was taken by FBI agents in Florida. Although Mr. Cortez was in the USA while his wife and son got involved in the disablement of the Iranian nuclear plant, the authorities believe he has knowledge of what has been going on. We believe that detaining him will facilitate the surrender of Anne and Mark Cortez."

A correspondent raised his hand to ask a question. "Basically, you are holding a person you know has not committed any crime. You are holding him hostage to make his wife and son surrender. Was it a crime to disable the nuclear plant when we all know that previous administrations spent money to accomplish that very task, by covert or by diplomatic means?"

The press secretary grasped for words. "Well, we need to know the truth."

Another correspondent simply said, "You have violated human rights in so doing."

"Do you anticipate the Cortez family pursuing a lawsuit against the administration for this illegal detention?" another correspondent said. "Is this the lowest yet, or how low are we going in this mess? The mess is actually the administration." The correspondent walked out.

The other correspondents followed.

The press secretary was left without an audience.

The next TV picture was Edward Cortez with his tousled white hair. His eyeglasses, with one lens broken, was hanging askew on his nose. "Mr. Cortez seems to have put up a fight," the announcer said, followed by a black screen.

"Oh God!" Anne said.

"You shit!" Mark uncharacteristically exploded.

"I'm gonna get you, man! I'm gonna get you!" Guzman said through clenched teeth.

"I'm calling Luke," Anne said.

Almost instantly Luke answered. "Where are you? I've been trying to reach you! Have you seen the TV?"

"Yes! We just did! We got here and roamed around and got new cell phones. Maybe the battery is dead on the other ones. Oh Luke! What's going on?" Anne's voice mirrored her fear—not for herself but for her family.

"I've been frantically trying to stave off these idiots without revealing that I was there. That's so I can represent you guys in court. They don't know about Guzman. They are after you and Mark. It's a perverse way of trying to show that they are in command, but instead the people are turned off. Just the same, they want a trial of sorts. The Speaker of the House is making it a congressional hearing instead. If you don't come voluntarily, they will keep Edward in prison. They are aware that you went to the Philippines because there is no extradition treaty with that country. Anne, you and Mark have to come back here."

"No! Dammit!" Anne cussed.

"Anne, please. This would be easy in a fair court—there's no case. But the attorney general himself is calling the shots, and his minions are just obeying. I'll arrange for you and Mark to come to clear your name. Even your son Jim will be harassed. You were right; they are hostages now, but I still believe in this country. We will fight this out."

Anne had turned on the phone speaker so that Mark and Guzman could hear what was going on. There was silence for a while as her mind went through the different options.

"Anne! Anne?" Luke sounded lost.

"I'm still thinking!"

Luke sighed audibly. "Higgins is up and about already, and he's very angry. We are calling in all supports. Tell me when you are coming."

"Okay," Anne said. "I'll call you after I make the arrangements. Only our team knows about it. How are Levi and Alain? Have you heard from Andre and his family?"

"Levi is a lot better and was examined by several specialists," Luke said. "The doctor thinks that Levi will be back to normal in due time, although his liver enzymes are still high, indicating he has hepatitis, probably drug induced or due to the needle injections. The doctors are still testing. Alain was discharged from the hospital, but he is staying with us. Andre's relatives were able to send word that his mother and sister are in Syria. Problem is, there's a rebellion there. We are trying to find some reliable agents who can get them out," Luke said. "What's your plan with Guzman?"

"He's staying here as our weapon!" Anne said.

"Huh? Anne, please don't do anything drastic. Tell Guzman I have a job ready for him. Please, guys, stay with me on this!" Luke pleaded.

"We'll let you know when we are nearby," Anne said, and she ended the call.

The phone rang again.

"Anne! Don't you hang up on me! Dammit!" Luke said angrily.

"Oh! For heaven's sake! No offense intended! Luke, we need to think together and plan. Give us time," Anne said irritably.

"Okay! But you keep me posted!" Luke said, and he hung up.

Mark and Guzman shook their heads.

"Crap!" Anne said. "What a mess!" She let out a long sigh and sat limply across from Mark and Guzman. "Your ideas, please."

"I'll shut them down," Guzman said quietly.

Anne looked at Guzman, and then her eyes widened. She suddenly realized that he meant it. She pondered his attitude and weighed the possibilities, but she was unable to come up with a plan. "What would you do?" she finally asked.

"I can shut down the electricity on the East Coast and in Washington, DC, if they don't release your husband."

Anne had to shake her head to wake up and concentrate. "That might be too radical. Let's think of something else."

Through the night, they tried to think, until they all decided to get some sleep. They had no plan.

They all tossed and turned in bed, unable to sleep. When they fell asleep, they could not wake up.

Anne woke up to persistent knocking at the door. She stumbled out of her sofa bed and opened the door for the breakfast trays brought by the maid. "Thank you," she said, struggling to wake up.

"Good morning, ma'am," the hotel maid said, and with a smile, she placed the trays on the table and left.

Anne decided to shower first. She needed to wake up, and it was also good to be ahead. She was pouring coffee when Mark and Guzman began to stir. Anne then turned on the TV. It was the usual chitchat on Fox News, so she switched to CNBC.

"The S&P is forecast to be up tomorrow because of the deal being brokered by the IMF for the faltering economies in Europe," the announcer said.

Anne glanced at Guzman, suddenly concentrating on the ticker tape on the screen. "That's from yesterday, since they are twelve hours behind. The stock market will open at nine thirty a.m. Eastern Time. That's tonight our time." She meant to explain further, but she was also observing Guzman light up with ideas. "Don't do anything funny until we talk about it." Anne picked up Guzman's trend of thought.

"You have to explain a lot of things to me regarding how things work," Guzman said.

"Don't go that route," Anne said. "It's the whole world you are fighting instead of the people who are doing this." Anne started to feel uncomfortable. "Let's eat first; then you guys take your showers. We need to clear our minds."

Mark got up, and soon they were all eating breakfast in silence.

When Anne finished all the coffee, she went for the soda in the food bags they had brought in. By the time Mark and Guzman were ready, she had formulated the semblance of a plan.

"All right, Mark and I need to get back there just so they will release Edward. I don't know whether they will put us in prison first before asking questions, or whether we will be on house arrest. If we go back and notify them, we will be at their mercy. If we go back on our own, unknown to them, then we can stay hidden until the terms are favorable. Guzman, you have to stay here and stay in touch with Luke and Higgins. Let's get all the information available as to how to contact their office; that way, we have other options if one method is not working. We will have all the info in triplicate, so if one of us is down, the others can take over. If we have to be in prison, Mark and I will be separated. You know I'm against being alone without protection, since there are too many perverts there. If that happens, spring me out of prison—can you do that?"

"If most of the locks are electronic, easy; if it is manual, Luke or Levi would need to be there to help," Guzman said.

"Wow! Where would Dad and Jim be?" Mark asked.

"I can't even predict the diabolical twists these people are introducing. I don't know," Anne said. Then she saw the funny expression on Guzman's face.

"You have a family; I don't," Guzman said.

"You know, we haven't even talked with each other about our personal lives," Anne said. "We just kept going through danger and presumed each one will be there for us. Do you want to tell us now about your family?"

Guzman sat looking sad. "I don't really have any. My mother was considered a math whiz and went to the University of the Philippines. She married her childhood sweetheart—her neighbor, my father. I was twelve years old, a happy child, and my mother called me Roland, like 'The Song of Roland,' the nephew of Charlemagne. One day, my mother visited her relatives during a fiesta in Bulacan. They rode in a barge that was overcrowded. It sank, and she drowned. My father remarried and forgot about me. He spent my mother's inheritance to please his new wife. I did not even have money for college, so I worked as a waiter, with very little money to finish at a technical computer school. One day, when I'd just finished an exam, I went out drinking with my classmates. We dared each other to see who could do the most fantastic thing on a computer. That's when I made what I called the Love Virus. My friends laughed and cheered me when it went worldwide; then it caused damage to defense systems and a lot of companies. My friends became quiet, but it was my father who told the police where I was. I thought it was the end of me. Luckily there was no law in effect that I broke, so I was released. My father disowned me, but I had already disowned him when I found out that he was the one who betrayed me. I have no family now. You were the first people who really cared for me."

Mark touched Guzman's shoulder in sympathy. "Roland it is," he said.

Anne held back her tears and said, "You know we will be there for you. You have shown character in the face of all the difficulties we've been through." She held Roland's shoulder. "Your mother is watching over you."

Roland nodded.

They were silent for a while; then the phone rang.

"Hello, Anne? You and Mark hop on the plane already. We have to talk about our defense," Luke said.

"Where exactly are we going when we get there? Are you sure we are not going straight to prison?" Anne asked.

"Definitely not. If they try something like that, we will raise a big howl," Luke said.

"You are not sure," Anne said. "We will be there when you see us. You are the first one we will call, but not before we are ready. By the way, what is the Israeli embassy saying in all this?"

"Nothing to the public, but they are offering asylum and all the financial help necessary. You three also have bounty money coming to you."

"How much?" Anne said.

"That's eight million to you, seven each to Mark and Guzman, five for Andre, and one million to Alain. Levi made the recommendation. Even though Guzman got involved later, he was highly instrumental in decrypting the code."

"Does Levi have a double citizenship, then?"

"Yes."

"We are planning to come," Anne said, "but on our terms. Roland will stay in the Philippines to monitor the situation."

"What situation?" Luke said.

"Whatever," Anne said.

"C'mon, Anne, don't be dangerous," Luke said worriedly.

"We'll see you in twenty four hours, something like that. I'll give the phone to Roland, and you give us all the e-mail addresses and phone numbers we can safely use."

"Uh . . . Who's Roland?"

"That's Guzman. That's what we'll call him now," Anne said, and she handed the phone to Roland.

Roland put it on speakerphone, and he and Mark wrote down the information Luke gave them. Mark then also gave Luke a list.

"Okay. I have the primary and secondary phone lines and e-mail addresses for each of you—Luke, Levi, and Higgins," Mark said.

"Right! Enter those into your cell phones, computers, and iPads. Always send a copy to each of us when sending a message," Luke confirmed. "Anne? Give us a ballpark of what to expect."

"We're still in the planning process. As usual, we will use a circuitous route to get there. We will be calling you—bye for now," Anne said.

"Okay. Bye for now," Luke said uncertainly.

Anne sighed. "I miss working in my garden! What a summer this has been!" She turned down the TV and then sat on her sofa bed. Still restless, she moved to the seats by the table. "Why don't we write it down?" She looked for paper and grabbed their old ticket printouts. She wrote on the back, first listing *Anne*, followed by *Mark* in the left column; then she left a big space and wrote *Roland*. She placed arrows after her name and Mark's. The arrows pointed to DC, followed by a series of emanating lines. The first line was prison, the next was Israeli asylum, the third was house arrest, and the fourth was hiding. "Will you check again to see whether Israel has an extradition treaty with the USA?"

Mark and Roland sat across from her.

"Yes," Roland answered. "That's one option out."

"I'm worried about your dad staying in prison if we don't show up." Anne turned to Mark. "Why don't we let Luke arrange a press conference as soon as we arrive? We will disclose the time and location with only a short notice. It will give the press the chance to ask all their questions without the administration messing things up. With or without bias, most of the news will come out the way we tell it. When it is a congressional hearing, we don't have control of which direction it goes."

"They can still take you to prison," Roland said.

"We can negotiate for Dad's release before we agree to show up," Mark said.

"We don't have much choice, do we?" Anne said.

"I can announce our position, and what really happened, on the Internet," Roland said.

"But that would not be admissible evidence. Besides, we want to keep you out of this if we can help it, Roland. You see, you are the ace up our sleeve. Also, Roland," Anne added gently, "your life will be in danger if people know what you are capable of. We have to keep you hidden. We will have to leave you with money here. Wait until it is safe to come out."

Roland looked at Anne and Mark for a while; then he nodded.

"Okay. Today we'll open an account for you at the bank. We'll just make a moderate deposit. Keep most of your money in cash. Don't ever get drunk and tell people who you are or that you have money. You have to be very discreet." Anne paused. "You might get lonely." She thought for a while. "I don't know if any of my classmates can hide you. There are a few I can really trust. My family here cannot be approached. I'm sure people will rat on them if anything unusual happens. Could you stay strong by yourself? If you cannot handle it, that's when I'll get some classmates involved."

Roland nodded solemnly.

"After you have your account, we will get our tickets. We will use PAL. I feel there will be some loyalty, and also we will probably be protected. Will you check your passport, Roland? Do you still have a valid visa to enter the USA if necessary?"

Roland checked his passport. "Oh! I only have a temporary visa that Luke got for me. It will expire by next month."

"Oh! I remember now," Anne said. "Your visa was for Sweden, right?"

"Right! Maybe I should just come with you now but stay hidden somewhere." Roland scratched his head.

Anne glanced at Roland, who for once looked vulnerable. "It looks like we're back to square one. How about a Residence Inn in Washington, DC? Let's do that. Get a suite, and we can hide there for as long as necessary. It should have Wi-Fi."

"I'll get the tickets using Higgins's card. How soon?" Mark said.

"Take the soonest nonstop departure available. Make all flight reservations round-trip, one-week return. Would that flight out be tonight or in the morning? Book for LA, and then we'll go to Baltimore, Maryland. We'll sleep there one night. The next morning, we'll take the Amtrak to Washington, DC, but we'll go to our Residence Inn suite first, spruce up our appearance, and show up at the DC conference after noontime."

"I'll do the Marriott Residence Inn. What's that number?" Roland said. "Wait, let's do it together. It's half a day later there. Then we have a sequence. Let's double-check the dates."

While Mark and Roland were doing the booking, Anne got her pen out and made a list. "We'll buy some clothes so they don't have to think we are begging to them," Anne said. "I still have my jewelry."

"Okay. We can leave at ten p.m. tonight, fly nonstop, and arrive at LAX at 8:05 p.m. the same day because of the time difference. However, the reasonable connection to Baltimore is six a.m. the next day. The other option is an eleven p.m. flight, which is obviously impossible, considering customs and all that," Mark said, looking up while Roland wrote notes on a piece of paper.

"So we sleep in the airport," Anne said, "and arrive in Baltimore the next day. We'll stay in a hotel there for the day, get some sleep, and go to DC the next morning. So you book the Residence Inn suite for the day after. We don't even know if we will have problems when we arrive;

if so, we'll call the DC people." She was amused at the thought. "I can imagine what a mess it would be if anybody detected us while in transit. Otherwise, we'll let Luke know when we leave from Baltimore."

"Isn't that too close?" Mark asked.

"I don't know. What do you think? I just don't want these people to know we are coming. They might look for us."

"I think that's good." Roland nodded.

"E-mail Luke now to say that we are demanding the release of Edward Cortez before we show up. Proof that he has been released is necessary before we make an effort at all."

Roland typed frantically and then said, "Done!"

"Okay. Let's eat lunch, do some shopping, come back to our room to get everything ready, and head for the airport three hours before departure. We'll pay the hotel for tonight even if we leave early, so we can do stuff here in peace."

They locked their room and went out feeling good, knowing what was next. They had a good lunch, took their time shopping, and bought nice-looking clothes. Anne needed a secondary bag aside from her purse and carry-on.

"We'll dress up for the airport. Somehow there's an intimidation factor when people don't think they can mess with you," she said.

They ate an early light supper of Chinese take-out and fruits; then they headed for the airport.

They had no problem with their tickets, but Roland was scrutinized for a while by the security check. Anne went back for him, her beads making a loud clanging noise.

"What are you doing there, Roland? Hurry up—the delegation is waiting!"

The man let Roland go.

## 22. Facing Interrogation

They proceeded to the boarding area but sat a little toward the back, keeping in mind an escape route. There was no further incident until they were in the Los Angeles port of entry.

Anne coached Roland. "You'd better smile and look happy. Look confident, and be just a tad friendly to the customs and INS agents. Tell them your temporary visa is by special request of the US government. Give Higgins's number if they want to call."

That worked. Anne and Mark waited for Roland past the customs area, and they settled in an area of the airport where other passengers were hanging out for the night, prior to the early morning flights.

"I'm surprised we got through without authorities coming after us," Mark commented.

"I was banking on the premise that most ordinary people don't bother to listen to the news. They just do their own thing. Not a good prognosis for the country, but it worked in our favor for now," Anne said with a shake of her head. "Besides, we don't look like fugitives."

They tried to sleep, or at least closed their eyes. Their flight was on time, so they arrived in Baltimore by noontime. They ate at the airport and then took a taxi to their hotel.

"Is there news of your dad being released yet?" Anne asked aloud while turning on the TV in their room. "No? We'll try to stay awake till five p.m. Then we'll eat an early supper and sleep early. Our wake-up call will be for six a.m. We can talk more on the Amtrak to Washington. Let's clear up the kinks in our strategy then. You guys set up the cell phones and the computers."

They went to the harbor and walked around to ward off the jet lag, and then they ordered crab for their early dinner.

They were able to sleep, and by morning there was an e-mail from Luke: "Edward has been released but is under house arrest at Higgins's residence."

Mark e-mailed back the following: "Please schedule a press conference at Higgins's office at one thirty p.m."

They were on the Amtrak, already close to Washington when Luke responded. "What? Where are you?"

"Can't tell. Is it on or off?" Anne directed the message.

"I told you to call me, Anne! All right! Press conference it is! I was busy with a meeting this morning! Why aren't you calling? What's your phone number?"

"Touchy, touchy! He's beginning to sound normal," Anne said to Mark and Roland, who couldn't help smiling. "Just say that we're on our way."

From the Amtrak, they went to their hotel just to change and freshen up.

"Roland, remember that you don't leave the hotel unless we call you," she said, touching his shoulder.

Mark gave him a high five.

Anne and Mark then went to the lobby, got a taxi, and directed it to Higgins's office.

Roland watched them leave in the taxi and hurriedly went to his computer. He had a lot to do—things he could do only if Anne was away.

Anne called Luke's cell phone number when the taxi turned the corner unto the street where Higgins's office building was located. In the office lobby, a crowd of media people had gathered. Correspondents, technicians, and TV cameramen were getting on the elevator, and recognizing Anne and Mark, they made way for them.

Luke was waiting to board the elevator when they showed up. "Anne! Mark! You guys!" He hugged them for a while, and Anne cried.

Luke led them to the office where Higgins and Levi were waiting.

"Could we do this without naming Senawi and Roland? I'm just afraid of the repercussions for them," Anne said.

"Let's see," Luke answered. "I think it's possible here but not if we are testifying before Congress. However, you can always withhold information on the grounds that you are protecting a source. This will set a precedent. I'll get my team to check it out."

They huddled for a while, and then Anne went to check her makeup. They were ready.

The conference room was full despite the short notice. Mark called Roland to tell him what TV news channels were carrying the press conference. As it happened, all the major channels were carrying it.

Luke started the conference and introduced himself as one of the lawyers. He then proceeded to tell their story, including the time that Anne and Mark were asked to save a hostage during the cruise, the fear for their lives, and how they ended up at Higgins's office. He traced their journey that followed the shoot-out at Higgins's office and the race to save the hostage from the North Koreans. He pointed out the danger that the team encountered after deciding to follow the hostage's desire to bring his father's remains home and retrieve the rest of the code. The path over Europe was in a big chart behind him, and he followed that with the escape from Iran, the chase in Budapest, and the decision to disable the Iranian nuclear site.

"Could you have done anything differently if you had been in their place? The only other option was to back out and turn your back to a boy who needed your help to survive. After that, would you be a patriot or a traitor if you decided to go on with a mission whose objective was to disable the nuclear capability of a hostile country that we have been cajoling to stop the proliferation of nuclear bombs?

"How much money do we spend for defense? How much money have we spent on covert activity and putting human assets over there to stop that program? Shall we give reward money to these people who made it possible and did it for us, succeeding where we failed?

"Or are you going to go along with an administration that has instead decided to prosecute them, ostensibly for not letting the government know what this group was doing? Are you seriously saying that people running for their lives will go out of their way to call the administration?

"The administration was unable to stop the North Koreans who left with a hostage, an adolescent male, who was later crucial to revealing the secret of the disablement code. Could you blame these people, who were running for their lives, for turning to the only other country that would fight to stamp out the nuclear threat when we, the number-one country in this world, did not have the heart to make the right decision?

"Could you imagine that instead their family member was held hostage by the administration?"

Luke had held the audience in rapt attention, and he was able to get away without mentioning himself, Senawi, or Roland by name. Anne looked at him speaking from the podium and wondered how soon the reporters would realize that there must have been other characters involved. As it was, they were so mesmerized by the story that they asked questions mostly about the details of how it was done.

They looked at Anne, who was dressed in a lilac short-sleeved dress that extended several inches below her knee, pearl earrings, a pearl necklace, and diamond rings on her fingers.

"How could you run around looking like that? Wouldn't you draw attention?" one reporter asked.

"I hid my jewelry, for I do travel with it. I was actually running around wearing my son's shorts, no makeup, wearing eyeglasses, and with smudges on my face. I suppose even the enemy did not give me a second look. Believe me. I saved a lot of manpower hours by not having to paint my face on a daily basis."

The male reporters laughed.

The female reporters were not easily convinced. "I don't believe it; women are usually vain," one said.

"If you are running for your life, maybe you'll have a change of heart. Besides, if I'd died, the mortician could have the job of making me look presentable," Anne countered.

The men laughed. Then they turned their attention to Mark, who was wearing a dress shirt and a tie.

"How come you and your mother know that much mythology?" one reporter asked.

"Our mother always read to us when we were children, and we usually watch movies together and talk about them," Mark answered.

The reporters asked more questions, and then the conference ended. As much as they would have liked to continue with the questions, there was so much to digest, and the reporters needed time to get out their scoops. They soon hurried out of the conference room to file their reports. Some stayed to have their say on camera before heading back to their stations. Nobody noticed when another "reporter" also came out and climbed into a car that was ready to go. Her cameraman had an ID tag and a knapsack that did not look like a camera bag.

Anne and Mark had prepared for this event with a change of costume. The car was driven by Luke, who'd also quickly changed. Beside him sat Higgins. Levi, Mark, and Anne were in the backseat. They had left Alain at Higgins's house in Alexandria, Virginia.

"Let's go," Higgins said, and Luke quickly eased the car ahead of the reporters' pack.

## 23. Family Crisis

Anne, Mark, and Edward hugged each other when they arrived at Higgins's home. Anne and Mark warmly greeted Alain. The others then left the family to talk among themselves.

"By God! What have you done?" Edward suddenly confronted Anne.

"It had to be done," Anne said.

Mark nodded.

"You have destroyed his future. He should be in school!" Edward continued.

"What are you talking about?" Anne countered. "Mark can make his own decisions about what he wants for his future. He has some reward money coming his way. He can rest for a while after what we've been through." Anne tried to explain patiently, but Edward did not seem to hear.

"Look what you've done to Jim!" he said.

"What about Jim?" Anne asked.

"He also had to go into hiding when some people were looking for him in school," Edward said.

"Did you tell Higgins? Or Luke? Where is Jim now?" Anne asked, bewildered.

"I don't know," Edward said.

"Oh God!" Anne said. "Mark, call Roland to come here. What's the address here? I'll tell the other guys. Wait! Son, call Jim on your phone. Leave a message if he isn't answering. Text him also. Tell him we are in the USA, at Higgins's office. Give the address where we are. At least that's solid. Ask him where he is. Tell him we are coming for him."

She turned to her husband. "Where was Jim the last time you talked to him? I told you to go into hiding together. School can wait; this is a matter of life and death. The North Korean and Iranian agents are vicious! Oh, Edward! Why couldn't you just listen for once?" Anne sat down limply on a chair.

Higgins came walking in, followed by Luke, Levi, and Alain. They suddenly stopped in their tracks when they saw Anne crying. What would have been a joyful reunion turned into a crisis situation.

Roland Guzman arrived in a taxi twenty minutes later, bringing along their computers and other equipment. "What's his cell phone number, or iPhone?" he asked as he placed his computer on the table. "The last time you talked to him, he was in Chicago?"

Levi worked on his computer, and Luke called the local authorities. Higgins called his contacts in Chicago.

"Give me names of people who you know are his friends," Alain said.

"I know Tony Lazio, Chris Hawkins, and Betty Knapp," Mark answered.

Alain called the university and asked for the student affairs office. Nobody answered, and he realized that it was four o'clock in the afternoon CST already. He checked the registration file instead, but there was limited information. He next entered Jim's Facebook e-mail and focused on the same college, student activity, and class year, and he found phone numbers for the three names Mark had given, plus two more possibilities he could contact on the phone.

The first person he called was not available; the second on his list answered the phone.

"Hi, Tony! I'm trying to reach James Cortez. Would you happen to know where I can get in touch with him? I'm with the Washington, DC, Outstanding Young Men's Awards. James has been nominated. Please write my phone number down. Ready? . . . Well, tomorrow is Friday, but isn't it uncharacteristic of an outstanding young man not to attend school?"

He called the third person and repeated his inquiry. "You saw him last Monday? Where? Do you have the same class on Friday?" Alain continued writing notes.

Anne snapped back to life after a while. She wiped her tears, blew her nose, and was back in action. "All right, you said before that when we told you to hide while we were running around Europe, the CIA or FBI was watching you. You also said that it was the FBI that was watching Jim, right?" Anne confronted Edward. "When we met up in Kansas, you were able to come without a tail. Was the FBI still there when you got home? How come you were able to elude them and go to Florida? Who took you from Florida—local police or the FBI? When was the last time you spoke to Jim?"

Levi came over when he saw Anne waking up, getting geared for battle. He helped Edward clarify his answers, focusing on facts, not speculation.

"So you were still able to talk to him when you were in Florida, before the FBI took you to Washington, DC? Was that Monday? Is it possible that it was the FBI who took Jim?" Anne turned to Levi. "Could you check?"

"I've traced his cell phone by tapping into the Verizon computer," Roland said. "It's still in Chicago."

Levi was quickly beside Roland. "Try to pinpoint the address," he said, getting ready to write it down.

Mark quickly sidled up to them and looked up the address on the web's white pages. "Is that the Loyola library?"

"Looks like it," Levi said. "If he felt threatened, he could be hiding there. Or maybe he left it there as his trail . . . Sorry," Levi said when he realized he was thinking out a bad scenario.

"I'll contact the FBI agent assigned to Chicago," Levi said.

"I will send my own man there to look for him," Higgins said. "What's your emergency password?"

"Kidapawan," Anne and Mark said together.

"You are ready all right," Higgins remarked, and he looked up his phone list.

Mark signaled to Guzman, and they sent a text message to Jim preceded by the word *Kidapawan*. "How are you? We are in DC. Shall we come for you?"

Then the wait began. Anne, Mark, and Edward sat together while the others made phone calls.

Once more Higgins called the house help to bring food, coffee, soda, and fruits.

"The FBI agent was instructed to stop tailing Jim about two weeks ago," Levi announced to everybody. "That's about the time we disabled the nuclear plant, and you guys had your Israel tour. Things were quieting down then. When you guys arrived back in the USA, the furor started again because you called out the administration for taking credit. Then the agent was told to shadow Jim again, but there was already somebody else tailing Jim. The agent called for backup, but he was mugged by two Iranian agents. After that, the agent lost track of Jim."

Alain's phone rang. "It's Jim's friend Chris. He saw Jim on the campus on Tuesday, looking worried, but Jim did not say anything unusual," Alain said.

Higgins's phone rang. "My friend is on the Loyola campus. Which library is it?"

"The Cudahy Library is by Sheridan Street. It is also listed at 6515 North Kenmore, considering the large campus. That's what I see on the map," Roland said.

"Okay. That's a large library. My man Crawford might take a while if he has to be discreet," Higgins said.

"Is he armed and reliable?" Anne asked.

"Yes, former Navy SEAL. Why do you ask?" Higgins wondered.

"Mark, call Jim on his cell phone now. Roland, e-mail Jim again. Both of you start your messages with *Kidapawan*. Richard, if Jim doesn't answer in a few minutes, please tell your man not to bother to be discreet. He will have to holler out Jim's name. I feel that he must find Jim at once."

"I have to agree. I'll tell him right now . . . He said the library is closed. Crawford! Get security to open the library—now!" Higgins looked tense.

"I hear the phone ringing!" Mark said. "There's no answer. It's been turned off. Somebody is there!"

"Crawford, are you in? Get the security guard to help you. Guns ready. Start yelling, 'Kidapawan! Jim where are you?'" Higgins ordered. "Right! Start at the lower level, and go up. Does the security guard have a walkie-talkie? Somebody might need to guard the door. Tell the guard to call for backup. Call out to Jim, and tell him to let you know where he is."

Crawford kept his phone on so that they could hear him calling out. He told the guard to stay by the door until the backup arrived; then the other guard could help him. Crawford started calling out to Jim on the lower level; the echoing sound could be heard on Higgins's phone, which had been set on speaker mode. They could hear him go up to the first level and then the second.

"Hurry up!" Anne said under her breath.

They heard the backup security guard joining Crawford on the third floor, calling out.

"He's not in the graduate reading room. The guard is on Deck E, and I'm checking the main stacks, one by one . . . A body! Jim! Are you Jim?"

"Send us a photo from your cell," Anne nervously said. "That's Jim! Thank God! What happened? How is he?"

"It looks like he passed out. His pulse is weak—might be from dehydration. He was locked in here. I'll call an ambulance," Crawford said.

Anne turned to Higgins. "Is that safe?"

"Crawford! Please stay with Jim until he is absolutely safe. Stay with him in the ambulance. Wait for further orders. We might come over or have him transported here. What does it look like to you? Is he hurt?"

"I'm not sure if he was drugged," Crawford answered, "or whether he fainted from hunger. He looks dehydrated, possibly from hiding. It's not clear. I'll try to rouse him. Jim? Jim? I'm your mother's friend. He's waking up. Jim? What happened? . . . Two guys . . . You ran to hide here and did not want to come out . . . Hungry, afraid to come out . . ."

"Okay," Higgins said. "Please accompany him to the hospital. Hostile parties might be watching, so be careful. Can you get some help?"

Anne had been crying with relief and a sense of regret. *How could I have gotten into this?* She thought. "I'm flying out there as soon as possible, or is it better to bring Jim here?"

"Okay," Higgins said. "Roland, check the flight schedule heading to Chicago. Let's hear from Crawford first and find out what the doctor's diagnosis is. I hope it's not something serious."

They all spent the next hour being restless, just waiting, and then the phone rang. Higgins turned it on speakerphone.

"Crawford here. The doctor said that Jim fainted from hunger and dehydration. He has an IV and is being hydrated. Here he is."

"Mom? Mark? How are you guys? Is Dad there?" Jim's voice was soft, as though from weakness.

"We're all here, Son. How are you?" Anne said in a choked voice.

"I'm feeling better. What a mess! Those guys chased me when I came out of my apartment. I ran to the university campus, and they slowed down when they saw a group of guards. I made a turn where they wouldn't see me and then came inside the back door of the library. I didn't realize that the building was actually closed, but I didn't want to come out either. I was afraid to call you, just in case I was found. I must have fainted before I could answer your call."

"Jim, this is Richard Higgins, working with counterintelligence. You've been very brave, and your family has been relentless in finding you. Do you think you can take the airplane to Washington, DC, tomorrow? Crawford and another agent will guard you. Otherwise, your family will come down there tonight."

"Oh, wow! If I have guards, I'll come over. Those Iranians tackled the FBI agent who was tailing me and then came after me," Jim answered.

"Okay, you're coming over tomorrow then. We'll have backups," Higgins said.

"Get well, Son. We'll wait for you here. We love you!" Anne, Mark, and Edward chorused.

"Good night," Jim said.

"We're not waiting for tomorrow. Loyola University Hospital is not equipped for warfare if the Iranians decide to kidnap him. As soon as we have four people on the ground, we'll move them to the airport and bring him here," Higgins said.

He conferred with Luke and Levi; then each made several phone calls.

Roland prepared a spreadsheet of departure schedules from O'Hare airport. After a while, Higgins sidled over to Roland, and they bought five round-trip tickets from O'Hare to Washington, DC. He talked to Crawford on the phone.

"We'll wait for them here," Higgins said. "Those guardsmen are veterans, but it's easier if they are just guarding one, rather than all of us. We need to reinforce this fort if the enemy decides to take us on."

"We still have our things at the hotel," Anne said.

"I'll send an agent to bring all your things here," Higgins answered. "You will all have to camp here until it settles down a bit."

They ate desultorily, and after some small talk, they retired to assigned rooms. Anne and Edward shared a room, and Mark was in another by himself. Roland and Alain shared a room, as did Luke and Levi. Jim would be placed in Mark's room.

They all went to bed early, aware of the busy day ahead.

Anne slept fitfully, but she got up early to start the coffee. On her way to look for the kitchen, she only had to follow her nose; somebody had started the brew already. "Good morning," she said as she came in.

Luke turned from bringing out coffee cups. "Good morning," he said solemnly.

Just then Higgins appeared. "Am I interrupting something?"

"Oh! I just got here myself," Anne said, sounding confused as she blushed without knowing why. "I would have been proud to help with the coffee, but Luke was here ahead of me. Can I help with anything?"

The housemaid arrived with croissants and Danish. She also prepared sausage and bacon.

"I can do the eggs," Anne volunteered. "How do you want them? How many?" She sprayed the nonstick pan and started warming it on the stove top.

"Two for me, sunny-side up," Higgins said.

"Also two for me, but use some cooking oil; I don't want them too dry," Luke said.

The others started arriving, and Anne was glad they were all back to normal, talking about the coming arrival of Jim and the preparation for the congressional hearing.

## 24. Congressional Hearing

Anne ate a quick breakfast and excused herself. She borrowed Mark's computer and went to the library to work on her statement for the testimony. She then sent copies of her statement to the other computers.

They worked through the morning, with only a coffee break. Anne was going to read through the sequence of events from beginning to end, and Mark was going to put in the human factor.

"Is it clear enough as we've put it, without using Senawi's name, and evading the use of Luke's and Roland's names? It's not perjury to attribute an action to a person without specifying exactly who did it, right? If they ask me point-blank, I'll say who it is, with advice of legal counsel." Anne turned to Higgins. "This is your framework, and I agree, but I'm not so comfortable."

"Luke and I will be right there with you and Mark at the hearing," Higgins said. "Don't feel that you absolutely can't mention the names; do so if they have to be said. As we have agreed, we need to shield Roland from the hearing. You have to stay at home, Roland, and just watch us on TV. It's too dangerous if someone outside of our group learns about you."

"Okay. I feel better now," Anne said.

"I was having the same trouble, but okay, I feel all right now," Mark said.

At noon, Higgins called a break. "Let's have lunch. Jim will be arriving shortly after lunchtime."

Anne and Mark were visibly lighthearted as they ate, and Edward also started smiling.

The group had just finished coffee and dessert when the car arrived.

Anne and Mark ran to the door.

"Hey, guys!" Jim was out of the car first.

The family hugged each other for a long time.

Higgins introduced everyone to Jim and the four agents. "We're lucky the Iranians did not challenge our agents," Higgins commented.

The newcomers were led to the dining room, where more food was served as they conversed and bantered a bit.

After the brief respite, the whole team, including Jim and the four agents, gathered again in the library. Jim had to tell his side of the story, and Roland typed everything on the computer, afterward e-mailing a copy to everyone.

"We will work through this weekend to polish your testimonies while Luke works on all the legal ramifications," Higgins said before they retired. "You can have some down time to exercise or play ball, but only on the grounds. We have guards posted around the perimeter; stay inside."

Anne whispered to Higgins, "I'd like to hear Sunday Mass."

Higgins nodded. "I'll request Father Connor."

Father Connor came the next morning.

The group sang hymns with the Mass and thanked the priest.

"I can't stay for lunch, but I'll take a rain check," Father Connor said when Higgins invited him.

Higgins, Luke, and Levi worked extensively in the library in preparation for the hearing. They took a short respite by jogging around the compound.

The others played tennis, even without tennis shoes.

"I just hope we don't get hurt," Mark said.

Jim and Anne played against Mark and Alain; then they played one against two so that Alain could teach Roland to play tennis.

Higgins then called everybody for a conference. "Everybody, come to the library in one hour," he said.

They worked together to polish Anne, Mark, Levi, and Alain's testimony. They had an early supper, went to bed early, and started early the next day for the congressional hearing.

Escort cars flanked their cars, one in front and the other behind them. The agents were armed.

Levi and Luke each drove a car, and the others divided themselves between the two cars. Roland was left at the house with two agents. Anne and Mark were quite tense.

The spectator seats had filled up early, and the people who had been turned away became noisy and jostled each other to get a glimpse of the arriving witnesses.

Anne wore a navy-blue short-sleeved suit with a brooch on the lapel. Mark wore a suit with a light blue dress shirt and a striped tie.

The hearing began on time.

Anne read the prepared text that their team had printed out. Next, Mark read his statement. Then the question-and-answer process started.

"How did this nuclear physicist choose you to carry the disc?" the committee chair asked.

"I do not know if it was an active selection or a random choice. We just happened to be there. One speculation is whether, having seen us pray, he thought he could trust us," Anne answered.

"The man involved in a blockbuster event—definitely a world changer in the balance of power—trusted you because of religion?" the next inquisitor asked.

Anne looked around to see if she needed to answer the preposterous question. "Trust is a very important factor in human events. It is true that most people would trust somebody they believe is God-fearing; albeit so much of what we hear today is an abuse of that trust. Certainly we did not seek this responsibility. It has been a burden," Anne replied.

"Why did you not run to the US embassy right there in Stockholm, considering the resourcefulness that you seem to have demonstrated?" the third inquisitor asked.

"In hindsight, that would have been easier, but then again, with the layers of bureaucracy, could you assure me that the end result would have been what we achieved?

"At the moment that the nuclear physicist was killed, we were afraid for our lives, and not knowing what we had, we came back to the USA to seek the person whom we knew could shed light on what we did not understand then. We were also sympathetic to the plight of the kidnapped son. We did not have much time to think; we just ran."

"Why did you turn to the Israeli agents instead of the CIA?" was the next question.

"We were attacked before we knew what the stakes were. I am aware that Iran has been threatening the very existence of Israel. As a Christian, I have sympathy for Israel. As a citizen of the world, could you stand by while one nation threatens the existence of another? I followed the Golden Rule, and the choice was easy.

"At the airport, when we saw the kidnapped son being taken as a hostage, the CIA did not move. Instead, the North Koreans were allowed to leave, ostensibly in deference to a CIA agent who was also kidnapped. I knew that the USA does not deal with terrorists and certainly would not be docile to their demands. As I understand from the news we've tried to gather, the order came from the attorney general's office. If I can be permitted to ask, as a citizen of the United States, may I ask why? Why? Have we become cowards, or is there an agenda that you, sir, have yet to explain?"

There was no answer. The next question took a while to come. "Why did you go to the Israeli embassy in Budapest?"

"We chose to take Higgins from the hospital to the Israeli embassy because there was not enough protection or assurance that we could glean out of the US government then. Higgins suffered an unnecessary setback because of a wrong medicine. Was that an error, or was that intentional? If he went under because of malice, would we just chart it to error and shrug, or would we get him out of there and make sure he lived to tell the tale?

"From the report that I read, you can imagine the speedy, accurate assessment that followed our decision to go to the Israeli embassy, and the immediate response that made it possible for us to completely decrypt the code. Would you please create a comparable time frame to reflect what would've happened if I had gone to the US embassy instead?"

The next question almost did not come. As she sat there waiting, Anne realized that she had become angry, answering questions with an equal contempt, and that was not the way to win. She took a deep breath and sipped some water. *I should kick my own shin for letting them get to me,* she thought.

"Who made the decision to disable the Iranian nuclear plant?" the next inquisitor said.

Anne thought for a while. She did not want to point a finger. "The decision must have come from somewhere high—I don't know. All I know is that the nuclear plant had to be disabled."

There was a recess, and Mark was going to be questioned next. Anne was getting hungry from the stress, and she had no idea how her performance had been. *I must have flunked. I'm not used to this. I'd better warn Mark.*

They sat in the side office for witnesses, and Anne had a pastry and some coffee. The other people on their team were quiet, and Anne felt like bolting out of the door, crying for freedom.

Instead she came closer to Mark and warned him. "Don't let them get to you. Try to answer in one sentence, unlike me. Stay cool."

Mark was obviously nervous; at first, his voice could hardly be heard.

"Speak up, son." The committee chair coaxed him a little. "Okay, are you saying that this nuclear physicist gave you the disc, just like that?"

"No, sir." Mark cleared his throat. "He must have placed the disc deliberately in my camera bag without telling me. I only found it in the airport when we were running away from his killers."

"So did you do the decrypting? Who exactly did the decrypting? You used random mythological names and places. How did you figure that out?" The senator looked at Mark testily.

Mark looked at Luke first and then decided on his own answer. "Levi Cohen did the initial attempt but made no headway at first. Then I remembered that once, in the computer room of the cruise ship, the physicist told me to use mythological names for passwords. We tried many words and just randomly chanced on the correct ones."

"You still have not answered my question regarding who the genius is, who worked on the system to finally disable the entire Iranian nuclear plant," the senator said.

"I'm sorry, Senator," Mark said, "but I'm not aware of a single genius. We all tried to figure it out, even when we were on the run. When we worked with the scientific team, I did not bother to get the names. It was surely a team effort. I was so tired; sometimes I would fall asleep."

The other members of the panel laughed.

The questioning continued, but these were friendlier senators, making comments more than asking questions, as if they just wanted to see their pictures in the evening news.

Mark's turn ended just when he thought he had it down pat.

The next day, it was Levi's and Alain's turns to be questioned. Anne and Mark sat in the third row with Edward and Jim.

The first question was hostile toward Levi. "You are a dual US-Israeli citizen—is it more like you are an Israeli citizen spying in the US?"

Levi did not even flinch. "The day anybody proves that I did something against the USA, you can execute me."

Luke intervened. "Mr. Levi Cohen has demonstrated time and again that the interest in which he acted was aligned with the proclaimed goal of the USA, based on all past administrations. Would the senator clarify if there has been a change in position by the administration, and also, is there a specific act that was against—instead of for—the USA?"

The first inquisitor demurred. "No comment" was the answer.

"What exactly is your classification?" the second inquisitor asked in a reasonable tone. "Are you a covert agent like James Bond, licensed to kill, or are you like the man behind the decoding machines?"

"I'm more of the man behind the computer, but I've also been trained to defend myself and those around me if there's trouble." Levi's tone was more even now.

"How come you were already being chased by the Iranian agents so soon after Higgins called you?" the third inquisitor said.

"Those guys were often tailing me, and it has not been an easy life to live. That day, I was badly outnumbered—four to one—so I had to run and dodge them. Unless we capture one of them, I don't know how many of them are out there, when they are not supposed to be here. Maybe the administration and the UN can give you that answer.

"All I could presume at the time was that when the nuclear physicist was killed, those Iranian agents were doubled up here to watch and find out who did it. At that time, only the two previous witnesses were aware that the North Koreans were involved. Then the North Koreans attacked Higgins's office."

The next question was more direct. "Would you please trace, in your own words, the events following the call you got from Anne Cortez? She called you to say that the North Koreans were about to leave with the kidnapped son, right?"

Levi took a deep breath, mentally checking himself not to divulge hidden names. "That's right. When Anne and Mark Cortez arrived at Higgins's office, they were the only ones who knew that the physicist's son had been kidnapped. They were asked for help by a dying father; he showed them his son's picture. Maybe it was a father's intuition to ask help from another family.

"Anyway, when she saw the TV report, the North Koreans were already in the airport, ready to leave. She called us to help stop the departure, but they were proceeding to go. I went to the airport after calling somebody I trusted, Ben. We were outnumbered, and the enemy gave us both injections and then took us with them as hostages.

"At the Swiss tunnel, it was Ben that the North Koreans strapped to the car as a ploy; then they tried to escape with me and the kidnapped son. Ben was badly burned in the explosion when the North Koreans detonated the bomb in the car; he later died. I was dressed as a North Korean by those bastards, and I was stabbed when our car was hit by the car driven by Alain. Luckily Anne Cortez had an uncanny intuition. She turned me face-up when I fell off the car.

"At the Swiss hospital, the Iranians came to kill Alain and me. Luckily the Swiss lockdown system was very efficient. I was out of commission for the rest of the affair."

The next inquisitor asked his question without waiting to be introduced. "If you started the decoding, who was responsible for the follow-up? It seems that these people were able to get the job done pretty quickly."

Levi was ready for this. "Anne and Mark Cortez thought along the same lines that the physicist did. Then, of course, the clues from the tomb of the Chaldean kings were necessary to solve the intricate code. All these, together with the hard work of a team of scientists, contributed to solving the entire code."

"Would it be possible to solve it without going to the tomb in Iran?" The next inquisitor was also impatient to know.

"I wasn't there, but I understand that it would not be possible to remember all the Chaldean kings from Nebuchadnezzar to the present."

"Where is that list now?" the next inquisitor asked while the chairman shook his head. The senators had been bypassing the introductions.

"Anne Cortez burned it. I heard that afterward she wanted to stop all the ethnic fighting, so she burned it." Levi lied without flinching.

Anne sat ramrod straight as she heard his words. She looked down as she tried to contemplate the implication, thinking it was for the best. Just the same, she knew that the panel had looked at her. She sighed, hoping it was better to keep the secret.

"Maybe we need to interrogate Anne Cortez again," the senator said.

"As I recall," Levi said, "she was not asked that question. Besides, it did not hurt US interests."

Most of the following questions were affirmations of what had been already said, or just comments from friendly members of the panel.

The break was just one hour, and the team went to the witness room for lunch. An agent brought in boxed lunches, chips, and fruits, along with lots of coffee.

Levi smiled at Anne. "Sorry to surprise you there. I had been wondering about that question coming up. My answer was purely intuition."

"That might put to rest a lot of speculation, although I would have chosen to say it got accidentally burned," Higgins said with a laugh.

Anne smiled woefully and patted Mark's shoulder. "At least you did not put it on Mark's lap. I was worried you'd slip up and mention names."

"All in all, we've come out okay," Luke remarked. "Alain is next, and we can look forward to easier sailing."

Alain took a sip of water before he calmly sat down.

"What were you doing there, and why did you just help these people when they asked you?" The first question came without preliminaries.

"I asked myself that too. All I know is that they looked like good guys, so I joined them," Alain answered.

"I repeat, what were you doing there?"

"Oh, I grew up in Switzerland and became an exchange visitor to the USA. I applied for citizenship here, but I visit Switzerland on a backpacking trip every summer."

"So you are a US citizen?"

"Yes, sir," Alain said respectfully.

"I don't understand why you rammed your car against two bigger cars, downslope. It sounds like suicide!" the senator said irritably.

"I happen to know that road, with a tree at the bottom of a winding road down the hill. There have been many accidents there. We would have been at the top of the heap if we'd crashed."

"If you crashed? You were going to crash! Were you not afraid to die?"

"Sir, I stepped on the accelerator and prayed. It was the only way. The bad guys were shooting at us and would have outdistanced us if we did not do something drastic," Alain said solemnly.

The senator rolled his eyes, and the others snickered.

"What do you do in the USA?" The next question sounded friendly at first. "Are you in some form of public assistance?"

"No, sir. I've been waiting tables, and I just finished business school, so I went on a cheap vacation. I'm waiting to sell my castle so that I can have capital to start a business here."

"What castle?" The senator looked nonplussed.

"The St. Geoffrey Castle outside of Bern, Switzerland."

"If you are rich, why are you waiting tables?"

"The castle upkeep is very expensive. Here, I work and survive. It's the American way. It's fun, and I like it," Alain said sincerely.

"I'm not even going to ask what your title is," the senator said, ending his questioning sarcastically.

The next inquisitor was smiling now. "Were you involved in some of the decrypting? I'm still not convinced who made it possible."

"I wish I had been there! That was brilliant work, but I was in the hospital," Alain said with a nod of his head.

The rest of the questions were softballs. The session ended twenty minutes earlier than expected.

Higgins got his team out as quickly as possible, and they returned to his home. During the drive back to his home, he was on the cell phone giving out orders.

## 25. Escape from Washington, DC

Roland met them at the door, but his excitement was dashed when he saw Higgins.

Higgins spoke to them as soon as everybody was in the foyer. "I got an e-mail that the administration is trying another tactic. Let's not rest on our laurels. There's trouble brewing. Everybody get your stuff and bags. We all leave in thirty minutes. Get going!"

Anne ran upstairs to pack. Mark and Jim were first downstairs with their bags and computers. Roland and Alain followed.

"We need help at the library!" Luke said as he came out with a suitcase full of papers.

All the men who were available ran to the library.

Higgins directed the traffic. "Roland, transfer everything that you can on discs. We have to destroy the computers that we cannot bring with us. Alain, take care of all the printouts; put them in this suitcase. Mark and Jim, haul all information equipment out of here. There's a rolling cart. I'll be back in five minutes; get it done. Luke and Levi, get some of your stuff before we leave. Hurry!"

The men were all sweating by the time they met up at the foyer. Roland and Levi brought up the rear.

"I think we got everything cleared up. You don't have to blow up the library," Levi said.

"All right, get into the cars. Same arrangement, except Roland will be in our car. We will meet up at the extended-stay hotel that Anne reserved in DC. We will be there only for a conference; then we scatter."

Crawford and one of his agents took the lead car, while the two other agents took the rear car. They flanked the two cars driven by Luke and Levi. The cars driven by Crawford and his agents screeched out of the formation right after they came out of the gate. Those cars turned left. The cars driven by Luke and Levi turned right.

Levi was sweating. He drove through smaller streets instead of the bigger avenues. He left some distance between their car and the one driven by Luke; then Luke's car disappeared.

"He knows these streets; we'll meet up there," Levi said.

Anne had been holding her breath while holding Mark's and Jim's hands. "Watch!" she said as a car came out of nowhere and almost hit them.

Levi's eyes widened. "That's the other party looking for us." Levi turned unto a small street just as another car sped from the opposite direction. Levi parked the car on the small side street. "Everybody, keep your head down." He took one revolver from his belt and gave one to Mark. "Be ready. Just stay quiet for a while."

They must have waited for five minutes; then Levi eased the car off the curb without headlights. He drove slowly until they reached a bigger avenue. He turned on his lights as he joined the speedy traffic.

Luke's group was already getting into the rooms when they arrived. They had used the side entrance and had come in by twos. They signaled to Levi without speaking, and their group did the same thing.

Higgins was already in the room and had turned on the TV at a soft volume.

"Good evening! This is Hal Kreiter of QNC News reporting with a scoop from our network. We just found out that something has happened. The attorney general's office has issued warrants for the arrest of Richard Higgins and the people who were last seen in the congressional hearings.

"This directive was in connection with the disablement of the nuclear plant in Natanz, Iran. The attorney general's office cites that some of the group's actions were contrary to the interests of the United States and therefore constitute acts of sedition.

"We can see that the US Army was sent out there—two trucks filled with armed soldiers . . . . Is that necessary? Are those soldiers just going to kill those US citizens? What's going on? Peter? Can you tell us what's going on there?"

The TV screen showed the open gate and the two trucks in front of Higgins's house. The armed soldiers jumped out of the trucks and ran through the door, and the cameraman followed right behind. There was a crash as a large porcelain vase in the foyer was knocked down and the pieces clattered on the floor. The soldiers rushed through one door and then another and went up the staircase.

"Is the house abandoned? Peter? What's going on? . . . What? Nobody there? Maybe that's good . . . Okay. Go ahead. We will now hear from Peter Collins what has happened."

"Good evening, folks. This is Peter Collins reporting in Alexandria, Virginia. I'm in front of the residence of Richard Higgins, the former head of counterintelligence in at least three past administrations. As you might have heard in the congressional hearings earlier today, he was co-counsel when the witnesses testified about the disablement of the nuclear plant in Natanz, Iran. As a matter of fact, Higgins was shot when the North Koreans came to his office, looking for a blueprint that the Iranian nuclear physicist was supposed to give in return for his kidnapped son. I don't understand why they are now raiding Higgins's office instead. It looks like it has been emptied of papers and computers. Are they going to haul that desk? Whoa—another big vase broken! Nobody is home. Wait, they have gone back to the library, looking for a safe . . . There is no safe. The painting or whatever is on the floor. Back to you, Hal."

The confused face of the TV anchor was shown, followed by a commercial break.

"So that's where we are," Higgins said with a sigh. "They are out to prosecute us because we did something they could not do, and now their popularity rating for the coming election is down. This is their revenge. We need to hide; obviously they are not paying attention to the law. We either hide or leave the country.

"The Philippines has no extradition treaty with the USA; that might be the only country worth going to. The other countries are unstable. So, Anne and company, if you go to the Philippines, do it your usual way—through a circuitous route.

"Alain, Switzerland has an extradition treaty with the USA.

"This has happened so fast that I haven't made up my mind where to go."

"Maybe Alain, you, Levi, and Luke should go to Israel," Anne said. "Those people there would at least stand their ground."

"Maybe we should all go to Israel," Levi offered. "We can all come back after the swearing in of the new president, definitely not before."

Anne looked at Edward. "I'm staying here," Edward said.

"Pardon me, Edward," Higgins interjected, "but even I would not dare challenge a vengeful administration that has no regard for the law. We will need to wait outside of the USA."

"We only have two choices, Edward," Anne said patiently. "We need to get our tickets now, before they discover what we are doing. We need to move, or it will be the same scenario as before, when you were arrested the first time." Anne turned to Jim and held her son's shoulder, unable to say what could have happened.

Roland was already on his computer, entering names. "By the way, Jim, you don't have your passport, right?"

"Right," Jim said, and he looked at Higgins. "Maybe Dad doesn't have his either."

"I came by ambulance flight; my backpack has not arrived yet," Alain said.

"Actually, neither do I, because we took a private plane to France," Luke said.

"I did not use the normal channels either," Levi said with a nod.

"All right, we are all going to the Israeli embassy. From there, we can discuss more. We just need to get out of here first," Higgins said.

"We used that route before; would it be safe? The bad guys might be lying in wait for us. Could we be better off leaving from the East Coast, going to the consulate office instead?" Anne asked.

They stopped to think.

"How would you like a limousine van?" Mark looked around, seemingly inspired. "It will fit us all, and it has tinted windows. We'll be dropped off at the Israeli consulate in New York."

Roland quickly tapped on his computer. Then he announced, "The limousine will be here in ten minutes. How do you like that?"

It was a white stretch limousine. All their backpacks, computers, and extra bags could fit in it. They sat comfortably in wide seats and drank some soda. Luke and Levi found the champagne, but Higgins warned them.

"Stay sober; we might run into trouble."

They each had a glass, including Mark and Jim. Most were able to sleep for an hour or so during the three-and-a-half-hour drive to New York.

The driver was a discreet middle-aged man. Higgins paid for the expenses, including the return of the car, and also gave the driver a nice tip.

It was late in the evening when they arrived in New York, but the consul had been waiting with several security guards. They went inside the consulate and camped there for the night. Two consulate cars with flags picked them up early the next morning. They took a private plane from La Guardia to London and then a chartered plane to Tel Aviv.

Part V

# THE PLIGHT OF THE WANDERERS

## 26. Refuge in Israel

They were housed in a walled-in private mansion near Tel Aviv. Considering their jet lag and the continuous travel, Higgins made an announcement.

"We have been on the run for a while and are still jet lagged. Let's sleep first and then hang around without a fixed schedule until tomorrow afternoon. We'll have a leisurely dinner meeting then."

The older members relaxed by catching up on the news or reading. Anne took a walk inside the walled compound and saw two tennis courts and a swimming pool.

They converged in a conference room after a leisurely dinner.

Higgins started the discussion. "We are safe in a walled compound, but you might want more freedom soon. The time between now and the inauguration of a new president is five months. If the president stays the same, we'll be waiting for four and a half years. Any ideas?"

Alain spoke up. "I would like a chance to visit here, make my own car tour, if it is safe. Maybe we could meander around for two weeks; then we could go to Switzerland, and you can all stay in my castle. We need some money, and Anne will cook."

"Huh?" Anne said, caught off guard. Then she thought it out. "That actually sounds like fun. I would have recommended the Philippines because there are a lot of beautiful sites. My problem is that we'll stick out like sore thumbs, and we need to get some protection. Wherever we visit, I'd give that a month or two; then probably the younger guys would get restless."

"If it gets boring, we can work on the computer. I've been watching the stock market," Roland said.

"Maybe you can try living in a kibutz," Levi said.

"For your information, guys," Higgins said, "Luke, Levi, and I have been working on a draft for a new law. There must be some accountability when government decisions are made. People cannot just break the law when they work for the government. Signatures will be required if an order is given by someone. If abuse of power or miscarriage of justice occur, those guilty should be punished, more so because they have broken the public trust."

"Great! That's been a long time coming!" Anne said.

"Hopefully we will distribute it to members of Congress as soon as they sit down for session so that this law will quickly pass. I want justice for each of us," Higgins said.

"There should be mandatory prison time for these offenses," Anne said. "Put them alongside criminals in a maximum-security prison, because they are that dangerous. They cannot hide behind the government that they have betrayed. If financial damage has to be reimbursed, it has to come from their own pockets because they have used their positions in government to settle their personal scores. That abuse is just beyond me," she said passionately.

"I will make sure they don't have any money at all!" Roland said.

"Oh! Don't do that!" Anne quickly touched Roland's shoulder.

"Okay, I'm willing to settle for a fistfight," Alain said.

"Oh! Maybe we did need to get that off our chests," Anne said.

"Seriously, I'd like that tour to help me unwind," Jim said.

"The last tour we took did help a lot," Mark said.

"What's that then? Two or three weeks in Israel, the same in Switzerland, then the Philippines, and then we come back here to draft that law," Anne said, and then she laughed. "What a dream! Where's our money?"

They all laughed.

"Seriously," Higgins said after a while, "it would be good to take a break. Anne, Mark, Luke, Roland, and Andre are due some money from the Israeli government. That should come soon. At least that's money that has not gone to the USA yet. You can probably open an account here and transfer it later.

"Since it is dangerous for us to be on US soil, and since it will be a while before we can go back, we can actually unwind first, before we get serious drafting this law. Maybe when we are not so angry anymore, we can frame the law in a more reasonable context.

"I say, why don't we do the Israel tour, making sure we are in safe, not-too-public places? As Anne did before, we can be discreet in our appearances, and also we will be on guard and carry arms. There's no other way after what we've been through," Higgins said.

"I'm all for it!" Levi said.

"Me too!" Luke and Alain said, followed by Roland, Mark, and Jim.

"Let's get that map; I'm sure there's so much we can visit!" Anne said.

"You've been here several times already," Mark said to Anne.

"There are some places we've bypassed on a hectic schedule, and this time nobody's rushing us," Anne said with enthusiasm.

"Here's the map." Levi spread it out.

Mark, Jim, Alain, and Roland swarmed all over it.

"This was our path last time," Roland said as he traced it.

"I'd like to see this Mt. Hebron here, with St. Catherine's Monastery," Mark said.

Anne turned to Luke and Higgins. "I've been thinking of Andre and Janan. How are they? Has there been word about Andre's mother and sister?"

"Andre is still waiting," Luke said. "There has been no communication from them. He's between despair and boredom."

"Maybe we can meet up," Anne said. "Andre enjoyed our trip when we were last here. I'm sure he is worried, so maybe a little distraction will be good while he is waiting for word about his mother."

"Andre carries the fortune of his family," Higgins said. "He can move to whichever country he decides later on. His main consideration will be his safety. So, like us, he might want to come to the USA later."

"There are more rooms in the lower level of this house. Maybe they can stay with us if Janan is already out of the hospital," Anne wondered.

"Let me make a call," Luke said. After a while, Luke smiled. "They'll be here in a short while."

"Andre's coming? Great!" Mark said, and he made a high-five sign with Roland.

"You know that I don't know the whole story, right?" Jim said. "Not everything was in the testimony."

"Right," Mark said. "Mom, maybe we have to talk this over again?"

Higgins answered for her. "When Andre and Janan arrive, we will update everyone and fill in some of those gaps. Okay?"

"Okay," Jim and Alain said.

While waiting, the younger men returned to the map, and Anne resumed making a list.

"We all need sports shoes, but I also need slip-ons or espadrilles. Maybe the guys can also use driving loafers or something. We will need bathing trunks for the men, one bathing suit for me, and possibly one for Janan. Is that allowed in their custom? Maybe we will just hide out in one corner of the pool," she said, and she burst out laughing.

Levi and Luke laughed with her, while Higgins just shook his head.

"Nuts! This is becoming like D-day! That's a lot of stuff!"

"You know we are still spending the money from your account, right? Don't worry. I'll replenish it with one million if the Israeli government comes across with the reward money. That has saved our lives! Thank you for thinking about it." Anne came over to touch Higgins's shoulder.

Higgins touched her hand too. "Once in a while, there are true patriots like you, Anne. Glad to do it." He looked at the younger men poring over the map. "I hope some of those guys will carry our torch when we get too old for this. That account is there for these situations."

"We have a good group," Anne said.

Luke and Levi nodded, and then they heard the sound of an arriving car.

Andre came running through the open door. "Anne! Luke! Mark and Roland!"

They all hugged each other in a circle. Janan came in walking slowly and hugged Anne and Mark first. The ladies cried.

Anne brought Andre and Janan forward to meet the others. They spent some time getting acquainted with each other and ate the leftover pastries and fruits. They opened two wine bottles and had a glass each; then they were ready for their conference.

Luke updated everyone on the events that had taken place from the time that Senawi had contacted Anne and Mark, up until their recent escape to Israel. It was a long story, with the important points emphasized. Then he turned to Higgins.

"You see, not all of you knew all the events," Higgins said. "Only Anne and Mark knew everything, and then Luke, after they told him. When Anne, Mark, Levi, and Alain had to testify at the congressional hearing, Luke and I prepared the text of what they had to say, which was necessary so that we neither disclosed Luke's presence there, nor mentioned Roland's involvement.

"I also notified the panel that we were going to keep Andre's and Dr. Senawi's names out so that we would lessen the chance of retaliation from random Iranians and North Koreans. We kept Luke's name secret because, as a lawyer, he was there and could plan the defense necessary if you were to be charged by an adverse administration. We were afraid of that, and our hunch was correct. We also kept Roland's name out because it would be very dangerous if bad guys got ahold of him. There's no telling what the ramifications would be if they made him do evil things, mostly computer-related disruptions of legal commerce. Having observed Roland, I think he will be loyal to our cause. His religion and sense of family with us are probably our best bets that he will stay on the good side." Higgins paused, watching Roland nodding to himself.

"So we have our sense of family with this team. Our younger men are welcome to join us on an official basis, and you are on our list of reliable sources on an unofficial basis. Any questions?"

Roland raised his hand. "Are you saying you'll hire me? Can you take care of my papers?"

"Done!" Higgins said, and Roland broke into a smile.

Mark and Alain looked at each other.

"I'm seriously thinking," Alain said.

"Me too," Mark said.

"In the meantime, we will go on a tour here. Anne wants to shop first. Maybe everybody needs something. Just remember, we have to be careful wherever we are," Higgins added.

Two Mossad agents went with the group when they shopped. They divided into small groups, stayed in one area at a time, and looked out for each other.

After they returned to the compound, the Mossad agents were replaced by two others who had brought several small arms. The arms were distributed to the men, and the young men were taught how to use them. Anne and Janan were given a short course on how to fire a gun, but they did not have to carry weapons.

They packed before they went to bed, looking forward to their tour.

## 27. Search for the Family

Roland was first in the foyer area that morning. His computer was open, and he was waiting for Andre. Andre came hurrying when he heard Roland calling.

"You have an idea?" Andre asked.

"Yes. Give me the e-mail addresses of your family and friends. We will contact them and fish for information among their e-mails," Roland said.

"Is that legal? Are you hacking?" Anne asked as she reached the foyer.

"No. We're just e-mailing them. If there's a curious answer, we will see," Roland said. He started typing the addresses.

Shortly afterward, a van carrying a group of tourists came out of the compound. They only had one Mossad agent guarding them now—their driver, Shimon.

The tourists brought along their computers, and the male members carried hidden weapons. They were arranged into three groups of four, and the Cortez family was up front. The groups would rotate forward every day.

Anne took her seat and prayed for their safety. She smiled and took a deep breath to savor a bright, pleasant morning. She then looked at the itinerary printout that the younger men had proudly handed to each one. They were going south first, along the coast, toward Ashdod, before swinging east to go to the Dead Sea and then Masada. They would turn north through Mt. Hebron, go up to St. Catherine's Monastery, and then go to Bethlehem and Jerusalem. They would continue north through the biblical Samaria, Nazareth, Tiberias, and the Sea of Galilee and then continue farther north before swinging west to Acre, down to Haifa, Caesarea . . . Something was bothering her. She looked at the map printout. *Are they purposely going near the Syrian border? What are these guys up to? I'd better corner these guys later,* she thought.

They ate lunch in a café along the coast, lured by the advertisement of fresh seafood galore. A gust of sea breeze blew Anne's scarf to her face, and it also blew off Higgins's beret. He ran after his beret, but it escaped his grasp. It went tumbling through the sidewalk and into another table, where four men sat. Andre went to retrieve it and came right back, handing it to Higgins.

Anne was facing the group of men at the other table, and she saw an expression of dislike from one and a downright scowl from another. She looked at Luke and Levi while wiping clean her sunglasses; she saw that their men were aware of the animosity of those exchanged glances. Anne watched as she quickly ate.

One of the men came to Andre and scolded him for helping those foreigners, and he also said that his sister should be wearing a head scarf.

Andre did not understand the Arabic, but Shimon did. Shimon said calmly that the hat belonged to Andre's uncle who lived in America and that his sister had been living in France and needed to readjust, since the head scarf was banned there.

The man backed off and reported to his friends. They nodded their heads together, and somebody left.

"Hurry!" Anne said to Mark and Jim. She called for the check and paid at once. "Why don't we go?" she said to the younger men.

Higgins's group had already stood up, ready to leave, but the younger guys were not fully aware of the situation.

"We are leaving right now!" Anne ordered, and she held Janan's arm to help her up. "Let's go!"

Only then did the younger men seem to realize that something was wrong. They all went back to the van, and Shimon quickly drove off.

Levi looked back at the café. There was a group of workers arriving, and they did not look friendly at all.

"I don't understand what happened!" Andre said.

Shimon explained only after he had driven a good distance away. "I'm sorry to have brought you there. I did not realize that there was a road construction site nearby. I presume those were Arabic workers, and they resented Andre for being nice to Higgins, mistaking Andre for one of their own. Those people would have ganged up on us. From now on, we stay only in guarded tourist spots. We don't need trouble when we are just sightseeing."

"I'm glad you were aware of the situation, Anne," Higgins commented.

"That's only because I was facing in that direction. I saw one man scowl, and the other made a hissing reply. Maybe we were just lucky."

The younger men were silent for a while.

Levi tried to cheer them up. "You learn along the way if you have to be in covert operations. That situation was not usual, but we came out okay because the other members of the group were aware. Cheer up. Forget about those quaint little places; we will stay in safe places from here on."

"Mark, do you have the iPad?" Luke asked. "Would you check out a place for us to stay tonight? The recommended safe hotels will be listed separately by area."

"Okay," Mark said. "I'm on it. Hmm . . . There's nothing less than a big, at least four-star hotel. Shall I book the Sheraton?"

"That would be it," Levi said with a sigh.

There were no further untoward incidents that day.

At breakfast the next day, Anne finally cornered the young men.

"Roland, could you explain something to me? Whose idea was it for us to go so near the Syrian border?"

Roland looked from Alain and Andre to Mark and Jim. "Oh! . . . Ah! . . . Oh! We thought it would be easier to go for Andre's mother and sister if we are that close."

Luke spilled his coffee, and Higgins suddenly looked up.

Anne turned to the older men. "Are you telling me that you did not notice?"

Levi laughed. "Obviously not! It looks like we just trusted these guys. It's not a bad idea, actually!" He laughed again. Luke reddened, and Higgins started laughing too.

"Unbelievable!" Anne said, sitting down.

The younger men, especially Andre, looked forlorn after they were busted.

Anne felt sorry for being too hard on them. "Actually, that is the correct connection point if they are in Syria, but we shouldn't go there unless it is warranted. Andre has to wait and see if any of your e-mails will yield something. It is better for his mom and sister to come down near the border. So far Assad has been good to Christians. I hope that, because of the rebellion, they come down south or southwest, actually."

"Yes! Yes! I hope they do that!" Andre went to Anne and hugged her.

Anne looked at Higgins, Luke, and Levi as she hugged Andre back. "Let's hope so," she echoed.

Andre was crying with happiness, and Anne sympathized with him. She had been through that too, but all she could do at that moment was pray.

With Andre's infectious optimism, everybody began to really enjoy the trip.

The younger men, Luke, and Levi forgot their worries when they climbed Mt. Hebron at dawn. They reached the mountaintop just as the sun was rising, and they were touched when they reached the site of the burning bush.

"It's like a miracle," Alain said, and the others nodded.

Higgins, Edward, Anne, and Janan waited at the mountaintop already, not wanting to do the climb. "I wish I were younger," Anne said.

They were in safe areas, and they were relaxed. Often, when they reached their hotel, they would swim in the pool or play tennis. Roland and Andre became frequent opponents since they were on the same level. Jim matched with Alain, and Anne played against Mark. While they played, the older men included Edward in their work on the legislation.

Their visit to Jerusalem lasted just two days. Three more Mossad agents were added to guard them while they were in the area. They visited the old city and put their prayers on the Wailing Wall. Levi was solemn during the visit, and most of the others were solemn as well, trying to connect to that time in history.

Anne bought filigreed bracelets for her and Janan in one of the shops. "I'm not buying anything heavy," Anne reasoned before the guys could comment.

Anne had been observing Janan, giving her room yet realizing the terrible trauma Janan had experienced. "I'm here if you want to talk," she had said.

Janan's response had been to cry; afterward, she'd nodded.

They visited the different churches and the Mount of Olives. It made a big impression on the young men, and even Higgins realized that this was an excellent idea.

They were in Samaria when Roland noticed a cryptic remark on Facebook from one of Andre's friends, Abel:

*Esther is not my fiancée anymore. It has been so boring to wait. She will take very long to come all the way from Damascus, what with the war going on. I'm now going out with Helen Towers.*

Roland told Andre when he saw it.

They were in the lounge room for their usual after-dinner relaxation. As usual, instead of relaxing with conversation and listening to the piano at the bar, Roland had gone up to the room to get his computer.

"How well do you know this guy, Andre? Is he really your sister's fiancée?" Anne asked.

Janan answered. "I don't know this guy. Maybe it is a trap."

"I have met him," Andre said. "He visited Esther when we were in Sanandaz. He is from Tehran. I don't know if he is engaged to Esther. Father did not mention it to me."

"Is he a Chaldean Catholic or not?" Anne tried to narrow the possibilities.

"I think so, but I am not sure," Andre said.

"If he is of your tribe, he could be loyal to you; perhaps he is sending you information in an indirect way. If he is not, either he is a careless braggart or he has been incited to lay down a trap," Anne said, and she waited for other comments.

They were silent for a while.

"Andre," Roland whispered, "we can talk back to him on Facebook and find out more. Let's see, what do you want me to say?"

Andre looked at Anne and Janan. "What should I say?"

"Say something about Sanandaz, and say you are sad you did not see your sister. Don't say you were there recently." Anne groped for words.

"That would work," Levi said. "Did you visit parks or any special places in Sanandaz? Mention it with either a wrong date or wrong information. If he corrects you, that's him. If he does not, it's a trap."

Andre lit up. "I remember now! He was an older friend of mine, not Esther's. I met him at Tehran, and he liked Esther but was not so serious. I invited him, and our family had a picnic at the foothills of Abidar Mountain. I remember it was a Sunday, because we went after going to Mass!"

"It could still be a trap if he was too enthusiastic with befriending you," Anne said. "Also, we are not sure if this is indeed your friend."

"Okay," Roland said. "We bait him. What do we say?"

Levi sidled up to Roland. "Say, 'I remember our visit to the museum that Saturday. Esther has missed our hometown since she went to school.'"

"Done!" Roland said. "Now we wait."

The next morning, Andre was so agitated that Roland rolled his eyes.

"Maybe somebody has a sedative?" Alain asked.

"He'll calm down," Mark said hopefully.

They were now heading north toward Nazareth. Away from the commercial areas, the rolling hills, farms, and villages looked like scenery from a period long ago. Anne prayed her rosary, and the young men dozed off.

There was nothing on the e-mail for the next two days. They had arrived in Tiberias, and their hotel was by the shore of the Sea of Galiliee. They toured the town and then spent the afternoon by the shore of the Sea of Galilee, swimming, chatting, and eating snacks.

When they changed for dinner, Roland announced, "There's something in the e-mail. I'll show you later."

They conferred in the lounge area after dinner. Roland opened his computer to the e-mail message.

*I'm sorry to dump Esther, but it can't be helped. When she left Sanandaz, she said she'd return after a short vacation. Instead, I hear she went to Syria. Now I hear she is in Damascus without telling me. I remember the delicious pomegranates we ate that Sunday.*

"Okay. It's him, but I don't know if Esther is really in Damascus," Andre said.

"We're back to square one," Levi said.

"Do you know people in Damascus, Andre and Janan?" Anne asked. "With just a few names, maybe Roland can check the white pages and we can use an international SIM card to call them by phone. If you happen to remember some people, they might talk on the phone but not on e-mail."

Andre and Janan both thought hard and then looked at each other.

Janan nodded. "President Aziz was a friend of Fawzi. They were friends when they were studying in the USA."

"Is that all?" Anne asked. "I was hoping for someone more approachable, not a president in a country with a civil war. Actually, he is better than his predecessor, but all this Arab Spring has been like a loose-cannon movement. Hmm . . . Come to think of it, actually it is possible for him to hide them. What do you think?" Anne turned to Higgins, Luke, and Levi.

"Actually, it makes sense," Higgins said, thinking aloud. "But since Aziz is getting help from the Iranians in quashing this rebellion, we need reliable people to be able to get in there without being detected by the Iranians."

"I can speak Farsi and Arabic," Levi said. "What do you think?"

"Approach Aziz directly through high channels only," Luke said. "A high State Department official can probably talk to him privately; then Levi and Shimon can go in disguise to fetch Andre's mother and sister. We need to find out first if Aziz is harboring them. I don't want to sound like I'm shoving this job to you, but it has to be done by people who can speak Arabic and Farsi, maybe also Aramaic."

"I'll call the department tomorrow," Levi said. "I'm eager to find out."

"We can wait at the border and be ready to come for you," Luke added.

"You don't think that this Arab Spring in Syria is what our journalists say it is?" Higgins held Anne eyes.

"I don't," Anne said. "What do you think?"

"I agree with you," Higgins said. "It actually makes our planned extraction of Andre's family more difficult."

"You agree that it has to be a small excursion, as a large party would otherwise call unwanted attention, right?" Anne asked.

"Right," Higgins said. "Let's see what tomorrow brings."

Levi got up early, ate a hasty breakfast, and went back to his room to take care of business. Higgins, Luke, and Shimon joined him.

Anne and Janan squirmed at being left out of the discussion, while Edward read his papers. Roland surfed the net looking for information, while Alain, who also became restless, played tennis with Mark and Jim.

Andre went to his room to pray and chanted his prayers, but finally he got tired of waiting and joined the other guys on the tennis court.

The older men ate lunch in a hurry and conferred in their room again. Anne and Janan prayed the rosary together and then went back to their rooms.

"Let those guys tell us later what's going to happen; I'm tired of waiting. Let's take a nap. I did not sleep well last night," Anne said.

"I did not sleep well either," Janan said, and she went to her room too.

The younger men channeled their restlessness into swimming and playing card games.

At dinnertime, Higgins announced, "We'll talk after dinner."

They gathered at the hotel conference room.

Higgins began. "We have confirmed that Andre's mother and sister are indeed in Damascus. Aziz has protected them, and they live just like ordinary people, working on a daily basis. The mother, Fatima, works as a payroll clerk at an oil refinery company, and Esther works as a teacher's aide in an elementary school. Their cover is that they moved when they lost their home to a fire. It's true that there was a fire in one town, so they've had no problem with their cover.

"They have been waiting to hear from Andre, and they will come to the border in the area of Baniyas, which is near to Dan on the Israeli side. All of you not involved in the operation may wait in Dan.

"Baniyas is in the area of the Golan Heights under Israeli control, so it is already a safe zone, but they have to be met at the UN Disengagement Observation Force zone, which may be a problem, considering how unclear the UN is about their own mandate. As you are aware, the UN has already withdrawn their people, ostensibly observing the rebellion in Syria.

"If Andre's mother and sister cannot manage to get to the UNDOF Zone, Levi and Shimon will meet them as far as Hadar, which is already Syrian territory.

"If they still cannot get to Hadar, Levi and Shimon may have to go deeper into Syrian territory. Their advantage is that they can speak Arabic, and the Druze communities are not hostile to them. As a matter of fact, Aziz is having them escorted by Druze members of his army. Levi and Shimon will also be augmented by two Druze soldiers from the Israeli army.

"Fatima and Esther will have to travel discreetly during daytime, maybe several hundred miles at a time, so that they do not arouse suspicion. They would probably be in the Israeli territory in two days, give or take a day.

"All parties, including Fatima and Esther, will be issued cell phones with international SIM cards, but we don't know who could be listening and how discreet they will be. By the way, we will give the numbers to Roland so that he can try to trace them if possible."

"Are women allowed to drive there?" Anne asked. "Even if she can, does she have a car? How could they reach a relatively long distance without arousing suspicion?"

"That's the problem," Higgins continued. "Under her disguise, Fatima Senawi does not have a car. She can rent one or buy one, but we don't want to arouse suspicion. Aziz has a problem with labor shortage. There's this rebellion, and he cannot just trust anybody, so although he has escorts for them, he is strongly recommending that we be prepared to extract them if necessary."

"Oh!" Anne said.

"By tomorrow morning," Higgins continued, "we will drive to Dan. We hope that the people involved will have finished the arrangements by the time we get there and have the necessary cell phones distributed on both sides of the border. If not, we'll wait there for our plan to be in place before Levi and Shimon get started."

"I'd like to go with them," Andre pleaded.

"It is an unpredictable scenario made more dangerous by the ongoing rebellion. The rebels now have the upper hand north of Damascus. There are too many possible enemies, especially since Aziz has welcomed some reinforcements from Iran. You might just slow Levi and Shimon down, as they would have to protect you," Higgins explained. "Please just stay with the rest of us, waiting at the border."

Andre was crestfallen. Janan and Anne tried to console him.

The next day, Shimon drove their van to Dan. The group was quiet, feeling a mixture of anticipation and apprehension.

There had been no calls while they were driving, so Roland hurried to his room and turned on the computer.

"There's no message," he said with a frown to the men around him.

"We wait," Higgins said, and they all went to bed.

It must have been an unsettling night for Janan. Anne watched her friend coming to breakfast looking exhausted already. Andre looked half-asleep. They just sighed as they ate.

Finally Anne spoke. "An operation like this could take time for plans to be in place. Fatima and Esther have done quite well so far. Let's not jeopardize it. We are already so lucky that you and Andre are here now. Let's be patient."

Janan cried, and Andre sulked.

"Please, Andre, you are the leader of your people now. Levi and Shimon will already be augmented with support on both sides," Anne said patiently.

"Okay," Andre said, "but if something bad happens, I'm going."

"Let's hope you don't have to," Anne said.

The older men arrived for breakfast but went back to their room without talking to the others. They were holed up in their room, just requesting lunch trays to be brought to them.

Anne and Janan were getting edgy just looking at Andre, but they did not want to go out without security escorts. Anne finally suggested that they all go to the tennis grounds, whether they played or not.

"For those who don't want to play, the fresh air will help. It's better than being confined indoors, waiting for something to happen," she said.

That helped. Alain decided to give Andre a workout by hitting the tennis ball left, right, and center so that Andre ended up running from side to side and receiving hard-hit balls. In the end, Andre worked up a sweat and forgot about complaining.

They swam in the pool afterward and then hurried to dinner. The older men were already waiting for them.

"We're all right," Higgins said. "Let's enjoy dinner, and then we can talk."

Once more they used the hotel's conference room.

Higgins began. "There was a delay in confirming your mother and sister's coming, Andre. Esther did not want to come unless a special person could come with her. When we had doubts about it, your mother did not want to come without Esther."

"Why?" Andre asked with a frown, his tone almost harsh. They all looked at him, as though seeing him in a different light.

"Esther has feelings for a man in Syria, a distant cousin of Aziz. His name is Ibrahim, and he did not want to leave Syria. Your mother, Fatima, did not want to leave Syria without Esther, thinking that Esther would be vulnerable without her. We gave them twenty-four hours to make up their minds, whether we extract them or not. Now they are coming, with Ibrahim.

"That was one reason for the delay; the other reason was that we could not be sure about Ibrahim. Esther had not told him about her being Chaldean Catholic. Ibrahim is an active member of the Wahabi sect. In spite of that, we found out that he had been a playboy in the past.

"So we had to sort out this information before we could proceed. Esther finally told Ibrahim about her predicament, and Ibrahim has now agreed to come.

"Tomorrow, Levi and Shimon will go with their escorts through Golan Heights and beyond. It may take just four days; it may take a week. We don't know what conditions they will face." Higgins looked at Andre.

Andre was quiet, but there was anger in his bearing.

Anne looked at the older men and then at Andre. "Andre, tell us what you think," she said softly.

Andre seemed to have transformed into a mature man suddenly. "We don't have to get them back then."

Janan cried, but Andre was determined.

For the first time, Anne realized that the stoicism and determination she saw on and off were all part of Andre's training, despite the inadvertent displays of spontaneity in a yet-maturing young man.

Higgins cleared his throat before saying, "We have until tomorrow morning to abort the mission."

They all went to bed feeling uncertain and tired.

The next morning, Roland made the rounds, knocking at their rooms.

"Early breakfast and conference," he said.

They hurriedly ate breakfast and went straight to the conference room. Most of them looked like they hadn't slept well, including Higgins.

"We received an early call from Damascus," Higgins said. "They have already left by car, without escort. Ibrahim is driving, planning to drive during the day, one segment at a time. As it happens, the rebellion has erupted in some segments of Damascus, specifically in the area where Esther works. They hope to be in Hadar in less than two days. We will have to meet up with them as previously planned."

Andre just nodded. Janan sighed in relief.

Levi and Shimon left shortly afterward.

They spent the next couple of days restlessly. Higgins and Luke continued work on their legislative proposal, Edward read newspapers and watched TV news, and the younger men played tennis or swam. Anne played tennis and then would spend time with Janan painting, each working on different scenes they had just encountered. It also gave Janan a chance to slowly open up and mention some of her experiences as a hostage.

Roland kept them updated on where Levi's team was. He laconically reported the news to the group for a week; then, one day, he came late for breakfast and excitedly whispered at their table.

"They're now in Baniyas! They could arrive here today."

Andre showed no reaction, which rattled Anne. Janan closed her eyes in prayer, and everybody else sounded happy.

"Yeah!" Mark high-fived Jim and Alain.

Higgins and Luke looked closely at Andre but said nothing.

Nobody really knew what to do after that. Andre's reaction bothered Anne, and she knew that Higgins and Luke were aware of it. The other younger men also realized the subdued reaction, and not knowing what else to do, they played tennis and then went swimming. Andre joined them without saying much.

After lunch, they were just waiting. Anne and Janan tried to continue painting but did not make progress. They all took naps and then waited some more. Levi called Higgins by phone and said they were arriving soon.

Higgins told everybody to wait in the conference room. When the army vehicle stopped at the hotel front, they all sat forward in their chairs.

Levi led the way, gently holding the elbow of Andre's mother. Fatima Senawi held her daughter Esther's hand. Shimon led Ibrahim Aziz and came forward.

Higgins stood up to welcome them, but Andre did not. Janan got up, but seeing Andre, she hesitated and sat down.

Higgins did his best by introducing each one to the new arrivals.

Anne tried to infuse enthusiasm in her voice as she said, "Nice to meet you," but it somehow fell flat.

The other younger men looked confused. What would have been a joyful scene became a cold reception for the people who had been reluctantly saved.

Fatima Senawi came forward to Andre, but he did not move.

"Welcome, Mother," he said without emotion.

Esther came forward and then stopped. "Hi!" she said, and she turned back to take a seat.

"Why don't you tell us about your trip, Levi?" Higgins said, struggling to salvage the situation.

Anne couldn't believe that even Higgins could lose his cool.

Levi stood up. He started with a knitted brow but thankfully warmed up to his topic. "We drove our jeep through Baniyas and Majdal Shams. Since we hold the Golan Heights, our problem was more of the terrain and the need to travel lightly so that we could move fast. Once we got to the UNDOF Zone, it was a little dicey. We got challenged as to what we were doing and where we were going. We explained that we were from the Golan Heights and that we were just a little off our base. We had a fistfight with two persistent soldiers, and we decided to knock them off and duct-tape their mouths shut. When we moved forward and saw more UN soldiers, we had to circumvent to a longer distance, so it was past the second day when we reached Hadar.

"Ibrahim called and told us that they were still at Bayt Jinn, with a broken-down car, so we went to extract them. Coming back was a little faster since by then we knew where the UN stations were." Levi sat down.

"Thank you, Levi." Higgins was sounding more animated. "Could you tell us about your experience, Ibrahim?"

Ibrahim was a little uncertain at first. He stroked his mustache before he began. "The rebels were getting bolder north of Damascus. There were clashes also between civilians and police because of frustrations arising from the inability to get a constant food supply.

"Esther had not told me about her tribal origin, so when she told me, I was at first hesitant to leave my family. Her mother explained to me about your responsibility to your tribe. I love Esther and cannot bear to be separated from her, so we decided to come. By then, our two Druze escorts were not available, because they were fighting the rebels—but we left anyway. We already had our cell phones, so when our car broke down outside of Bayt Jinn, we were able to contact Levi. So, thankfully, here we are."

"So glad to hear you are safe!" Anne could not stand the cold reception. She got up and came toward Fatima and Esther. She gave each a hug and shook hands with Ibrahim. "Welcome! We ordered dinner to be served here, so we can have some privacy. We knew it would be a suspenseful story, and certainly you all need a lot of rest and a good night's sleep. The food should be here any minute. What would you like to drink? Tea? Soda?"

Anne rambled on as the food arrived, and the silence was replaced with the tinkering sound of flatware and the comments on the pasta, potatoes, lamb stew, chicken curry, beef kebabs, and fruits.

Anne sat with Fatima and Esther, and Levi sat beside Ibrahim. There was a little more animation when they ate that somehow blunted the awkwardness.

After dinner, Anne accompanied Fatima and Esther to their room and brought them other essentials they needed. Ibrahim was in a room by himself, while Andre remained in the same room as Janan.

A sense of restlessness pervaded Anne, and she could not sleep. Just as she got up to drink some water, she heard a soft knock on her door. She opened it slowly, and Janan stood outside crying.

"Could you talk to Andre? He is still very angry, but I think he will listen to you."

"I imagine that's possible," Anne said. "Maybe I should have done something sooner."

When they entered the room, Andre was standing by the window, looking sad. Without speaking, Anne went over and led Andre to sit on the bed, across from Janan, who sat down too.

"Andre," Anne said, and held his hand. "I'm sorry I had to make them comfortable, for the situation was too awkward. I understand how you feel. You have been through so much, and you were going out there by yourself to bring them here, and they at first preferred to stay in Syria. That has been so disappointing to you.

"You and Janan have been very strong, just like your father, but families are a mixture of the strong and the weak. You are now the leader of your tribe, with all the responsibilities, but a good leader has to have compassion—and the first people who need it most are your mother and sister.

"You still have a future to face and a family to build, and Janan is right there beside you. Plan your future, Andre. You have a fortune that you can provide for them, even if they are away from you. Don't let this get you down."

"I don't want to see them for a while," Andre said sadly.

"Try to be courteous to them while they are here. We can have them taken for repatriation to Tel Aviv, or wherever they want, while we proceed with our original plan. I know you have to heal too."

Andre wiped away the silent tears and nodded.

"Let's get some sleep," Anne said, kissing Andre's and Janan's cheeks. Then she closed the door gently after her.

Anne made herself get up early the next morning. She knew Higgins, Luke, and Levi were always first at breakfast, and she needed to talk to them. She joined them after getting her coffee, waffles, and eggs.

"I talked to Andre last night. Janan asked me to come. Andre was so hurt with their indifference that it might take a while to heal. I suggested that those three proceed to Tel Aviv, and Andre can spend some of his own money to repatriate them. Is that possible?"

"That might be a good idea," Higgins said. "Last night was really awkward. I had no idea that this kid could grow up so fast."

"He's just a kid until his leadership is being called on. He was stoic when those North Korean agents had him," Luke commented.

"I'll call Tel Aviv after breakfast. Maybe we can speed it up," Levi said.

"I'll check on his financial status and explain it to him and Janan," Luke said. "I take it we continue with our plans of going by the coast on the way back?"

"Yes, if that's okay." Anne looked at the men. "I think it's good for Andre to be around his friends."

The three men left to make the arrangements just as the others arrived. Andre and Janan ate their breakfast quickly and left just before Fatima, Esther, and Ibrahim arrived.

"Where is Andre?" Fatima asked.

Anne greeted them with a smile. "Good morning! The men are preparing your papers to stay here. They need to talk to Andre and then to each of you before they can finalize them. Did you sleep well?"

"Not so good, but better than the previous nights," Fatima said, and she let Esther bring her the coffee.

Esther and Ibrahim then helped themselves at the buffet and sat at a table for two, holding hands.

Fatima went to get her breakfast and sat with Anne's family.

The younger men approached them. "What's on the agenda?" Alain said.

"Higgins, Levi, and Luke are arranging the papers for the Senawis and Ibrahim," Anne said. "Since that might take the entire morning, why don't you play tennis or swim? After that, we might proceed with our original tour schedule."

Higgins was waiting for them at the hotel café for lunch. "They may leave for Tel Aviv after lunch. Then we can proceed going south along the coast."

That made everybody hurry up to pack right after lunch.

"Andre, your mother is looking for you," Anne said softly to him and Janan. "Could you just say good-bye before they go? Please?"

Janan nodded and nudged the reluctant Andre forward. They said their good-byes, albeit not too warmly, and then Fatima, Esther, and Ibrahim waved from the car. The soldier-driven car then left for Tel Aviv.

"Okay," Higgins said, "let's get going."

The others got their bags and possessions and hopped on the van. Their tour proceeded southwest toward the coast. It was like a fog lifting. The younger men were back to their bantering, and Andre was smiling again.

They went to Acre first. When they became aware that Shimon had a master of history degree, the younger members became particularly interested with his views on the movie *The Kingdom of Heaven*. Shimon could weave a tale of the Crusader Period in history, and he showed them the actual historical site in comparison to what was in the movie. Shimon ended up telling them more background history and information—so much so that the younger members really had a sense of the past.

"We are so lucky. I'm learning more," Anne said with a smile. "What an unusual stroke of luck and opportunity we've had."

"I'm learning more too." Higgins nodded in assent.

From there they proceeded to Haifa and then Mount Carmel and Caesarea. They were all sunburned even though they'd taken care to apply sunscreen. After a long day of walking around the tourist sites, they just waded in the pool, too tired to really swim.

They arrived at their compound in Tel Aviv feeling content yet sorry that it had to end.

"Shimon has been such a good guide. It's a shame we are forbidden to give him anything!" Anne said.

"I heard that!" Shimon said. "You have all been good, and I enjoyed the company. That's more than enough. Shalom!"

"Shalom!" they all said, and they shook his hands.

They were all issued Israeli passports, and Roland was so relieved that this problem was solved, as was everyone else. They had forgotten that they needed new ones to disguise their past and to be able to travel.

Higgins shook his head. "Didn't you realize that we all needed new passports?"

"No," Anne said jokingly. "My brain is still on tour; it was left at Acre."

## 28. Touring Italy and Switzerland

They left Tel Aviv on a commercial plane that took them to Italy. Luke and Levi were in charge of customs, and the rest just lined up where they were told.

Higgins had arranged for them to be on a ten-day tour of Italy. It was a regular motor-coach-driven land tour, except that their driver was a disguised Italian soldier who used to be a tour guide.

Roland's assignment was to get each of their cell phones adapted to the country where they were. He also made sure there were backups with international SIM cards. At night they would gather around the computer and stay updated with current events, evaluating any news that could affect them.

Levi made firearms available for the men to carry, and three times a week, Levi drilled the young men on how to use the weapons. Just the same, they were more relaxed in a land with no overt conflicts, so they enjoyed their trip.

From Italy, they went by rail to Switzerland. They stopped for sightseeing wherever Alain said. They all snickered, not having realized earlier that he could be another control freak.

"No! No! No! I said we go east first to visit St. Moritz and Liechtenstein, then we swing west through Lucernne and Bern, and when we reach Neuchatel, we go south through Lausanne and Geneva. Then we go back east to Zermatt."

"This had better be good," Roland challenged irritably. "It's like a jigsaw map."

"Believe me. We then go to my castle," Alain said.

That stopped the complaining.

True enough, it was a good itinerary. It was Alain's country, and he was used to traveling through it. They were, like most tourists, booked for an evening dinner and a show, and they enjoyed themselves.

When they arrived at Alain's castle, they were overwhelmed at the task of fixing it. It seemed to be a grand castle—until they looked more closely and saw the faded curtains and the beams and flooring in need of repair.

Alain had called ahead to the house help, and food was ready when they arrived. They toured the castle after their meal, and they appreciated that their rooms were spacious, with views of beautiful scenery, but they had to share bathrooms.

"We don't have enough money for maintenance since our farm tenants gave up farming and went to the cities," Alain explained. "My parents died in a car accident, and after a few years, even if I was too young to know about business, I plunged right into the fray, so I lost money. Now I have to make sense of my future."

"You came to America as an exchange student," Anne said, "and then went on to finish college there, right?"

"Right," Alain answered sadly. "I finished business, but I don't know where to start. I was thinking of making my castle into a bed-and-breakfast, but I do not have the capital to repair and refurbish my castle, much less decorate it."

"If that's where your heart is, you can start either small—that is, a few rooms at a time—or big, meaning getting capital from other people. My question is this: Is that what you really want to do, or do you feel tied down here just because of tradition? If you just feel tied down, you can lease it to a hotel chain or subcontract it to a tourist group. That way, you still own it," Anne said, thinking out loud.

"When we get back to the States," Higgins said, "you can ask around—try different real-estate investment groups, or ask a tour owner. Switzerland is a frequent tourist destination."

"What do you mean about him feeling tied down to Switzerland by tradition?" Andre asked.

"It means that he does not have to feel obligated to live all the time in Switzerland. It can still be a home that he comes to visit. That often happens among people who have to move to places where their jobs are located," Anne explained.

Andre was thoughtful and then asked again, "So it means that I don't have to feel obligated to return to Iran?"

Anne had seen this coming, so she answered gently. "That's right. It is too dangerous to go back there now. There is religious persecution going on. You know in your heart where your homeland is. You can wait for an opportunity to help shape its future. Let's hope that one day peace will come, and then you can go home.

"In the meantime, traditions are important for you to keep faith with your heritage. Watch all the news coming out of your tribal area, but don't rush to go home if it is futile. This is the reason why there are Chaldean Catholic communities in the USA. Mark and I have looked through some of the information before."

"Oh! I'd love to stay in the USA!" Andre said.

"Your mother and sister might want to do the same," Anne said, and she watched Andre's expression.

He thought for some time and then gave Anne a hug. "Thank you, Anne!"

They finished the tour on a top turret without a bell. The sun had just set, and the beautiful hills were shaded with a pinkish glow just as the electric lights started to turn on.

"I'm home!" Alain said.

It was a cold evening, but the blankets kept them warm.

Higgins had preordered a Mercedes van big enough to fit a dozen.

The group looked it over before they ate breakfast. Everybody seemed to be in a good mood.

*Maybe it's because we are in a home,* Anne thought.

That morning they went over the castle with a more critical eye and offered suggestions. Mark had his iPad ready.

"How expensive is labor here?" Luke asked.

"Labor is expensive, but I hope to get a more reasonable rate when the tourist season is over," Alain said.

"Maybe we can just use ready-made drapery first. We can order embossed cloth with a shimmery thread so that it looks expensive and elegant," Anne said.

"There's loose flooring here," Levi said.

"Morning room, right-hand corner," Jim dictated to Mark, who started to keep a record on his iPad.

After lunch, they rode in the van and went to the market area at Berne. They walked the streets just like tourists. The vendors were precise and courteous, and people enjoyed looking and asking before they bought anything. There was no haggling.

Anne and Janan bought some fruits. When they reached the flower market area, the ladies smiled and started their noisy purchase of flowers.

"What are you going to do with that?" Edward asked.

"We'll put flowers in the rooms!" Anne said.

"Leave the ladies alone," Higgins answered with an amused look. "It's been awhile since they've looked so happy."

"Right! I've missed my garden," Anne said.

Mark and Jim took the fruits from Anne's hands so that she could hold the flowers, and Andre did the same for Janan.

"All right," Alain said. "It's our turn. We're buying some crusty bread we make in these parts, cheese, and wine." Alain led the way to make his purchases.

"Let me buy some newspapers, including past editions," Edward said.

They then went to the wine shop, and everybody came inside. The men took their time talking about wine and arguing.

Anne and Janan stepped aside and talked about their flower arrangements instead.

"This flower is similar to what grows in Sanandaz. Andre would surely like it in the room," Janan said.

"We can put the mums mixed with some roses in the men's rooms. The flowers will brighten the room, even if it's only in the men's subconscious," Anne said.

When they went back to the castle for dinner, a feast awaited them.

The ladies hurriedly made a flower arrangement for the dinner table and put the rest of the flowers into a pail of water. They ate in their street clothes.

They retired to the smoking room for after-dinner drinks and canapés.

"This castle is really a wonderful place to stay," Jim commented.

"I'm enjoying it here," Roland seconded.

"Maybe our plan to stay here for a month is a good idea, but we might need Wi-Fi," Mark said.

"By the way, I was just getting to that," Higgins said. "Tomorrow we will divide the labor. Roland, Luke, Levi, and I will take our computers with us and check in for a day at a hotel with Wi-Fi. We need to get caught up with some recent news and also get a chance to continue with our legislative proposals. Yes, that's plural.

"We have gotten in touch with reliable senators and congressmen who will work with us in drafting much-needed laws. We will discuss these recommendations later on with everybody, especially our young men, who have already demonstrated character and conviction. These future leaders will have a say in the final wording of these documents.

"We will be there for the day, so don't wait for us, not even at dinnertime. We might be back late at night or the next morning.

"In the meantime, Alain and Edward can see to the connection for Wi-Fi. The rest of you can see to helping Alain here with his plans. Please keep your cell phones on and stay connected. There's no relaxation as far as safety is concerned. Any comments? Oh! I've ordered two TV sets, which might arrive tomorrow or the day after."

There were no comments. They finished the evening with a contented feeling and looked forward to a busy day ahead.

"Oh, what peace!" Andre remarked with a smile after the older men left and the cell phone ringing finally stopped.

"Okay," Alain said. "It's my turn to call for the Wi-Fi. These technicians don't work so early around here, following labor laws."

Edward and Alain inspected several ground-floor rooms for a Wi-Fi connection. When the technician arrived, they began at once.

The ladies and the younger men continued their inventory of the rooms and the castle grounds.

Anne looked at Mark's iPad and counted through the inventory. "Maybe Alain can use the three large rooms on the upper floor for himself and his family or guests. The four large rooms on the second floor can be used as suites, and we can convert the other rooms into twenty smaller rooms. Five rooms on the ground floor can be used as hotel rooms. The big hall can be used for balls, wedding receptions, banquets, and other functions."

"I agree," Janan said. "Also, the umbrella room with a large closet can be used as a coat check-in for big receptions."

"Right," Anne replied. "Alain will need a full-time maintenance man and gardener from now on if this is going to be a business. Then, of course, let's add another cook and maids for the rooms and cleaning. Hmm. It actually sounds doable."

"It's a good challenge!" Janan replied.

"Are you interested?" Anne asked.

"I'm just thinking," Janan said.

The younger men nodded.

"This place does make you want to stay," Andre said.

Anne and Janan looked around the garden and decided to start clearing up some overgrown bushes. They worked with the younger men through the afternoon, taking only a quick lunch. When they were sweating and tired, they marched for their showers and took their naps.

They were awakened by the sound of running feet. Roland was running from room to room, waking them up. Edward and Alain rushed to the newly wired rooms and checked the recent news reports from the web.

Alain read aloud the news headlines. "Syrian troops broke into Damascus suburb in attempt to retake areas from rebels," "Iranian opposition leader Mir Hossein Mousavi, who has been under house arrest, suffers heart attack, taken to hospital," "US drought worsens to involve areas producing corn and soybeans," "Monsoon rains in Pakistan caused 26 deaths," "Over 3,000 people in Taiwan evacuated as typhoon nears island," "Tourist reports spotting Levi Cohen and Alain Deneuve in Rome airport," and "Tourist in Florence reports seeing Anne and Mark Cortez."

Higgins let them look at the two computers that searched on the same news site. "I haven't really mentioned to you before that there has been a bounty of five thousand dollars for information leading to the capture of Levi, Alain, Anne, Mark, and me. I thought it would be unlikely for fellow Americans to turn us in. However, I did not count on our pictures being posted in US embassies and consulates. As it happens, sooner or later somebody will take the bait.

"Our advantage is that we are several steps ahead, and the governments of other countries refused the administration's request to help hunt us. So although it is not widespread, we are still prey for bounty hunters. The reward money is not much if taken individually, but since we are together, the sum result might be enough incentive.

"Remember that we are traveling on Israeli passports with different names, so that should throw off those hounds, should any one of us be caught. Since we have continued to address each other using our real names, when we are in public we have to address each other with our new names. That's not easy to memorize, so we will put a name tag on our chest for the next couple of days until we get used to it.

"I do not recommend that we separate; our strength is still in numbers, in case we are attacked. Remember that we also still have the Iranians and the North Koreans out there, seeking revenge. We will, however, take the trouble to be in uneven pairs when we are out in public. We will mix it up so that our appearance doesn't easily trigger people's memories. This is what Anne and Luke's group did before.

"Also, we have taken pains not to reveal Roland in public, but his face, along with Janan's and Andre's, is being studied now for being part of our group.

"We will have to leave Alain's castle because this information was disclosed during the hearing. The cook is now compromised, as well as the technician who came to set up the Wi-Fi. It may just be better for the cook to say that we came but left very quickly. That way, the cook gets off the hook." Higgins paused to think.

"Our cook is very loyal and has been with us since I can remember," Alain said.

"All the more reason that we can protect her better if she says that we have been here," Higgins said. "By the way, that's as far as the authorities are concerned, Alain. She may still have to go somewhere. Those Iranians and North Koreans might come calling."

Alain nodded sadly.

"We were just getting warmed up with a lot of plans here," Anne said, touching Alain's shoulder. "We'll leave those plans on hold. In the meantime, we will remove all traces that we've been here." She looked at Janan, who nodded in understanding.

"When do we leave?" Jim asked.

"We leave tomorrow. Tonight after supper we clean up our traces and pack. We will sleep early and leave after an early breakfast," Higgins answered.

"Where are we going?" Andre asked.

"We are close enough to France, at least another country away from where we were last seen," Luke answered. "Roland has been searching for a place where we can stay that is close enough to either the Israeli embassy in Paris or the Marseille consulate. Since those are highly populated areas, a reasonable distance will be tolerable as long as we have an escape route."

Levi and Roland did computer searches to find places where they could stay. There was no suitable choice among the bed-and-breakfast hotels or in the monasteries and hostels.

"How about renting a villa?" Anne kept wondering. "I've heard of some villas being rented out for weeks."

Roland and Levi searched again while everybody stood restless or looked over their shoulders.

"There's quite a choice, actually," Levi said, "but we need something quite suitable. There's Les Vieux Chenes in Toulon, Cote d'Azur, which sleeps eight; has five bedrooms, two bathrooms, Wi-Fi, and a private pool; is five hundred meters from the shops and the sea; is a pleasant villa with enclosed grounds, terraces, and a conservatory; and is peaceful without being isolated."

"Here's another one called Les Amories in Le Tignet, Cote d'Azur," Roland said, and he read the description aloud. "This sleeps ten and has five bedrooms, two bathrooms, a private fenced pool, a spa, and Internet. It's a lovely south-facing villa, decorated, with terraced grounds and lovely views. The green countryside has oak, pine, and olive trees. The Siagne Canal borders the villa. It is close to St. Cassien Lake and is twenty-five kilometers from Cannes."

"Hmm." Higgins thought aloud. "The Le Vieux Chenes is smaller, but it is enclosed, and we can improvise with the sleeping quarters. The Les Amories is more spacious, but it is also more accessible to the public. Which one is available now?"

Levi looked it up and shook his head. "Neither is available now, but the Les Vieux Chenes will be available next week."

"We can stay in bed-and-breakfasts on the way there; the wait is not too long," Luke said.

"Okay," Higgins said. "Considering that those villas are down south and near enough to the Marseille consulate, I think that's a good option. Let's get started tomorrow, heading in that direction; something might come up along the way. Get the list of name changes from Roland. Acquaint yourselves with how each of you is named on the Israeli passport."

Roland listed each name, followed by the new name, and distributed the copies:

Richard Higgins—Samuel Klein
Luke Mattheson—Daniel Weisman
Levi Cohen—Ezra Grossman
Edward Cortez—Felix Segal
Anne Cortez—Hannah Segal
Mark Cortez—Micah Segal
James Cortez—Jesse Segal
Janan Senawi—Judith Goldberg
Andre Senawi—Aaron Goldberg
Rolando Guzman—Joshua Rosen
Alain Deneuve—Cyrus Steinberg

They adjourned and started putting things back the way they had been when they arrived. The ladies pitched the flowers in plastic bags, cleaned the vases, and returned them to the storage shelves.

After breakfast, they finished packing and wiped their fingerprints from the castle. They left with a sense of reluctance.

"I'm not sorry we worked in the garden. Maybe we will have continuing visions of what we can do with this place in the future," Anne said wistfully. She then distributed name tags for each person to put on his or her lapel, to get them more used to their passport pseudonyms.

Luke, Levi, and Alain took turns driving. They made good time heading directly west into France.

## 29. In France

Once they were in France, they drove more leisurely. They ate in marketplaces with their disguised appearances, always breaking up into smaller groups to avoid triggering memory by association. They were always within sight of each other.

Luke, Roland, and Jim took care of checking into hotels. Roland and Levi always checked on their computers for current events and updated the rest.

Two days after they left Alain's castle, they were in Savoy. They went sightseeing and had supper in the market. They checked into their hotel and, as usual, gathered at the lounge area to screen the news on their computers. They were not ready for something dreadful.

### Fugitive's Cook Found Slain

The police entered the castle grounds of Alain Deneuve earlier today after being summoned by a man delivering TV sets ordered by Mr. Deneuve. Nobody was answering the door, so the delivery man went to the back door. He found the cook's body on the pathway. The delivery man said that the TV sets were supposed to be delivered yesterday, but the second set was not in stock, so the delivery could only be done today.

The police had actually been to the castle yesterday, questioning the deceased—Helga Vorst, who was the cook for the castle. Mrs. Vorst was questioned about the whereabouts of Mr. Deneuve, the castle's owner, who is being sought by the USA regarding the disablement of the Iranian nuclear plant. Mrs. Vorst said that Mr. Deneuve came home the other day but left quickly.

Preliminary reports indicate that Mrs. Vorst was shot from the back, apparently after attempting to flee. She had bruises on her face, body, and arms, probably from blunt trauma. She was dead when the police arrived.

Alain bowed his head and made the sign of the cross. The others prayed.

There was nothing more to say; they all went sadly to their rooms.

"I want to bury her properly," Alain said over breakfast the next day.

"Do you have a plan?" Luke asked.

"Yes," Alain said seriously. "Helga has no more family here. I was her family, and she has been very loyal. Her sister died last year, and Helga's only daughter has not been heard from since she went to the USA. Maybe somebody can pretend to be the estate administrator of her daughter, Lena, who has appropriated money for Helga from the States. I don't have to be there; I just want her buried properly in the cemetery." Alain looked around.

"That might work," Luke answered. "I can pretend to be that administrator and make some papers to claim her body. I'll put on a fake beard and other props, but Levi, Alain, and Higgins have to be nearby in case of trouble."

"I'm glad we paid euros for the TV sets," Higgins said. "We need a smaller car so that when the four of us use the van, those left here have a car to use. Everybody should be alert with weapons and cell phones ready. Let's map out a fallback location."

Roland and Levi searched on the computer.

"The Church of St. Michael will do," Levi said, pointing to the screen. It was a small church on the outskirts of town, surrounded by houses, with several trees in the parking lot.

"Okay," Higgins said. "We can actually leave today after Luke prepares the necessary papers. I suppose he needs to use a print shop to make them look official."

Luke took care of his papers, and they bought a small brand-new car.

The four left in the van after lunch.

Roland extended their hotel room reservations for an extra five days. He did it all by computer and then checked all the cell phones twice. Still, he just kept fidgeting.

"Calm down," Edward said.

"Maybe we can go to the grocery in threes and buy some food so that we don't have to go out so often," Janan suggested.

"That might be a good idea to help Roland settle down," Mark said.

"Let's buy some table games; then we don't have to be so bored," Jim said. "There is no tennis court here, and we cannot be out in public too often."

"Can we go out this afternoon then?" Roland said. "I do feel edgy."

"Maybe we should buy some books to read also," Andre said.

"Okay, we'll go out this afternoon," Anne said, "but we'd better put on disguises and also do the unlikely pairing."

Edward drove the car to the western side of town, far from their hotel. "Even small grocery stores have cameras now," he said.

They shopped for food that would keep for a long time in their room refrigerators. They also bought drinks, extra toiletries, flashlights, batteries, table games, playing cards, and books.

They finished their errands just before dark and ate supper at a casual café.

The Cortezes had a bigger room, so they converged there to play poker. Since most were new to the game, Roland and Andre argued in whispers and kept checking the rules. By the time they finished, they were tired enough and at least forgot their troubles.

The next morning, Anne woke up to a cell phone call. Luke and Levi had alternated driving, so they were already near Konolfingen. So far everything had gone smoothly.

Those left at the hotel had been sitting in small groups for their hotel breakfasts, carefully watching each other's back, but Anne could sense the anxiety creeping over the younger men.

As they gathered in the Cortez bedroom for their update, Andre asked, "Are we going to be hiding so much?"

"Be patient," Anne said. "If it gets worse, we will go back to Israel. There was more freedom there because we had the support of the government. The other alternative is to go to the Philippines, as long as we can go incognito."

"I'm curious to go there," Janan said, looking at Anne.

"So we can put that on our to-do list," Anne said. "You know, we can get bored doing nothing when there are so many things we are capable of doing. As soon as we are not hunted anymore, we can even spend our time volunteering for the nations suffering from famine."

"I'd really like to do that," Roland said. "I can give some of my reward money for that."

"Right! Let's hope we can come out of this problem without getting hurt," Anne said.

"Yeah! Okay. Who wants to play chess?" Mark asked.

"Me!" Andre and Roland said, so Jim evened up the pairing.

Edward read the news and searched on the web, while Anne and Janan checked for what other things they might need.

The next report call was after they've had lunch in the room. Levi called on Edward's cell phone, telling him how the funeral service was being arranged.

The next call was from Alain to Mark's cell phone. A police siren could be heard, and Alain said that they would be getting out of there.

The room was suddenly quiet, and they stopped what they were doing. Mark put the call on speakerphone, and they could hear the sound of running, a scuffle, and heaving bodies. Then they heard the sound of screeching tires and a police siren in the distance.

"Now what?" Jim said.

"Oh God!" Anne said.

"God have mercy!" Janan said.

"Was that necessary?" Jim wondered.

"Sometimes we are not totally ruled by reason, Son," Anne said patiently. "We have all stood for each other as family, that's why we were able to do what we did. On the other hand, this administration has made criminals out of us. If the historians are fair, they'll realize that we have done something good, regardless of how others want to paint the picture."

Mark and Andre nodded.

"We've been right all along, but we need to fight back," Roland said. "I'm going to do something about this; it's high time."

"What are you going to do?" Anne said in alarm. "Don't you scare me!"

"I'll work within the bounds of the law, mind you," Roland said, and then he burst out laughing. "There are so many ways to skin a cat."

"Seriously," Jim said.

"I've been checking the law regarding web releases and Internet rules," Roland said. "There are things I can do in France that I cannot do in Switzerland—and vice versa."

"Mark, Jim, and Andre!" Anne ordered. "You look over Roland's shoulder and make sure he does not do anything illegal!"

"Here's for starters," Roland said. "Sent!"

The item he'd sent was a picture of a politician kissing somebody else's wife passionately.

"Who was that?" Anne said. "Good Lord!"

"They were in a public place, although they did not think there was a camera around. A person took the picture and was trying to sell it to the tabloid papers, but nobody was buying it, out of fear for that vicious idiot. It will go viral in seconds, and I bet in less than ten minutes, the networks will carry it."

Mark, Jim, and Andre looked confused, but Edward started laughing. They all started laughing; covering their mouths to be sure nobody else heard them.

True enough, in less than ten minutes, one station after another covered the news. The TV screen was edited to cover either just the faces or the whole bodies, but when one station showed the full picture, the other stations followed. Less than an hour later, the irate wife of the high official said there has been a mistake. This was followed thirty minutes later by the other woman's husband declaring that he was divorcing his wife. The Citizens for Good Government issued a release entitled "We Are Ruled by Scumbags."

They were preoccupied with the news since it was morning in America. The other political news regarding the coming election was sidelined because of the scandal.

Andre's cell phone rang, and they all jumped. It was Higgins, calling to say they'd just crossed the French border, and although they had some scrapes, they were all right. The group looked guiltily at each other and smiled.

"Let's pray," Anne said, turning off the TV for a while.

When turned on the TV, they burst out laughing again. The "other woman" was livid. She said she had not been there, that it was her maid in the photo. But the photographer got mad and went to the

TV station to show exclusive photos of different scenes in sequence. He also brought pictures from other trysts. The other woman threatened to sue the photographer for stalking. The photographer then released pictures that this woman had ordered to be taken of her in order to land a job. The wronged husband said that under their prenuptial agreement, this other woman was not entitled to any alimony.

The Citizens for Good Government bewailed in a new release, "We Have Sunk to the Gutter!'"

They finally had their fill of diversion and played table games.

"Let's have an early supper and sleep early," Anne said. "Those guys might arrive sooner than we expect. We need not bother to make their room look like it's been used. Whoever is called when they arrive, please inform the others."

They all got ready for bed early, and for once, they were not focused on being worried.

True enough, the guys arrived before ten o'clock that night. They greeted each other in the hallway with muted high fives and a promise to talk more in the morning.

"Are you all right?" Anne asked.

"A little bruised and dusty, that's all," Higgins said. "We can rejoice tomorrow. How are you people?"

The people looked at each other and snickered. Anne and Janan struggled to suppress their giggle.

"We have a lot of stories tomorrow," Anne said. "We better sleep first."

They left the hotel after breakfast and went to a small park for a walk, using unlikely pairing. Later on, the group sat on the grass with their lunches and drinks before them.

Higgins started asking questions. "What was that thing on TV? Did you have something to do with that?"

"Yes, sir," Roland admitted readily.

"Explain," Higgins said testily.

"Well, we are, or I am, tired of always running without fighting back. We are always watching our backs, even if we are having fun; still it is not good to be afraid when we have not done anything wrong. I checked the law. I am in France doing something on the Internet about the States, and this photographer needs money. So I did him a favor."

Levi burst out laughing, followed by Luke, and then everybody but Higgins, who was red-faced.

"I'm not sure about that," Higgins said, and then he smiled wryly. "Obviously, I'm outnumbered."

After the laughter died down, Anne looked at Higgins.

"You tell it, Luke," Higgins said.

"I showed up at the mortician's with the papers," Luke said, "so the others could remain unknown. The mortician agreed that the papers were in order, so he inquired at the police station if the autopsy was over, and whether the body could be released. The body was released, so he took care of it. In the cemetery, we prayed with the priest, and after I put on the flowers, the body was lowered. Suddenly we heard the police siren.

"A detective had belatedly gone to the police station to request an examination of the body. He wanted to compare the gunshot to some syndicate executions. Since the body had already been released to the mortician, the detective hurried to the cemetery and used his police siren. The detective demanded that the body be brought up, but the mortician refused to do it, so they had an altercation.

"I protested that this old lady was being victimized again. The priest scolded the detective. Then another police group arrived looking for Alain, causing more confusion. They argued about who had more priority.

"I left them, complaining that I would go to the magistrate to protest. I walked quickly to where the van was hidden. Higgins and Levi hurried out of their hiding places, but Higgins tripped. We lifted him, and Alain drove the van out of there.

"Another police car with sirens blaring was just arriving. We let it pass; then we continued on our way, without looking back.

"When we reached France, we checked the news report, and it seems that the latter group of police was actually out looking for us. We decided to keep going to our hotel because it might be better to get to the villa already."

Levi informed the younger men, "We bought more small arms in Switzerland. We will fortify the villa where we will stay, and the van will be hidden most of the time. We also have a path plan if we get attacked. Our sanctuary point will be the consulate in Marseille. If anyone gets cornered and can't get there, hide in a church.

"Always have your cell phones handy. We will all practice the use of arms when we are in the villa. If you are swimming in the pool and hear a helicopter, duck first; then get back to the house."

They finished their lunch and then drove around in the van sightseeing, just like tourists. The older men made an effort to calm the others' anxiety, and they were able to enjoy a day outdoors.

Anne looked at the relaxed faces of the younger men and smiled with understanding at the older group. After supper in a market square, they went back to the hotel.

As usual, Roland's first task was the computer, and when he checked it, he announced, "The villa is now available."

## 30. The Villa

They left their hotel the next day. They ate lunch at a small café in Grasse, and they bought food. The villa was in Toulon, on the Cote d'Azur.

They unloaded their things quickly, eager to inspect the safety of the villa. The walls surrounding the compound were thick enough to cause an obstacle; just the same, all the men worked on putting small bombs and incendiary devices at strategic points along the walls. The van was in the garage, but the small car was placed closer to the back exit and covered with camouflage.

Luke listed other things that they still needed, while Levi gave the younger men a drill on using the available weapons.

The villa had been cleaned, so Anne and Janan took care of making it more comfortable and wrote down the room and bathroom assignments. They understood now why it was meant for eight persons. Some rooms were quite small.

There was a piano in the conservatory, which also had several wide sofas. They ended up fixing up the conservatory and putting bedding on the sofa, using throw pillows to make it more homely.

"Here's what we suggest," Anne said. "Higgins will take the small room by himself, and then there'll be a room each for Luke and Levi, me and Edward, and Janan and Andre. The four young men will draw lots as to whether a pair will sleep in the last room or the conservatory."

The four young men inspected the rooms, and as Anne had guessed, Mark and Jim preferred the conservatory with the piano.

"Wait a minute, I want the piano room too," Alain objected.

"You are going to draw lots then." Janan was ready and handed them two rolls of tiny paper.

Alain picked one and opened it. "We got the piano!"

"Boo!" Jim said in a friendly way, and he played a piece on the piano.

Alain sat beside him and played the bass part. When they finished, they gave each other a high five, while the others applauded.

"Let's relax tonight," Higgins said, smiling. "I think we deserve it."

They dined leisurely at the dining room with proper table settings. The ladies came up with beef stew with vegetables, wild rice, and a side dish of ziti with mushroom sauce.

They gathered at the conservatory after dinner for conversation, table games, and piano music.

"Okay," Higgins said. "Let's allow two hours of relaxation, but we need to sleep early. We have to stay disciplined; we are not home free yet."

Anne looked up from preparing the breakfast and wondered. "Where are those guys?"

Just then the younger men showed up. Mark and Jim came first, suppressing their smiles. Roland was behind Alain, who was trying not to snicker.

Higgins's brow went up while he ate his oatmeal. Luke and Levi looked up from their platefuls of pancakes and omelets.

Edward spoke up. "Now what?"

Anne looked suspiciously at them and turned on the kitchen TV.

"Earlier today, there was an Internet buzz when VP Max Levin's college transcript surfaced on YouTube. It showed several failing grades, many low grades, and the dates when he finally passed. When the VP was asked about it, he said it must be the transcript of another person with the same name. When it was verified that it was indeed him, he gave no comment. However, his appearance at an upcoming fundraiser has been canceled. Oh! This just in: other future appearances have been canceled until further notice."

"Oh!" Higgins hung his head, almost touching his oatmeal.

Anne and Janan tried not to laugh but burst out laughing instead.

Andre ran to Roland and gave him a high five.

Luke and Levi looked at the younger men.

"Fifty push-ups," Levi said.

"What?" Alain said. "They had it coming to them!"

"We are still in hiding," Luke explained. "Don't put any more heat on our trail."

"They think it is coming from Asia," Roland said.

Higgins sighed. "You said the same about the first one."

"They think the first one came from the USA," Roland said in a soft voice. "The photographer claimed he did it."

Luke and Levi laughed.

Higgins put up his hand. "Okay, the next time you want to do something, clear it with me first."

"Yes, sir!" Roland said.

The younger men then moved to the kitchen table and divided the pancakes and French toast among them. Anne passed on the sausage while Janan made more omelets.

The older men helped themselves to more coffee before heading out to buy more things they needed. The ladies cleaned up the kitchen and reminded the younger men about taking turns in the bathroom.

"You'd better take rotations with the washing machines too," Anne said.


"Shall we make a chicken casserole?" Janan asked, looking at their supplies in the refrigerator.

"Yes," Anne said. "That's just right with the ingredients we have. You know, I have a couple more ideas that Roland can work on."

The two ladies now had an easy camaraderie. Janan had moments when she would tell Anne some episodes of her ordeal, but she left out a lot of details, presuming that, being a doctor, Anne would know.

Anne let Janan take her time. "We have other resources to help you if it should be necessary. In the meantime, I'm here, and we're all here as a family."

"Fall will be upon us before we know it. Can you imagine how long we have been running?" Anne said while looking out the window.

"I've actually wondered what life will be like after we come out of hiding. I was making plans to run Alain's castle-hotel. It would be a gracious life, since I like to entertain and be around people who enjoy living. But then again, Andre and I are looking forward to a life in the USA afterward. What you told him made a lot of sense. He has looked up the Chaldean community in California."

Anne smiled. "I've had misgivings too about having to give up our home, but if anybody harasses us later, it'll be because of this affair.

"I want to get back at those bad guys, but we'd better confer with the others first; after all, we are under the same roof," Anne said.

"I have some ideas too," Janan said resolutely, and she looked at Anne.

They talked about the possibilities while they did their chores.

Edward came in to say that Levi had called.

"Thanks!" Anne said. "Maybe we will just eat the casserole for lunch, and you can grill some seafood tonight. Can you call Levi back and tell him what you want to grill? After all, you are the expert on grilling." Anne turned to Janan. "That's how I divide labor. Let's have wild rice with it."

"Levi said okay," Edward said, and he went out to check the grill.

The door bell sounded with a French lullaby, and both ladies looked up. Edward signaled with a finger on his lips before he went to open the door.

"It's the villa's supply of bed linens and towels!" Edward called, opening the gate.

Anne called Jim. "You'd better do this. Your face has not been shown on TV."

Edward handed Jim the fresh linens and placed the used ones in the basket.

"Merci!" Jim said.

"Merci!" the delivery man said, placing the address label on the basket. The van left, and Edward closed the gate after it.

"Whew!" Anne said to the gathered group. "I did not expect that. Guys! Will you check the procedures in this villa? We could have trouble without realizing it. Did somebody put down the plate number?"

Mark handed it to Anne.

"Thanks!" Anne continued. "Edward and Jim were seen by the delivery man. These two have not been shown as wanted fugitives on TV, but we need to talk about warnings and preparation."

Roland made the report after lunch. "Linens are delivered between ten a.m. and noon every other day. If you want more service, you pay more. Here are numbers to call for electricity problems, house repair problems, et cetera. The maintenance company services several villas."

"I don't agree with some of their procedures," Alain said. "Also, we don't want these people to come."

"We face a risk with these comings and goings of personnel," Anne said. "Let's talk about it tonight."

The older guys arrived in the van that afternoon. Without much fuss, they went on with fortifying the villa, assigning the easier tasks to the younger men.

Edward grilled the seafood, which was a welcome change of menu.

After dinner, they updated each other. Anne told the other men about the linens being delivered.

Higgins was worried. "Levi's contact said that Iranians and North Koreans have made discreet visits to Italy and Switzerland, wherever any one of us was spotted. It will just be a matter of time before they decide to cast a wider net.

"The Israeli government has drafted a formal protest to the UN on our behalf, regarding why the administration made fugitives of us instead. The conservative groups have been trying to make more noise on our behalf, but the administration has been muscling down any TV network that ever mention our plight.

"I hope the French will have enough guts to turn down the request to other governments to hand us in, wherever we show up."

"My God!" Anne said.

"High noon!" Roland said.

The older men looked at Roland, who then looked at the ceiling.

Higgins continued. "We took a while to get what we need to fortify this place, but what we have is not enough. We will need to go out again tomorrow, to a different location, after lunch. Levi needs to drill everybody on self-defense after breakfast."

"If we cancel the linen service," Anne said, "we'll have to buy our own bed linens and towels. Is it safe to do that tomorrow? We will also get groceries and make some cash withdrawals."

"We actually made some withdrawals for you," Luke said, "but go ahead. It pays to have cash. So far, with our different debit cards, small withdrawals from foreign banks have not been noticeable. Be careful, and let Alain talk in French for you. Use the van; we'll take the smaller car."

The others nodded. The younger men then relaxed with Alain on the piano, but the older men worked on their papers.

The next day went as planned. The older men left in the smaller car, while the rest used the van.

They shopped at a town thirty miles from the villa, observing the usual precautions. Roland took charge of purchasing the computer equipment, while the ladies bought the bed linens and towels. Everybody helped with the groceries, other household items, and books.

"Did you find all the things you need?" Anne asked Roland.

"Yes, I'm surprised that the store had everything I needed. Thanks for trusting us. We will work on it when we get to the villa. We won't do anything without explaining it to everybody first, as ordered by Higgins, but trust me, these things are necessary."

Anne looked at the guys and realized that they had been thinking about this, and there was determination on their faces. She smiled and patted Roland's shoulder. "This had better be good."

"Spaghetti with meat sauce, and let's sauté the eggplants and zucchini," Anne said.

Dinner was ready, but they had to wait for the other men, so the younger men started eating the fruits and some nuts. When the older men arrived, they looked worried.

"Shall we dine first?" Anne asked.

Higgins just nodded, and the older men sat down. The younger men seemed more upbeat, conversing about the shopping spree, but the older men were quiet. They gathered at the conservatory after dinner.

"There's a lot of static going on," Higgins began. "Our sources believe that there will be more teams coming out after us: Iranians, North Koreans, and bounty hunters. By tomorrow, the bounty price for each person listed will be doubled, courtesy of Mort Horus, a friend of our high official. As you know, this billionaire friend has been very cozy with the administration, with oil exploration money in Brazil having been lent to him by the administration.

"If there are more hunters after us, we need to not only fortify this villa, but also practice our exits and do more drills. Our last resort would be to get to the Israeli consulate and return to Israel. I share the feeling with you that we resent very much not having our freedom, and we are willing to fight for it." Higgins paused and looked at Levi.

"We were delayed," Levi said, "waiting for a person I trusted to show up. He had to take circuitous routes in order to bring us the things we needed. He detected several bounty hunters and notified us to be careful and just wait for him to come. We are feeling the heat. We will go out tomorrow for the other things we need, but after that, we will spend more time staying in and making sure we can handle an assault."

"None of you will go out tomorrow," Luke said.

Anne nodded toward Roland and the younger men.

Roland began. "We have talked among ourselves and decided to fight back. We went out to buy the things we would need. Here is what we plan to do. I will hack into their computers and make this Mort Horus's account a zero balance."

"What? Wait! Wait . . . Wait! Darn it! Don't do that!" Higgins said.

"Why not?" Roland was determined. "This bastard has the nerve to do this to us just because he has money. How about if we remove his money? I'm going to expose his business dealings too!"

"Uh . . ." Luke said.

"Duh! Oh!" Levi said.

"You see," Roland continued, "I'm still a Filipino citizen in spite of this passport. Back home, after the furor of my Love Virus died down, Congress could not agree on how to frame a law to stop me. I'm not

189

being evil, as you think. I'm fighting these bad guys with their own weapons.

"I'll hit Mort Horus's account tomorrow if he should want to make his offer. I'll also hit the New York Stock Exchange and the Chicago Mercantile Exchange with a freeze virus. Let's see what these people will do next. They want to make us miserable? I'll make them miserable—watch me."

Higgins sat down, stooped and tired. He sighed without saying anything. Luke was pensive but could not say anything. Levi scratched his head and did not say anything either.

"I told our young men about the prediction for 2016 that the Elliott Wave theorists made," Anne said. "By 2016, Larry Prechter believes that the DJIA—the Dow Jones Industrial Average—will be in triple digits. That is very possible if the current administration wins the coming election and goes on with destroying the fiber of our country. He is a socialist who is going to destroy us from within. We don't need an enemy that is visible from outside; a *paminyatchik* has come in, and the destruction is underway. We have to fight on several fronts, but we can do this together."

"So you think this is a factor leading to the prediction?" Higgins asked.

"Yes," Anne said, "but I hope that the prediction will be revised if we do something about it now. The future of the next generation is at stake."

"What exactly are we doing with the stock market, and why?" Higgins asked.

"We are not touching the stock market now," Anne said solemnly. "Not yet, anyway. After all, our sense of wealth is reflected by how high the stock market is. On that same breath, however, the DJIA can be manipulated to go up on a narrow trading range, and even with a low trading volume. I suspect that this is going on just so most people will think that our economy is all right, even if the bubble is about to burst. Obviously, with productivity not going up, high unemployment, and tight credit, the best possible economic outcome is a sideways market.

"Should the current spending, entitlement, and misdirected programs of the administration continue, along with further reduction of federal lending rates to almost zero, then we will face a point of no return, because we just cannot pay for all those debts that have been generated.

"On the other hand, I believe that we can help out by exposing those shady deals for all the public to see. I admit that indirectly we are influencing the outcome of the coming election for the Nationalist Party."

They were all quiet for some time, each one trying to absorb the implication.

"Like Senawi said, 'You could be Cassandra,'" Higgins said.

"I don't want to be Cassandra," Anne said, "but what an ironic twist of fate."

"My father said that?" Andre whispered to Mark.

Mark just nodded and patted Andre's shoulder.

"We have to pick up our other orders tomorrow," Levi said. "After that, we'll stay in most of the time and finish the fortifications."

"So you are waiting for Mort Horus's offer to come out tomorrow, and then you will hit him?" Luke asked Roland.

"Yes, it will be a limited attack on his accounts. As it happens, cyberattacks have been going on in the Middle East, and that is what they will attribute this to."

"We can charge this villa to that account if this gets blown up," Alain said with a nod of his head.

"I admit I did not see this coming," Higgins said. "You caught me off guard with your resilience and desire to fight back. You are right; I just did not realize this form of battle. Okay. Let's all try to think these ideas out and then get some sleep."

They went to bed in a pensive mood.

Anne hurriedly showered the next morning, followed by Janan. Roland was already on the computer with Alain. The ladies prepared breakfast quickly, just as the men started coming in.

"Yup!" Alain said. "Mort Horus made his offer."

"All right, limited cyberattack on Horus only," Higgins said, and he waited for Roland to nod. "We need to talk more when we get back."

"Please get us more copy paper," Mark said.

"Will do," Luke said.

The older men ate quickly and left.

The young men went to the conservatory right after breakfast and pored over the business and stock market books that they had purchased. They asked Anne, Edward, or Janan when they had questions; and together they formulated a game plan. Whenever they could not resolve something, Anne wrote it down for their evening discussion with the other men.

"Watch the DAX, the FTSE 100, and the CAC 40; that's our time here. For the DJIA, wait until four p.m. our time," Anne said.

They ended up just eating hot sandwiches and soup for lunch. They continued studying together until the afternoon, when Anne called for a break.

"Roland, it is now four o'clock. Everybody should take a dip in the pool and take a nap or rest after," Anne said. "Maybe we will be refreshed and ready for more discussion tonight."

Anne took a fifteen-minute rest to clear her mind and then started preparing dinner while monitoring the TV news. The younger men came to the kitchen right after her.

"This is a recap of events from about two hours ago. Mort Horus, the billionaire investor, was being interviewed by the morning news anchor regarding his reward offer to bounty hunters. Let's roll the tape."

"So," the interviewer said, "you doubled your bounty price to ten thousand dollars, adding to the five thousand that the administration offered? That makes it fifteen thousand dollars per person. You think that this is enough incentive to catch those whom you call criminals. Can you clarify why you call them criminals? Our poll shows that seventy-eight percent of respondents think they are heroes." The news anchor smiled in spite of her question.

"My dear, criminals are people who break the law. These people broke the law. By increasing the bounty price, there will be tips that we should receive soon. Considering that these criminals tend to travel in clusters, when one is spotted, chances are that the others are nearby. That would be a good price to encourage bounty hunters."

"Could you clarify what laws were broken?" the anchor persisted. "Also, I understand that you are a naturalized US citizen; what is your own incentive in offering this bounty?"

"They broke the law according to the attorney general! I care about this country as a US citizen!" Horus answered irritably. Just then, a commercial break suddenly occurred.

It was followed by another commercial and then another.

The news anchor finally came back on the screen. "We are sorry to report that Mr. Horus was called away to his office suddenly by an emergency. We will now report on the flooding in Southeast Asia. The first report is from Nelia Roberts."

The tape showing Horus's interrupted interview was stopped, and the original news anchor returned to the screen. "Mort Horus was called to his office while we were interviewing him. It seems that there has been a problem with his hedge fund and other investments. Right now, the DJIA is down 100 points and falling. Most of the stocks that are down are stocks related to Mr. Horus's accounts. We are not sure what the repercussions will be.

"So there you are, folks! This is what happened about two hours ago. From what we hear, there was a cyberattack on Mr. Horus's hedge fund, causing a sudden fall of 100 points on the DJIA. The DJIA lost 300 points before it stabilized."

They kept the TV on a softer volume as they listened to the stock market news. Janan, Andre, and Jim came in just as the news shifted to the international scene. A picture of Mort Horus returned to the screen. Anne quickly turned up the volume.

"Mr. Horus is vowing to get to the bottom of this fiasco. The Securities and Exchange Commissioner pointed to an errant trade on Mr. Horus's investment that came from his Hong Kong and Russia accounts. They had made very huge bets that the price of oil would come down. Those were put options on the price of oil, placed before Hurricane Isaac came into the picture. We now know that although Hurricane Isaac was downgraded to a storm, it changed direction toward the oil rigs on the Gulf Coast, causing the price of oil to go up."

Anne gave a thumbs-up sign to the younger guys just as the older men arrived.

"We heard," Higgins said. "We'll talk after dinner. We'll just wash up first."

They converged in the conservatory after dinner.

"Quite a job," Higgins said, "considering that you covered your tracks. Obviously, there are other similar things we can do, but let's focus on another pressing concern. Although you've restrained Mort Horus, there has been an increase in Iranian and North Korean chatter."

"It is not easy to measure that threat. I said earlier that we should be done with our purchases today; however, with a large threat looming like this, we will have to do more. We will have to buy a generator, a large refrigerator, canned goods, baking supplies, et cetera. We know that although our gate opens on a handheld door opener, it takes a minute for the door to open and close. We will have to fix that to make it move faster. We will build an underground tunnel that exits outside of the compound."

"That's really a lot of work!" Anne said. "Maybe we should just move to another place?"

"That's the other option," Luke replied. "Our choices are these: going back to Israel, which we've already visited, still with the same precaution; going to the Philippines, where you said we will stick out like sore thumbs, but the conditions are not so bad; or going to another country with no extradition treaty with the US. Until there is a change in administration, until we are free to go back to the USA, we are in hiding and must learn to defend ourselves. We might as well start here now."

"We can split up," Roland said. "It's easier to disguise ourselves. We'll go to the Philippines."

"Can you assure everybody that you can survive an armed attack of six or ten men?" Levi asked. "That's the chatter we are hearing."

"Whoa!" Alain said. "Won't the police find those people if there are so many armed men?"

"Not easily," Levi answered. "These people are professional assassins. They pair up in smaller groups and suddenly converge to attack. This is serious. We need to be prepared. We will continue practicing you in the use of firearms and we need to augment the fortifications on this place."

"Oh, by the way," Anne said, "the delivery man from the service company still has a door opener for the villa, and he can open the gate even if we are not home."

"That too—thanks for the reminder," Higgins said. "We will have to change the gate system completely. We might just have to buy this villa. We have a lot of digging to do, you know. We need the van tomorrow for buying the appliances and other things."

They all went to bed in a state of anxiety.

The men left right after breakfast and came home just before dinner. They unloaded a refrigerator, an extra freezer, a generator, and a lot of plows, cement mix, and other hardware.

"We start work tomorrow," Higgins said. "You ladies may shop for groceries with Levi, Alain, and Edward. That way you can do some unlikely pairing while somebody stays with the van."

The ladies prepared a casserole and sandwiches for those working at the villa, and then Levi drove the van to a town two hours away for their shopping. Anne thought it was a bit much, but she was humbled to realize the pains that the men took to waylay whoever was watching them. No wonder they often came just in time for dinner.

They were all in disguise, and they shopped in different places so that they wouldn't arouse suspicion with too many purchases.

The shoppers arrived back at the villa to the sound of plows hitting the ground with an occasional clink. Off on one side was the heap of dirt from the digging, and on the other side was the initial dugout.

The ladies hurriedly prepared dinner, and at least everybody relaxed afterward with some bantering among the younger men, now becoming more confident with their training. They all went to bed early.

Levi and Roland reported the computer news during breakfast.

"The IAEA thinks that Iran has another nuclear plant," Levi said. "This one is in Fordow, and they are speeding up the enrichment of uranium. We'll need to keep an eye on this one. The Israeli government is also sending feelers to determine whether we could help with disabling it."

"That would be our next project," Higgins said, "but one at a time. Defending ourselves in this villa is first priority."

The men practiced self-defense for two hours in the morning and continued digging the rest of the day. After a week, they had a hideout bunker that connected to a tunnel that ran five meters out of the compound, close to a tree. The tunnel was reinforced with wood and concrete; it was rather narrow, but it was well built. They used the soil from the dugout as an extra wall, thick enough against bullets, and was also cemented.

The steel gate opened and closed faster, with a new opener.

They then relaxed a bit, with the older men continuing to teach the younger men about the stock market and business principles. They could now leave their compound for errands and to go to church, following safety precaution. The laundry schedule worked well, and they were glad of their luck. One day the doorbell rang.

"Don't answer it," Luke said. "I'll check our camera."

Edward looked at the picture of a would-be linen-delivery van. "That's not the man who came the first time around. Also, that's not the van."

The van with the delivery man left.

"That's not a good sign," Higgins said.

They checked on the computer for a van matching the delivery van.

"There is a delivery service company by that name," Luke said.

"I checked the delivery service company for our villa, and there was a breakdown of service because of several malfunctioning vans," Roland said.

"The delivery service company that was here has been muscling itself into the smaller service companies." Levi thought for a while. "Let me check whether it has been going on for a while or is recent, which would mean it could be a camouflaged fishing expedition."

"It looks recent," Roland said, "but it could also be coincidental. Hmm . . . This company bought some delivery service business in Switzerland. Switzerland?"

"All right, today we do the hard drill for our escape route," Higgins said.

They only had soup and sandwiches for supper. They were all dirty and sweating by the end of the day. They slept early.

The next morning, Higgins briefed them. "We will go out to stock up on cash, emergency first aid, and food. Both cars will go out through the back at fifteen-minute intervals; the smaller car will go first. Persons sitting in the back will be the lookouts. We will meet in front of the film theater in Cannes before we proceed to another town. Cell phones should be ready on speed dial. Let's take the computers, the iPad, and all printout instruction papers with us."

Levi drove the smaller car with the two ladies, Edward, and Alain. Luke drove the van for the other guys.

They got back to the villa late that afternoon without incident. The ladies prepared their supper of take-out pizza, soup, and fruits while the men unloaded. Roland checked the computers. Anne had the TV on, but saw nothing unusual. Levi checked the cameras and called Higgins and Luke over.

After supper, Higgins addressed them. "There was another fishing attempt to find us. We left through the back door because we had left nails and broken glass in front. Under usual circumstances, there is no traffic in front of our gate, but today, a van got a flat tire just before our gate. The flat tire resulted from the rusty nails we put in the road from the tool shed. This could send a signal to our enemies, or they might ignore it as coincidence, but they are looking. We will mostly stay in the villa, but from now on, we stay packed, as in ready to go any moment."

The men played card games to unwind, but everybody was feeling tense, so they slept early.

The ladies could only come up with a haphazard lunch menu of stir-fried shrimp, minestrone soup, and salad. They made up for it with roast pork for dinner, served with tossed asparagus, rice, and potatoes.

Even if they swam in the pool, they couldn't relax.

"Let's just smile," Anne said to Janan as they prepared breakfast. "Maybe if we just smile, our spirits will be lifted out of this gloom."

"What now?" Higgins asked when he saw the ladies smiling.

"Ohh . . ." Janan said in frustration; Anne just laughed.

"We've been so worried lately that we decided to make today Smile Day," Anne kidded. "We want to replace your oatmeal with an omelet and bacon, if you let us," Anne kidded, turning on the TV automatically.

"Thanks, but no thanks!" Higgins smiled. "You ladies are spoiling us! This is my last bastion so I don't gain so much weight."

Levi came in just as his cell phone rang, followed by Roland.

"My contact called to say he saw two known Iranian agents in Lyon," Levi said. "Another contact saw other agents in Paris."

"There are quite a number of new arrivals listed for the Chinese and Iranian embassies," Roland said.

Luke came in, followed by Edward and the younger men.

The TV news reported some unusual US financial news. The news anchor was interviewing a computer specialist. "Do you believe the report about the new virus called Gauss?"

"I do," the computer specialist said. "Karpersky Lab is a Moscow-based computer-security firm, and they discovered this new cybersurveillance virus. They called it Gauss. The virus spies on banking transactions and steals log-in information for social networking sites, e-mail, and instant messaging. This virus began in the Middle East, affecting Israel, Lebanon, and the Palestinian territories. Thousands of personal computers have been compromised. They think that this virus is capable of attacking critical infrastructure and may have been built in the same lab as the Stuxnet cyberworm."

"Wasn't the Stuxnet cyberworm made in the USA? So the USA could not have made this virus that originated in the Middle East, right?" the news anchor said.

"Right now, all we know is that there is a virus," the computer expert said. "We do not know its full destructive ability. This analysis of Kaspersky Lab is preliminary. All I can say is that we've got to put in more antivirus and also double-check our own accounts."

The Dow Jones Industrial Average was down by eighty points.

"Well, just when we've got to run!" Higgins said. "Of course we don't have anything to do with that Gauss virus, but we might need to help contain it. Right now, however, the enemy is coming after us."

Janan hurried up with the eggs while Anne served the bacon. They started filling coffee cups one after the other, putting the creamer and sugar on the table. Anne sliced some oranges and sat down, signaling Janan to sit. They mostly ate in silence.

"We are leaving after breakfast, before they all descend on us," Higgins said. "We'll go through the back door in the van. We just armor-plated that. Levi, use code to notify the Israeli consulate in Marseille.

"Those who need to shower still have time, so take turns.

"Roland, be sure all computers, iPads, printers, and other equipment are packed according to assignment. Luke, please take care that we clean up the conservatory. Alain, help in the conservatory. Anne and Janan, clean up the kitchen and wipe fingerprints. Mark and Jim, make sure we've removed all our stuff from the rooms. Andre, help Anne and your aunt.

"Edward and I will start loading the van as soon as we can. We will try to bring with us whatever we brought in, including food. Why? Because it could give information about us to people who might come, directly or indirectly. Of course we'll leave the appliances that we bought but wipe them clean of fingerprints also. Get the food out, even if we'll just throw it away later. We must try not to leave something that tells our pursuers about us. We'll try to leave in one hour, maybe an extra thirty minutes."

There was a sudden flurry of activities. Anne and Janan took care of putting the food in boxes, separating the frozen foods from the dry goods. They put the filled boxes outside the kitchen door for the guys to pick up and bring to the van. They were leaving the cleaning and toilet supplies, so they wiped the fingerprints off the containers. They wiped fingerprints off the appliances and everything they touched, including the doors that they closed after they were done with the room. They then rushed to pack their things from their rooms.

"The towels and bedding we bought!" Anne suddenly remembered and asked Mark and Jim to get those from the other rooms.

They closed the door of each room as they finished with it, and in less than an hour, they were almost finished.

"We have to do the shed!" Mark said, and he rushed there with Jim, carrying towels to wipe the fingerprints off the plows and other equipment.

They closed the toolshed and found Andre and Alain putting camouflage on the bunker. They covered the opening with more dirt.

"The bedding and towels actually have some use against these protruding plates," Anne said when she saw what the van looked like inside.

Higgins and Edward were sweating from loading up the van. It was quite cramped with so many things. Luke and Levi double-checked all the rooms and wiped their fingerprints off. They had left a camera facing the gate, the villa entrance, and the car garage. They were the last to come into the van. Levi took the wheel and eased the van out through the back door and closed it. Everybody sighed in relief.

The first hour was uneventful; then a car with a wailing siren overtook them on a narrow one-lane road along a mountainside. The car suddenly stopped ahead of them and started firing.

"Duck!" Levi yelled, and he accelerated.

Luke and Higgins were ready. Higgins was on the side and threw a grenade. Luke aimed a revolver through the open window and hit the driver just as the car exploded. Higgins called on his cell phone as the van continued on its way.

Alain and Roland held their revolvers ready from the backseat.

"There could be more coming," Levi said.

The next obstacle came just as they were entering Marseille. There was an unexplained roadblock. Many motorists got out of their cars and complained to each other.

Luke called on his cell phone to the Marseille police, asking what the roadblock was about. "There's not supposed to be a roadblock. Get ready. An armed police helicopter is on the way."

The motorists were slowly moving their cars forward for inspection, one by one. Each car was inspected by men dressed as gendarmes. They made every person get out of the car and then pointed a device at them, as though checking for bombs or explosives.

As the line in front of the van got shorter, Anne looked up at the skies, waiting for the helicopter. There were now just two cars ahead of them, and Anne could see two gendarmes performing the inspections while two more watched. On the roadside, parked under the shade of a tree, another car was waiting.

Just then they heard the sound of a helicopter from above, and then the helicopter appeared from out of the clouds. A bullhorn protruded from the helicopter as it descended.

"Surrender, you terrorists!"

The reaction was swift. The terrorists pointed their guns at the helicopter. One fired a rocket-propelled grenade. The officer holding the bullhorn flew across the sky with the force of the impact.

Police cars with blaring sirens arrived at the scene to return fire. The motorists ducked for cover behind their cars. The gunfight was brief, but the mortality rate was high. All the police from the helicopter died in the explosion. All the terrorists were slain, some from Levi's and Luke's revolvers, which they fired while hidden behind the cars.

It took two hours for the carnage to be cleared up. The ambulance left quite quickly. There were no wounded individuals; the dead bodies just had to be taken away.

The motorists were not questioned. The police were overwhelmed by the surge of curious and angry motorists wanting to take revenge on these terrorists who had the nerve to cause them trouble and give them such a hard time in the morning.

The van left the scene and cruised into the town proper. Levi updated the consulate on his cell phone. They came in from a one-way side street and drove quickly into the consulate, where the gates had already been opened. Everybody ducked as Levi drove full speed ahead. There were gunshots behind them.

They were met by armed security guards, and the gate was closed as soon as they were in. The consul general met them with a smile.

"Welcome! I am Consul General Michael Goldberg," he said, shaking hands with each of them as they said their names. "That was quite a feat to escape that roadblock. You saw the situation ahead and realized that those men were not the official gendarmes. They attacked your villa too, but let's hope they came out with nothing. The police arrived as soon as they broke in."

They went inside and entered a conference room. The consul general placed their computer on the table, and they connected it to a projector. They watched the villa as a car crashed through the front gate. There was an explosion, and the lead car was wrecked. A second car was behind it, and the intruders from the second car helped the survivors out of the first car. Suddenly police sirens could be heard, and the intruders were cornered. A policeman was wounded by one of the intruders who fought back.

The group in the conference room then turned to a TV screen where the scene from the roadblock was being sorted out. The anchor was very indignant and spoke in a shrill voice.

"Can you imagine these foreigners posing as French police? They put up a roadblock, causing inconvenience to hundreds of people, in an attempt to find some persons connected to the disablement of the nuclear plant in Natanz, Iran. Our preliminary report indicates that these were Iranian agents. The French government is asking the Iranian ambassador to explain. The government is also protesting to the UN. Furthermore, if the explanation is not satisfactory, the Iranian delegation will be asked to leave the country.

"There was also a big assault at a villa near Cannes. The police believe that this villa was vacated by those people involved in disabling the Iranian nuclear plant. Preliminary reports indicate that the intruders were North Korean agents who came in with visas from China. The French government is very upset with these foreign trespassers and their lack of respect. They will be tried in French courts."

The consul general shook his head. "I agree. No respect whatsoever. The nerve! Let's have lunch first. Have a seat."

They were served lunch, followed by coffee.

"Have you heard the recent Internet buzz?" the consul asked. "The Gauss virus is causing us a big headache. It is a real threat—not just to us, but to the entire industrialized world. Of course we have to prioritize the disablement of the Fordow plant as soon as possible, but this Gauss is a looming threat. We would like you to help us, whether you do it here or in Israel. We have enough housing here if you want. My instruction is to let you have whatever you need."

"I have actually given the Gauss more thought by now," Higgins said. "It actually sounds like a mutation of the Stuxnet cyberworm. If that is so, then the surest way to counter it is by restudying the original Stuxnet cyberworm." Higgins looked at his brood. "What do you say, folks?

"Working in either place is fine with me, although that task might not be as easy as we think. I think we should prioritize the disablement of the Fordow plant. Maybe Aaron could join us."

"Aaron is willing to come here," Goldberg said. "He could also wait for you in Tel Aviv. The acceleration of the Iranian uranium enrichment process is very worrisome. It equally surprised us that Dr. Senawi only worked in one plant. Now we realize that he was deceived into thinking that Dr. Iravani was not active anymore, the same way that Iravani was made to believe that Senawi had fallen out of grace.

"Our physicists believe that the set-up of the Fordow plant has some variation in comparison to the one in Natanz.

"Why don't you get some rest? You were suddenly thrown off schedule by these goons, and I'm sure you want to discuss things. I would not mind being called on if you need me. The secretary will show you to your rooms, and we will have dinner together here at seven o'clock tonight."

"Thank you," Anne said.

Everybody nodded and went to their rooms.

That evening, the group came down for dinner looking pretty decent. They exchanged pleasantries with the consul general, and they talked of the beautiful places they had seen, only alluding to the defensive precautions they had to take.

It was quite an elaborate dinner, which started with salad, followed by cordon bleu and grilled salmon, with potatoes on the side. They had a choice of wine or soda with their meal, and they had sorbet for dessert. After coffee was served, Higgins canvassed their opinions.

"It looks like we are willing to go back to Israel," Higgins said to Mr. Goldberg. "Thank you, but we will just have to take a more extensive tour of France some other time. Right now, I do sense that most of my group feels duty-bound to get this problem solved.

"You might have been briefed as to how they disabled the plant in Natanz by teamwork. So many lives were lost in that process. We have been under constant threat from unexpected enemies because of that, and we might not only strain your resources by being here, but also distract you from other pressing concerns. We will be ready to leave at any time."

## 31. The Anti-Fordow

The next day, an escorted armored van took the group to the airport, where a private plane was waiting. It was a comfortable flight to Tel Aviv, and they arrived in the afternoon. Back in their enclosed compound, they had a swim before the catered dinner arrived, along with Aaron. It was a nice reunion for the team, and they spent the night sifting for clues as they discussed the project ahead.

Their meals were going to be mostly catered, with a lot of fruits and snacks for them to munch on. A trusted helper was going to arrive every morning, along with breakfast, and she would stay until after dinner. There would be two helpers alternating. The idea was for them to unwind and just think of the project. Aaron was going to room with Levi, while Luke would be with Higgins.

They would have to work eight-hour workdays—more when they got inspired—with time for drills and swimming to unwind. They could be driven to the nuclear plant if they wanted to consult with the scientists there or wanted to see something. They could also just invite the scientists to come over.

The next morning they had an early breakfast and met at the library/conference room to start work. Roland and Alain whistled at the two newly installed industrial computers. The screens were also projected on a white wall, so everybody could see at the same time. There were chairs on either side of the computer seats. There were a dozen chairs with desks facing the projection wall. The desks had notepapers, pens, and pencils.

"They mean business," Jim commented as he sat down.

"Wow! What speed!" Roland eagerly tapped on the keyboard. "We're ready."

"It is connected to the scientists' room at the nuclear plant, so we can simultaneously work on any given data," Levi said. "We are starting from scratch practically, since Senawi's work was completely independent from Iravani's."

"Let's see what data the scientists have then." Roland moved the cursor, and different images appeared on the screen.

"That Fordow facility looks very active, based on the heat activity index of our map," Higgins said. "It is underground and has antiaircraft batteries, so it has evaded detection and would be impregnable to air attacks. We need to disable it in a way they have not thought of. Considering that the IAEA—the International Atomic Energy Agency—only states its protest and Iran continues their program unabated, we have to do the task of disabling it ourselves."

"Question is, where do we begin?" Levi said. "The Israeli scientists showed us what they found, but they have no plan yet."

Roland and Aaron scratched their heads.

Mark handed Roland his copy of Senawi's original disc. "This might help," he said.

"Right!" Roland said, inserting it in his computer. The others simultaneously saw the information on their screens.

"Thank you!" their Israeli counterparts said.

"What next?" Levi stared blankly at the data.

"Can you hack into Dr. Iravani's computer, Roland?" Anne asked.

"That's it!" Roland said. "We can gather data from their e-mails and their papers; then we can plan how to get inside."

"Maybe we can create a worm when we see their formulas and other data," Luke said.

"Right," Higgins said. "Just remember, this time the Israeli government is taking the responsibility without lawyers."

"Make a random e-mail group connected to Dr. Senawi's e-mail address, and then pool together the address books. Is there such a thing? You can infect them with a virus, but we are firewalled, so they cannot infect us," Anne said, continuing to think aloud.

Roland and Levi continued tapping on their computers as Anne talked.

"Let's also make a group out of the friends who answered on Andre's Facebook search," Roland said. "That could yield something unexpected. I'll also make a new address for Andre and one for Janan."

Levi suddenly became excited. "I just checked out one of the scientists who worked under Dr. Senawi, Anne. He's now in the Fordow plant! I'll show you guys the connections. Do you see it, Roland? They actually transferred all the scientists from Natanz to Fordow, and a lot of them still use the same e-mail addresses! Good suggestion!"

"Do those scientists use their e-mail addresses for personal purposes also, in addition to professional?" Anne asked.

"I see that a Dr. Abbasid e-mails his family before he comes home from work," Roland said.

"Bingo!" Luke said. "There's our opening."

Higgins moved to the seat beside Roland, while Alain took the other seat. Luke and Aaron were beside Levi.

Roland started hacking at the computers, printing out copies of any information he thought was pertinent to their goal. Mark went to the printer, and Jim and Andre sorted the papers and stapled them together for each member of the team.

"Do you see what I see?" Roland said. "I detect a pattern of behavior in Dr. Yazdi."

"I see what you mean," Aaron answered. "If data or information comes late in the afternoon, he does not stay in the lab to finish working. He sends a copy of the work to his computer at home and works at home instead."

"What a break!" Levi said just as their computer received a "Nice job!" compliment from the team in Tel Aviv.

They had a short lunch break and then went right back to work, making diagrams of their findings, trying to detect a pattern. At five o'clock in the afternoon, Higgins called a halt and gave instructions.

"The men will have a short drill and can then go to the pool; the ladies can take a walk or jog. Dinner will be at seven p.m. We must adhere to time limits, or else we won't be able to think straight. Tomorrow the drill will be before breakfast, since we wake up early anyway. That way, we can have a more relaxing afternoon."

"I did not realize it, but I'm quite tired," Janan said.

"I am too," Anne said. "We must have tensed up trying to solve this problem. How about if we go straight for the pool? That way, we can leave ahead of the guys and be in the shower first."

With a nod from Janan, Anne led the way upstairs to change.

Dinner was a quiet affair. Andre was nodding off, looking tired. Jim and Mark yawned. Anne and Janan were quiet too. Luke smiled, and Higgins made his proclamation.

"I see that everybody is exhausted. We worked hard today and made headway. Tomorrow we will take some breaks in between our work."

They went to bed early.

After more than a week, the group made the connections and fashioned a virus, but it was unable to gain a foothold. Roland scratched his head, and Aaron threw up his hands in frustration.

"We are missing something—something that will make it stick," Levi said.

The other members of the team were already tired of drinking too much coffee. The younger ones switched to soda, but the older ones took one cup after another, trying their best to think.

"Why don't we start from the beginning?" Anne asked in between sips. "The Stuxnet cyberworm was fashioned on a four-step process, right? What model are those machines? Where were they manufactured? What are the serial numbers? Once we have that information, we can probably go one step further than that and also build a defense against its mutation."

"Serial numbers! The serial numbers on the centrifuges! The nine thousand serial numbers on the centrifuges!" Roland exclaimed, and he typed the information at the same time for the Tel Aviv team.

The Tel Aviv team answered at once: "Let's try that! We are sending you the information now."

Everybody was suddenly awake. Reams of copy paper came out of the computer printer so fast that the younger men had a hard time trying to collate the copies. The printer was overheating. They stopped the printer for fifteen minutes while the collation was going on, and then they resumed printing.

"Either it is straightforward, or we have to detect a pattern," Higgins said, adjusting his eyeglasses.

They spent the next two days figuring out if there was a pattern.

"All nine thousand serial numbers are too cumbersome. There's got to be a pattern," Higgins said.

Mark, Alain, and Jim were aligning the sheets of copy paper this way and that, while Andre just turned his copy upside down.

"Son, would you and Alain get the smaller computers so that we can do random searches here and there?" Anne asked. "There's something that occurred to me."

"What?" Luke said.

"Just you wait," Anne said. After receiving the computer, she said, "Thanks, Mark! Let's do random searches depending on whatever comes to mind. There's got to be something we've missed. Didn't we encounter a report once that Dr. Iravani was a close friend of Dr. Senawi but had a falling out with him?" Anne asked.

"Let me check that," Roland said.

"If I'm not mistaken," Anne continued, "they were good friends and for some years were together at Tehran University, actually as undergrads studying medicine. A math professor felt they were promising young men, so they were sent as scholars to the California

Institute of Technology. From there, they went on to be doctors of physics and were groomed to head the nuclear plant ambitions of the government."

"All right, here's more," Levi said. "Dr. Senawi was the face that the Iranian government put on their nuclear program at Natanz. People were made to believe that there was a falling out between the two, and the name of Iravani was not mentioned. Actually, Dr. Iravani was in the Fordow facility, the progress of which was slower than Natanz. When Dr. Senawi was killed, the Iranian government put out the face of Iravani as the head of the nuclear program. All the scientists at Natanz moved to Fordow."

"This one here is the clarification," Roland said. "Both men liked history, and both men were ethnic minorities: Senawi was Chaldean Catholic, and Iravani is an Azeri Muslim. There was no real falling out. The government simply prohibited each from talking to the other, probably so the government could hide the existence of another facility from the public."

"If both had practically the same background," Anne said, "and both liked history, is it possible that they would think along the same lines? Take the use of passwords, for instance. Iravani might have used the same levels, with historical names, and then had it cascade to several points using numbers."

"What names come to mind?" Levi asked as he typed.

"Qom, for instance, which is near the Fordow plant," Anne said. "What is its significance? What are the important names or places in it?"

"Qom is a holy city," Levi read aloud, "ninety-seven miles southwest of Tehran. There is a religious university where men come to study in order to become mullahs. The name is Howzeh-ye Elmieh. The most important site in Qom is the burial place of Fatima, the daughter of the seventh imam, and sister of Reza, the eighth imam. The holy shrine is called Hazrat-e Masumeh. Other heritage sites in Qom are Kahak Cave, Vashnaveh Cave, Howz-e Soltan Salt Lake, Namak Great Salt Lake, Marashi Najafi Library, Astaneh Moqadasseh Museum, Qom Bazaar, Feyzieh Seminary, Jamkaran Mosque . . ."

Roland was typing the information as Levi read; then he asked for help. "Jim, could you hand me a copy of the printouts? I can't remember all the spellings as I enter them for passwords."

"Are we going to try it first, like we did with the Natanz plant?" Aaron asked. "This is beginning to make sense. Some of those words just mentioned are lighting up like passwords."

"Right," Levi said. "I need help too. Could somebody give me those printouts? . . . Thanks, Andre."

"You know what?" Anne lit up with an idea. "The guys were trying to find a pattern, and they spread out the printouts to see if they could detect something. Andre, however, turned the page upside down. Out of curiosity, I wrote the numbers one through nine and turned them upside down. Only three numbers are left viable when you do that: nine becomes six, eight is eight, and one is one. I wonder if that helps."

Roland looked at the nine thousand serial numbers on the copy paper and started entering only the numbers one, six, or eight from each serial number.

"We're on to something!" Levi said.

Andre ran to Anne and gave her a high five. "Maybe I can stop drinking coffee for a while," Anne said.

The men on the computer worked feverishly on the new idea.

"There are still a lot of matchups we have to work on." Higgins looked at the clock. "Let's call it a day."

They all went to the pool and had an early supper. They slept early, as usual.

Before that week was over, things began to fall into place.

"Are the scientists in Tel Aviv going to craft a stealth scientific formula for the nuclear plant so that it implodes slowly?" Anne asked. "It can be put on the home e-mail addresses of Dr. Yazdi and Dr. Abbasid."

"That too," said Higgins.

Their Tel Aviv partners took a week to make an imperceptible change to the Fordow plant formulas.

The final virus was shaping up; they called it Anti-Fordow. The Tel Aviv group tested it on their model and then rechecked it. The results were good.

"Let's enter it in Dr. Abbasid's computer when he e-mails home," Higgins said. "I see that we can also put it on Dr. Yazdi's computer when he takes his job home."

The next day, the group eagerly awaited the release of the virus. They stayed in their compound where their closed-circuit TV would simulcast with the Tel Aviv lab. The prime minister and the defense minister were arriving at the nuclear research laboratory. The head nuclear physicist was going to press the send button.

The group gathered in the conference room of their compound and watched the button being pressed.

The assessment would be based on the heat emitting from the Fordow nuclear plant, signified by a very dark green spot on their TV screen. The color slowly transformed into a paler green. It would take five days for the green to change to gray, then black.

The Tel Aviv facility greeted them with congratulations. The prime minister called to congratulate them as well. Higgins took the call.

"Take this as usual, Mark," Higgins said, handing him one disc copy. "I'll keep one too."

The food caterer sent them champagne along with steaks that evening. They were laughing and joking, finally able to relax after a long period of tension. The young men ate with a good appetite.

"Let's get some rest—like two days maybe," Higgins said. "I am worried about the Gauss, and I'd like us to work on it. What do you say?" He addressed the group.

"No problem," they all said confidently.

The young men went to the beach the next day and then spent another day just playing card games, playing piano, and hanging out. The ladies relaxed and tried to get more sleep. After that, they returned to work.

Higgins updated them on some news first. "Iran is unleashing more cyberattacks on US banks. These are supposed to be ten times more damaging than the previous denial-of-service attacks; they are now disrupting service at major US banks. The cyberweapon is called itsoknoproblembro.

"Next, Swiss banks don't want to service US citizens because of a pending regulation aimed at tracking down tax cheats. Foreign banks are supposed to identify Americans among their clients and provide their financial information to the IRS. Swiss banks just don't want to do the IRS's job for them. Take note, Alain.

"Now let's try to tackle the Gauss virus," Higgins said.

Alain looked dispirited. The others shook their heads.

"Come on. Let's solve one problem at a time," Roland said. He tried to tackle the Gauss. "What's this thing?" Roland complained. "It's different from our other projects!"

"Well, we don't have a disc to work with, so we are starting from scratch. It took years to fashion the Stuxnet, and it was released without defense. Therefore, I really expected this to be more difficult. Let's try, but if we can't solve this, we will just have to wait until I can retrieve my copy of the Stuxnet disc. Okay?"

"Okay," the young men chorused.

Roland cussed as all his entries went nowhere.

"Let's see what happens if I do this on pure numbers," Alain said.

"Did you use passwords on any level at all?" Anne asked.

"It was purely mathematical, and I can't remember those formulas now," Higgins said, shaking his head.

After many attempts, they did not succeed.

"We might as well wait until I get my disc," Higgins said.


"It has been an honor working with you people, but I'm going back to my house tomorrow," Aaron said. "Thank you!"

"Oh! We'll miss you," each of them said.

"I'm so used to working with you already!" Roland said, shaking Aaron's hand.

All of the group members said their farewells to Aaron and shook his hand.


"All right, let's take a break. We have nothing on the agenda. Do what you want," Higgins said.

Later he was almost sorry he'd said that. The young men played poker all night. Levi and Luke duked it out on one chess game after another. Edward read all the Internet news he had missed. Higgins dozed off reading back issues of the *Financial Times* and the *Wall Street Journal*. Anne and Janan chatted all night, making lists and exchanging recipes.


The next morning, Higgins was alone in the breakfast room, except for Tova, the cook. It was already ten o'clock, and he watched the TV news. It had been a week already since they had disabled the Fordow plant, but still there was no news about it from Iran. Anne and Janan finally came down, followed by the older men and then the younger men.

"Let's play soccer!" Alain challenged.

"Yes!" Andre said.

"We're going shopping," Anne said.

"Oh no!" Edward said.

"Yes!" Anne laughed delightedly.

"We're just buying painting supplies, hair stuff, and a few other things," Janan added.

"I'll drive," Higgins said. "I'm too old for soccer. Are we okay with that?"

"I suppose so," Levi said. "Let me make a call so that you have backup."

"I'd better just come too," Edward said. "I'm too old for soccer, and I've been reading good reviews on Tom Clancy's latest novel."

The shoppers arrived after lunch. They left their parcels in the foyer to check on some noises they heard in the back. They went through the kitchen and saw a mess. Tova, the cook, was muttering to herself. The players had decided to have a soccer rematch after lunch. The guys were grimy with dust, running back and forth in the back lot. Andre was sidelined, nursing a bruised knee.

"Oh my goodness!" Janan exclaimed. "I hope you did not break a bone!"

Anne saw Mark running with a torn shirt, trying to kick the ball from Alain. Jim came out of nowhere and kicked the ball the other way. The three collided while Roland ran after the ball.

"Stop it! Stop it!" Anne said, running to the middle of the field. "You crazy people!"

"Aw, Mom!" Mark said, getting up.

Anne helped Jim, and Levi helped Alain up. Luke stood aside.

"Looks like their energy has become unleashed," Higgins said. "We'd better keep these people occupied."

"Looks like he did not break a bone," Janan said.

"We'll make these people stick to military drills and tennis," Higgins said.

"It was fun while it lasted," Luke said sheepishly. "Let's take our shower, guys. The police are here."

The players marched off to take their showers.

They had a leisurely dinner with lamb stew, couscous, and sautéed vegetables. Anne and Janan helped Tova clean up and were rewarded with smiles.

"Next time, you tell them to put things back," Anne said.

Tova just smiled.

"We have chocolates and also jigsaw puzzles," Anne said. "Let's have a contest! We can have three teams."

They had a raffle to see which team got what puzzle. They started at the same time and stopped at eleven o'clock that night.

"Okay," Higgins said. "Puzzles stay as they are until we resume tomorrow, but let's not make a habit of staying up too late."

That was better. They were all at breakfast by nine o'clock the next morning. The TV was on, updating them on the news they'd been waiting for.

"There seems to be a problem at Iran's nuclear site in Fordow. Note that the other nuclear site in Natanz was disabled by a group that was later sought by our government. That's another long story. In Fordow, which is close to the Iranian holy city of Qom, although the authorities are mum about it, word is filtering out that some of the clerks and nonessential personnel were given a few days off. A watchdog agency says that the thermal pickup on their heat monitors shows a lower than usual temperature." The anchor paused, and then a scientist from South Africa made an assessment.

"You think, but you are not sure, that an event happened—either a malfunction or an accident? Is that not dangerous to the people living in the area? Would it not be necessary to evacuate those living within a certain radius from the plant?"

Higgins listened closely to the assessment. Everybody else stopped eating, and tried not to make any noise.

Higgins then changed the TV station. Different scientists had varying opinions as to the cause, but they agreed that the nuclear plant looked impaired.

"We'll stay in today. We can have a one-hour drill and then study at the conference room starting at ten a.m. Lunch break will be from twelve to one thirty p.m. That gives you more time; then we'll work until five thirty p.m. Dinner will be at seven.

"You saw the reaction from our administration when we disabled the Natanz nuclear site. Now that we have disabled the second site, I'm expecting an almost violent response from the Iranian authorities. Of course we also have to think of the North Koreans.

"We are in Israel, where we are one with the government in wanting this done. In spite of that, I am worried and have requested for more protection. Whatever we need would be brought to us, and we will even fortify this compound, just like we did in France.

"We will do studies, from history to philosophy, and certainly the nuclear bomb. This will be good in warding off boredom and also enriching our knowledge of some areas we have not visited for a while."

"Oh!" Andre sounded disappointed, but everybody else nodded in agreement.

They were back to a strict schedule. After lunch, two scientists from the Israeli nuclear site arrived. One lectured about the principles of the nuclear bomb; the other one lectured on how the Natanz nuclear site and then the Fordow nuclear plant were disabled.

Anne watched Higgins survey his group while the lectures were progressing. He smiled with satisfaction to see that the young men were paying attention, and Andre was actually soaking it up. Anne was having another cup of coffee, something she forced herself to do; otherwise, she might get sleepy. Her mind sometimes wandered off when she was off guard, and her last out-of-order idea was to have the swimming pool water be replaced.

The supplies for fortifying the compound arrived. Their plan was a mirror image of the plan they had in France: install cameras, change the lock on the steel gate, dig a bunker, construct defense obstacles and camouflage them, and dig a tunnel to the outside, five meters from the cement fence.

The men worked long hours since this was a bigger compound. The swimming-pool water was replaced. Tova, the cook, slept in a room just off the kitchen. Food supplies were going to be brought in every third day. The ladies laundered all the bedding in the washing machine, but each person had to do his or her own laundry, so a schedule was posted on everyone's doors.

Anne and Janan worked in the kitchen with Tova, but they also had to keep the house in order and pick up in the other rooms. They usually took a swim after five in the afternoon, just before dinner at seven. The time they spent on after-dinner games and other diversions was shorter now. They had not even finished their jigsaw puzzle; they were usually ready for bed at nine p.m.

After the compound was fortified, the men continued their daily two-hour drills, but the younger men were distracted in their study sessions. Everybody was feeling tense because of the increased anti-Israeli rhetoric from Iran.

Anne also started noticing that Higgins looked worried. "What's bothering you, Richard?" she asked after dinner.

"The Gauss could be anything, from a weaponized mutation of the Stuxnet cyberworm, damaging our defense infrastructure, to a recipe for financial disaster. It has already started disrupting banking transactions—in the Middle East, Canada, and the USA. This will soon extend not only to banking but also to trading in international stock markets.

"The latter impact will be worldwide, from governments to civilians. This will result in loss of monetary assets, extending to bonds and commodities, not stocks alone. That's the threat we face."

"You have mentioned that before," Anne said, "but I've put it in the back of my mind. It's too dismal. This could be another scenario for the triple-digit Dow!"

Higgins nodded. "Yes, without actually looking at a crystal ball, these theorists stumbled on a possible scenario whereby, due to mankind's self-destructive stupidity, we will lose all our decades of progress. When there is chaos, most people will look out for themselves, and in the end, if there is no order, all our financial and civic institutions will crumble.

"I won't be able to shake off the sense of guilt if it attacks us and we have not prepared a defense. The only way to counter it may be for us to get the original disc and fashion a countervirus."

Anne looked at Higgins with a knitted brow. "I thought you just wanted us to get some rest and that's why you did not press for us to finish work on countering the Gauss. We used Senawi's disc to disable the nuclear plants, based on how the cyberworm functioned, but you still don't think that we can counter the Gauss without the disc? You don't mean we have to get the original disc from Arlington, Virginia?"

"I'm afraid that since this is a mutation of the original, I need to compare the blueprint so that we can counter that malware. It's difficult because it is not straightforward. Let's hope it can wait," Higgins said.

The group was deep in thought when they went to bed.

The news the next day was different. The news anchor on TV was solemn while reporting the death of the ambassador to Libya, along with three US citizens. "According to the administration, this occurred after a demonstration outside the consulate in Benghazi, triggered by the release of a YouTube video that was derogatory to Islam."

"Let me see that video! It was so bad that the ambassador was killed?" Roland checked his computer and then scratched his head. "Why can't I see it?"

Levi also looked up from his computer. "I can't see it either. There's talk of a video, but I don't see the video. How could those demonstrators have seen it? Why can't we?"

Higgins looked grim. "It occurred on 9/11—maybe it was a terrorist act."

They followed the news. Administration and State Officials went through several TV shows to emphasize the video connection. The producer of the video was jailed for violating parole conditions for a previous bank-fraud conviction.

In the end, congressional hearings and subsequent investigations would prove that it was a terrorist act. There had been no prior demonstration; it was a premeditated murder.

This turn of events saddened Higgins even more. Anne looked at her friend and wondered if she should just block out the bad news. But there was a more pressing problem to face. She could hear rockets being fired toward them.

The Iranians were irate. The friends of Iran in Lebanon, the Hezbollah, denounced Israel, and their members launched some

Katyusha rockets toward Israel. Border patrols and the coast guard were on heightened alert and caught some Iranian agents trying to sneak in using fishing boats. The border patrol also caught some North Korean agents, which heightened the alert even more.

## 32. Enemies at the Gate

The group stopped their study sessions and went on alert. They monitored the computers and Internet chatter. Egypt's head was by now an Islamist. There were skirmishes between youth protesters and the Israeli police in the Palestinian-occupied territories. The Palestinian Liberation Organization authorities also denounced Israel and canceled an upcoming summit between their prime ministers.

One day it all came to a head. The dark evening sky across Tel Aviv suddenly lit up with incoming bombs. Wailing sirens woke the sleeping citizens just after midnight. Missile attacks rained from Iran, and in spite of the Israeli air-defense system, two bombs went through. One landed in the commercial downtown district; the other landed off the coast of Haifa. Although the bombs themselves did not cause a lot of damage, they were enough to galvanize the radical factions from the Gaza Strip and the West Bank.

Hezbollah forces unleashed Katyusha rockets; then their soldiers descended from Lebanon. Israeli soldiers were fighting in Gaza and at the Lebanese border. Egyptian Islamist radicals attacked from the south, but they were not trained soldiers and thus were repulsed with a lot of mortality. The Golan Heights area was relatively quiet since the Syrians were fighting their own civil war.

Most Israeli cities were vulnerable to attacks from within—the radical Arabs were surprisingly well armed to fight group battles with the Israeli militia.

Higgins sounded the house alarm, and everybody scampered out of his or her bed. They finished arming themselves for battle just as they heard a loud noise outside their gate.

Higgins was at the foot of the staircase, directing everybody. "Ladies, go to the bunker! Mark, Jim, and Andre, go with them and protect them. Be sure the connection to the outside is intact, Mark. If not, throw a grenade at anybody who comes through, and all of you come back to the house. Go!"

The entry to the bunker and adjacent tunnel was just off the kitchen storage area.

"Tova! Let's go!" Anne called the cook, and Janan gave the cook a helping hand.

"I did not hear the siren," Tova said, putting on her hearing aid.

Mark opened the door and, with a battery lamp, led the way while Jim guarded the rear.

The older men could hear the noise from outside the steel gate. Although the gate was rigged to explode unless opened electronically, it was still not a good option to let their enemy come in.

Higgins and Luke guarded the house entrance behind a cement pedestal with adjoining shrubbery. Their positions were preplanned to include steel and cement reinforcement. Alain and Edward were deployed at the second floor, behind an armored, steel-reinforced wall. Levi was on higher ground just before the house door, with a lookout view of the entire house front.

"Grenade!" Levi shouted as he saw the object thrown over their cement fence.

All the men took cover. The grenade exploded with a lot of shrapnel and dust as it hit a decorative plant urn.

"Grenade!" Levi shouted again.

This one landed close to Luke. He ran to it and gave it a strong kick toward the cement fence. He then dived toward the area where Higgins was taking cover. The grenade exploded on the corner with a lot of shrapnel, flying leaves, and debris. The men looked at the fence, wondering if that would be a weak spot. The enemies outside aimed their machine guns at that part of the cement fence. Levi ran toward that spot and lobbed a grenade over the fence to hit the enemy crowded in that area. He lobbed two more. The cries of pain and agony were mixed with a lot of cursing.

There was silence for a while; then the older men could hear the sound of a car. It tried to smash through the steel gate. The steel gate exploded with a fire that engulfed the car and its occupants.

Levi moved closer to the burning gate. As he expected, what was left of their enemy soon attempted to get through the gate, firing indiscriminately with machine guns.

The enemy had no defense against the submachine guns from the second floor and the three men in front of the house who were waiting. The burst of gunfire was long, enough for anyone else who would have attempted a comeback to let reason prevail and walk away. Silence followed as lifeless bodies strewn outside the fence lay unattended.

Levi tried calling for an ambulance several times before somebody answered his call. He was told that the ambulance service was for the living; those bodies would have to wait. The list of sites for pickup was quite long. The men had to continue their guard.

Higgins briefly left his post to check on the others in the bunker. "How are you guys doing? Okay? We're all right. It's almost over, but stay where you are until we come for you."

Aaron arrived on a truck with six armed men just before daybreak. He used the hidden back-door entrance and evacuated the entire group to the soldiers' barracks.

"We're back to square one," Anne commented over a breakfast of bagels, cream cheese, orange juice, and coffee.

They were all dusty and so tired that they took their time to eat.

Higgins answered the unspoken question. "Let's stay here for a week. The country is fighting a war outside and inside its borders. We'll not bother them with our plans yet. In the meantime, our young men can train along with the soldiers, so they will know about the armed forces and learn something for their own self-defense.

"Israel has to thank the foresight of General Gold, who made it possible for them to have this Iron Dome defense. Right now I am concerned about the threat this country faces, and this might preoccupy me. We have all functioned in the past as individuals aligned with this country in the name of world peace. Should any one of you feel otherwise, you are free to go.

"When it settles down a bit, we can ask to be transported to another country. Let's send our votes by mail for the coming presidential election. Remember that we are not out of the woods until a new administration is in who will see things our way. January is still a few months away."

They all nodded.

"We're with you," Andre said.

The group then went to their different quarters. The Cortezes had the biggest quarters, which was intended for a family. Tova, the cook, was taken home by Aaron.

The group was going to eat all their meals at the soldiers' mess hall. They converged there at lunchtime but were so tired from lack of sleep that Higgins told them all to get some sleep and he would update them all after supper. That worked well.

When the group returned for supper, they had gotten some sleep and felt better. Higgins gathered them in an improvised room just off the mess hall. The room had a TV, a projector, and several computers.

Higgins updated them. "There were more missiles fired from Iran than had previously been thought. Israel was lucky to have an antimissile defense shield. Two missiles fell on Syria; one hit a rebel stronghold, and another fell on the UN observer post just before the Golan Heights. One fell right on the border between Jordan and the West Bank. Skirmishes are still going on in the streets, and the mortality rate could run in the thousands, not counting the foreigners.

"The diplomatic channels are hot with accusations and counteraccusations between the nonaligned countries and the other countries that used to be called allies.

"Saudi Arabia, with its fleet of fighter planes, is being encouraged to join the radical block. So far the Saudi king has refused. Riots against the monarchy have erupted in Saudi Arabia.

"Alain, Roland, Mark, Jim, and Andre will follow the soldiers' daily schedule of drills and classes. Luke and Levi will join the officers' group for daily activities. Edward and I will man the TV news and other reports from here so that we can update you every evening. Maybe Anne and Janan can have more time to do their painting."

The next morning, the younger men woke up to the morning call and, in spite of some grumbling, got to the mess hall on time. Higgins and Edward had a more leisurely schedule, while Janan joined Anne on the porch of the Cortezes' quarters to do their painting.

After supper, Higgins gave his update.

"There are a lot of radical Islamist prisoners, but a platoon of Israeli soldiers was trapped at the Lebanon border. A Lebanese living in a border town had worn an Israeli uniform, pretending to need help.

When the platoon came toward him, the platoon was ambushed. Now the platoon soldiers are being paraded in Beirut and will be used as hostages or pawns in an uneven prisoner swap.

"Diplomats from the USA and several second-world countries are shuttling back and forth, supposedly to negotiate and to calm things down. There is so much anger because of the missile attack that has triggered a cascade of events. Iran is instead blaming Israel because their fury was caused by the disablement of the nuclear plant."

Higgins kept a wary eye on the goings-on by watching TV, reading newspapers, and searching the web. Every now and then, he would call his Israeli liaison, or they would call him.

The younger men adapted to the soldiers' routine and became tan and lean. Anne and Janan were almost done with their painting, except for a finishing touch here and there.

The group hadn't really conversed with each other since the men had started the soldiers' schedule. At first, the young men would fall asleep right after Higgins's update. Later on, they became acclimatized and could tolerate a short card game. It was already October.

"It is quieting down here," Higgins said. "We can request where we want to go. I recommend that we stay together, since our strength has been in watching each other's back. We just need to while away the time until it is safe to go back to the USA. Wherever we go, we have the funds for it. Give me your opinion tomorrow. We will talk again here after supper."

The item on the agenda was where to go next.

The vote was unanimous among the younger men. "We are going to the Philippines!" Roland said it for them.

Higgins was not so sure. "How safe would it be?"

Anne thought aloud. "We can rent a house in an exclusive district and be discreet when we go out. We will hire a live-in maid, a gardener, a cook, an additional washing woman, even if there's a washing machine—"

"What? Why are we hiring so many?" Luke asked.

"That's the way it is. Labor is cheap; not all households have the necessary appliances, and those people need the jobs. We have to let the help live in the compound, without outside communication;

otherwise, they could easily be indiscreet and divulge our presence. It's not because they want to betray us, but these people like to boast about who they are working for."

Luke chuckled. "What do those people do at home? You mean the housewives are just sitting pretty?"

Anne just smiled. "A lot of women work nowadays, and some of those who don't work get involved in charitable causes and other community work. Still others spend their time socializing, playing mah-jong, and stuff like that."

"It sounds like we are back to the Spanish colonial times," Higgins commented.

"Right," Anne said. "When it was only Mark, Roland, and me, we were able to stay discreet and safe. With our number, we will be obvious if we go out; but if we don't, the younger men will get bored.

"Asking for help from the government is out. Any information about us could not be kept discreet." Anne sighed.

"If we look through other countries with no extradition treaty with the USA, there's not really much to choose from," Levi said.

"We've already done a lot of touring over the course of this travail," Alain said. "Could our guys be interested in touring another region, like Eastern Europe? The tourist season is winding down. Let's travel in an armed van and carry weapons."

Luke nodded and helped think it out. "It may be more feasible to get help from these countries' governments than with other hostile areas. We could stay in smaller hotels and check in by Internet. We should notify the Israeli embassy where we are."

"Ohh," Jim said. "I've been looking forward to visiting the Philippines."

"We'll visit there when this crisis is over," Anne said, touching Jim's and Mark's shoulders. "You've learned more in these few months than you could have learned in school for a year."

The young men nodded.

"Well," Higgins said, "are we still voting, or are we going to Eastern Europe?"

# Part VI

# CYBERFIGHT AND THE QUEST

## 33. Eastern Europe

"Eastern Europe!" the young men chorused.

"Where do we start?" Edward asked, looking surprised at the young men.

"Huh?" Andre said.

"Bulgaria or Greece?" Luke said helpfully. "Wait, not Greece."

"Okay. Bulgaria! What's there?" Mark said.

The young men then gathered around the computer to map out their plan.

"They won," Higgins said. "We leave the day after tomorrow. You still have to do your drill before you can pack."

The young men gave Higgins a dirty look, but each went to bed with a spring in his step.


It was evening when the EL AL plane arrived in Sofia, Bulgaria. They disembarked in a quiet part of the airport, all dressed in white uniforms, as though training for some service job. They headed straight for the waiting van. It was driven by an Israeli agent. Levi went in first and spoke to the driver in Hebrew.

The driver greeted them as they hopped into the van. "Hello! Welcome to Bulgaria! I'm Shlomo. I'll be your guide in eastern Europe."

"Hello!" They all greeted Shlomo and introduced themselves.

Anne looked at Levi with an unspoken question.

"The best defense is a good offense," Levi explained. "It is better to be proactive. Our van is armor plated, and we have weapons in the car for each one of us."

"Let's hope we don't have to use them," Anne said with a nod.


They first stayed in a small inn by the city suburb. It was owned by a Jewish family. They had a big breakfast, a light lunch while touring the city, and then a big, homemade dinner with wine as they relaxed at the end of the day.

"Look at this picture! It's blurred, and I'm so tiny!" Edward complained.

"It's the Alexander Nevsky Cathedral that I was taking a picture of, not you. You got in there, and the motion made my picture blurred!"

Anne retorted. "I need a panoramic picture of this thing! How'd your picture turn out, Jim?"

"Wait! I was still taking pictures against the sun! Why wouldn't the camera make that correction? Look how dark it was!" Roland said.

"Ahh . . ." Higgins decided not to add to the commotion.

They were all enjoying themselves now. In a way, it was good to be young and quickly forget your troubles.

"But, Shlomo, I want to see Kardzali!" Alain said.

"But if we go to Asenovgrad and Kardzali, which is south, we will be so far from Vidin, which is north. If you want to see the Belogradchik Fortress and rock formations, we'll go north and then east to pass by Pleven on the way to Bucharest. That way, we will see southern Romania before we reach Bucharest."

"Huh? Let me see that map!" Mark said.

"Let's print more information here. We're getting confused," Jim said, and he put more paper in the printer.

"Guys," intervened Levi, "look at the recommended tourist sites and tell Shlomo what you want, but he will have to make the final decision; otherwise, we will be going around in circles."

"We were just about to go around in circles," Andre said with a grin.

The younger guys studied their printouts and maps.

"So we go north from here to see Belogradchik and then Pleven to Bucharest? Isn't that the same distance if we go south?" Roland looked up from the map.

Shlomo consulted the map too. "From Pleven to Bucharest is shorter than from Kardzali to Bucharest. Besides, we can drive along the Danube with the quaint villages along the way."

"Oh! Maybe that makes more sense," Alain conceded.

"But we are not in a hurry," Roland said.

"Guys," Higgins said patiently, "we have to limit a country to seven days; there's a lot to see in Romania and six more countries to go."

"Oh, wow!" Mark said, and he looked at the map again.

They left the inn with profuse thanks to their host. Shlomo took the wheel, and after a while Levi and Luke alternated. The younger guys were preoccupied with looking at maps and discussing, but later they either dozed off or just appreciated the unique countryside that they passed.

"Pictures!" Mark commented as Jim bypassed him to a higher ground, aiming for a panoramic view of the Belogradchik Fortress and rock formations. Mark sidled up to Anne. "I remember Dr. Senawi on and off when we take these tourist pictures."

"I have those flashbacks too," Anne said. "We've been on the run so much that it's not that frequent. Later on, we might even have more of those. We've been through a lot, Son. Just pray." Anne held Mark's shoulder, and he nodded.

Luke was nearby. "Memories?" he asked.

"Yes," Anne said serenely. "I hope that with time we will remember it with hope, rather than with fear and terror."

When they reached Bucharest, Shlomo had to arbitrate between too many ideas. They talked together at the hotel lounge after dinner.

"I have an outline of where we are going; we cannot do everything. I will read the entire plan so you have an idea. We can still alter our route, but if we stick to this, it will be orderly, and it would make sense.

"There are a lot of things to see in Romania: castles, fortified churches, painted churches, medieval towns. We will go by region.

We are near most of the sites listed in central Romania. We will go first to Sinaia, where you will see Peles Castle and the Pelisor Castle. We will pass by Predeal and go to the village of Bran, to see Dracula's castle. Between Bran and Brasov, we will visit a fortified church in Harman; then we'll overshoot Brasov to see the Prejmer Fortified Church. We then proceed to Brasov to see their Saint Nicholas Church, Council Square, Brasov Fortress, Franciscan Monastery, and Black Church. We'll sleep in Brasov.

"Okay. In your printout is a list of what you will see in Brasov, Ramnicu Valcea, Sibiu, Cluj Napoca, Sighisoara, Bucovina, and Maramures. We then continue west to cross over to Hungary.

"We will see a lot in Budapest, Hungary, before we go through the Czech Republic; then we'll visit Krakow, Auschwitz, Czestochowa, and Warsaw in Poland.

"From Warsaw, we'll pass through Poznan and sleep in Berlin."

Anne and Mark looked at each other; Janan bowed her head.

Shlomo continued. "We'll stay two nights in Berlin, proceed to Dresden, and go to Prague, Czech Republic. We will then drive south to Vienna. From Vienna, we can go west to Salzburg, Munich, and then Innsbruck; or we can go south to Zagreb in Croatia. Maybe by this time, you might get tired of the tour, or something else will happen."

Shlomo took a deep breath and then distributed copies of the itineraries with the help of Andre. When they saw the long list, the young men took the itineraries to their rooms without further comment.

The next morning, they discussed the itinerary over breakfast.

"Let's get going," Higgins said, and the half-confused lot marched toward the van.

"We are in Bucharest, Romania," Mark kidded Andre as he sat down.

Andre looked up from his confused scanning of the itinerary and grinned.

The day went smoothly, and as usual, Higgins always checked the news both on the TV and through the Internet. If he could lay his hands on a newspaper, he read that too, either on the van or later in his room.

That night, the group listened as the TV news anchor asked a senior correspondent about his forecast for the election.

"You learned that the presidential challenger will not visit anymore in Michigan and Pennsylvania. Why?"

"I think it's stupid," answered Trent Woods. "Not putting up a fight is like conceding you've lost, when the election is just weeks away."

"Is the problem money?" The news anchor pressed for answers. "They have a lot of money, don't they?"

"Yes, they have money," answered Trent Woods. "If you ask me, I'd fire the advisers for making this recommendation. Those advisers are just unbelievable! Imagine releasing a picture of the candidate with his wife Jet Skiing, like they've got it made, instead of their picture having a family barbecue with all the grandchildren. You'd think that these are nouveau riche people who flaunt what they have now because they've never had it before. That's not the case here. It is so frustrating to watch it."

"Whoa! You're not even the candidate!" The anchor laughed.

"Well, what would you do if you were in his place?" Trent Woods asked.

"I'd fire the whole lot of advisers!" the anchor responded.

The interview continued, but Anne could see Higgins frown. The others looked thoughtful.

"How do you like the idea of not going back to our country?" Higgins said sarcastically. "If this keeps up, we are like the myth of the Wandering Jew. That's not all. I'm worried about where our country is headed."

Anne sat thinking aloud. "I suppose we should become more aware of the Elliott Wave Theory prediction?" she said to Higgins, and he nodded. She then addressed the younger men. "An Elliott Wave theorist thinks that by 2016 the DJIA will be down to triple digits. At the rate the USA is going, we will be worse than Greece. Greece could default and completely be in chaos without much effect on Western civilization, but if the US economy falters that much, the whole civilized world will be thrown into chaos. If our sense of wealth crumbles, people will lose their faith even in themselves. They would be unable to provide for their families or make sense of how to progress to a bright future. Without a concrete evidence of wealth, as seen in our monetary possessions, their beacon to a future is lost."

"Huh?" Roland said. "What happens to our money?"

"It will be of undetermined value," Luke commented. "If the stock market collapses, people who were once rich will not even be able to buy what they need. We will be reduced to the basic necessities: food, clothing, and shelter. If you have those, you'll survive, but you will not be wealthy. Nobody will even be interested in gold, because it cannot get you what you basically need. Farmers might be better off as long as the harvest is good, but not if there is a drought; the insurance companies will not be able to pay them enough if their crops fail. There will be no law and order, because the monetary pay for services will have no value. People might just barter for goods. Gold starts to have value only if people have more than enough after providing for their basic needs. We will return to the Dark Ages."

"Heaven forbid," Janan said.

"How about oil?" Andre asked.

"Oil is only useful if there is an ongoing demand from industry," Luke explained. "Without industry, there is no need to refine oil.

People will just use coal, but then the system for distribution would also break down."

"Whoa!" Alain said.

"There is still hope," Anne said. "In 1987, Larry Prechter of the Elliott Wave Theory predicted that the DJIA would go up to 3,000. Consider that at that time, the bull market spawned by President Keegan's economic policies caused the DJIA to rise from 776.92 in 1982 to 2,722 in August 1987, a two hundred fifty percent increase. People then became interested in the rapid rise of the stock market and began trading speculatively. As the market peaked, Prechter sensed a change of sentiment, and he predicted a stock market crash. Before October, Larry Prechter advised his followers to sell. On October 19, a Friday, the DJIA lost 508 points, a twenty-two percent fall, on top of previous losses, and the DJIA was at 1,738. When asked, President Keegan said that there was nothing wrong with the economy. Some people attributed it to the US trade deficit and an Iranian attack on a US tanker in the Middle East. Larry Prechter attributed it to a sudden change in consumer sentiment, or emotional sense of well-being, replacing the previous speculative wave in the market. The DJIA would recover within two years, back to its previous level. Prechter advised his followers to stay in blue chips, foretelling that the boom market would return. True enough, we now know that the DJIA went up to more than 14,000 before it went to the lowest point of 6,547 in March 2009 due to the mortgage and banking crisis. It has come up since, to the 12,000 to 13,000 level now.

"In the past, the stock market crash of 1929 was considered the harbinger of the Great Depression. That one was preceded by the optimism that pervaded after the end of World War I. People were enamored with stocks. By 1927, and into 1928, the bull market was on. People began speculating on the rich rewards of owning stocks. There was a great disparity in income. People borrowed money to keep buying more stocks, not thinking of the downside. The stock market peaked in the summer of 1929 at 381.17, but on that Black Thursday of October 24, it lost eleven percent. There was panic as the ticker prices could not keep up. A group of bankers pooled their resources to invest in the stock market, reassuring the people, and the panic subsided. But four days later, on Monday, the DJIA fell another 12.8 percent, and again the next day, October 29, it fell another 11.7

percent. October 29, 1929, was called Black Tuesday, the beginning of the Great Depression. The DJIA went up slightly and down again, and it reached a nadir of 41.22 on July 8, 1932. It would not reach the previous peak of 381 again until November 1954.

"The Great Depression was all over the Western world, made worse by bad economic policies, protectionist tariff acts, the drought that affected the USA, and the dust storms that occurred following bad cultivation practices. Businesses failed, industrial production fell, banks closed, and the unemployment rate reached twenty-five percent, with an additional twenty-five percent working for less pay or just working part-time. People went hungry.

"Although there were work programs and social programs, the misery would not be lifted until the USA entered World War II.

"So you see, we learn from the past that there are conditions that predispose us to disaster. With our increasing sophistication and some degree of anticipation, we can at least try to forestall the prediction by helping remove the factors that could cause it. There is no certainty in what we can do, since we don't have a crystal ball, but we have a responsibility if we know better. We can also at least protect ourselves, even if we just can't help our country with all the obstacles we are facing." Anne looked around.

The young men heaved a collective sigh, unable to say anything. They went to their rooms in a pensive mood.

The next morning, Higgins was ahead of everybody at breakfast. He looked at Andre and cleared his throat before saying anything. "There are protests all over Iran. Their currency has plunged to 40,000 rials to the dollar—up to 225,000 in some black markets. People have varying opinions regarding the cause, including the preoccupation of the government to accelerate their nuclear program, the economic sanctions put in place by other countries to deter them, the revelation of Standard Chartered PLC's use as a money-laundering haven, and the involvement of Iran on the side of Syria in that country's rebellion. I think it is because of their central bank restricting the availability of the dollar to a country that has done badly economically, in addition to fiscal mismanagement.

"Be glad a lot of your assets are in gold. Just the same, you might need to accelerate your study about geopolitics and the economy so that you can be ready to help your country."

Andre sat stunned in his seat. Anne and Janan held his shoulder for a while. Andre was thoughtful throughout the day, and the group was a little subdued in deference to him. That night, Andre took the economics books to his room and read through the night.

## 34. Campaigning from Abroad

They were in Sighisoara when the looming presidential election really got on Anne's nerves.

It was Higgins's turn to speak to her. "The question is this: What do we do now, since we are far away?" Higgins said.

"There's something we can do," Anne said. "We can use the computer to let our voice be heard. I have more ideas too."

"Such as?" Higgins asked.

"Is everybody aboard?" Anne looked around, and with a nod from everyone, she explained. "Roland will release the YouTube videos of the falsehoods the Liberal Party is spreading. We will work on a fact-check sheet complete with citations and proper data, showing the false claims against reality. We will examine Medicare, the health-care law, the unemployment numbers, the property assessment per household, the manufacturing productivity, and more. I have a copy on file of the pathogenesis on how the hedge funds, credit-default swaps, derivatives, and other esoteric funds were born during the Hinton administration. We have to look that up on the web. It was a well-written article from *Time Magazine*."

"All right," Higgins said. "Let's get one suite in this hotel for all our work. We will work until we finish, whether it takes a few days or a whole week. Our work has to be accurate and clear. We all need to sleep well so our minds are clear tomorrow when we start."

They all nodded and went off to their rooms.

After breakfast, they all went straight to the suite and worked. Shlomo had brought a wall board, printing paper, rulers, and other things they might need. The group correlated current events with statistical data from both government and private sources and then analyzed it before making drafts on how to present it.

They took an hour for their lunch break, during which Roland and Shlomo went to buy more software and some computer programs. The others went to the gym while Anne and Janan took a short stroll in town accompanied by Edward and Higgins. They worked through the afternoon until five thirty, had an early dinner, and went back for more work until nine. Anne had bought snacks and drinks, which they ate when they adjourned at nine thirty.

The more data they processed, the angrier the young men became. They were now just getting to know more about government and politics, and Higgins had to counsel them on keeping their cool.

Roland was the safest person to press the button when any of their information was ready for release. They had several releases coming out on any given day, and Higgins, Luke, and Levi had to approve the final form first. Mark, Jim, and Andre worked on the math, especially the statistics when they needed to portray comparisons, inflation adjusted.

"You were really fast on that data, Andre," Mark said. "You must have taken after your father."

Mark said it before he realized that it might be insensitive; then he touched Andre's shoulder.

"You think so?" Andre asked without taking offense.

"Yes, and he was a very good man," Mark said, and Andre nodded.

"Is that flow chart ready yet regarding the chronology of the debt swap and hedge funds? Don't forget to acknowledge the author." Higgins looked up from other data.

"I'm still on it," Alain said, showing a proof to Luke. "Mark et al. are working on an addendum for the last four to six years. The ladies are checking on the color contrasts to make it clearer."

By the fourth day, they were in full swing, regularly releasing data via YouTube videos.

"It is now two weeks until November 6," Anne said. "How effective have our releases been? We have generated a buzz on the Internet, but only Century network has talked about it. Could we release information on other networks by buying advertisement time? We could go undercover as a tax-free organization supporting one party."

"I've been thinking of that too, but we have to contribute to the organization, and they sometimes take time to release it," Luke said.

"Roland can go directly on their website, contribute, and get an answer regarding the ad," Anne said.

"Right! We can do that," Roland said. "We can offer five releases to one organization, and another set to another. Whoever answers first releases it to a network. Pretty soon they will have a contest, because the quick responders will keep getting the publicity."

"Do it," Higgins said.

"Okay. Here are the first five ones," Mark said.

"Here is another set of five," Jim said.

"Let me see first," Higgins said as Luke and Levi took another look at each set. "Use my account. Route it, of course."

"There's an organization that is not answering," Levi said. "When any of you encounter that, exit out of communication without a trace; those are wolves in sheeps' clothing."

"Maybe we can wrap this up in two days or so and then monitor the results as we continue to travel," Higgins said.

"There's one more thing I'd really like to do," Anne added. "Let's contact Michael Keegan. I talked with him during one of the rallies for the Nationalist Party. He is a true Keeganite. He strongly believes in the principles of democracy that his father espoused during Keegan's presidency.

"Suppose we ask Michael to sponsor a series of soapbox debates. It can be done through the Rotary Club or one of those organizations. The debate can be done in a park, a school, even somebody's yard. The debaters will be ordinary people, one from each party. In the middle will be the fact-check chart. They will be arguing about the points that we released.

"This common-man's debate will draw a lot of previously unknowing people to the real facts. It will also rouse the apathetic people who just vote the usual party line without thinking about whether the government is doing its job. At least, it will be fun. At most, we can cover the states that the Nationalist party has not been able to carry because of its own ineptitude or lack of the will to fight."

"That's crazy," Edward said.

"That will actually work," Higgins said. "I was thinking along those lines myself but could not visualize the exact logistics. Let's call Michael on a routed phone line when it's morning their time."

"Great!" Anne said.

"Wow! I have feedback already from the Breitbart sister organization. The ads will air tomorrow on four major networks!" Roland said happily.

"Yes!" Levi said. "The other set was picked up by the Democracy Guardians. They are paying for it with their own funds."

"Hooray!" Andre and Jim said.

"Can we open some champagne?" Alain said.

"Let's have our snack," Anne said, "and sleep early if we have to call the USA tomorrow."

"Our phone lines are all set," Shlomo said.

Higgins made his call from the suite early the next morning. The older members were there early too.

Michael Keegan was enthusiastic. "I can start tomorrow. I'm in DC right now. I'll make the calls to the Pennsylvania Nationalist Party chair," he said.

"We are also contacting Michigan, Florida, and North Carolina now by e-mail," Higgins said. "Can you be the moderator at each state, or find somebody reliable to take your place where you cannot physically make it? We will provide funds through your organization."

"Between now and election time, I can lease a campaign bus, so I can do two per state in one day and be at the next state the next day. Wait. That might be good for Pennsylvania and then Ohio, but I'll be flying to the other states with my three staffers. We'll go first to North Carolina and then Florida, Iowa, and Wisconsin."

"Sounds good! Communicate to us on this e-mail address I'm sending: HALL6789@yahoo.com. We'll monitor this. In case of emergency, please reach us through this phone number. Ready? We are still in hiding but might have to come out if things go awry," Higgins said.

"Well, best regards to everyone. I'll do my job from this end," Michael said.

"Good luck!" Higgins said, closing the phone. He then looked at the expectant faces around him. "Let's eat. We deserve a good breakfast!"

The group was excited with their progress and ate a hearty breakfast. They were actually burning calories from the tension of bringing out their data for release. They were back at the suite working before nine o'clock.

Edward was at the TV monitor and changed channels again. "It's coming now!" he said.

The network news flashed the advertisement; then the anchorman interviewed the Nationalist Party and the Liberal Party chairpersons.

"This advertisement is so clear in making people realize that the current president has no excuse for saying that he needs more time to fix the economy because it was so bad. When then President Keegan came into office, his predecessor had made a mess of the economy too, in inflation terms. That scenario was even worse than the one that the current president inherited. President Keegan, however, was able to resurrect the American economy before his first term was over. So what's your excuse?" He addressed the Liberal Party chairman.

"I resent the connotation of the question. The conditions are different; the person is different. I'm not making excuses."

"What? Okay, let's hear it from the Nationalist Party chairman."

"President Keegan was one of those visionaries that the historians of today, and the politicos, completely underestimated. He had a unique gift, like Abraham Lincoln had. These visionaries are able to see the future of the country because they genuinely love this country and can think for it. One hundred years from now, you will see Keegan's name among the greats, and the rest will be in the dustbin. That reminds me of the Impressionist Movement, by the way."

The anchor sighed. "The chatter on the Internet is even more than anticipated. I suppose it's because the regular networks turned a blind eye to all this information. Why is that?"

"Bias!" the Nationalist Party chairman said. "The networks have always been biased to the left."

"Sir?" The anchor turned to the Liberal Party chairman.

"No comment," he answered.

"How much was Mr. Horus a factor in all the negative ads, which came to a full stop after he lost his money?"

"No comment!" the Liberal Party chairman said.

A commercial followed. On the screen was the student ID of the president, showing that he was a foreign student.

The chairman of the Liberal party left in a huff.

"Yeah!" Mark and Jim said.

Luke and Levi went back to their computers.

"We'll let Edward monitor the TV reports," Higgins said. "Let's get more work done so we can at least move to another vacation spot."

They were able to leave Sighisoara, Romania, the day after, and Shlomo drove toward Suceava. Before they did, they released another big chart both on the Internet and as a TV advertisement. It was the chart of cascading events that occurred after financial restrictions were lifted, and it looked at the rise of the debt swap, default swaps, derivatives, and hedge funds.

Higgins was answering his phone even in the van, and he announced that Michael Keegan was going to start the soapbox debates the next day.

"That would be fun to watch," Mark said.

"We'll watch it in Maramures," Higgins said with a smile.

That morning, Roland enumerated some Internet news over breakfast. "WSJ reports that in Egypt, with the victory of a Muslim Brotherhood member as the president, secular-minded politicians and intellectuals are raising an alarm regarding the Islamists' efforts to change the post-revolution constitution to impose Islamic law. Next, with Congress out of session until the election is over, the White House will issue an executive order on cybersecurity, which will give power to a DHS-led council to regulate cybertechnology and combat cyberthreats."

"Are they trying me?" Roland said.

"Those clowns just can't stop." Levi interrupted to address the younger men. "It reminds me of Hal More claiming to have invented the Internet. What hubris! The inspiration came from a presidential science adviser in World War II, and the Pentagon was involved. The Internet's backbone and the hyperlinks were invented through private companies, and so was the ability to link different computer networks, the personal computer, and the graphical user interface."

Roland nodded and then continued. "They now refer to Social Security as Federal Benefit Payment/Entitlement."

Anne sighed. The bad news was making Higgins look worried.

At least the trip to Maramures diverted their attention, and the TV news that evening was fun.

It showed Michael Keegan standing in the center of a platform in a town square, flanked by two debaters, each running for Congress. A rowdy group of people kept offering their comments after each candidate addressed a point. The police began to intervene, and there was order for a while.

When the last discussion point was being debated, the Liberal Party candidate got frustrated when he could not explain the anemic recovery he was bragging about. The rowdy group added to his frustration when they started asking him directly for proper answers. The Liberal Party candidate cussed under his breath as an old lady stood up to berate him for the state of the economy.

The Liberal Party candidate let loose a barrage of expletives out of sheer frustration, and the old lady's son—a huge, ponytailed weight lifter—went up onto the platform to smack the Liberal Party candidate. As the weight lifter raised his hand to smack the candidate again, the dizzy candidate ran toward Michael Keegan to take cover, putting Michael off balance, and they both fell to the floor.

"Wow!" Mark said.

"SOB!" Roland said.

Anne and Janan laughed, and soon everybody else laughed too.

Michael Keegan was next shown with a Band-Aid on his forehead.

"Are you proceeding as planned to your second soapbox debate tomorrow?" the news anchor asked.

"You bet I am! The fun is just beginning!" Michael Keegan gave a thumbs-up sign.

"Yay!" Andre said.

They checked the Internet chatter and the other news channels. They were all carrying the incident, and people started discussing the points that were raised. Some people aired their opinions on Facebook and Twitter, for anyone who cared to read them.

"Great job, guys!" Higgins said. "We will release another chart tonight. Michael already has the particulars."

"I can't wait to see what happens next!" Jim said.

"We sure hit on something that clicked. That was a great idea, Anne!" Higgins shook her hand.

"We're thinking this out together," Anne said modestly. "I'm glad you went for it too!"

They all went to bed feeling very optimistic.

Higgins checked the TV the next morning, and he received briefing reports by phone while they traveled.

In spite of a hectic day touring the sites at Budapest, the group was being energized by the good news, and they sat down together after dinner to watch the TV news.

There was Michael Keegan again, with crowds getting bigger and bigger. There were more police, but actually a lot were off-duty police officers and army and other military officers showing up to be given a badge by the Rotary Club officers who were managing the event.

The people had signs reading PROUD of AMERICA: Keep This Place Clean. They listened to both sides and were more orderly this time.

"See?" Michael said. "This is what democracy is all about! Let our voices be heard; let us debate in an orderly way."

They started with the national anthem and the Pledge of Allegiance.

The next day, the group watched Michael amid a sea of people in Ohio. There was a rock band that got there ahead of him, and a lot of younger generation people were there. The air was thick with smoke.

"No! We are not going to have a serious debate in this atmosphere!" Michael said. "Do you have a permit?"

The head of the rock band shook his head.

"Then you have to leave, sir!" Michael said.

The band started another song. It contained expletives.

"Police!" Michael called, but the rock band would not budge.

Firefighters arrived and hosed the band off the platform. In the next picture of Michael, he and the debaters were all wet, but they continued the debate. Every now and then, they had to wipe the water off their faces, and the microphone would suddenly let off a high-pitched shrieking sound because the equipment had gotten wet. The people laughed, but they stayed.

The event was shown all over the world, and people laughed but also saw how democracy works.

"Michael is becoming a celebrity!" Anne said. "He's also reacting to different situations with skill. I hope he can really have a larger role with the government in the future."

"You were right," Higgins said. "He is carrying his father's torch."

The TV screen next showed a poll chart. "The Nationalists are ahead in the polls!" the TV anchor said.

By the time the group reached Vienna, the Nationalists were ahead in the polls, and Higgins was more relaxed. They had released the last of their charts, and Michael Keegan was in Grand Rapids, Michigan.

However, the debate did not happen. Michael Keegan was surrounded by burly men and the police. He had to leave.

The mayor explained, "There were several threats to his life, and the police could not guarantee his safety."

"Bullshit!" Higgins said.

Roland got mad and hacked into the Grand Rapids City Hall account. He transferred all the money to the state coffers.

The next morning Higgins could not focus on his breakfast. He was waiting for Roland.

"To the TV room, everyone, right after breakfast," he said.

When they were all in there, Higgins asked Roland, "What on earth did you do?"

The TV screen showed the angry mayor of Grand Rapids, Michigan. "Today is payday, but the city has no money in its account. Who stole our money? I want that person to be executed!" he screamed.

Roland was not apologetic. "The money is there. They just have to find it! I'm not telling."

Higgins glared at Roland.

"C'mon," Luke said. "This mystery might unravel by the time we stop tonight."

They proceeded on their tour. Higgins was still upset, but Anne defended Roland.

"He did not break any law that applies to him," she said. "The money is there. It would come out with their dirty linen. Serves them right!"

It would take two weeks before the Grand Rapids city treasurer could find out where their money was. It would be in the state coffers, but the governor's office would give the city a hard time. By then the city would be dirty because city civil employees had refused to work; and the mayor would be in the process of being recalled. The state treasurer would later ask about some bills and find out that those burly men had been put on the payroll. There would also be a furor about an expense for the mayor's lady friend. Instead of a recall, the mayor would resign.

There was a strong backlash, and people boycotted Michigan products. The TV audience even boycotted the prime-time Spartans football game.

Roland went back to the situation by putting out the pictures of the burly guys surrounding Michael Keegan. The people identified them, and those guys went into hiding.

The younger guys were celebrating, and Higgins complained to Anne. "I'm wondering if we will lose control of these younger men!"

"Live with it Richard! I'll talk to Roland and make him promise to clear things with you before releasing anything. But really, I would have done the same thing myself!"

"Oh Anne!" Higgins said in exasperation.

"I warned you that I'm not a politician," she retorted.

Higgins resigned himself to the rebellion. Luke and Levi looked at each other and then at the group.

"Maybe we are becoming toxic after too much vacation," Levi wondered.

"It's a good eye-opener, actually," Luke said. "We have different temperaments, but we've been able to work together."

Anne wished she had awakened earlier just to shield the news from Higgins, but Roland was there at the breakfast table already, nodding his head as he gave an update.

"WSJ news says that Islamists and secularists are clashing in Cairo. Next, with Iran's rial plunging, their economy is getting worse and will probably contract next year. There have been cyberattacks on US banks, namely JPMorgan Chase, US Bancorp, PNC Financial Services,

Wells Fargo, Capital One Financial Corporation, Regions Financial, and SunTrust Banks Inc. The attacks have taken the form of denials of service, and the Qassam Cyber Fighters are taking credit. Some people think that this is payback for the US release of the Stuxnet cyberworm. Note that this follows the previous January's small-scale attacks against banks; the cyberattack on Saudi Arabian Oil Co. by a virus called Shamoon; and the cyberattack on Rasgas, a Qatari natural gas company."

Even Anne looked gloomy after the report. The older men had knitted brows; Andre and all the younger men looked solemn afterward.

"We have our hands full with this election still," Higgins said. "We need to work on a counterattack as soon as we get our chance. I'm almost impatient to get home to do something."

Anne saw how the inability to counter this was eating up Higgins, and she tried to reassure him. "Let's focus on one thing at a time. We're getting results on our fighting for this election."

The group was now in Munich, Germany, feeling comfortable with the events at home, but that night, they were unsettled by the TV news.

Larry Prechter was being interviewed. "You made a prediction that the DJIA will just be triple digits in 2016. Why is that? Is there a connection with our coming election?" The news anchor did not sound friendly.

"The Elliott Wave Theory follows the Fibonacci principle, where there's a wave that goes up two steps, and one wave down. The election per se is not the determining factor as to where the Dow Jones Industrial Average goes. We instead indirectly measure the psyche, or the emotional well-being, of people, whether they are optimistic about their futures or not. Right now, the DJIA is trending upward, but on a small scale, as though it is being manipulated to show improvement of the economy. It is going up on small volume swings, so it would be easy for that to practically spiral downward when those propping mechanisms fail."

"I'll be honest and say that I can't imagine this at all," the news anchorman said. "The world is more civilized, and with so much at stake, there will be a concerted effort to let the stock market go up."

"Let's hope so; I don't want it to happen either. Do you know where the DJIA was in the first stock market crash of 1929?"

"No," the anchor said, a bit put off.

"It was 381; then it fell to 50 and then 41." Prechter continued, "In Eisenhower's term, the DJIA hit 734, and it went up and down during subsequent presidencies, until Keegan arrived. It then rose from 1,000 to 2,722 in spite of a transient fall. From then on, there has been a zigzag but a continuous upward movement of the DJIA overall.

"The general public has simply been more aware that their money earns more if placed in stocks and not in bonds. State pension funds, IRAs, personal savings—all got into the picture.

"The peak of 14,164.53 in 2007 was followed by a fall to 6,547 in 2009, but we are now back to about 13,000. More people now participate in the stock market. A precipitous fall is going to be acutely felt. Our chart is looking at a fall toward triple digits. I hope it does not happen."

"I certainly hope not. I can't imagine myself begging," the anchor said.

"Go buy yourself a farm," advised Prechter.

"Not again!" Alain said. "When we first talked about this, it sounded terrible. Hearing it again really brings home the point. I just hope it does not happen."

"We're all trying not to let it happen," Anne said. "The administration discredits any criticism, and claims to have accomplished what they have not done. They claim credit for a future they have not delivered. I cannot imagine people being so egregious, so bent on telling lies without shame. Can you imagine a life outside of our beloved country? By the time we come back, it may be so depraved that we won't recognize it; nor would we really want to come back. Let's do our best to fight where we are. The time to fight back is now."

Anne looked at Higgins. "Well, are we putting out a supplement to Larry Prechter's theory?"

"Like what?" Higgins asked.

"We'll say that it will happen if we let negative karma prevail and cause a downward stock market. Even if the interest rate goes down to zero, if there is continued class warfare and there is no incentive for increased production, we will be like Greece, Spain, and other countries that had to be saved by the EU!"

"Okay! Okay! Gosh! What a fighter! Luke, Levi, and Alain will work with you on the draft," Higgins said.

The whole group worked on the draft that night.

"Maybe we'll strive to make it relatively short and concise, with chart flows and statistics. Then we will post it on the Internet as a YouTube video and also send it to Michael Keegan so he can use it in his soapbox debate."

"Let's do it," Higgins said. "Good call, Anne, guys!"

Anne smiled. They were all becoming aware of each other's gifts and the need to share them for the common goal.

The group then decided to go toward Innsbruck, Austria. The election was just a few days ahead now. Even Higgins was a bit edgy.

"They'd think you're a candidate." Anne couldn't help kidding Higgins when he spilled his coffee answering the phone call.

Higgins was getting used to Anne's bantering now and then, but he had yet to come up with an answer. "Hmm . . . I give up. One day I'll be able to come up with a repartee, Anne. I need to get used to your comments that come out of the blue."

The TV news that night caused more agitation to Higgins. There was a controversy about the early voters.

"Why does the Liberal Party insist on not counting the overseas and military votes now?" the news anchor said. "Is that not the reason why they voted early—so that come Election Day, their votes would be counted with the rest?"

"We have to be sure there is no fraud on those early ballots!" the Liberal Party spokesman said.

"Aren't the overseas and military votes even more fraud-proof because of the strict ID checks?"

"In a way, yes," the Liberal Party spokesman said. "But we insist that they be counted later so as not to hinder the polling place count."

"But it's not affecting the polling place count! What are you talking about?" the anchor said irritably.

"Well, that's our position," the Liberal Party spokesperson insisted lamely.

Alain was mad. "I could slap that idiot if he were nearby."

"I might not want to become a US citizen," Roland said. "Too many idiots are allowed to speak, and it becomes a battle of the dumb and dumber."

Higgins just sat in his chair, sighing. Luke and Levi smiled.

On October 29, one week before the election, calamity struck.

"Superstorm Sandy, a hurricane turned cyclone with a central pressure of 940 millibars, hit the US East Coast Monday evening after killing sixty-nine in the Caribbean Islands," the newscaster reported. "Damage is estimated at more than twenty billion dollars. Thirty-nine more died, seven and a half million people and businesses lost power across fifteen states, and the New York subway system and other transportation systems had to be closed. The governor of New Jersey accompanied the president in touring the devastated area."

"Sellout!" Jim said to the TV monitor.

"Crap!" Mark said.

## 35. The Election

By the time they were in Liechtenstein, it was Election Day in the USA.

"The exit polls reveal toss-up states," Higgins said. "Let's wait for tonight's report and also tomorrow morning," he said, struggling to be patient.

"It's still too close to call," the news anchor said. "It's a toss-up for the battleground states. People will be staying up just to count the votes. Most precincts have poll watchers to be sure that the vote count is correct."

Luke sighed. "Since some polls will close as late as five a.m. our time, maybe only then will they announce the winner. We might as well sleep early and wake up early."

"Unless it's as clear-cut as California going on the Liberal Party's side," Levi said.

"Right," Higgins said. "'Early to bed, early to rise' it is."

They all went to bed.

Higgins, Luke, and Levi were first in the lounge room with their cups of coffee before five o'clock in the morning. Alain, Roland, and the Cortezes arrived at the same time, followed by Andre and Janan.

"It's over," Higgins said. "Olama won."

"The toss-up states mostly went blue," Levi said.

"New York and New Jersey stayed blue even though they didn't have much help when struck by the storm," Luke said.

Anne laid down the cookies and assorted snacks on the coffee table and sat down on a chair. The group sat there feeling dispirited for a while.

Anne sighed. "I don't believe it. I can't believe it. However, it would be impossible for us to sequester those voting machines and compare the registered voter count to the vote count."

"Let's have breakfast first and get on with our tour," Higgins said. "We need to think out our options."

"I have a headache," Andre said. "I'm very disappointed."

"Be patient, Andre," Anne said. "No system is perfect. We might be able to think more clearly after we shake off this defeat." She turned to the older men. "We're all awake now and can start looking around Liechtenstein after breakfast, but how about a nap or rest after lunch? We can resume with a stroll after three p.m. and have a leisurely dinner."

Most felt better after their naps. They had dinner at a nice restaurant and then went back to watch the news. The talk was mostly an analysis of how one party won and how the other lost.

"Let's finish our tour of this place," Higgins said. "We'll just monitor the news wherever we are."

"Where do we go from here?" Alain asked.

"How about meandering through Germany?" Shlomo said. "As long as we don't let our guard down, there are a lot of historical places to see. We can visit the Black Forest and Stuttgart."

They did that and then went north to Heidelberg and Mannheim, west through Luxemburg, and north again through Aachen and Cologne. They came down through central Germany.

They watched TV that night, and Higgins kept changing the TV stations to avoid bad news. They watched a news anchor interviewing a *Wall Street Journal* reporter about the fiscal cliff.

"The fiscal cliff is a scenario that could happen by the end of 2012. That's because last year, in the negotiations to lift the federal debt ceiling, Congress and Mr. Olama set the spending cuts to take effect by year's end. That's December 31, 2012. If no agreement can be reached on how to reduce the deficit, tax cuts dating from the previous administration, and extended by the present administration, are set to expire the same day. Therefore, at the end of the year, spending cuts are set to take effect just as the tax hike begins. That's why a lot of small and big businesses are afraid of a recession."

"What's that?" Roland scratched his head.

Luke explained it to the younger guys.

"Oh . . ." Alain groaned.

Most of them sighed and sat gloomily in their chairs.

"I should run for Congress when I grow up," Andre said.

"Everybody to bed," Higgins said. "This is depressing."

A few days later they heard news of the CIA chief resigning over an affair with a female who was in uniform and who had written his biography. Roland looked up the correspondents' report confirming that the White House had known about the investigation since spring but waited for the election to be over before accepting the resignation.

"Is that why they made a false report about the video, causing four Americans to be murdered?" Mark asked irritably.

"Yes," Higgins replied.

"SOB," Roland said.

"Let's enjoy this tour, but we might want to return to the USA afterward. We need to plan our future," Higgins said.

The others nodded.

"How about you, Shlomo?" Levi asked.

"I have a lot of vacation time," Shlomo said. "I'm not in a hurry. The van will be left in Munich."

By the time they had gone through Hannover, Bremen, and Hamburg, Anne often caught Higgins looking worried. There were times when he was deep in thought as Anne watched him from a distance.

Anne was thankful that the younger men were enjoying the tour by shaking off the Damocles's sword over their heads. The older men with responsibilities and a more visionary outlook were feeling frustrated.

She asked for a consensus on the itinerary. She wanted to pass by Magdeburg, Leipzig, Erfurt, and Eisenach. "Let's see that triptych that Malachi Martin mentioned in his novel."

"Huh?" Roland scratched his head.

"Let's pick up some books too, since we have a leisurely schedule now," Anne added. "We can then continue south through Wurzburg, Nurnberg, and Augsburg before flying out of Munich. Is that all right? We could go west from Eisenach to Frankfurt if you'd rather leave soon."

"Through Munich is fine," Higgins said, realizing that Anne was reading him again.

"Flying out of Munich is actually better." Luke glanced at the map. "We'll make Minneapolis our port of entry and go east toward Richmond, Virginia. We'll stay in my aunt's house until our situation is clarified. Maybe our enemies will not be looking there because it's a different family name. She's from my mother's side."

"I like that," Levi said.

Higgins and Edward nodded.

"I'll fly through Munich to Paris," Shlomo said.

In Munich, they took a stroll at Marienplatz, took more pictures with the Glockenspiel, and then had dinner in the area, along with some wine.

Whenever they were out in the open, the men were armed, but they took risks; otherwise, they'd have been giving up on the beauty of life itself.

They each said their good-byes to Shlomo.

"Thank you, Shlomo, and take care," Anne said as she shook his hand.

"I'm thanking you guys," Shlomo said. "I'm ready to help you whichever way you need me. It took so much courage for you to be able to do what you accomplished. I pray for you and wish you luck! Shalom!"

"Shalom!" they all said.

Shlomo dropped them off at the Munich airport the next day. He would have to drop off the van at the safe house before taking a flight himself.

The group was quiet on the flight back to the USA. The men had no weapons and were a bit tense. They were divided into unlikely pairs, with their cell phones ready. Their port of entry was Minneapolis, and they arrived safely in Richmond, Virginia.

A Cadillac car and a van were ready for them. Luke was handed the keys by an attendant. Luke drove the van, while Levi followed in the car.

The house of Luke's aunt was a huge, walled enclosure with an electronic gate. It had many rooms that were seldom used. His aunt was past eighty years old, a white-haired patrician preferring to stand with her cane, although she sat in a wheelchair if she had to be with people for a longer time.

"Aunt Mary, let me introduce my friends," Luke started.

Aunt Mary was welcoming and gracious. "What a nice bunch of friends you have! You'll have to tell me more about your adventures. After I saw you on TV, you disappeared without telling me."

"I'm sorry, Aunt," Luke apologized. "As you saw on TV, the senators were all right, but the administration wanted to prosecute us, so we had to leave in a hurry."

"What?" she said. "Nonsense! I'll call my lawyer."

"I can only tell you some information, not all, and you know what that means." Luke gave his aunt a look.

"All right, I'll settle for that. Let's have dinner first." Mary Hartford sat in the wheelchair, and Luke pushed it toward the dining room.

There were two dinner entrées: orange-glazed duck and seared salmon with mango sauce, served over wild rice.

"Don't spoil us, Aunt Mary," Luke kidded.

"Oh, you know it's all going to you," she said. "When are you getting married? I'd like to see some grandchildren."

Luke turned red; Higgins and Levi laughed.

"That's off limits, Aunt Mary—highly confidential. I'll let Higgins brief you about our adventure instead."

Higgins had to finish laughing before he gave Mary Hartford a concise summary of their adventure, leaving out some intelligence information that might compromise her.

"I can tell what's in between the lines; I'll probably still need an outside lawyer to request papers through the Freedom of Information Act. I'll get that started," Mary said decidedly; then she laughed. "I'm so glad you are here! Life has been boring."

"Aunt Mary," Luke started.

"Oh, hush!" she said, and she turned to Roland. "I know you too."

Roland was at a loss for words; then he laughed. "Okay, I can't hide."

From there on, they talked about their impressions of the tour, what they'd done on the Internet, and their work with Michael Keegan.

"I knew that somebody I know was doing it! That's exactly what I would have done!" Mary exclaimed.

"You could get in trouble here, Aunt Mary," Luke said.

"That too, but you do have an asset nobody knew about," Mary said with a spark in her eye. "There are still things to do."

Luke looked at Higgins helplessly, but Higgins and Levi were taking Mary seriously. The others looked at his aunt with a mixture of amusement and admiration. Luke sipped his wine and, sighing, decided to keep his peace. He was not ready for his aunt fighting with him instead of him protecting her.

They all went to bed past midnight, after just relaxing with an enjoyable conversation.

Anne felt refreshed after having slept well. She could hear the birds chirping, and the smell of bacon and eggs beaconed her to the kitchen.

"No TV while we eat, but there's one in the next room," Mary said eagerly. "Some of you may still be sleepy; otherwise, there's a tennis court, and I had the swimming pool cleaned. After you are rested, maybe we can still do something. I want to get the facts straight as I join your cause."

Mary was not one to mince words. "We have no proof if there was cheating in this election; it's all gut feeling. As you know, they are good at turning the tables on us, blaming us for what they did wrong and claiming the work we've done as theirs. I've never seen such egregious malice for a long time."

Luke took his coffee to the next room, which looked like a sitting/ lounge room with a TV. Higgins, Levi, and Edward stood up, and everybody else followed to listen to the morning news. Mary gave instructions to the help before she wheeled herself to the next room.

A political pundit was on the air. "Kitt Rooney lost the Hispanic vote because they did not like his immigration policy. Next, Rooney did not articulate a convincing argument to get the women's vote. Rooney also had several other missteps, such as his comment about the forty-seven percent of people whose votes he could not count on. He should have gone down to the gutter politics that his opponent was using, if that was the only way to get through to the consciousness of the voters. Instead of keeping the argument on the economy, his opponents just painted him as an unbelievably evil person who fired people and sent jobs abroad.

"He did not attack Olama on the Libya fiasco in which four Americans died. The U.S.A. demonstrated pure ineptness to act, or there may be something more sinister. The CIA director was already being investigated since spring and did not resign until after the election. Our government has a situation room and knew from the offshoot that the Benghazi attack was by terrorists. Our ambassador to the UN made the rounds of TV stations, proclaiming that the attack was related to an anti-Islam video. Who ordered her to do that? I'd also like to know who gave the order to stand down. That coward is the murderer of our men at the Benghazi consulate.

"Lastly, Superstorm Sandy came around, and TV stations showed Olama with the New Jersey governor, touring the stricken area. It did not show them helping, just walking around. People bought it, oblivious of the third-world conditions those people in New Jersey and New York would be suffering from." The pundit looked grim.

"So this is Monday morning quarterbacking," the news anchor said. "Do you think the Nationalist will ever win a presidential election again?"

"I won't hazard a guess," the pundit replied. "They are now talking about averting the fiscal cliff, but neither side has budged from their previous positions. We will be facing a recession—and, worse, maybe another depression. I'm so disgusted that I want to give up this line of work. Maybe I should be working for their newly created Consumer Financial Protection Bureau. The head of the bureau was installed as a recess appointee, and out of 958 employees, sixty percent of them make $100,000 a year. This offshoot of the Dodd-Frank Act has not accomplished anything, yet they have an annual budget of half a billion dollars."

"Right!" The news anchor also sounded agitated. "Those two idiots are not in Congress anymore, but they sure left a mess. We should enact a law to make those clowns pay!"

Luke changed to another station, but it was another political analysis. He changed the TV station again to hear instead about the DJIA falling some more. The next station showed the storm victims who were still without electric power. Another station showed an interview with a former nun who had become an MD and a lawyer. She had spoken out against the administration, and then her job contract had not been renewed.

"I quit," Luke said, and he sat on the sofa. "What do you guys want to do?"

"Actually, if we have a foundation, we should help that ex-nun," Anne said.

"Right!" Mary said.

"Let's get back to the business channel," Edward said worriedly. "The Dow Jones is now down to 10,000."

"Why don't we just have a relaxing day?" Anne said. "Maybe the guys can go for a swim or play tennis; then we can play table games."

Luckily for them, it had warmed up a bit and it was a sunny day. After sweating it out at tennis, the gloom was lifted among the younger men, and they were in a better mood. They stayed up late that night, playing table games.

Most of them woke up for brunch the next morning, and Higgins soon went to the sitting room to watch the TV news. Anne exchanged glances with Mary, Luke, and Levi. Higgins was obviously preoccupied with a lot of problems—not just their situation, but also his other responsibilities.

The group followed Higgins to the lounge room, where he sat watching the TV news with a faraway look.

"We need to make constructive plans for our future," Anne said, interrupting his reverie. "We will be captured the moment we set foot in our house. Under our assumed names, we can buy a different house in another state. I would need somebody I trust to help me remove my important papers and things from the house. The rest will have to be done by a mover."

"I have to check my assets and accounts so I can liquidate those that will be cumbersome to own," Edward said.

"I won't go back to my house in Alexandria," Higgins said. "I have another apartment in Washington, DC, which is registered under an assumed name. Luke and Levi also have other condos."

"You guys can stay in any of our other apartments and condos here, on the East Coast, or in California," Luke said.

"You are all welcome to stay here forever," Mary said seriously. "If you are Luke's family, then you are my family too. I could not see eye to eye with his sister, Amanda, and Luke has been like my son since his mother died. I've been pretty lonely since you people went around the globe on account of that Stuxnet hullabaloo. I would just love to join the fray.

"Anne and Edward, Andre and Janan, why don't you start your house search from here? It would be easier if things are set to go by the time you leave."

"Oh," Anne said. "I meant to get a security system for the house while we were away but just did not get around to it."

"It's done." Luke smiled. "I arranged for it when they took Edward to prison."

"Thanks." Anne smiled. "No wonder you always have all those papers around you."

"You're welcome," Luke said. "As a matter of fact, I've done a preliminary check of a house in the San Diego area for the Senawis. I'm checking first if we can get it under Andre's assumed name if he likes it."

"Where?" Andre suddenly brightened up. "Show me, Luke!" He and Janan eagerly went toward Luke's computer.

"Roland and Alain can stay with any one of us guys," Higgins said. "They could also choose to buy their own houses wherever they please with their reward money, using their assumed names. Just avoid living near Washington, DC, for it could get dicey if those bad guys decide to prosecute us.

"All of us could have made a living by investing in the stock market, but times have changed. Whether the fiscal cliff happens or not, I am too well aware of the 2016 prediction. We have to stay short in the market. Over and beyond our own problems, however, I have this nagging sense that we have to release a countermand to the Stuxnet cyberworm. I'll feel selfish if I don't do something, because we are the ones who are aware of this prediction, and therefore we have the responsibility to solve it."

"You are obsessed with this responsibility, Richard," Anne said worriedly. "It's different when we are trying to do something good but an adverse administration turns against us instead."

"Would you do otherwise?" Richard Higgins asked.

"No," Anne answered candidly. "I've simply put it on the back burner because I can't see the light on how to solve it."

"I need to get my original disc in the safe," Higgins said. "That would be a big help for us to solve it."

"It's still too dangerous, Richard!" Anne argued. "Those guys will be drunk with power by now."

"We need to work on it soon; the clock is ticking," Higgins said. "Being able to stay in any of our safe houses should be okay at first, but after a while, our younger men might get restless and get into trouble. I've actually considered moving to Texas for all of us."

"Huh?" the young men said in unison.

Higgins explained. "In Texas we can carry arms and can be certain that our neighbors will protect us and have the guts to do it too. Okay, let's all think about it for a few days and try to come up with solutions."

"Why don't we eat an early supper on the patio tonight?" Mary said. "Then you can do your house search before we tackle the Stuxnet II."

"Thank you," Anne said with a smile.

That night all of them were busy looking at homes. Streams of copy paper were coming out of the printer as each of them made comparisons among the different choices.

Alain and Roland searched for homes too, but the other younger men were discussing their predicament. Pretty soon they were back to talking about legal matters and ethics. Andre had a pile of books he'd taken from the house library, so did Alain and Roland. Higgins, Luke, and Levi were back on their in-service mode.

It was a lively discussion, with the older ones exchanging opinions and sharing them with the younger ones. They were up quite late that night, and the younger ones began to have a better comprehension of what laws applied to their situation.

Most of them ended up choosing some books from the house library.

"This thing is getting on my nerves," Roland said. "I'm getting to the bottom of it."

"Choosing a house, arranging the papers, and waiting for it to be ready will take some time," Luke said. "Settle down and be patient. You need to visit the house before you buy it." He was addressing Alain and Roland, who got tired of their search and played table games instead.

"I did not know that it gets pretty intense," Alain said. "I'll take a break."

Most of them were now looking at Texas, and they decided to be within a close distance of each other. The Cortezes would need extra rooms for Aunt Mary and everybody else, just in case they came under attack again.

"It seems that we need another walled compound," Higgins said.

"There's really nothing suitable for our needs," Levi said. "I'm for building something out of what is there, rather than building a new one."

"Ohhh!" Anne said. "I'm having a headache, but you are right. We're back to looking for a fortress."

"I don't know if we should look for a large acreage with an open space or something with a lot of trees." Mark looked up from his computer screen. "Each kind of layout has its own disadvantage."

"Be patient," Mary said. "We're fine where we are right now."

"Since we do have to wait here before we can move," Higgins proposed, "we will have to divide the labor once again. Luke will put up part of our cash assets in the stock market, and we will do some trading to make money. While the older group supervises our younger group regarding stock and options trade, the others will continue the house search. If it's okay with Aunt Mary, we will add more fitness equipment in the basement so we can all stay fit through the winter. Let's keep a regular schedule with the usual rest on weekends."

"I agree," Mary said.

Higgins, Levi, and Anne gave the younger members a crash course and made them work on simulated trading. Luke transferred money into one of Mary's accounts, and he and Alain started trading. Edward watched the stock market news and stock gyrations.

By the November expiration of the options trade, the account managed by Anne made $1 million.

"Way to go!" Higgins said. "You're a gutsy trader, Anne."

"We have the advantage of paying attention to the news and knowing what to expect," Anne said modestly. "Let's not rest on our laurels. It's going to be a choppy market."

That Saturday, Anne addressed some concerns. "It's getting cold. We need to shop for warmer clothing and sweaters for everybody. We must also stock up the food pantry and prepare our Thanksgiving feast."

Levi and Edward went with the ladies to Petersburg, Virginia.

"It's big enough and far enough from Richmond that people will not easily make the connection," Levi said.

They bought warmer clothing for everybody, along with pumpkin pie, seafood, lamb, and specialty food for Anne's stuffed chicken recipe.

"Even if we have a turkey dinner, I'll still cook the stuffed chicken, which my sons like. It's a Spanish recipe from my mother," Anne said.

"I'd like that," Janan said. "Also, Andre wants some lamb."

# 36. Higgins's Quest

That Sunday, they went to church in a small town and relaxed. They rewarded themselves with a good dinner and champagne. The young men were ebullient, as they'd also made good profits from their stock trades.

"Remember," Higgins cautioned, "money can be earned and lost. This is a good way to earn a living, but we have to be on our toes and always read up on the news, both domestic and international. Also, we have to read in between the lines."

They earned more even during the short week before Thanksgiving.

The temperature dropped, but it did not dampen their spirits. They celebrated like a big, happy family.

"Happy Thanksgiving!" they greeted each other.

Anne and Janan were in the kitchen most of the time, cooking different treats. Mary gladly gave a suggestion here and there.

Lucinda, the cook, was happily learning some tips from Anne when the phone rang. As though anticipating it, she picked it up and beamed after putting it down.

"She has a special someone!" Mary teased.

Lucinda smiled but did not tell them anything.

"I'm stuffed," Jim complained. "I should not have touched the cheesecake after I ate the pumpkin pie."

The other guys just grunted. They had eaten the turkey with all the trimmings at lunch; then they had the stuffed chicken for supper, which was actually another dinner with all the trimmings. In between, they watched movies and football on TV.

The younger guys were sitting in different positions in the lounge room, obviously contented but too full to be really awake.

Levi couldn't help laughing at the younger guys. "Take it easy, guys. Sleep earlier if necessary. Obviously the food was too good."

Alain started playing some favorite songs on the piano, and they had fun doing sing-along songs, especially Mary. After ten o'clock, the young men were just too sleepy; they went to bed like contented cats.

Mary was first at breakfast the next morning. "You have to help me put up the Christmas tree," she said to Anne and Janan.

"You plotted this all along, didn't you?" Anne said with a grin. "Oh my goodness," she suddenly said. "I need to buy my Christmas cards, stamps, and presents! We really lost track of time! I don't have the complete list of addresses."

"We'll get started tomorrow—oh, happy day!" Mary said.

They all laughed. They spent the day just relaxing. Alain, Mark, and Jim alternated on the piano or played table games. Higgins played chess with Levi. Edward, Andre, and Roland looked at more houses on the Internet. Luke was busy with his papers, as usual. Anne, Mary, and Janan started bringing out the Christmas decorations.

The next day, Anne and Janan got ready to go shopping. The young men were sleeping in.

"We need more cold-weather things for us, and we need some things for Aunt Mary," Anne said.

"Luke and Edward will go with you," Higgins said. "I need to pick up some things in my Arlington office. Levi and Alain will come with me."

"Is it safe yet?" Anne stopped in her tracks. "Those guys were really vicious. Could you have the place combed or whatever first?"

"I've already sent a preliminary team," Higgins said. "They said it is okay. Even if the opponents won the election, we need to do the Stuxnet II. I'll get the disc containing the blueprint of the Stuxnet cyberworm. I feel that this is the only way to counter the Gauss virus."

"Richard, I know you're obsessed with it, but can it wait? I'm just not comfortable with that," Anne persisted. "We've been attacked in your DC office and your compound. Is a preliminary team enough?"

"Yes, Anne!" Higgins said. "You worry too much! We'll be back even before you are done with all your shopping. Buy me an extra box of cards, please."

Anne frowned. She impulsively went over to Higgins and buzzed his cheek. "You be careful."

"Hey! When do I get a kiss?" Levi asked.

Anne just smiled and pointed to Higgins. "That guy's stubborn."

Higgins and company took the car.

Luke drove the van with Edward and the ladies to Petersburg, Virginia. The light snow mixed with the cold, blustery wind, and they shivered a bit in their sweaters.

"It's really quite cold," Edward said.

"Do we need to buy coats?" Anne wondered aloud. "At the rate that Aunt Mary is going, we might not be able to leave, not that it's an unpleasant thought."

"Buy coats," Luke said.

Anne looked at Luke with consternation. "You know your aunt that well, huh?"

"I wonder if our purchases will fit in the van!" Janan said. "There are eleven of us, and with more warm clothing and presents . . ."

"We'd better not forget the smaller things," Anne said. "How about the Christmas cards and stamps first, or else we will forget those. I don't have my complete address book, but with you guys and Aunt Mary, would a dozen boxes be enough?" she asked Luke.

"Oh! Make that fourteen, then. I have no idea," Luke said.

They picked up the stamps and cards first.

After lunch at a small café, Luke checked with his aunt. She asked him to get some croissants and cocoa for the next day.

"Okay," Luke said. "I'll get some popcorn and chips for the guys too."

"We're supposed to think about that! On another shopping day maybe!" Anne said, and she exchanged amused glances with Janan.

"Don't forget more ice cream," Edward said.

The ladies burst out laughing.

"What's funny?" Edward asked.

"It's cold and snowing! But you really have a sweet tooth, Edward," Anne said.

It was almost three o'clock in the afternoon when they finished up and loaded the van.

"We're heading back. Did Higgins call?" Luke called his aunt.

"Not recently. The last time he called was when they were parking the car at the Arlington office." Mary sounded worried.

"What time was that?" Luke said.

"That was before noon. I wanted to call you earlier, but I felt like a worrywart."

"I'll call them right now. Take proper precaution there. Tell Mark, Jim, Roland, and Andre to make sure everybody is safe," Luke said. He pressed the numbers on his cell phone to call Higgins. There was no answer. He called Levi, and then Alain. There was no answer.

They all turned pale in the van. Luke called the Arlington police.

Anne called Mark. "Higgins, Levi, and Alain are not answering their cell phones. Have any of you heard from them? No? Take proper precautions, and be armed. Take care of Aunt Mary. Luke said there is a safety room in the house. One of you guard just outside of it so we don't lose contact on the cell phone. Wait . . . Go in. Luke said there's a land line in the safe room. He knows the number. Please check it. Come out to make a call if that phone is not working. Take the computer with you."

"The Arlington police is not aware of any problem in the vicinity of Higgins's office," Luke said worriedly. "It is not possible for three cell phones to not be working. I'll have to drop off you ladies first. Edward and I also need the younger guys with us. I don't trust anybody else."

"Luke, if your aunt's house is on the way, fine; if not, Janan and I can take a cab if it saves you guys some time. Mark, Jim, Roland, and Andre can use our cab to catch up with you and Edward," Anne said worriedly.

"It's on the way," Luke said, stepping on the gas. "Besides, I feel better knowing that you ladies are together and safe."

"Okay," Anne conceded. "I'll call Mark to check if the phone land line is working . . . It is. Mark? We are coming over so your dad and Luke can pick you guys up. Have your weapons ready, and leave some for us . . . Okay. Bye . . . I'm calling the DC police. Edward, will you give me the number from your iPhone? . . . There is no report about anything regarding Higgins . . . I'll call those guys again . . . No answer."

Janan and the others were silent the rest of the way while Anne kept calling Higgins's, Levi's, and Alain's cell phones.

As soon as they entered the compound of Luke's aunt, Mark's head bobbed out of his hiding place; then Jim, Roland, and Andre unloaded the packages. Their weapons were ready, and they left after kissing Anne's cheeks. She gave them a blessing.

The ladies hurriedly brought the packages inside the door and locked it. They brought food, lamps, and a radio to the safe room and locked it. The long wait began. They spoke in whispers.

"I wish we could be there to help, but they would end up worrying about us and would just be hampered by our presence." Anne sighed.

Aunt Mary was in a cushioned seat, looking frail now that she could not control the situation. "What could have happened?" she asked.

"Let's check if our cell phones work here, Janan. I'll call your number," Anne said, and she pressed the keys. "It's not working. They can communicate with us only through the land line. We have food for three days. Where's the cook, Aunt Mary?"

"She asked for a day off today," Mary said. "I was surprised since she usually just stays in the servants' quarters for weeks. She has a home there with TV and everything she needs, and she just did some shopping the other week."

"Does she use the Internet? Does she know about the safe room? How long has she been in your employ?" Anne asked.

"One at a time," Mary protested. "She was learning to use the Internet and confided to me that she has a new friend. I suspect that this person wants to have a relationship with her."

"Does she know about the safe room?" Anne asked gently.

"No. I don't think so," Mary said. "You see, she is the daughter of our trusted help, and her grandparents worked for us before that. Her grandparents knew about the safe room from way back, but we told her parents that we discontinued using the safe room because it was full of water. We have not mentioned the safe room at all to her."

Anne suddenly raised a finger across her lips. The sound they heard was first a soft, scratching sound—the footsteps of somebody trying to walk in a stealthy way. Then they heard steady, heavy footsteps on the floor above them. Anne's eyes widened, and she held Mary's and Janan's hands, pursing her lips. She opened her mouth to let out her breath without making a sound, and she showed Mary and Janan how to do it.

Two more sets of footsteps came; one set was heavy and slow, while the other was a regular, medium cadence. The last set belonged to somebody who walked quickly and carelessly, toppling a stool to the floor. Then the cook's voice could be heard.

"They must have all of a sudden left; I don't know why. The cars are all gone."

"Did you warn them?" a voice asked.

"I did not even know what your plan was," the cook said in a whimper, as though in pain. "How could I warn them? What are you doing, anyway?"

"It's none of your business! Somebody wants those people out of the way," the voice said.

"What for? They don't harm nobody!" the cook said indignantly.

The voice disregarded her. "When are they coming back?"

"I don't know. You told me to ask for an off day, so they did not have a chance to tell me what they were doing. Maybe they went to New York for Christmas."

"Do you know what hotel they usually stay in?"

"No, they stay in different hotels," the cook said.

"Let's go! There's nothing to do here. Our boss might want us to help out in Arlington."

"What's in Arlington?" the cook asked.

"Well, baby, them guys got even with that other boss, but I hear they might have not finished up smoothly. Maybe we should tell our boss now . . . Hello? Boss, there's nobody here; they all left . . . No, there was no warning. Maybe they suddenly decided to go to New York. That's what the cook here said, like they always do that . . . Okay, we're coming to Arlington . . . Not there? Where? . . . Alexandria, the cemetery—and bring plows. Will do, boss. Yes . . ."

Anne tried her best not to make a sound as tears fell onto her cheeks. The footsteps receded, and there was silence. Anne presumed those people had left the house. She waited. Suddenly there was the simultaneous sound of a gunshot and a bloodcurdling shriek.

Mary and Janan were in shock, and Anne waited for a while to make sure there was nobody else around.

She dialed noiselessly on the land line, calling Luke's cell phone.

"Try the Alexandria cemetery. We're okay," she whispered.

Luke had driven at full speed to Arlington after picking up the four young men. "There's six of us against we don't know how many. We only have M-16 submachine guns, revolvers, and grenades against we don't know what. Whatever training you've had will be put to the test now. Let's hope it is not too late to save them. Roland, keep calling our guys' numbers. Mark, keep your phone line open; your mom will be calling you or me."

They arrived at Higgins's office building in Arlington and surveyed it from the van, without getting out first. Luke got out of the van after it looked clear, and then Edward and the others followed. Roland and Jim walked behind Luke, and Andre and Mark walked behind Edward. Luke's group went into the building while Edward's group patrolled the grounds and the foyer. There was no sign of Higgins, Levi, or Alain.

"They would have left a clue or dropped a sign if they'd come inside. Let's stay together, arms ready. Roland, call Edward and the others to come up. Jim, you'll be the lookout; I'll look farther inside." Luke came right back with a ghastly look. He waited for Edward's group to come inside and then led them to Higgins's inner office.

Inside a small storage-like area was the body of a uniformed guard. There was a stab wound to the heart, and the blood that had gushed out was now caked and black. The corpse was already stiff.

In another inner room, there was a safe in its enclave within the wall. It lay open and empty; a painting was on the floor.

"The guard must have been attacked right after he said that the coast was clear," Luke said. "Higgins spoke to him yesterday. After they talked, Higgins said that he would be coming, without specifying when. I'm not sure that Higgins, Alain, and Levi were here, but only Higgins could open this safe, with a code that neither Levi nor I know. If it is forcibly opened, it will blow up and destroy all the secrets with it. I'm sure that the bad guys have been lying in wait for them. If this office looks undisturbed, our clue might be just outside the building or in the parking lot."

Just then his cell phone rang.

"That was Anne. She whispered, 'Alexandria cemetery,' and said that they are okay. Oh! I don't know if we should split up so that some of us can make sure the ladies are safe," Luke said.

"If Mom says she's okay, then we can proceed to the Alexandria cemetery," Mark said. "Of course we'll communicate with her, but I think only the land line is working now. She did not answer when I first called on her cell phone."

"All right, let's go directly to the cemetery, then," Luke said.

It was just after five o'clock in the afternoon, but it was late November and the sun was already setting.

"Do we have flashlights?" Luke asked as he parked the car.

"Two. They have stands, but they are small," Mark said, turning one on and giving it to Edward and then turning on the other, which he carried.

They headed for the cemetery grounds, uncertain at first regarding the direction.

"Wait!" Jim went toward his dad and turned off the light. Mark did the same with his.

They listened and, in the descending darkness, turned toward where they could hear the sound of digging. They tried to walk noiselessly toward the diggers, but the fallen leaves made a crunching noise when they stepped on them. The howling wind, however, camouflaged their sound, and the rustling sounds of dried leaves being blown by the wind helped even more.

Luke advanced with Roland and Edward, guns pointing at the diggers. "Stop! Who are you?" Luke said.

For an answer, one digger turned to hit Luke with his plow. Luke barely got out of the way. The other diggers pulled out their guns, but Mark and Roland had their M-16 rifles ready and killed the four diggers.

Just then the four men who had come from Aunt Mary's house arrived.

"Hands up!" they said to Luke, Edward, and Roland, but Mark, Jim, and Andre were behind them.

"Hands up!" Mark said.

The four men turned around to face Mark, but he readily unloaded his M-16 on them.

Mark stood transfixed for a while, somehow realizing he had become one of the killers now.

Luke came toward him and held him by the shoulder. "Sooner or later it happens."

Mark nodded and tried to shake off his shock.

They all proceeded to check on what the bad guys had been doing.

"They were burying somebody or some bodies. Hurry!" Luke raised the lamp over the excavation.

"Oh God!" Jim said when the light shone on some covered figures.

Luke jumped on one side, and Edward on the other. They both lifted the wrapped bodies and handed one after another to the younger men, who in turn got busy uncovering the figures.

"It's Higgins! Oh my God!" Mark felt for the pulse, but Higgins was just staring, lifeless. "He's gone," Mark said in a choked voice.

"Hurry! Check the others!" Luke said as he and Edward climbed up from the hole.

"This one is Alain! He still has a pulse!" Jim said.

Luke immediately called 911 on his cell phone. "Mark and Roland, stand guard! We don't know if there are enemies out there still. How's Levi?"

"Barely alive!" Andre said.

"Well, well!" said a voice behind Luke. Three men were standing in the shadows.

"What more do you want?' Luke said angrily, turning to the thugs.

Roland had already stepped backward as the three men went forward to face Luke.

"Your lives, of course!" The speaker moved to press his AK-47 trigger.

Roland was faster. The speaker did not get farther than a twitch of his hand. Roland unloaded his M-16 bullets on the three.

There was a noise from behind a tree. Mark let out a burst from his M-16, and a body fell to the ground.

"Damn! Are there any more?" Luke asked, picking up an AK-47 nearby.

There was another noise from behind Roland. They all hit the ground, but Luke dived while still looking up and unleashed a fusillade of bullets toward the area. They heard a grunt and a whimper; then another body collapsed face-down on the ground.

Luke pressed the emergency numbers on his cell phone again. "There's been a shoot-out at the Alexandria cemetery," he said. "Send police and ambulances ASAP."

"Isn't it a rather long wait?" Mark said in a worried tone. "Shall we bring them to the hospital ourselves?"

"Okay," Luke said. He went back to the van and moved it closer to where they stood. "Why don't we open up those wraps and see if there is any bleeding we can stop while we wait. Line them all up on one blanket, and use the other for cover. I'll take the third."

"Levi's pulse is getting weak," Mark said. "He has a bullet wound on the stomach. Jim, do the heart resuscitation while I put a pressure band on this wound."

"Alain's wound is on the right side of the chest. He is having difficulty of breathing now," Roland said.

Mark moved over to Alain. "Andre, take one light, and would you run to the van to get the medical kit? I think we need an airway for Alain."

They did what they could, sweating as they hurried.

"Mark and Jim, stay with the wounded," Luke said, picking up some pairs of gloves from the kit. "We're putting on gloves. Andre, empty all our men's pockets, and put their belongings in one place. Roland, do the same with our opponents' pockets," Luke said calmly. "We're taking those with us. Edward and I will take the contents from these guys' cars. I'm looking for what they took from Higgins." Luke took one lamp and motioned to Edward, giving him a pair of gloves.

They went to the cars used by their opponents and emptied each of their contents, including papers from the glove compartment. Among the three cars, they found the M-16 rifles of Higgins, Levi, and Alain. They also found scattered reams of paper. The blanket used to hold the items was full and heavy. Luke and Edward placed it in their van and hurried back to the others.

"Ten minutes have passed without an ambulance," Mark said.

"Let's load them up and drive to the hospital ourselves," Luke said grimly. "Let Roland hold his M-16, with me in the front; the rest can help resuscitate those guys. Gotta go! Hurry!"

They loaded up the bodies quickly. Luke stepped on the gas.

"Near the medical kit is a siren light. If you can find it, that will be some help. Roland, place the siren light on our van roof. Don't worry—there's a magnet on it."

Andre handed Roland the siren light, and soon enough, the traffic parted for them all the way to the hospital.

Luke stopped the van right at the emergency entrance. Mark jumped out of the van and ran to the surgery section.

"Help! I have several critically wounded patients!" Mark directed his plea to the sitting surgeon.

They both picked up stretchers and wheeled them out to meet the patients being brought out of the van.

"Straight to OR! Code blue!" the surgeon shouted, and all of a sudden, other doctors and nurses came rushing back and forth.

Luke took care of the registration and paperwork, Edward stood guard just outside, Roland and Andre sat on one side with their M-16s ready, and Mark and Jim helped with the personnel traffic, explaining what the emergency was about.

"There was a shoot-out at the Alexandria cemetery."

The next day, the news headline was: Spies Shoot It Out at Alexandria Cemetery. The article read: "Surprisingly, the bullets were mostly from M-16s; only a few were from AK-47s. The authorities could not explain the events. There was no paper trail; in fact, there were no ID papers."

Mark had called by ten o'clock that night to tell Anne that the ladies should sit tight in the safe room. Later, Roland told the ladies that the men would be coming home and asked them to stay in the safe room until they arrived. The men arrived at past three o'clock in the morning, waking up the ladies who had dozed on and off while waiting.

When Luke saw the cook's body in the front yard, he and Edward put on gloves, wrapped the body in a blanket from the cook's house, and took it by van to the river, where they dumped it.

"Sorry, but it is already very difficult to explain things. I don't want the police here," Luke said.

Anne cried when she looked at her sons, Roland, and Andre. "Sooner or later, you lose your innocence and suddenly become a man you thought you'd never be. Just remember that it was a case of 'kill or be killed'."

They formed a circle, with their arms on each other's shoulders, and prayed for Higgins, Levi, and Alain. They also asked for forgiveness for themselves and for God's mercy and blessing.

They were all sad; then Anne realized that everybody must be hungry. They ate an improvised meal the ladies cooked up and then went to bed.

None of them could really sleep, and they came down for a late lunch of leftover food. They moved listlessly, pervaded by a sense of gloom.

"I have called my other lawyer to request records of the 911 and police calls from yesterday. I want to know if indeed they did not receive your call," Mary Hartford announced, wearing a black dress and her cameo pin, drinking her second cup of coffee.

Luke sat stunned, still unable to accept the loss. Roland was angry and grim. Anne's eyes were red, and she looked pale and tired. Janan and Andre were openly crying. Mark's eyes were red, but he was also very angry. Jim and Edward sat forlornly.

"We missed Sunday Mass just when we really needed to go," Anne said. "Let's just pray here for Richard. He was like a father to us." She started crying again.

Mark sat beside Anne, holding his mother's shoulder, letting her cry; then they said a prayer for Higgins, Levi, and Alain.

Luke called the hospital. "Alain is still in critical condition, but they might transfer Levi to the floor this afternoon. We can visit then."

"How safe is that?" Anne asked. "Sorry, I don't really know what we can do. Just imagine how many times Levi and Alain had to be operated on. Remember when we had to move Higgins? Is that a factor again?"

Luke looked at Anne. "I was thinking about that too. I suspect that Aunt Mary will find out that the police purposely left us out to hang last night. We're back to square one, and it will be like this for four years, even if we use assumed names. We can't even use a witness protection program.

"We might have to move Levi and Alain, and I'll ask you guys to stay here until that time too. We need to reinforce this estate. I don't even like the idea of Aunt Mary needing all that protection, but it cannot be avoided."

"I'm already old, Luke; I can take it," Mary assured him.

"Thank you, Aunt Mary. Believe it or not, we've been making fortresses out of the houses we've stayed in."

"Just remember, I've lived a life with some danger too. I'll be all right," she said with a smile.

The phone rang. Luke picked it up. "I'll come and identify the body. Also, I'm considered next of kin; the papers are in his lawyer's office. My memory fails me about the attorney's name. We will make the funeral arrangements ourselves. What time? Can you make that flexible? I'll be coming from the funeral home. Thank you."

The others looked at Luke.

"That was some kind of unusual morgue. I did not expect them to finish Higgins's autopsy so soon and give me a time to come. Here's the phone ID. Somebody write down this number: 202-927-7885 . . . What's that, Mark? Not the mortuary."

"All right, everybody, take on your guard positions. Get the armaments out. Aunt Mary and ladies, go to the safe room."

"No!" Mary Hartford said angrily.

"Please!" Luke gave her the look.

Anne took one of the old lady's arms, and Janan took the other. Anne grabbed some snacks, and they descended to the safe room.

The ladies could hear the men running for the armaments and taking positions. The attack started within a few minutes. It began with a blast, which was the electronic gate being blown by a car bomb that was used as a battering ram.

Three jeeps then raced inside the compound through the opening. Luke was on the second floor, and he aimed a grenade at the first jeep. Edward and Roland each threw a grenade on the other jeeps. Mark, Jim, and Andre unleashed continuous M-16 rounds on each jeep. Some men jumped out of exploding jeeps, but there was no mercy from the M-16 rifles that cut them all down. There was no movement from the three jeeps after that.

"Please maintain positions," Luke said to his team. "I don't trust these people."

True enough, the next vehicle that came charging was something else. The group's grenades bounced off the armor-plated car. The enemies inside were carrying RPGs, but they impatiently fired even with their car speeding forward. Their aim was widely off. One RPG hit the back wall; the other landed near the gazebo. The men inside the car got impatient and came out of the car.

That was just what Luke and company were waiting for. They mowed down the people as they came out. Not sure if there were still people inside the car, Roland crept between the cement garden urns and threw a hand grenade inside the car. He earned a bruise on his shoulder from a piece of flying metal when the car exploded.

Luke kept them in position for another thirty minutes. "Okay. Edward and I will stand guard for twenty minutes. Mark and Jim, pack your things and then take our positions. Roland and Andre, get the ladies out and tell them to pack—twenty minutes only. Leave your weapons where you can easily pick them up. Go!"

They kept standing guard while the others took turns packing. They loaded their things in the van, right on top of the things from the cemetery. They also brought the newly purchased things, the extra room made possible because three persons were not with them. Aunt Mary was excited, and Anne and Janan had to help her pack.

"I have a folding wheelchair; let's take that," Mary said.

"Okay, but we'll come back, Aunt Mary," Luke explained. "Just bring your essential things. Right now we have to leave because we can't protect you with a breached wall. I'll notify the local police."

"Give me a few seconds," Roland said, sprinting to the maid's quarters. He came back with the cook's computer. "I don't have to work from scratch; this will tell me a lot of things."

## 37. Averting a Prediction

Luke drove quickly out of the compound and headed east. When they passed the Virginia boundary, Luke paused to make some phone calls before they proceeded.

"Where are we going?" Aunt Mary could not help asking.

"New York," Luke said. "We'll use my condo hideout. It's under an alias that only Higgins and Levi knew. It has four rooms and four bathrooms, believe it or not. We'll be a little crowded, but we'll manage."

The condo was in Midtown Manhattan, facing Central Park. Judging from the papers that were on every table, it had to be a bachelor's lair.

"Ahhh . . ." Anne said when she entered, and Luke reddened. "Give us a chance to separate Luke's papers on one side, guys, while you bring up the things from the van.

"Aunt Mary, please take care of putting Luke's things in his room," Anne said with a smile as she handed her the heap of papers. "We'll clear some areas for our own stuff. Looks like Luke had been working on something; we don't want to mess it up."

The ladies hurriedly tried to clean one room after another while the men unloaded. Anne vacuumed, and Janan followed with wipes to get the dust off. They then cleared a section in the foyer area for the things from the cemetery.

"We'll do the bedding later," Anne said with a sigh. All their stuff was littered on the floor.

"So I'm in one room," Luke counted. "Roland can room with me or sleep on the sofa. Aunt Mary can take one room, either with or without Janan, or Janan can room with Andre. Edward and Anne will be in one room, and Jim and Mark will be in the last room, either with or without Andre."

"I'll room with Mark and Jim!" Andre said happily.

"Okay." Luke smiled. "Let's put the baggage in the assigned rooms; then we'll go out to eat."

"Oh! That's why I was feeling hungry." Andre looked out the window.

"Let's eat nearby," Luke said, "where we can see Central Park. We can take a short stroll afterward, with proper precaution. We are carrying weapons."

"Central Park! Finally, I'm here!" Roland said.

"Me too!" Andre said.

They had dinner in a restaurant with a view of the park. Luke then assisted his aunt in taking a stroll with her cane. The younger men walked deeper inside the park, with the direction of Edward, Anne, and Janan.

"Not too far, guys," Anne said.

All the men were armed, but even so, the ebullience of youth could be seen, with Andre laughing as the younger men ran back and forth on the quaint little bridges.

They bought pretzels on the way back, along with some chestnuts.

"We have cereal for tomorrow until we get a chance to shop," Luke told the ladies.

They returned to the condo feeling a little relaxed; then they sorted the things from the cemetery.

"Let's examine everything thoroughly," Luke instructed. "If you have doubts about something, check with me, please."

"I have the stack of IDs here, their money, and other personal things. You've seen the papers from Higgins's office." Roland sat back.

"The opponents' weapons were AK-47s, revolvers, and grenades," Luke said. "Their ID papers were from Iran and other foreign countries; maybe some were mercenaries, even some Hispanics.

"There's a container here of something that looks like a chemical, plus some gauze cloths. Maybe they chloroformed our guys and then tried to interrogate them. Was there an order to just bury our men? I don't understand it. We will enter those IDs on the Interpol database; maybe we can see some light from that angle.

"The cars were rentals, paid for with green money; but an ID had to be produced for the car to be released, so we can work on that angle too. However, I have a problem. I've been through our men's things, but they don't have what I'm looking for."

"What are you looking for?" Anne asked.

"I'm looking for the blueprint of the Stuxnet cyberworm. Maybe Higgins told you, but for the others, let me explain. You see, our group in the USA was involved in creating this cyberworm to counter the nuclear plant at Natanz, Iran. It took quite a while to create it, and Higgins was aware that there was still a flaw: it needed to have a defense before being released. Higgins was due for retirement when the cyberworm was released without the flaw being fixed. Without a defense, the malware could be used against us, whereby it could disrupt our defense, financial, and currency systems.

"When Anne and Mark came around, Higgins could not believe his luck. Instead of a simple deterrent, the disc from Dr. Senawi, and all the decoding that our team worked on, accomplished the disablement of the nuclear plant. Of course the team of physicists and nuclear scientists was there, but Anne and Mark brought a breakthrough we did not expect. Higgins couldn't have been happier when we disabled the Natanz and Fordow nuclear plants.

"When he heard of the Gauss virus, at first it did not ring a bell, but when he looked up Kaspersky Lab, Higgins recognized his old Russian nemesis. These people knew what they were talking about, and Higgins felt that they were sending him a message, asking for help.

"You see, disruptions of commerce have already begun in Israel, Lebanon, and Palestine; then the malware probably went on a sleep mode, lurking somewhere, ready to strike.

"The mathematical calculations in Stuxnet were so complex that a little tweaking of Stuxnet by diabolical hands could create a boomerang malware that would destroy data with numbers.

"So Higgins had a nagging feeling that Gauss was the mutated version of the Stuxnet gone awry. Aside from affecting worldwide monetary systems, that malware could bring down our nation's entire electronic infrastructure, including the power grid, banking and telecommunications, and even our military command system.

"Higgins studied it alone through the night. He tried to keep it to himself, trying not to dampen our spirits, but Levi, Anne, and I noticed it.

"Higgins hoped that our team of scientists, with Roland, would release a cyberworm to counter both Gauss and the defect of the first Stuxnet. This is our highest priority now.

"We need that disc not only to save time, but also to be sure that we release an efficient cyberworm that will address the previous defects. If we fail, this could be the scenario of the triple-digit Dow. The DJIA may go down following the Elliott Wave Theory, but Higgins became obsessed with making sure that the fault should not lie in our failure to stop what we began. Higgins became impatient and paid for it. I must find the disc; that's what Higgins was ready to die for."

"Ohh!" Anne said, and she sank in her chair.

"Ohh!" Aunt Mary echoed as everybody else slumped in his or her chair and suddenly felt tired.

"We might as well get some sleep," Edward said. "It is past midnight, and it's not easy to think anymore."

Anne woke up looking at the bright sun rays shining through the curtain gap. When she got to the kitchen, the others were drifting in too.

Mary was on another cup of coffee, munching on a pretzel. "I'm eating this just to remind me of New York," she said.

Anne smiled and helped herself to oatmeal; then she sat down crying. "Higgins was devoted to morning oatmeal," she said, and she made the sign of the cross.

They were silent for a while.

"Levi and Alain are now in Mt. Sinai Hospital," Luke announced when he came in. "They are being guarded by the Mossad. Let's settle down first. We can visit tomorrow in small groups, once more wearing disguises and unlikely pairing—even Aunt Mary."

"Why?" Mary said irritably.

"These guys are vicious," Luke said patiently. "They could use you as a hostage."

"I can't believe the world has come to this." Mary sighed.

"I'm going first with Edward; then others can follow by unlikely pairing. We are allowed to bring weapons. We'll come in through the side door and exit through another door. Levi and Alain have been placed in a big room, so it is easier to guard.

"I've also made arrangements for Higgins's funeral. It will be this coming Monday at Arlington Cemetery. There will be a visitation just before Mass, but we don't have to show ourselves until Mass. There will be a lot of CIA, but right now, I don't know who to trust. We can bring our weapons there too."

Anne and Janan cooked what was available in the food pantry. They were more aware of their grief after they have stopped running. They had no appetite.

They were anxious to visit the hospital the next day.

Luke parked the van on a side street and came out with Edward. They looked around and signaled for the two pairs to come out and wait inside the door. The hospital was quiet just before noon as they each paid a visit to the patients.

Alain was still intubated. Levi was grunting something to Luke that he could not understand. Luke signaled to Anne and Mark to listen. Mark tiptoed a bit to bring his ear near Levi's lips; then he nodded. The visitors each held the patients' hands tightly before leaving.

"Let's have lunch," Luke said. He parked the car at a deli on Madison Avenue, closer to Midtown. They looked around first and then sat with Luke's and Edward's backs against the wall. They ate pastramis.

"What's with this sandwich?" Roland asked. "Hmm, a bit sour, but I like it."

"This is the pastrami on rye that New York is known for," Luke explained. "I wanted you to try it."

"It's very filling," Janan commented.

"I like it!" Andre said.

"Did you understand what Levi said, Mark?" Luke asked after they finished eating.

"I'm not one hundred percent sure, but it makes sense. Levi said the word mail." Mark turned to Anne. "Do you still have the locker-room number, Mom? Higgins could have sent something to his box, or whatever that is. I remember that we passed by a mailbox on the street corner when we got out of the van to go to Higgins's Arlington office."

Anne quickly searched her bag. "I always keep these important little things; I hope it hasn't been misplaced . . . Here it is! It has the number of Higgins's locker."

"How did that work?" Luke asked. "Higgins had so many tricks that Levi and I still have to learn."

"Higgins gave us this locker number, which said 'Grand Central Station,'" Anne explained. "While doing a web search before we set out, Mark and I found out that there are no lockers at Grand Central Station itself; however, at this Fifth Avenue address, there is a locker-room service.

"Higgins had a bag there that we took. That's why we had some money, the revolvers, and the credit card to use when we were running around hiding.

"I suspect that Higgins may have had a special connection there, because we did not have to pay for the storage at all, and the attendant was quite helpful. He just let us take the bag.

"I suggest that Mark and I go there and ask for the stored material."

"We're nearby already," Mark said.

"Tell us where to drop you off," Luke said. "We need to post guards, and everybody has to go out in pairs."

"Here's the address," Anne handed Luke the card.

Luke drove the van to the address. Jim and Roland looked around first; then Mark and Anne got out of the van.

They were back in less than ten minutes, carrying a brown envelope.

Luke drove back to the condo, and they opened the envelope as soon as they were inside. Luke laid out the contents on a table: a bunch of official documents that looked like titles to Higgins's possessions, data, articles, a disc, and a jewelry box. Luke opened the jewelry box, and there was a paper on top labeled "For Anne Cortez." Luke handed it to Anne.

She looked at the others with a knitted brow and examined what was inside the box. "What's this?" she asked, and she read the paper on top of the box. "My name? Whose is this? Are they real emeralds?" There was a set of emerald earrings and a necklace.

"Yes," Mary answered. "The Maltese emeralds are for a woman in our family of fighters sworn to defend the country."

"That's not me. These are too expensive. You can have them." Anne quickly gave the box to Mary.

"Anne, you don't choose it; it chooses you," Mary explained. "Higgins, Luke, and my family belong to a line of old settlers who believed deeply in this country. Recently Levi was admitted, and I expect everybody in this room will be admitted too. It has no requirement, because we ask you to be part of the family after you have proven yourself to be a patriot.

"When one of our members became affluent, namely Higgins's great-grandfather, he gave his wife this emerald set. Owning this just signifies that you belong to our family of patriots. It's not a cult or anything. Higgins is the last of his line. Because he was too busy chasing spies, he never got married. Higgins gave this to you. Wear them with pride."

Anne sat down and cried; then she put the box on the table. "At first I didn't want to feel like I'd been bought. Also, I don't really accept expensive gifts from anyone outside of my family. Please keep it in the meantime; I'll think about it."

"All right," Luke said after a pause. "We have a lot of things to do. Roland, start deciphering this disc. Give the list of names to investigate to Mark and Jim. Andre, help Roland with some of the calculations. Edward will update us with the goings-on around us. I have to finish the funeral arrangements. Aunt Mary, give me a hand."

"Janan and I will tidy up the place," Anne said, but she just sat down on the chair, still stunned.

Luke looked at her and then proceeded to his table. Janan sat beside Anne and let her cry.

After a while the two ladies got up and tidied up the place. They visited the kitchen and frowned.

"There's not enough food for dinner," Janan said.

"They're too busy to come with us for guard duty," Anne said. "What do you think? Chinese takeout?"

They smiled woefully at the thought and then nodded together.

Luke watched them from a distance and looked at his aunt. "They're back to normal."

The ladies served coffee and snacks at four o'clock.

"By the way," Anne said, "give me your orders for Chinese takeout. We don't have enough food for dinner, and we did not want to disturb you."

"I'll have noodles," Roland said, and the others also gave their orders.

"We'll come with you to pick it up," Luke said. "We'll also buy food for the next couple of days. We need to work hard on this disc. I'll call in some help from the Israelis too."

Luke and Mary finished making all the arrangements for Higgins's funeral. The group heard Sunday Mass at St. Patrick's; then Luke drove the van to Washington, DC. They all slept at Luke's apartment for the night.

The service for Higgins lasted an hour. The CIA chief spoke, and in the tradition of very efficient people, he kept it short without missing the important details of Higgins's contribution to his country.

Most of the attendees wore black, or white and black, and the solemn service was partly carried on most TV stations. To the TV audience, it was fine to see only the hearse, the speakers, and the priest. The audience did not mind that the people attending the service were not shown. The people who came were advised not to use cell phones, iPhones, or cameras during the service. Anybody who tried to use them was blocked by special police. This was a special request by Mary Hartford, communicated through her lawyers.

Mary was in a special place, but Luke and the rest of the group wore disguises and stayed at a discreet distance from the important people.

More than two hundred yards away from the scene was an expensive telephoto camera perched on a tree. This was being used by a very experienced spy to take photos of all the interesting people who attended. The spy stayed in his lair and waited for all the people to leave before he came down. He straightened up and walked casually, like a regular park visitor, when suddenly a helicopter came from nowhere. It hovered right above him, so he ran. Bullets sprayed that direction, so the spy ran the other way. More bullets sprayed that direction, so he aimed his revolver at the whirring metal. His hand was hit by a bullet.

"Surrender!" The bullhorn did not have to be so loud. The spy lay spread-eagle on the ground. He was a CIA operative working for another government agency.

Roland later traced all the errant spy's connections and divulged them to information channels—never mind due process and the notion of "innocent till proven guilty." This was a criminal caught in the act. The spy had taken many pictures of the group. Luke destroyed the pictures.

The group went back to New York after the funeral and got busy tracking leads, trying to make the connection, and finding the traitors.

"One of the dead bodies in the cemetery was a former CIA agent," Luke said. "There are now two former CIA agents working for the enemy, or is the enemy from within?"

Mark and Jim got busy checking all the agents; the first clue was their bank accounts. Unless they had inherited a windfall, there was no reason for a number of CIA agents to suddenly make huge deposits.

Roland and Andre continued their attempt to counter the Gauss, using the original disc.

Luke was forever drafting letters. "I'm writing different proposals and counterproposals with our senators and representatives to avert the fiscal cliff. I've closed all our stock positions, since we do not know what will happen."

"Maybe the best thing would be to just extend the agreement for three months," Anne said. "That way, they save themselves from a haphazard job of trying to fix something that's not so easy to solve. Most people are already distracted by the holiday."

"That may be a good stopgap proposal," Luke said. "I'll send that too."

"Let's hope Congress comes to a solution," Edward said, looking up from monitoring the financial news. "The stock market is confused."

The ladies could now cook a proper meal. Luke devised a plan whereby the younger men would alternate guarding the ladies while they shopped.

"It will soon be Christmas. We need some things. When will you guys be finished?" Anne asked.

"Sorry, Anne, we're not done," Luke said. "Two Israeli physicists are arriving tomorrow to help us finalize this virus."

"Where will they sleep?" Anne looked around.

"Next door," Luke answered. "That condo has actually been empty for some time. It was rented out periodically, but I never noticed."

"Okay," Anne said. "Better give us a chance to buy a Christmas tree tomorrow. Hmm . . . We need to shop too, if we can," she said, looking at Aunt Mary and Janan, who both nodded.

"Aunt Janan, don't forget what I want!" Andre looked up from the papers on his lap.

"I have my list," Janan answered.

"Maybe it's time we take a break," Luke said. "The scientists are not arriving till late evening. Tomorrow is Saturday, but we'll hear Sunday Mass at St. Patrick's in the afternoon.

"We'll shop in between, and we'll eat out. I'm sending somebody else to meet those who are arriving.

"By the way, folks, we are going to the annual Patriots' Ball in DC. We'll rent tuxes for you guys."

"Wow!" the younger men chorused.

Luke explained. "The Patriots' Ball coincides with the inaugural balls held during presidential election years. If the Nationalists win, the president-elect usually comes to our ball. Since we lost, we still have a ball, attended by people with a conservative ideology. I'd like to introduce you guys."

"Oh! Even my father would have loved this," Andre said, and then he looked down.

Janan and Anne held Andre's shoulder.

They went shopping the next day.

"I know where the Best Buy and Apple stores are," Mark said.

"Remember that you are carrying weapons, so take turns going inside stores," Luke warned. "I'll be accompanying Aunt Mary and the ladies."

"I'll go with the guys," Edward said.

The younger men went for the electronic gadgets while the ladies went to Bergdorf Goodman and Saks. They brought Mary's wheelchair with them.

After supper, Luke and Mary went back to the condo to wait for the arriving Israelis. The others headed to Midtown for more shopping.

"The Israeli scientists arrived early," Luke told Edward after calling him on his cell phone. "It's good we were here. I'll update them on what we've done so far. Bring us some warm snacks."

"We'll pick up some food on the way back," Edward said.

The shoppers arrived at the condo just before nine o'clock that night. The young men had bought a lot of electronic stuff, while the ladies brought warm pizza and food for the next two days.

The men worked on their Stuxnet II: Anti-Gauss that night and well into the morning.

"I hope our brains don't get fried," Mark said; then he paused, "Uh . . . Sorry."

Anne and Mary laughed along with the scientists, Dr. Goldberg and Dr. Rabin.

"We don't have a dull moment here." Luke smiled. "Our work is fun."

They worked through Christmastime.

"This will give us an opportunity to share our Christmas tradition with you," Anne said.

They had decorated a small foil Christmas tree and placed their wrapped presents around it. They had gifts for Goldberg and Rabin too. They all went to Mass and celebrated the day by relaxing, doing sing-along Christmas carols on iTunes, and playing table games. There was a lot of food and champagne.

"I like this Christmas," Goldberg said.

Luke was up early after Christmas. "Come on!" he said to the computer just as Roland was coming in. "Congress might agree on the three-month extension, averting the fiscal cliff."

Edward arrived and looked at the TV news. "The rumor alone is making the DJIA go up."

Roland sighed. "This world is getting too complicated. My project here can't get through this stumbling block," he complained.

Goldberg and Rabin were getting frustrated too.

"There is a difference between this disc and the one from Senawi," Goldberg said.

"Well, Stuxnet did not have a defense to start with, so aren't you just proceeding from there?" Anne asked.

"Yes, we were, but it always failed the test. It won't stick," Rabin answered.

"Higgins said that the formulations were complex, and he also said that they were numbers. But we know that Senawi used passwords, and even the Fordow facility was disabled using passwords, not just numbers, right?" Anne thought aloud.

Roland looked at her askance. "How about that!" he said.

"What do you mean?" Goldberg said.

"Let's try something," Roland said. "What do you say, Anne?"

"Use our trip itinerary by sets, for instance. Start at Belogradchik," she said.

Roland hurried to the computer and started entering set words. "Belogradchik. Next! Just give the names of the places," he said.

"Okay," Anne said, also running to check her notes and the map. "We'll skip two-letter words. First set: Nevsky, Kurdzali, Belogradchik, Asenovgrad, Pleven. Next set: Sighisoara, Sinaia, Pelisor, Prejmer, Brasov. Let me write down the rest while you work on that."

"Okay!" Roland said.

Anne took a piece of paper and wrote more names: Hunyadi, Turul, Krakow, Wawel, Jagiellonian, Auschwitz, Czestochowa, Poznan, Tiergarten. She was bent over from the pressure of hurrying to write; then she straightened up. "Is it working?"

"So far, yes." Roland paused to show what he was doing to Goldberg and Rabin.

Luke smiled, but upon looking at his computer, he sighed. "There's no compromise yet."

It took a haywire act by Congress on the morning of December 28 to approve the three-month extension.

"For this, I'll drink champagne even before lunch," Luke said.

"Me too," Rabin and Goldberg chorused. "The whole world is looking up to America. Even we would have been affected by your disaster," Rabin said.

They took a break on New Year's Eve. The young men wanted to go over to Times Square for the New Year's countdown.

"It's hard with your M-16s in the crowd; better step back a bit. Don't get crushed," Luke said worriedly. "I'd better come."

The others stayed at the condo, watching TV. They celebrated the New Year when the other guys got back.

"We're almost done," Goldberg said a week after. "I did not think we would finish this soon."

"It has been great working with you!" Luke said. "So you take one disc for your government to release when you get to Israel; we have two copies. One is for Higgins's box, and the other I will put in my safe."

"Thank you very much," Rabin said. "I hope that the world order will be preserved with this great work."

"Let's drink to that!" Mary said, and they toasted their success with champagne.

Goldberg and Rabin left that week. They were all looking happy and shook hands.

"Come and visit us again," Goldberg said.

"After weeks of tension, I'm ready to scream," Roland said. "Just kidding," he added.

The two extra copies of the Stuxnet II: Anti-Gauss had to be deposited: one in Luke's New York safe and the other at Higgins's locker near Grand Central Station. Mark and Edward deposited the disc there the next day.

Roland gave Anne the original. "I give this to you and Mark, the unlikely keepers, as per Higgins's rule. You keep it for whatever need there may be in the future."

Anne was hesitant yet thoughtful. She looked from Roland to Luke and then to Mary. They all nodded. She went to her room and placed the disc in her bag.

"Levi will be out of the hospital in a few days," Luke said, "but Alain might take another week. Levi would have been named CIA chief, and I would have been the Attorney General. Instead we will be hiding for another four years.

"When we go to the Patriots' Ball in DC, we are touching base with our people, our resource in the future. They will see us, but all of us are there to declare, by our presence, our love of country. Are you all right with that?"

With a nod from everyone, Luke continued.

"Aunt Mary's compound has been redone, with more up-to-date defenses and even a helipad. We added an extra foot of thickness to the surrounding wall. It is also equipped with some kind of anti-air-assault defense.

"Basically, that's for all of you to know; so you can take shelter there, should there be trouble. By the way, we still don't have a helper there. There are many applicants, but it's not easy to trust just anybody nowadays.

"We can leave for Richmond the day after tomorrow and stay at Aunt Mary's house. For the Patriots' Ball, you can choose to change at my apartment in DC.

"By the way, would you like to see a Broadway show or an opera before we leave New York?"

"What shows are there?" Roland went to his computer and checked. "I've never been to any one of those. This week, the Met has Il *Trovatore*, *Turandot*, *La Rondine*, and *Maria Stuarda*.

"On Broadway, there's *Wicked*, *Phantom of the Opera* . . ."

Janan, Mark, and Jim looked at the computer too.

"The only thing worth watching on Broadway is *Wicked* or *Phantom of the Opera*," Mark said.

"I'd like to see the opera," Andre said. "My father said he would take me to see one in New York someday."

The words were out before Andre realized it. Janan held his hand, and Anne came over to touch his shoulder.

"Opera it is, guys," Luke said with a smile. "After you've left New York, only then will you realize what you'll be missing."

Mary went over to Roland. "Let's see what tickets are available, young man. We don't have much choice if we have only one day."

Luke drove the van even though they were going only a short distance. He let them off at the front of Lincoln Center and parked the van near Fordham, instead of using the underground garage.

They had gone to the opera after an early, light supper; then they went to a bistro afterward and had tapas and some drinks. There was a subdued excitement when the young men exchanged opinions and expressed their impressions of *Turandot*.

"We have to do it again," Mary commented with a smile.

## 38. The Patriots' Ball

The young men fell asleep on and off during the drive to Richmond, Virginia. Edward relieved Luke in driving, and they bought food supplies.

"This place looks new!" Edward commented when they arrived. "How did that Cadillac get here?"

"I contacted Aunt Mary's lawyer to have it brought here," Luke said. "It was still where Higgins had parked it that day."

"It actually feels very safe with the thick walls," Andre said.

Mary looked around her and said, "If anybody tries to mess with my home next time, I'll be willing to kill."

Luke sighed. He knew the memories would not be all pleasant; that's why he had the house repainted.

They drove again to Petersburg, Virginia, the next day.

"Haircut first," Luke said. "Remember to use your assumed names when renting your tuxes, and say we're all going to a wedding."

The young men nodded.

Anne and Janan had chosen gowns at Saks.

Anne was not so happy with her gold-colored gown. "Never mind, it's just one night."

"I'm quite happy with mine," Janan said. "It's my favorite shade of blue."

"Are you not going to ask me?" Mary asked, and she smiled when Anne and Janan turned.

Anne and Janan laughed at the old lady's expression.

"I bet you have a surprise up your sleeve!" Anne said. "I presume you have a designer gown from Bergdorf."

"I do have a surprise, mind you!" Mary put one finger on her lips.

Luke visited one of the patriot men's homes in DC, accompanied by Roland and Mark. They went armed. Luke gave Senator Evans copies of the issues and papers that Higgins had worked on.

The ladies stayed home, guarded by Edward, Jim, and Andre. They sighed in relief when Mark called on the way home.

Luke convened them after supper. "Stuxnet II: Anti-Gauss has still not been released. We know that the tension is escalating between the Israelis and Hamas after the assassination of the Gaza Hamas commander. I have not yet directly asked the upper levels of government, because of their war, but I'm worried. Let's investigate."

The group searched the local and worldwide news on their computer.

"There's a small news report here that may be relevant," Jim said. "There was a car accident in the traffic flow from the Tel Aviv airport last week. The casualty names have not been released."

They all looked at each other. The ladies made the sign of the cross.

Roland was determined. "I'm willing to release Stuxnet II, using the disc that Anne has. After all, I'm the safest person to do it."

Anne got the disc from her room without saying anything. She gave it to Roland, touching his shoulder.

Roland nodded. He placed the disc in his computer while everybody else watched. Roland then released Stuxnet II: Anti-Gauss.

They all heaved a sigh, feeling a mixture of relief and apprehension.

"Anne, it's time to wear the emeralds." Mary looked seriously at Anne as she handed Anne the jewelry box.

The others were rushing to their rooms to get dressed.

"What? Oh! . . ." Anne frowned.

"Higgins did not make an empty gesture," Mary said with a faraway look. "You have more than earned this. Higgins wanted you to wear them because wearing the Maltese emeralds is a sign that there will be patriots fighting for this country. It takes courage to wear them, like answering a challenge. It's a tradition. Some persons will be revealed as either friend or foe when they see the emeralds."

Anne's look of dread gradually changed to determination, and she nodded.

"I bought you a gown that goes with the jewelry too—that was my other secret," Mary added, and she brought over a large gown box.

The young men tried hard to tone down their excitement as they converged in the foyer before departing for the ball.

"Well! What a fine bunch of gentlemen!" Mary said as she came out of her room, dressed in an elegant black gown.

Roland let out a wolf whistle.

"You watch yourself, young man!" Mary bantered.

Janan came out in her blue gown.

"Wow! You look wonderful, Aunt Janan!" Andre said proudly.

Anne hurriedly came out of her room and said, "I'm ready."

They were quiet.

"What?" she said, looking around.

"You look stunning, Anne!" Mary said.

Luke drove the van to the Patriots' Ball. "Please remember, these people are supposed to be our friends. Just the same, there could be bad apples around. Some will ask you questions, trying to pry for information. Do not give out info; instead, evade them or ask questions in return. If you can't handle it, refer to me. Don't ever get drunk and lose control. This is your test. Sorry, it should really be enjoyable. I'll be introducing you to people."

The young men were set to enjoy the marvel of it all, including the elegance, the exquisite food, and the company of others—some powerful, some just rich, mostly friends. They were not disappointed; rather, their idea of adventure and intrigue was piqued by the array of interesting men and women.

Anne had arrived feeling guarded but determined. She had expected a somber atmosphere of defeat; instead, the ball was an upbeat celebration, and she sensed a confident willingness to fight back.

Luke was a good dancer and used it to advantage by dancing with some female congresswomen and female power brokers. Roland was in a discussion with some men introduced by Luke. Mark, Jim, and Andre hit it off with the younger set, mostly the daughters of senators and congressmen.

Anne's gown was emerald-green silk, as green as the emerald necklace and earrings that she wore. She had put them on as if she had to put on a costume, without realizing that the color set off her unusual complexion and beautiful shoulders. The effect was stunning, and people's heads turned to look at her; then they noticed the emeralds.

"The Maltese emeralds!" she heard them say.

"The Maltese emeralds!" the society matrons whispered to each other.

Edward danced the first waltz with her, but different senators and congressmen started cutting in. She danced one number after another, gradually feeling game and enjoying the party. Luke cut in, and after dancing with her, he led her to a table far from the dance floor, where Edward and Mary were seated.

"Thank me for rescuing you," Luke said, blocking the view from the dance floor.

"Thanks," Anne said, kicking off her shoes under her long gown and stretching her toes. "If that's a test, then that was a test!"

"You've come to conquer, Anne," Mary said. "Most of the important men have danced with you."

"Levi will come later and will join us at Aunt Mary's home," Luke said.

"Luke! Don't monopolize Anne," a senator said. "It is a cha-cha they are playing. It's my turn to dance with her. I'm Senator Curran, just in case you forgot." The senator led Anne by the hand back to the dance floor.

Anne only realized that Levi had arrived when he cut in to dance with her.

"Levi!" she said with a choked voice.

"You look so beautiful, Anne," he said, kissing her hand. "You've saved my life twice."

She cried silently. "I can't believe what you and Alain had to go through!"

"We're all in this, like you said." Levi glanced toward their group. "We need to leave soon; we have a lot to talk about."

She just nodded, and Levi led the way back.

They all left shortly afterward. Luke drove the van back to his aunt's house. Edward drove with the other members in the SUV that Levi had arrived in.

"Get changed into something comfortable," Luke said to everyone. "We need to talk about a lot of things. We'll meet at the lounge room in ten minutes; bring your computers."

Most of them changed into pajamas, topped with robes. The younger men were prepared with small tables for their computers. Anne brought paper, pens, and pencils for the older members.

Levi still looked pale now that he could be seen under a better light. "You may all be wondering what really happened that day," he started. "The guard must have been already compromised for some time when Higgins called; otherwise, Higgins would have detected any tone or voice change.

"Higgins arrived the day after he called so that those thugs would not have enough time to prepare. The thugs must have learned that the safe would explode if forcibly opened, so they had to wait for Higgins. They had been lying in wait for a while. When Higgins finally came, the thugs were almost not ready.

"They had planted bugs at Higgins's office, so after Higgins called the guard, one of them came in to kill the guard. They then hid the guard.

"The enemy lookout was still gathering his men when we arrived. Higgins took the disc, papers, and jewelry box and mailed them at the postal collection box on the street. We were walking to the car when eight men surrounded us and then chloroformed us from behind. They interrogated—or, rather, tortured—us at the cemetery. Higgins would not reveal his secret; instead, he kept asking them, 'Who is the head of this bunch of snakes, the traitors to my country?' They tortured Higgins, but they did not get anything out of him, for he seemed to know that he was going to die. He just kept asking who their head was and finally succumbed after multiple stab wounds. Higgins never told us what he took from the safe and where he sent it; all I knew was that he mailed it.

"After Higgins died, those thugs tortured Alain and me separately. They liked to stab us, one part at a time, asking for information. They did not want to kill us all until their leader arrived. Apparently, their leader had gone to New York, ostensibly to look for leads, but they thought he was just having a good time.

"One of their guys had already seduced Aunt Mary's cook so that they could be let in to kill whoever was at home. The thugs who went to Richmond grumbled that nobody was home. They were then told to come to the Alexandria cemetery instead. As you know, they killed the cook first. It was really provident that Anne was able to tell Luke to go to the Alexandria cemetery.

"The thugs were having a go at torturing Alain and me, when their boss from New York told them to just bury us. Their boss was coming to Washington, DC, to meet with other important people.

"The persons calling the shots were Middle Eastern, but the henchmen were Hispanics and some Asians, so I presume that they were mercenaries." Levi looked tired and pale after narrating his ordeal.

"So the head of the snakes is still out there," Luke said. "Higgins did not take a shot in the dark. He was sending a message through you, should anyone survive, that he suspected somebody else was pulling the strings to kill us or give us a hard time.

"Among Higgins's papers was a diagram that he had been working on. It contains the names of people he thought were behind this network of traitors. Higgins suspected that there was an international network with a sinister goal.

"For sure they wanted the Stuxnet disc, but after we disabled the Natanz and Fordow nuclear plants, Higgins was puzzled about why they were still after us. I believe that aside from the disc, they also wanted to get the position papers, the ideas, and the resource list Higgins had. They wanted Higgins out of the way too, because our group was an obstacle in the way of their committing mayhem against our country. Those thugs are after us. This sinister network is not just in the USA; it is possibly international.

"We already know that two ex-CIA men were involved: one was at the cemetery, and the other was the photographer snooping at Higgins's funeral.

"I have spoken with Senator Evans and other men that I trust in the patriots' group. Our commitment to our country will be severely tried in the coming years. Although there are people we can trust, we have to sift through each government agency to figure out how compromised they are.

"As you know, the attack of the terrorists at our Consulate in Benghazi, Libya was covered up. The congressional hearings are revealing a deepening scandal. Obviously, there is somebody from up there who told our guys to stand down.

"Now there are fifty states wanting to secede from the Union.

"Higgins's death was a warning shot. You would think that we accomplished something by disabling the Natanz and Fordow nuclear plants and releasing the Stuxnet II: Anti-Gauss. We have done our best to avert an ominous prediction. Instead, we made this group of conspirators unhappy with us. These guys are big. Our hands will be full, and we need people we can trust.

"Roland has to be hidden as much as possible. When Alain is released from the hospital, I have asked that he be taken directly to the Israeli consulate. From there, we will arrange for him to be moved to our hideout.

"We will have a financial arm, so we can earn a living and finance our activities in safeguarding our country. Our young men will continue with their studies through a special program and finish their course.

"We showed our face today as a signal that we are ready to fight; albeit we have to do it behind a façade. We need to move now that we've shown ourselves, for we face a threat. We can discuss more of our plans when we get to Texas, our destination. There is a compound there that we can use." Luke looked around at the young men when he finished.

The young men all nodded in assent.

"Let's get moving; load up our armaments," Luke said. "I'll drive the van. Levi is not fully healed yet, so Edward will drive Levi's SUV. We'll leave Aunt Mary's Cadillac here so we have something to use if we come over."

They all hurried to their rooms and packed as quickly as possible. They did not bother to change out of their pajamas. Anne and Janan helped Mary pack, and they took with them as much of the food as they could.

As the van and the SUV sped out of the compound, all the lights turned off on the compound.

Anne tapped Roland's shoulder as he sat beside Edward at the front.

"That's just for the next eight hours," Roland said. "Afterward, a timer will keep a minimum temperature during the winter, and there will be alternating room lights with cameras. Luke had the house wired so that I can adjust the settings from his computer."

Roland made reservations under their assumed names at a Residence Inn outside of Raleigh, North Carolina. After more than four hours, they arrived there. Janan, Andre, Roland, and Jim collected the room keys. They converged at the Cortezes' suite and checked the TV news.

The news anchor had a garbled account of something he could not understand. "There are spotty power outages on the East Coast and in Maryland, Virginia, and Washington, DC. There were accidents reported, some involving cars with drivers using GPS. There was an unusual accident in Richmond, Virginia; two cars landed in a ditch, and a truck with some soldiers slammed against a tree."

"Let's get some sleep," Luke said. "We'll lie low until I can switch our cars for something those bad guys can't track. I'm hoping to get a chartered plane to take us to Texas; otherwise, we will drive until we get to our compound just outside Houston."

The others nodded sleepily, and they dispersed to get some sleep.

END

# Bibliography

AP News. "Lawmakers Say Libya Security Pleas Were Rejected." *Wall Street Journal*, October 3, 2012,

Bradley, Matt. "Alarm Raised over Egypt Constitution." *Wall Street Journal*, September 26, 2012.

Bradley, Matt. "Islamists, Secularists Clash in Cairo." *Wall Street Journal*, October 12, 2012.

Crovitz, L. Gordon. "We Helped Build That.com." *Wall Street Journal*, July 30, 2012.

Dagher, Sam, Nour Malas, and Joe Lauria. "Syria Rebels Take Battle to Capital's Streets." *Wall Street Journal*, July 17, 2012.

Fassihi, Farnaz. "Iran Currency Woes Spark Rare Strike." *Wall Street Journal*, October 4, 2012.

Fassihi, Farnaz. "Gaza Fight Hints at Hezbollah Arsenal." *Wall Street Journal*, December 5, 2012.

Fassihi, Farnaz. "Quake in Iran Kills More Than 200." *Wall Street Journal*, August 13, 2012.

Gorman, Siobhan. "Iran Renews Internet Attacks on U.S. Banks." *Wall Street Journal*, October 18, 2012.

Gorman, Siobhan, and Julian Barnes. "Iran Blamed for Cyberattacks." *Wall Street Journal*, October 13, 2012.

Gray, C. Boyden, and Jim Purcell. "Why Dodd-Frank Is Unconstitutional." *Wall Street Journal*, June 22, 2012.

Greil, Anita. "Wary Swiss Banks Turn Away Yanks." Wall Street Journal, October 20-21, 2012.

Ignatius, David. "Iran Digs in on Nuclear Program." *Quad City Times*, July 6, 2012.

Jamaluddin, Ayad. "Political Islam and the Battle for Najaf." *Wall Street Journal*, July 17, 2012.

King, Rachel. "Virus Aimed at Iran Infected Chevron's Computer Network." Wall Street Journal, November 9, 2012.

Lahart, Justin. "Stocks Will Indicate When the Tide Is Turning." *Wall Street Journal*, March 2, 2009.

Levinson, Charles, Matt Bradley, and Sam Dagher. "Israel Mobilizes as Rockets Target Jerusalem." *Wall Street Journal*, November 17-18, 2012.

Levinson, Charles, and Adam Entous. "Israel's Iron Dome Defense Battled to Get off the Ground." *Wall Street Journal*, November 26, 2012.

Maltby, Emily. "Entrepreneurs Fear Fiscal Cliff Awaits at Year-End." *Wall Street Journal*, October 4, 2012.

McGurn, William. "Obama's IRS Snoops Abroad." *Wall Street Journal*, July 17, 2012.

Neugebauer, Randy. "$447 Million Consumer Alert." *Wall Street Journal*, September 20, 2012.

Opinion. Review and Outlook. "From Busher to the Bomb." *Wall Street Journal*, December 6, 2012.

Opinion. Review and Outlook. "Obama's Cyberattack." *Wall Street Journal*, September 24, 2012.

Opinion. Review and Outlook. "Soros: The Super Pac Man." *The Wall Street Journal*, September 9, 2012.

Rosenbaum, Ron. "Cassandra Syndrome." *Smithsonian Magazine*, April 2012.

Reuters. "New Computer Spy Virus Hits Financial Institutions." *Wall Street Journal*, August 10, 2012.

Solomon, Jay. "Enrichment Capacity Seen to Double at Site." *Wall Street Journal*, August 31, 2012.

Solomon, Jay. "Iran Economy Seen Worsening." *Wall Street Journal*, October 13, 2012.

Solomon, Jay. "Iran Seen as Closer to Bomb-Grade Fuel." *Wall Street Journal*, October 10, 2012.

Solomon, Jay. "Iran's Nuclear Arms Guru Resurfaces." *Wall Street Journal*, August 30, 2012.

Solomon, Jay, Julian Barnes. "U.S. Raises Monitoring of Iranian Reactor." *Wall Street Journal*, December 3, 2012.

Tadros, Samuel. "The Christian Exodus from Egypt." Wall Street Journal, October 12, 2012.

Taylor, John. "Monetary Policy and the Next Crisis." *Wall Street Journal*, July 5, 2012.

World/Iran. "Iran's Currency Fails." *Time Magazine*, September 24, 2012.